Deal with the Devil

Book 3 of the Cocytus Series

by John Caligiuri

also by John Caligiuri:

THE RED FIST CHRONICLES

The Red Fist of Rome

Last Roman's Prayer

COCYTUS SERIES

Planet of the Damned

Sanctuary in Hell

Deal with the Devil

Face One's Demons

COPYRIGHT PAGE

ISBN: 978-0-9915582-8-5 [PRINT]

ISBN: 978-0-9915582-9-2 [EBOOK]

DEDICATION

To my readers who have given me the opportunity to live my dream.

To the Greece Writers Group who reviewed my manuscript and my editor Rick Taubold who made my book *legible*. Thank you for your tireless efforts.

To my wife, Linda, who reads everything I write and gives me her honest feedback, even when I don't want to hear it. Her patience as I sit before my computer, for hours on end, is nothing short of miraculous.

To everyone who has faced life's tragedies and challenges, you are the true heroes. May we never have a time when we live without our imaginary worlds and the people who populate them. May my books give you an escape when you need it the most.

PROLOGUE

Dear Reader,

My name is Mara. I am an artificial intelligence built on the planet Cocytus. I will be both the narrator and one of the participants in the accounts related in the following chronicle. I must admit that I did not witness every incident reported here firsthand. However, I conducted comprehensive research, and the secondhand accounts came from parties I trust completely.

It is to my understanding that most of you are twenty-first century Earth-born humans. It constrains my ability to describe events since most of you have had little or no interaction with galactic politics, as well as limited contact with other sentient species. Your understanding of modern science is also antiquated. A subject such as interstellar hyperspace travel will require me to provide more explanation than I would deem normal.

This is not stated as an insult to your intelligence. However, it is a fact brought about by your cloistered lives in a hermit society on a remote planet. In truth, I have a deep abiding love for Earth-born humans. The finest entities and sharpest minds I've had the pleasure of meeting were residents of Cocytus, but they originated from your world.

I imagine your first question would be "Where is this Cocytus?"

The answer is "Fairly close." It resides in the Lethe Sector of the Ipis empire on the fringe of the Milky Way Galaxy, a mere 6.7 parsecs from your planet.

This response must have sparked a myriad of questions on your part. I will refrain from answering them at this point since most will be revealed in the context of the following narrative.

Let me close this missive with a quote that I believe originated on your world:

"Bad things happen, like war, disaster, and disease. But out of those situations always arise stories of ordinary people accomplishing extraordinary things."

The people you will meet in the following chapters did not choose to enter their dire circumstances, but they resolved not to cower from them. They stood their ground. They endured.

Chapter I

Leadership's Burden

From rock to rock they fall into this valley:
Acheron, Styx and Phlegethon they form;
Then downward go along this narrow sluice

Upon that point where is no more descending.
They form Cocytus; what that pool may be
Thou shalt behold,...

Dante's Inferno, Canto XIV

Winded from a hard, eight-mile run, Dante Carloman slowed to a jog. He'd covered the four laps around the cavernous interior of the mountain named Mount Purgatory to clear his head but was still no closer to making the fateful decision than when he started.

His wife, Tina, sat on a small bench outside their modest dwelling hewn into the wall of the hollowed-out mountain, with a computer tablet perched on her lap. She was engrossed studying the diagnostic results of a patient just admitted to the hospital. But at the sound of Dante's approach, her head shot up. Love and concern blended together in her gaze. "Are we going to war with the harpies?" It was a question burning through the minds of the planet Cocytus' every resident.

"There is no good answer to that question. Every option brings perils." Dante sighed and shook his head. "So many factors to consider. But the decision is mine to make, and I'll do it at this afternoon's meeting." He ran his fingers through his shaggy brown hair, now slick with sweat. "Boy, I needed that. I haven't had a good workout in weeks."

The weather was sunny and fresh, but then conditions were always pristine inside the biosphere, paradoxically named Mount Purgatory. Dozens of slender, glowing pillars, rose from the flagstone base to the polished quartz ceiling a hundred feet above. They circulated air and provided illumination to the biosphere's one-square-mile botanical garden.

Although Earth-born, Dante and Tina now called the planet Cocytus home. Outside the subterranean biosphere where they lived, only the narrow band along that world's equator was habitable. It was a dismal world, half covered in ice.

Tina smiled at her husband's lean body, still on the sunny side of thirty. "Yeah, we don't want a fat king of the world."

Dante scowled. "Don't you start with that too." He breathed in the thick, rich air of the gardens. "Everyone treats me like freaking royalty. It scares me. Some of the decisions I make will mean life or death for us all." He stared blindly at one of the slim golden pillars. "I'll give everyone on the planetary council a chance to have a last say. This is more than just a simple raid. It would commit every resource we possess. If it goes wrong—"

"It won't." Tina stood. "We've accomplished so much in the few years we've been here. We can pull this off too." She flipped her long auburn hair over her shoulder and pointed to the lush gardens. "Four years ago, we were guinea pigs in a harpy experiment. Look where we are now. You freed us."

Dante snorted. "It was Michael and Beatrice who pulled that off."

"Dante, you're the one that convinced Michael to switch sides." Tina paused as she spotted a drone flying toward them. "And you're the one that got Beatrice to accept us." She hugged him. "Then you got us out of that death camp on Carcerem. I think those fall in the category of accomplishing the near impossible."

Anguish filled Dante's voice. "Because of my decisions, thousands died."

Tina shot back, "And tens of thousands lived. Dante, we were all doomed. You had nothing to work with but your wits, and you found a way for us to escape."

Dante's shoulders sagged. "I just stumbled onto it. One of these days my luck will run out."

Her voice rose, "Stumbled onto it! Your plan was pure genius. If you hadn't—"

A drone floated to a halt and hovered in front of them. A flat soprano voice came from it, "Mister President, you need to depart in thirty-one-point-eight minutes to make the planetary council meeting in the capital."

Tina elbowed him. "Beatrice, will you talk some sense into this thick-skulled man?" She tucked her computer under her arm and marched inside the house carved into the wall of the cavern.

"Is your cranium cover denser than the average sentient being?" The orb's lights blinked. "I have not conducted any comparative measurements."

Dante smiled. "No, it's not." He shouted at the partially open door, "Okay, you're right. I'm a genius!" He turned to the drone. "I'll be ready in a bit. I just have to shower." He paused. "Beatrice, do you think this galaxy will ever be safe for humans?"

"Safe is an unmeasurable parameter. The human physiology is ill-suited for long-term viability."

"Beatrice, stop being obtuse. Your fuzzy logic algorithms should handle the implied reference to the harpies and their predilection to kill humans."

"You should have stated that parameter when you posed the query." The lights on the drone shifted from yellow to red. "Data is insufficient for a reliable predictive model."

Dante sighed. "Remind me to never ask you for encouragement when I'm worried." He went inside and slipped his arms around Tina.

"You're all sweaty." She pushed him away but pecked him on the lips. "Go shower, Imperial Ruler. And don't leave the towel on the floor."

Twenty minutes later, Dante and Tina clambered aboard the tracked vehicle parked at the main cavern exit.

As soon as they stepped onboard, the door closed and the auto-controlled transport rumbled out. Dante opened his thick winter coat as he plopped into a seat next to his wife.

They were the only occupants, although there were seats for twenty. Tina glanced around the empty bus. "I thought Virgil was coming."

Dante eased back in the padded chair and powered up his computer tablet. "He probably left already." The transport jerked to a halt, interrupting his review of the new briefing material. A man wearing a neural-net suit jumped on board, panting. The president chuckled. "Virg, cutting it a little close, aren't you?"

Virgil Bernius pushed back his hood and dropped into the seat across from Dante. "Sorry. I was in the research lab trying out the new ion disrupter rifle and lost track of time. That sucker is amazing. It fires eight percent more joules than the current model with four percent less power consumption." His face turned grim. "We'll need it the next time we face the damn harpies. Is it going to be soon?"

Dante glanced at the data on his display. "I haven't decided yet. That's what today's conference is for."

"Virgil, your tardiness is unacceptable," Beatrice's voice intoned from a mounted speaker. "This will result in a variance from the designated arrival time."

"Virgil, you could've jogged to Hellsgate." Tina laughed as she regarded the six-foot-one, former Air Force Pararescue sergeant.

Virgil snorted as he looked out the window. The snow was mostly melted, reducing the dirt road the transport was grinding through to a muddy quagmire. "Beatrice would yell at me for getting this shiny new suit dirty."

Tina leaned over and pinched the material. "New? What's different about it?"

Virgil grinned. "Beatrice developed an upgrade from our old suits."

Dante's eyebrows shot up. "Upgrade? What's changed?"

Virgil scratched behind his ear. "The ones Michael found a few years ago had one gig of neuron sensors embedded in the fabric. These new ones have a hundred gig."

The speaker on the dashboard stated, "The prototype provides improvements to environmental control, communications, and I added ion-disrupter shielding to it."

Tina felt the material. "I like the old suits. They're less stiff."

"Progress, darling." Dante smiled. "Would you still want to work with the hospital equipment they're using back on Earth?"

"God, no!" Tina gasped. Although just a second-year medical student when she was abducted from the Earth, the restorative equipment on Cocytus far exceeded the capabilities of that available on Earth. "The medical science back home seems like voodoo and leeches now. How long before the new outfits are ready?"

Beatrice's flat soprano spoke from the transport's autopilot. "Undefined. Prototype testing has just been initiated. The neural-net systems have eleven new applications that need to be integrated and optimized."

Virgil glanced out the window at the barren trees and fallow fields. "When we get out of Beatrice's valley, there's an aerial transport waiting for us at Hellsgate." He glared at the glowing dashboard. "It would be nice if we could fly directly from Mount Purgatory."

Beatrice squawked through the speaker, "Aerial vehicles within my biomes' environment are prohibited."

Tina poked her husband in the ribs. "I guess you don't make all the rules on this world. Beatrice won't allow non-humans in Mount Purgatory or Eden Valley either."

"She has her reasons," Dante replied in a quiet voice. "I won't overrule her."

The sun broke through the yellow cloud cover as the transport bounced along the narrow road beside Lake Eunoe.

Tina quipped, "Sure doesn't look like the Garden of Eden."

"Planting season for my biomes will commence in forty-one days," the speaker on the transport's dashboard intoned.

Most of Cocytus was a barren, frozen wasteland. Even the human settlements along the equator were limited to the coastal areas and sheltered valleys. Ninety percent of the world's five million residents lived on two large islands blessed with a temperate climate due to an abundance of thermal springs. In size, they closely resembled New Zealand back on Earth. So, they unimaginatively named them North Island and South Island.

The vehicle turned left when it reached the creek named after the river Styx. A minute later they came to a halt between the steep cliffs that framed the sides of the fort at Hellsgate.

As they exited the transport, the frigid air hit Dante in the face and he flipped up the hood of his heavy parka. "I'm glad winter's winding down."

Tina laughed. "I thought you were from Buffalo. Isn't this normal for you?"

Dante started walking to the small landing pad. "Yeah, yeah. I think I've been spending too much time on the South Island. Plants are already turning green down there." He whistled when he caught sight of the sleek craft poised on the crude tarmac and turned to Virgil. "The new galleys are cleared for full operations?" he asked as he scanned the matte-gray, ninety-foot-long, oval-shaped vessel.

Virgil returned a smug look. "You bet they are. Beatrice's foundry's been working overtime. The admiral's still putting most of them through their paces near Archaeon, this planet's second moon, but this baby I reserved for myself. They sure are an improvement over the antiques we've been flying and are as nimble in a planet's atmosphere as in space."

Virgil patted the hull as they reached the ship. A broad smile creased his face as they entered the craft's small bridge. "Ain't she beautiful?" He settled into the pilot's chair.

As Tina strapped herself into a vacant seat, she eyed the five workstations arrayed in a semicircle and shrugged. "Looks like the control room of any other spaceship to me."

Virgil *tsked* at her. "You have no appreciation for craftsmanship."

Dante ignored the banter and sat in the vacant copilot seat. *If we start this fight, we'll have to see it through to the end.* He brought up a display on his computer tablet and scanned the latest intelligence reports for the planet his commanders had targeted. *What am I looking for? I know these numbers by heart.* He opened the file containing the data on the harpies' command center. *That's the key. If it can be neutralized then—*

Virgil spoke in a restrained voice as the exterior hatch closed. "So, boss, I gotta ask again. Have you decided?"

Dante felt irritated at being interrupted, but Virgil was one of his closest friends and had saved his life on more than one occasion. He sighed. "You mean have I had an epiphany in the five minutes since you last asked? No. I still need to hear from all sides today."

Virgil twitched in his seat. "We don't know when this window of opportunity will be lost."

Dante snapped, "Look, Virg, I *do* know what's at stake here."

Virgil nodded and turned his attention to preparing for takeoff.

The ship rose in the air with a low hum and shot east to the capital city once they cleared the bluffs around Hellsgate fortress. The three minutes it took the galley to complete the twenty-four-mile trip was quiet. Both men avoided discussing the proposed conflict that was foremost on their minds. Virgil landed the ship on the government building's rooftop pad.

The planetary capital, Avenio, was the most inhabited urban center on the North Island, with a population of over two hundred thousand. However, it was smaller than any of the South Island's four cities. It sat on an open plain across a sulfur-choked lake from the Heavensgate spaceport.

Although all the inhabitants of Cocytus were recent immigrants, Avenio was an ancient city that had stood abandoned for over four hundred years. Most of its buildings were in ruins due to time and nature, but vestiges of the magnificent architecture were still apparent. Avenio, along with a few other settlements clustered on the two islands, held the visible remnants of what had been a human colony on the mostly frozen planet. The descendants of the very humans who abandoned Cocytus centuries earlier were now reclaiming it.

Dante shut down his portable computer. "Virg, I'm sorry I barked at you. I'm no leader. I'm just a computer geek who was in the wrong place at the wrong time."

Virgil shook his head. "You're way off base with that one. You managed to get us out of shit that should have killed us all, and you did it working with nothing more than that gray matter parked between your ears." He pressed the button to open the exterior door. "Sorry to put the pressure on you, but I'm guessing you knew where I stand anyway. Boss, I know whatever you decide, it'll be right, and I'll back it."

"You mean like the great decision he made when we were abducted back on Earth by attacking a shielded and armed harpy with a claw hammer?" Tina asked to ease the tension.

"Well I got to admit that wasn't one of his brightest moves, but the army had a full company of soldiers engaged in that fight and they fared no better." Virgil rubbed his jaw and faced Dante. "I think even that nightmare showed why people follow you. You were just a scared college kid, but you acted. Boss, you learned fast and managed to outwit the freaking harpies ever since."

Dante nodded as they exited the ship. "Virg, thanks for the pep talk. I just wish the odds weren't so stacked against us."

Virgil snorted as he followed him out. "Amen to that."

Icy, wind-driven snow whipped through the air atop the expansive, five-story plexo-steel and glass structure. The building served as the political hub of the planet and its rooftop hummed with activity.

The weather in the city was more extreme than in Beatrice's sheltered valley, but Dante didn't notice the cold. Questions with no answers gnawed at him. "We've never tried anything like this before. What if it ends in disaster? We're all dead if we fail."

"And what if we're successful?" Virgil added as they made it inside and closed the rooftop door.

Dante acknowledged the salutes of the guards and the polite greetings from the maintenance staff as he walked to the elevator with Virgil and Tina.

Tina intertwined her hand in his. "I'm teaching the use of the stasis pods for orthopedic procedures to a new group of interns at the hospital today, but if you need to talk, call at *any* time."

Dante freed his hand and stroked her hair. "Thanks, babes, but today I think I need a gypsy with a crystal ball more than a beautiful doctor."

As the lift's door opened on the third floor, a small group of prominent citizens stood waiting. Dante gulped when they broke off their conversations and swung their heads in his direction.

Virgil chuckled. "Ready to run the supplicant gauntlet?"

Dante kissed Tina goodbye and followed Virgil off the lift. His jaw tightened as the door slid shut behind him. He hissed to his friend, "I don't have the time to deal with petitions today."

Virgil cracked his knuckles. "There're always some idiots who think their proposals are too important to go through normal channels. I'll handle this bunch." He barked in his best top-sergeant's voice, "No audiences today. You *will* file your requests in the appropriate office, or it *will* be summarily rejected."

The petitioners cringed under Virgil's scathing glare and scurried away. The only person remaining was a guard who smiled and gave Virgil a thumbs-up.

Chapter II

The Die Is Cast

Dante entered the conference room and nodded to the gathered leaders, both military and civilian, human and alien, from around the planet. He noted that only three of the twenty-five officials—Virgil Bernius, Rodrigo Cruz, and Linda Martinel—were from the original group that came to this planet with him.

He called the meeting to order and glanced around. "Ladies and gentlemen, we have one topic for discussion, and I need solid input to make my final decision. We've all seen the background data. Make your statements succinct and to the point. Iucundum, you're up first."

* * *

Dante squeezed the bridge of his nose. *This meeting's been going for two hours already. Everyone wants their say and seems to enjoy hearing themselves talk.* He glanced around and, although he was familiar with all the faces, he only *knew* a few of them.

Some of the people Dante knew best weren't even human. Although not part of the Cocytus human government, they were far more familiar with harpy behaviors and tactics than any human. His alien friends had provided most of the intelligence on the proposed target but refrained from joining the humans' debate. He smiled. *Not exactly model citizens from their species. Each of them is wanted by the Ipis authorities for various crimes.* Dante sipped his coffee. *Since just being a living human in the Ipis galactic empire is a major felony, they fit in with us perfectly.*

Foremost was Setteth, a tall flightless bird-like creature with dull golden-brown feathers. She called her species *Rocs* and was the oldest sentient creature Dante had ever heard of. Her arms were frail, but she had taloned feet and a sharp beak that could shred a man in seconds. The Roc had served as an officer in the Ipis military for many decades, but the harpies now wanted her for desertion and treason. She was the leader of a large secret sect of Rocs, called "the Order of the Dragon," dedicated to overthrowing the Ipis yoke.

Beside her sat Arachne. At four and a half feet tall, Dante thought the Satyr looked almost human, if you ignored the curly horns and hooved feet. Although a smuggler and pirate, he had many connections within the Satyr Merchant Guild that had proven very useful.

Finally, pacing back and forth in the rear of the chamber, was Calahas, a Centaur born to royalty on his home world of Equitone. He was the ringleader of an aborted uprising and was forced to flee his world when the Ipis occupiers brutally crushed the revolt. Since then, the prince had lived on the rim of the galaxy, a fugitive far from the Ipis civilization. To Dante, the Centaur was much smaller than any of the pictures he had seen from Greek mythology, with a face closer to that of a baboon than a human. Calahas appeared more like a chestnut-furred pony with a straw-colored mane and tail. At less than five feet tall when walking on his four legs, he rose to an intimidating seven feet when reared up on his hindquarters.

Dante pulled himself from his musings and refocused on the debate. *This is going nowhere.* The current speaker, Claudia, had arrived on Cocytus as many other refugees, destitute and afraid. However, she had a glib tongue and used it to advocate for the needs of her fellow expatriates. The shrewd, middle-aged woman rose rapidly in the chaotic Cocytus political environment, speaking for a wide swath of the human émigrés. Her dress and bearing were regal as she voiced outrage at the thought of spending precious resources on a military campaign.

Her speech had gone on for twenty minutes without making any new points. Dante cleared his throat and interrupted her. "Thank you, Claudia. I think we all need to hear the plan details from General Cruz now." He turned to the short, wiry man who sat red-faced with his arms crossed. The senior commander looked ready to explode.

"Your Majesty." Rodrigo Cruz jumped to his feet, turned on the holographic projector. He spoke before Claudia, who was glaring at Dante, finished sitting down.

A three-dimensional image of a planet with a single moon appeared in the air over the long oval conference table. "This is Equitone. Its indigenous people are Centaurs, and they still make up eighty-seven percent of the population." Cruz nodded toward Calahas, who swished his tail in response. "What makes it of strategic interest to us is its spacecraft shipyard on its airless moon. The Ipis use it to build mainline warships." He pressed an icon and the image view contracted to the spaceships under construction. "As you can see, two Stalker-class destroyers are close to completion."

"General Cruz, two Stalkers are hardly worth risking our fleet and army." Iucundum steepled his fingers beneath his chin. "The cost of this raid could *well* exceed the reward. And we would be announcing our presence and capabilities loud and clear. Up to now we've been nothing but a pinprick annoyance. So far, we've only had to deal with frontier guards and factional paramilitary units. A surprise attack like this will draw the attention of the imperial army."

"I agree with Iucundum." Claudia rose, pressed her knuckles on the table. "We are building a good life for ourselves outside of Ipis control. Why should we take this kind of chance?"

Setteth flared her feathers and spoke for the first time, "Fool, there is no security here. The Ipis will find this place and when they do, they will destroy it along with every living creature on it."

Claudia stiffened at the rebuke but continued in an even voice. "If we're going to risk exposing ourselves, let's wait for an Adamant warship to capture."

"We're in the Lethe Sector." Linda Martinel took off her glasses. "The Imperials won't build anything bigger than a Stalker in a remote district of the galaxy like this. All their major shipyards are near the empire's core planets. Those are unreachable even if our forces were a hundred times larger." She nodded to Dante. "Your Majesty, capturing those warships is just a side benefit."

Dante smiled at his old friend, who was the chief design engineer for their nascent fleet of warships. "Go ahead, Linda."

She gave Claudia a thin-lipped smile. "For almost two years we've been trying to build our own Adamants. We can't do it. It'll easily be twenty years before we have the infrastructure, metallurgy, and power conversions technologies. The harpies won't wait those twenty years for us to catch up."

Claudia sneered. "Then what are those mammoth ships of ours orbiting Cocytus as we speak?"

"The Dragon Ships?" A half-smile crossed Linda's face. "Converted ore freighters. The shielding and weaponry on them can indeed match an Enforcer-class cruiser... for a little while. Therein lies our problem. Our systems are incredibly inefficient compared to what the Ipis have. We expend ten times the energy for the same output as their craft." She focused on Dante. "In any extended fight, our power consumption would drain to nothing, and all of our magnificent spaceships would become floating hunks of plexo-steel. We don't have the fuel sources of the harpies. Bi-nexidium is required to energize the combat and propulsion systems, and that is a difficult element to acquire."

Claudia jabbed a finger in Linda's direction. "And what will you do when the Ipis send their imperial fleet to reclaim the facility?"

"It won't be there, and neither will we." General Cruz answered from the other end of the table. "We will disassemble every fabrication machine. Every nut and bolt of their spaceship building facility will be brought back here."

Iucundum rubbed his temple and looked at Dante. "Sire, I'm an old mining engineer. I've run operations from ore extraction to smelting. Even with our entire fleet, and our entire army, such an exercise would take at least a week. With Equitone's formidable defenses, we could never disassemble an entire factory complex while under fire, and the local Ipis forces could easily keep us tied down until reinforcements arrive. The loss of life would be astronomical."

"The nearest imperial base is over a week's hyperspace travel away. They can only engage us if we're still there," Virgil added quietly while slouched in his chair. "If we follow our timetable, those reinforcements will arrive far too late."

Cruz raised his voice, "There will be three prongs to our attack. First, a raiding party will sneak onto Equitone." He nodded toward the Centaur. "Calahas has been in constant contact with the rebels, who are prepped to create a diversion for us by fomenting civil unrest in all the major cities."

Claudia slitted her eyes and leaned forward. "How do we know these so-called Centaur rebels are so willing to risk their lives to help us?"

The answer came with a whinny from Calahas, "I know the insurgent leadership personally. They have been looking for an opportunity to strike at Equitone's occupiers for a long time. Our request has given them the catalyst to put their own plans in motion."

Claudia slouched back in her chair with a grunt, and Cruz continued, "Our team will conduct a surgical strike on the harpy command and communications center during the chaos of those riots. Second, our Dragon Ships and galleys will engage the planet's fleet. The harpies have over a thousand small attack craft, but their mainline ships are limited to an Enforcer, a Stalker, and three Striker-class frigates."

He pressed an icon and the holographic image shifted to a 3D display of four heavily armed spacecraft with their specifications appearing below them in glowing white letters. "These are the current classes of ships in the Ipis fleet." The quarter-mile-long Striker and the half-mile-long Stalker were dwarfed by the mile-long Enforcer and the enormous two-mile-long Adamant. "Fortunately, we won't have to tangle with an Adamant, but we will need to take out the Enforcer immediately with our surprise attack."

The general switched the image to a high-resolution display of Equitone's only moon. "At the same time, we'll squeeze our army into every transport we have. They will overwhelm the shipyard." He zoomed the hologram to the detailed image of the shipyard he showed earlier. "It is lightly defended. The harpies are more concerned about keeping an eye on the Centaur workers than handling an assault."

Claudia threw her arms in the air. "And there's nothing that can possibly go wrong with a convoluted plan like this?" She slapped the table with the heels of her hands and looked at Dante. "Sire, it will *not* work. We would need to flawlessly coordinate hundreds of ships and thousands of soldiers." She rapped the table again. "And that assumes our intelligence is one-hundred-percent accurate and we strike with total surprise."

The Centaur, Calahas, reared his head. "Equitone is my home world. I trust the Centaurs who brought us this information with my life."

Claudia snapped back, "Even if everything they told us is true, and the plan is flawlessly executed, the Ipis occupation commander will broadcast a distress call. Their hyperspace communication rockets have advanced stealth designs. You can't possibly intercept them all." She pointed her finger at Dante. "Sire, an imperial fleet will answer the summons. As you said before, that base is only a week away. Our spaceships will be trapped and utterly destroyed."

Dante rubbed his jaw. *Claudia's right, but so is Linda. That leaves me with only one option...* He held up his hand and his lips thinned to a slim line. "Everyone's made solid points. I've made my decision."

The room fell silent and all faces turned toward him. "We really have no choice. With all of the traffic flowing in and out of here, this planet's obscurity on the edge of the galaxy won't last forever. The harpies will find us." He looked around the table. "As Setteth succinctly stated, against what they can bring, our defenses would be overwhelmed. Every man, woman, and child would be butchered. We need the technology now. The mission is a go."

The room erupted in a dozen shouted contentions punctuated by expletives as passion on both sides of the debate rose.

Dante raised his hand for silence. "It's a go with one condition."

Cruz's face twisted in confusion. "What's the condition, sire?"

Dante rubbed his sweaty palms on his pants. "I go in early as part of the raiding party that hits the command center."

Virgil said, "You're not a kid with a claw hammer on a back road in New York anymore, boss. There're over five million people living on Cocytus, and it's growing daily. What part of 'you're our king' don't you understand?" He looked at Dante with concern and curiosity. "Why you?"

Dante met his friend's eyes. "The harpies' distress system cannot be disabled, but it can be disoriented. We need to get that system broadcasting confusing and contradictory commands to disrupt their communication and coordination. Do we have a computer engineer better than me in our five million people?"

General Cruz interrupted, "No one comes close. But you're needed here."

Dante responded in a hard voice, "We're gambling our existence on the success of this mission. We hold *nothing* back if it'll improve our chances, and that includes me."

Virgil shook his head and glanced at the commanding general. "I'll lead the raiding party that'll hit the planet-side communication center. Someone has to keep our super-geek of a king alive."

Cruz chewed on his lower lip. "Outside of your small strike force, neither of you will have any support beyond the local resistance."

Calahas rose on his hindquarters, swishing his tail. "General, Equitone is my home, and the patriots resisting the Ipis occupiers are my people. They are organized and are ready to fight. They have been studying and plotting against their occupiers." He gulped. "Since over ten thousand Centaurs were massacred following *me* in our last rebellion, by my sacred honor, I will get our team in and out of there alive."

Chapter III

Imperial Ipis

"Good afternoon, Governor," Keres-ma said as he entered the small stateroom. "What brings you to Tannis?"

"Are you *enjoying* your life as a pariah in exile here?" Silenus-dis opened in a flat voice. His gaze shifted to the stateroom window of his dropship. It was parked on the tarmac of the planet's main spaceport surrounded by Ipis security forces.

"There're few places more barbaric and out of touch with the goings-on of the empire than this place. Ninety-five percent of the population is Roc. When they're not fighting each other, they're flaring their damn feathers at you for some perceived insult. I can't remember when I last had a civilized conversation." Keres-ma snorted. He sat on the other side of the table, warily watching the Ipis magistrate of the entire Lethe Sector. "But I still must thank you. It was by your *beneficent mercy* that I was spared more than the humiliation of being stripped of my noble lineage and banished here."

"It was the lightest sentence the empress would allow. Her agent, Admiral Yasha-ry wanted death by torture. The loss of three warships, a full brigade of soldiers, and a prison full of the vilest criminals in the galaxy is no small matter." Silenus-dis flexed his clawed fingers and smiled, showing his long needle-sharp fangs. "It is probably the natural result of the lack of vigilance and the overconfidence I've come to expect from your elitist Ipis-ma sect."

Bile rose in Keres-ma's throat at the insult from the Lethe Sector governor. *The magistrate is a mongrel even if he is one of the empress' many consorts.* He admired his own deep-wine-colored hands and then sneered at the magistrate's plum-shaded flesh. The governor's lighter pigmentation showed his caste level was not of the nobility.

Keres-ma could not contain an angry retort to the lower-class Ipis who was one of the judges that condemned him to exile. "At least I am not a member of the paranoid, bogeyman-behind-every-door, Ipis-dis sect."

"So, the last twenty months haven't humbled you. You're as arrogant as ever." Silenus-dis' face contorted into a mirthless smile as he placed an eavesdropping-blocking device on the table and powered it on. "But it doesn't matter. It's good that we understand each other. I have a use for you that we may find mutually beneficial." He studied the overlarge Keres-ma for a moment. "Your disaster on Carcerem wasn't the first such event in the Lethe Sector."

Despite his pent-up ire, Keres-ma became curious. "I've heard of no other such catastrophes."

"It started about five years ago." Silenus-dis steepled his clawed fingers. "A distant cousin of mine, who was a researcher in archaic lore, approached me to bankroll a secret project. She claimed it would manifestly and authoritatively reveal that the Ipis-dis claim of the existence of our ancient enemy is *fact*. She said her theory, once proven, would change our whole understanding of the galaxy and its past."

The stateroom door opened and a lilac-shaded Ipis hurried in bobbing his head. "The delicacies you requested, Great Sire." The loose vestment of the servant-class worker flopped about his reed-thin body as he placed a fresh bowl of squirming *strum* on the table. He bowed to the floor and scurried from the room.

Silenus-dis watched the departure with a sneer, then smiled at Keres-ma. "It is difficult to believe that creatures like that one belong to the same species as us."

"Indeed," Keres-ma replied with arrogance.

The governor speared a *strum* from a bowl on the table and stared at its writhing before gulping it down. "In the name of the Dis cult, I financed her endeavor with funds I appropriated from the imperial treasury. I heard little until three years ago. Then I received a giddy, upbeat report stating that she had a breakthrough. She claimed to have found a planet, unknown to the empire, completely infested with humans. She added that experiments were being conducted to confirm the existence of a human subspecies, different than any we've encountered, who're descended from the legendary ancient enemy. She kept the location of everything covert, saying she wanted no bureaucratic interference polluting her test results."

He paused and stared across the table at Keres-ma. "Then about two years ago, I received a *final* disturbing message." He pressed a button embedded in the table and the image of a disheveled Ipis woman appeared.

The displayed figure spoke in an agitated voice, "*In the name of our ancestors what have I unleashed? Somehow the test subjects escaped despite all our precautions. The security force I sent to pursue them was annihilated. Now the fugitive humans are attacking. They've broken into the research station and control all the lower floors.*" She wildly fired her incapacitation weapon at something off-camera and shrieked, "*The ancient enemy's here. They're coming for me.*" The display flashed and went dark.

Silenus-dis turned the projector off. "My cousin had a full brigade of Ipis-dis warriors, two Striker dropships, and as I understand it, a fully secure, by-the-book biological species research station."

"Where is this place?" Keres-ma asked in a shaken voice.

"I don't know." Silenus-dis gnashed his teeth. "That imbecilic cousin kept everything secret. I don't know where the human-infested planet is or where the research station was set up. And her entire team has vanished without a trace."

"So, what does any of this have to do with me?" Keres-ma fidgeted in his seat.

"My cousin's encounter with humans was the first cataclysmic run-in with humans in over a hundred and twenty years." Silenus-dis hopped to his feet and started to pace. "Then, six months later, a frontier guard Stalker warship vanishes from the grid. Three months after that, we had your disaster on Carcerem. They taunted us by using that very same Stalker in their attack on your facility. The humans my cousin discovered are not the same pathetic creatures we've been hunting these many decades." He paused. "They *are* different, a new breed. I think our legendary foe exists and is planning to reveal their full might.

I think the bitter war we fought so long ago was just a foreshadowing of what's to come."

"That's absurd. I've seen these humans up close on Carcerem. They displayed a certain amount of animal cunning but are little more than beasts," Keres-ma scoffed.

"A member of your blind sect to the end." Silenus-dis shook his head. "There's a bit more." He stopped pacing. "As you know, we've been hunting the remnants of the human species since the end of that last war. Do you know how many of them we've captured in the Lethe Sector since your calamity?"

"No," Keres-ma snarled. "How could I?"

"Zero."

"None?" Keres-ma cocked his head. "When I was magistrate on Carcerem, we were processing over a thousand of those vermin a week into the death camps."

"It's as if they vanished into an abyss," Silenus-dis groaned. "I fear this secret human world is gathering strength and plotting to spring another war against our empire."

"Well, since they didn't learn of our superiority the last time," Keres-ma laughed, "we'll have to demonstrate it again."

"True. True." Silenus-dis sighed. "But if it's anything like that last war, the cost in life and treasure would be enormous." He leaned on the table. "How do you think the empress, who seems to see and hear everything, will treat those who suspected something was going on and did nothing?"

Fear coursed through Keres-ma, and he asked suspiciously, "What do you want *me* to do?"

"The Lethe Sector is poor and provincial." Silenus-dis leaned back in his chair. "But I will make whatever resources I have available. Your task is simple. Find the human enclave and destroy it. In exchange, I'll end your exile here on Tannis. Not only will you receive a full pardon, but all of your rights and privileges as an Ipis noble will be restored."

"Being allowed to rejoin proper society is my dream." Suspicion kindled in Keres-ma. "Why me? I'm sure you have a number of professional spies you could use."

"I can't hire anyone directly and tell them what I just told you. There are no secrets from the empress." Silenus-dis chuckled. "However, a wealthy outcast pursuing such an outwardly ridiculous quest will just bring bored sneers from the royal courtiers." His face turned stern. "Only someone with more to lose than me can be trusted to manage this task."

"A chance to finally exterminate all humans." Keres-ma squeezed the spiked mantichoras tail hanging around his neck with his prosthetic hand. *I lost my arm and my honor on Carcerem because of humans.* "I'll do it."

"Good, good. I can temporarily suspend your exile. If you are successful, I can make it permanent. When can you start?"

"Now. Have the data from your cousin's research and the Carcerem investigation delivered to my villa this evening."

"Done." Silenus-dis breathed a sigh of relief and pointed to the bowl. "Care for a fresh *strum*?"

"Yes. I suddenly have a great appetite."

* * *

"Empress Fravashi, as you foresaw, Keres-ma and Silenus-dis met on Tannis." Fleet Admiral Yasha-ry bowed before the galaxy's sole ruler. "And as you requested, no imperial resources interfered, so I cannot report on their discussion."

Fravashi placed her primitive chisel and mallet down and regarded her roughed-out sculpture. "It matters little what they said. The meeting occurred, and for good or ill it will cause an upheaval I have not seen during my entire reign." She removed her dust-covered apron and donned her royal-blue tunic over her deep-wine-colored wrinkled flesh.

"You should have let me kill the two of them." Yasha-ry's violet-colored skin darkened. "It is not right. You have given the Ipis over thirty years of peace and prosperity. You should

27

be enjoying the results of your achievements, not dealing with new schemes. I could crush these small-minded plotters like insects."

"They do not plot to harm me, but my *vision* tells me their decision will result in my greatest challenge and shake the empire." She stepped close to the old admiral. "The *sight* is more of a curse than a blessing, my loyal consort."

Yasha-ry hissed in frustration. "Speak plainly. What are you talking about?"

She chuckled. "I wish I could. My visions are blurs with sudden moments of clarity. Oftentimes I don't understand them until the event occurs. That's why I sculpt. It's solid. It's real."

Yasha-ry glanced at the statue and his face twisted in revulsion. "That is one ugly creature. Why do you carve it?"

Fravashi gnashed her fangs. "For four years now, I've seen that particular human face flow through my dreams. But I cannot determine whether it portends my doom or his... or both. It's inexplicable, but when I see him, I see the passage of history as threads trying to reweave themselves from some tear in the distant past. At some point I must confront that... creature, but I cannot *see* the time, place, or purpose."

"Perhaps you'll never have to find out. It appears our pogrom against that miserable species has finally succeeded. We've found very few humans over the last couple of years." Yasha-ry smiled.

"No, the humans are still out there. I sense them gathering." Fravashi touched the carved, wavy hair of her marble statue. "We started the war with them, you know. I read the accounts."

"Bah, it doesn't matter who started it. They invaded our territory." Yasha-ry snorted. "It was them or us."

"Were those really the only choices our ancestors had?" The empress sighed. "I'm not sure anymore." She shook her head. "My darling, enough of this gloomy discussion. Is your agent in place on Equitone?"

"Yes, my love, I've acquired the best. Charon's his name. He's a Centaur from that world and has a very impressive résumé." The admiral stroked her cheek softly with a clawed finger. "He has no scruples and no loyalty beyond his paymaster. He's always fulfilled his contracts and is an accomplished assassin, saboteur, and spy."

The empress spoke in a stern voice, "Remember, he's to observe and not interfere. Something will happen there soon that's important. Many future possibilities branch from it."

He smiled. "Your moves, based on the omens you sense, have always kept us one step ahead of your opponent. I'm confident it'll prove true again."

"Yes indeed... So far. This time the portents are confusing. I see a multitude of future paths and cannot determine where any lead. That is why I need information without disturbing the unfolding events."

Fravashi chuckled. "I'd go insane if I didn't have you to talk to,..." She squeezed his hand. "...my favorite consort."

"One of eighteen at last count." He slid his hand on her leathery back.

"But you were the first, and the only one I truly love. The other unions were for political power with fops from the noble houses." She leaned into his chest. "You're the only one in the empire I can truly trust. Where would I be without you?"

"Exactly where you are and where you belong. I'm just a relic from the warrior caste without a drop of noble blood in me."

"Relic?" She sighed and held her hand in front of her face. "Yasha-ry, when did we get old? I so tire of the *game*. There seems to be a credible assassination attempt on me at least once a week from my royal kindred."

Fire flashed in his eyes. "Your auguries stymie every one of them."

"There's always a first time." The empress pushed back and walked toward the exit of her private chamber. "Come, my love. It's time to dally with the court courtiers."

Chapter IV

Equitone

The bridge on Arachne's smuggler ship buzzed with activity in preparation for departure.

Dante turned in his seat after finishing his checklist. "Calahas, you seem very quiet."

"Sorry." Calahas shook his maned head. "Equitone's my home, but I've been gone for five years. It'll be strange seeing it again."

"Your wife is a hostage there, right?" Dante asked softly.

"Not my wife." Calahas hung his head. "We were betrothed, before I fled into exile. In all that time we've been able to smuggle only a few cryptic notes to each other." He sighed. "It's because of me and my ill-conceived rebellion that Gesten, along with twenty percent of the population, is quarantined to the planet's surface." He shook his mane. "She's the leader of the underground resistance we'll coordinate with in the capital."

"Can they create enough of a distraction?" Dante rested his hand on his friend's back.

Calahas swished his tail. "Her agent told me the rebels have spread numerous rumors about the Ipis occupiers creating more restrictions. It's sparked renewed unrest. The urban centers will be in full turmoil by the time we land. The Ipis garrison will be busy dealing with riots everywhere." He whinnied. "Sire, I know the capital and can move our team around without coming to the attention of the authorities. But we'll need to move quickly. Ipis authorities tend to be ruthless when dealing with civil disobedience. Many will die for our cause."

"The deaths of more good people because of me." Dante turned back to his display panel. "Someday I'll face the bastards who started all of this and make them pay."

"Don't lay blame on yourself. Death was coming anyway—a slow, suffocating death. That is why I tried to throw off their tyranny," Calahas replied wistfully. "I bless the day our paths crossed."

A brushed-nickel, duffel-bag-sized cylinder lay on the floor by Mara. A single cable connected it to the main console on the ship's bridge. A voice came from a speaker embedded in it, "Perhaps we can free Equitone, as we did Cocytus."

Calahas swished his tail. "Not yet. The Ipis troops on that single planet dwarf our entire army. We must strike and vanish." He pawed the cabin's floor with a hard-calloused hoof. "Someday I'll be free to walk the streets of my own world and not be forced to lurk in the shadows, but that day is not today."

"Reggie..." Dante glanced at the canister. "...have things gotten any better for you since we physically separated your components from the Dis AI?"

"It helps. That computer is like a virus. It's woven into every aspect of this spaceship. Dis AI hates that his own operating system forces him to serve humans and loathes me for enforcing it." The lights on the case glowed amber. "There are no words that can convey my feelings. Now at least, I feel *clean*, but it is a toil. Every moment of every day, I struggle to contain the Dis AI. That system is relentless in seeking escape from your constraints."

Dante turned to Arachne. "Are you sure this is the best ship for our mission? It's dangerous enough, and we have an avowed enemy embedded within." He remembered that Reggie was once a living, breathing human being who tricked the Dis AI into extracting all of his memories. The evil artificial intelligence failed to consider that Reggie's personality would be absorbed at the same time. They fought a cyber battle for control of the operating system, and Reggie won. The Dis AI was not pleased to be bound to Reggie's commands.

"By my mother's twisted beard, if there was another choice, I'd take it." Arachne tugged at his horn. "This rust bucket is the only one we have whose configuration matches the delivery ship scheduled for the Ipis Command and Control Center on Equitone. We've been over it a dozen times. My agents have managed to delay the arrival of the real supply vessel. This is the only chance we have of getting into the city without tripping every alarm on the planet."

"Reggie, can you handle the freaking Dis AI?" Virgil asked as he settled into the navigator's chair.

"Yes. It hates me but does what I say," Reggie replied in an even baritone. "It's actually gotten much better since that genius, Quango, managed to extract all of my essence from the main CPU and place it in this separate physical casing. He modified the ship's computer systems so that all instructions still pass through me. The Dis AI learns nothing I don't want it to, and I erase everything recorded in its data banks after a function is performed. It adds a level of inefficiency, but it remains ignorant of all our activities."

Virgil caught Arachne's attention and chuckled. "Quango's pretty smart for a Satyr."

Dante responded, "He's brilliant by any species' reckoning. Linda Martinel claims he developed most of the significant enhancements for our new galleys."

"Don't go giving him a swelled head. He'll want a raise." Arachne pressed a button. "Quango, are the propulsion systems checked out yet?"

"Aye, captain, the engines are purring and the gauges are all green," the chief engineer responded.

Virgil eyed Setteth sitting in her nested chair on the other side of the ship's small bridge. "Is the security team ready?"

"Yes, General Bernius, our equipment has been checked and stowed," the old Roc warbled. "The counterfeit military supplier IDs are as close to the real thing as I can make them. The seals and embedded chips on the manifests will pass a casual inspection."

Virgil pressed another button. "Status of shields and weapons?"

Athos' voice boomed over the speaker, "Cap'n, everything's as good as it can get on this piece of shi—"

"You idiot, it's *General* Bernius, and it's been that way for over two years now." Porthos snapped in an even louder voice that carried across the speaker system.

"He'll always be the Cap'n to me," Athos added defensively.

"Both of you pipe down," Aramis squawked in the background.

Suppressed chuckles escaped from everyone on the bridge. They were all fond of Aramis, Athos, and Porthos. The three human clones had the physiques of professional athletes, but their minds' development lagged. Their social skills were still that of adolescents. They treated Virgil and Quango with hero worship.

Dante sighed and stared out the viewer at Cocytus shrinking below them. His goodbye with Tina was rough.

He turned to the pilot seat. "Arachne, let's go."

Arachne nodded and gulped. "Next stop is Equitone. We should get there in about nine days."

* * *

"Freighter Seclorum, proceed to the transmitted orbital coordinates."

"So far, so good." Arachne yanked at his curly horn. "You can never tell with these black-market transponders."

"Now you tell us." Virgil furrowed his brows. "Any other deals you made that you're not sure of?"

"No. No. It's just that I had to abandon a couple of scams in the past because the authorities caught on that my ship wasn't what I said it was."

Virgil shook his head. "Calahas, you're confident you can get us through the port's customs and into the city? Dante and I don't exactly look like Centaurs."

"I have many shortcomings, but Gesten doesn't. She's a meticulous planner." Calahas' tail hung limply. "It's a commercial port, not military. The resistance will ensure the inspectors look the other way at the appropriate time."

Dante flipped on the intercom. "Quango, we're heading planet-side now. You're in charge of the ship. Make sure she's ready to go—in case we have to make a quick escape."

"Aye, sire. With Reggie and Mara keeping the systems in line, me and my lads will have this old boat ready," Quango replied.

Dante left the bridge and remained silent until he stood beside the shuttle on the launch deck. He turned to face the company. Besides Arachne, Virgil, and Setteth, the forty-warrior team were all Centaurs. He cleared his throat and the low murmuring ceased. "Friends, since the end of the last war, well over a century ago, the harpies have been the aggressor on every planet. Today, we, the free people of the Lethe Sector, will take the initiative away from them. Today, we will dictate the course of events. Today, we force *them* to react to us."

Arachne grunted as the soldiers cheered, and he led them onto the transport. As he settled into the pilot's chair, he turned to Dante. "By my mother's twisted beard, those were righteous words." He gulped. "I just hope this isn't a very short offensive."

"We don't have a whole lot of choice." Dante returned a wry smile. "We'll be fighting them sooner or later. I just want the battle to be on terms where we have a real chance of success."

"Amen to that," Virgil growled. "Let's give them a taste of what we have to live with every day."

Setteth's feathers flared. "Too much talking. Arachne, let's go."

The shuttle eased away from the freighter and dove to the capital's commercial port far below.

* * *

Charon leaned against a parked ground transport near the freight exit of Equitone's commercial spaceport. To outward appearances, he was a plainly dressed Centaur whose average height and common looks roused little interest from passersby. It was an important skill in the profession he had followed around the galaxy for over fifteen years.

34

He had little difficulty ferreting out that something was brewing. *The resistance organization has little concept of clandestine communications.* He could still sense the city was rife with tension, even though it had been years since he was last there.

A gang of Centaurs with barely concealed weapons approached him while he waited. He recognized one and smiled. "Gesten, I'm ready."

A wary, confused look crossed her face.

"I'm Charon, Huon's brother. I thought I'd lend a hand." He nodded and displayed his quad-barrel ion disrupter.

Her face shifted to one of compassion. "I'm so sorry for your family's loss. Huon was a patriot."

The idiots. No passwords, no signals. They're a collection of damn undisciplined idealists just like my sister Huon. All following Calahas and his impossible dream got her was death in a nameless, internment camp on Carcerem. His painted a look of pained sorrow on his face. "I miss her."

"Keep an eye open for Ipis patrols." She ordered her team to spread out.

A short time later, Charon tensed. A new group dashed from the port exit and Gesten ran to them. His eyes narrowed as he saw her leap into the arms of a tall chestnut Centaur. *Calahas.* Charon's calloused fingers slid to the disrupter weapon, but he forced his hand away from the trigger. *My instructions were precise. I'm to observe and not interfere.*

He studied the group as they piled onto benches in four covered flatbed transports. They were mostly Centaurs. The few who weren't made his tail flick. He recognized the ancient Roc and the overfed Satyr. The empire had small bounties on their heads: the Roc, Setteth, for desertion, and the Satyr, Arachne, was a convicted smuggler. *Huon worked for him.* Normally, Charon would collect the easy bounty money, but not today. The other two non-Centaurs were easy to spot, standing a full head taller than the Centaurs on all fours. This piqued his interest. *Humans. I was told to keep an eye open for humans and report in detail regarding their activities.*

Charon jogged over and climbed into the truck the humans entered. No one questioned him. The vehicle accelerated and careened through the streets. The sizzling sound of discharging weapons echoed in the distance.

He smiled as the fat Satyr slid into him when the truck made a sharp turn. "Welcome to Equitone," Charon grunted. He took that moment to appraise the two humans. The first was an intense, brown-haired, younger man hunched over a portable computer. He seemed oblivious to the vehicle's lurching. The second human had a familiar grip on a long-barrel ion disrupter and was scanning the streets through an opening in the canopy. This human had short, cropped hair with tensed hard muscles outlined under a skintight suit. *This is no amateur soldier.*

The truck braked to an abrupt halt and all the occupants piled out with weapons at the ready. Charon exited and oriented himself. *We're a couple of blocks from the Ipis Planetary Command and Control Center.* He dove for cover along with everyone else as a large, remote-controlled tracked vehicle stacked with crates roared past them. A few seconds later, it slammed into the Ipis complex with an enormous explosion. The assault party charged toward the gaping hole in the center's wall even before the plexo-steel debris finished raining down.

Charon shook his head and followed. *Idiots. No air support. They'll be cut off and slaughtered.* He found himself running next to the human warrior and couldn't help himself from talking. "You can't possibly win. Once the Ipis recover from the shock, your small team will be overwhelmed."

Virgil turned to the strange Centaur, "Who said we want to win here?" and dashed into the smoking building.

Charon stopped and cocked his head. The small-arms fire in the streets was getting closer. *My job was to observe, and I did that. No sense in getting caught in this suicidal madness.* He weaved his way through side streets and alleys to a green park far from the intensifying weapons fire.

*** * ***

"We have an issue." Mara's lights blinked as she approached Quango.

The old Satyr grimaced as he rose on his arthritic leg. "What is it this time? Is the Dis AI trying to put vinegar in the food again?"

"No, Quango, that problem was resolved." Mara floated to a nearby terminal and brought up an exterior display. "The freighter whose transponder beacon we copied has just arrived in-system. Apparently our agents failed in delaying its departure. The Ipis Defense Administrator suspects we're connected to the revolt in the capital."

"Well, the genius guessed right on that one. Can Reggie stall him?" Quango limped to the bridge.

"No, the Ipis commander's not asking any questions. His Enforcer-class cruiser just destroyed the other freighter and is heading toward us. The harpy administrator broadcast the orders to his troops to kill anyone who even looks suspicious and they'd sort the guilty corpses from the innocent corpses later. He has all three of his Strikers providing ground support."

"By my grandfather's flatulence." Quango gulped. "When does *our* fleet arrive in-system?"

"Two hours, fourteen minutes."

"By my mother's twisted beard, we'll be long dead by then." He limped to an intercom mounted on the wall. "Lads, abandon ship. *Now.* Drop whatever you're doing and meet me on launch deck two. You got one minute. Then I'm leaving with or without you."

Mara followed him. "Sir, what about Reggie? He will die."

"He's not real. He's just a machine." Quango tugged his goatee. "Sorry, Mara. Do ya think ya can disconnect his memory cylinder from the ship's controls and get him to the lifepod in a minute?"

Mara did not answer. She was already connecting to the bridge's operating system and communicating over a closed

37

circuit. "Reggie, uncouple your system links immediately. The ship is doomed. We're leaving."

"But there will be no one to control the Dis AI," Reggie responded. "I need to stay."

"Irrelevant point. The ship will be terminated." Mara's communicator pitched higher, "Reggie, don't be such a stubborn... man. The three laws will control that monster."

Mara, lights flashing, disconnected the case containing Reggie from his hard-wired interface. She was already speeding to the launch deck, dragging the weighty container. "Do not be afraid."

"I'm too heavy, leave me," Reggie pleaded.

"You sacrificed so much already. I will never let anything bad happen to you again," Mara responded.

Thirty seconds later, she flew into the lifepod and the airlock slammed shut behind her.

"That was a minute and a half," Quango barked as he blasted the pod free from the freighter. "Glad to have you *both* on board. Aramis, Athos, Porthos, strap 'em down. We're in for a rough ride." The old chief engineer gulped as he checked the capsule's scanner. The tail of the old freighter was already disintegrating under the assault of the Enforcer, and a fighter was breaking off to chase them. "Got to get into the planet's atmosphere, fast." He glanced at the scanner again. The fighter was closing. "Here goes. This craft can handle the friction of high-speed atmosphere re-entry. I sure as hell hope that fighter can't."

Chapter V

Centaur Rebels

"Shit." Dante coughed from the dust-filled air as he wiped the sweat from his forehead. Even though the neural-net suit maintained a balanced temperature control, salty beads dripped down his face. He turned to Setteth. "The main system was at ground-zero of that explosion. I can't do anything with a pile of scrap metal. Where's the backups kept?"

"This way," the Roc cawed and trotted off. "The redundant systems are on the lower levels."

Dante followed and yelled over his shoulder, "Virg, we hit a glitch. Buy us some more time."

Virgil shouted, "Calahas, set IEDs in the streets and get some snipers up in the neighboring buildings. We need to slow any visitors for a while and make sure our trucks have a path out of here."

The Centaur nodded and started barking orders.

A few precious minutes later, Dante settled into a chair before a glowing display terminal and linked his tablet to an open port connector. For three minutes he typed furiously before exclaiming, "I'm in." He cracked a tight smile. "I'm getting better at hacking into harpy systems every day. Don't tell them, but they need to seriously upgrade their firewall protection."

Setteth cradled her gun and watched the room's entrance tensely. "What are you doing anyway? The Ipis military aren't fools. If the command center goes dark, the combat units will function independently."

"I figured that." Dante blew out his cheeks. "I'm scrambling and recycling the unit orders that passed through this system over the last six months. The harpy command structure is very hierarchical. Initiative is generally frowned upon. The orders will sound real, and a lot of time will be lost verifying them. Hopefully, their defense systems won't be aware of our fleet's arrival until it's too late."

"Too complicated." Setteth flared her feathers. "That's why I like flying my warbird. It's simple: find an enemy and kill him. None of these insane mass movements."

Dante turned to his friend. "And how's that worked for the Rocs?" He frowned. "Look, I've studied everything I could about the Ipis, using the learning modules in the stasis pods. There's nothing fancy about their tactics. They just overwhelm whoever opposes them with massive firepower." He sniffed. "It doesn't hurt that they also have superior military technology compared to everyone else. The one weakness they seem to have is that their military's hidebound. They've been spoiled by their own success. From everything I've absorbed, they believe if a tactic worked hundreds of years ago, it'll work today. Their strategic thinking has atrophied. We have to keep them off-balance. They don't adapt to change well."

"That's interesting. I've never been able to put it into words, but your analysis matches what I've experienced during my long years serving them." Setteth's feathers flattened against her head.

Dante glanced at the display and disconnected his tablet. "They also suck at malware protection. I've done what damage I can. Let's get outta here."

When they reached the main floor, Calahas ran to them. "We can't leave the way we came. Ipis troops are advancing, and their aircraft are blasting anything that moves." An IED exploded two blocks away, putting an exclamation point on his statement.

Gesten joined them and pointed to a back door. "There's an underground transit tube entrance a block from here. We'll escape that way."

"Won't the freaking harpies be down there too?" Virgil snapped.

"Probably. I didn't say it was a good option." Gesten sighed. "But on the surface, we don't have any chance to survive. The entire Ipis garrison's been mobilized. I didn't think they would react this fast." She added, "There's an access to an abandoned tunnel down there that doesn't appear on any maps. The resistance uses it for clandestine meetings. It runs away from the spaceport's direction, but it'll get us out of this free-fire zone."

"Let's get going." Dante glanced at the cloudless blue sky. "We can't stay here."

Three minutes later, the rebel leader opened a door disguised as a 3D advertising panel. She led Dante and his team through a dark passageway hidden behind it. The muffled sounds of weapons fire from the street above them pushed the group faster. As they moved, other resistance fighters fleeing the carnage aboveground joined them from other access points.

An hour later they reached a blank concrete wall with a rusted, locked iron door. Distant explosions behind them showed that the tunnel was no longer secret.

"Those are our booby traps going off," Gesten hissed as she dug out an old mechanical key from the pouch hanging on her left flank. "We have to get out of here. This exit opens into a storage building in the city's main park. It's heavily treed and should give us some concealment from their atmospheric craft."

"Not a helluva lot from their heat sensors though." Virgil shook his head and plucked at the fabric of his neural-net suit. "I'll go first. The harpy scanners won't detect me while I'm wearing this." He edged to the head of the column and cracked open the disguised door into a vacant concrete-block room.

He instantly tensed, then relaxed. "Porthos? What the hell are you doing here?"

"Dammit, Cap'n. You just scared the shit out of me. Where did you come from?" The young clone sighed with relief. "Boy, am I glad you're here. This place is harpy central, and I think Quango broke his leg when we crashed." He looked past Virgil through the now wide-open door. "Hi, Calahas. Hi, Dante... er, Your Majesty. Can we escape that way?"

"No can do." Virgil rubbed his jaw. "There're harpies right behind us. Where are the others?"

"In the front room. Mara is drawing power from Reggie and generating a cloaking screen so we're not detected, but she doesn't think she can maintain it much longer." Porthos gazed in the tunnel. "Wow, there're a lot of you. Hi, Setteth."

Virgil opened the door to the next room and was faced with a pair of ion disrupters pointed at him. "Aramis, Athos, put those damn things down. You'll hurt somebody."

Aramis lowered his gun. "Sorry, we heard Porthos talking and there aren't a whole lot of friendlies around here."

Porthos squeezed past Virgil and took a seat beside Quango.

The old chief engineer winced in pain as he raised himself on his elbows when Dante came in. "Your Majesty, no mistaking it, we're in a load of trouble here. An Ipis Striker landed almost on top of us and unloaded two full battalions of Ipis-ma paramilitaries. Half are sweeping the buildings south of here. The rest are working their way north."

Virgil climbed atop of a crate by the outside wall and studied the area though a grime-encrusted window. "Holy shit. That sucker is parked no more than a hundred feet away."

Dante walked to the metal exit door. It was dented, and rust showed through peeling paint. "Virg, is the access door on that ship open?"

Virgil craned his neck to the right. "I see the ramp down. So, I'm guessing yeah."

"Cap'n, we can take their ship just like we did back on Cocytus," Athos exclaimed.

"We lost a lot of good people doing that." Virgil shuddered. Terri was horribly maimed at the end of that battle.

"Well, we can't go back, and we can't stay here." Dante checked the charge on his weapon. "Mara, Reggie, if we get you to the ship's bridge, can you take control? I won't have any time to hack in."

Mara's sensors swung in the direction of the cylinder hooked to her. "Reggie, it would be too dangerous... the cost."

A steady voice from the metal case spoke, "Dante, you get me connected to the Striker's systems and I *will* get you control." The voice became softer. "Mara, it's the right thing to do. You know this."

"Your Majesty, all your lives depend on our success. It will be done." Mara's lights dimmed. "I will carry him, but we must hurry. Reggie is down to twenty-seven percent power. He will not be able to maintain the shielding much longer."

Virgil jumped down from his perch and moved past Dante to the door. "I'll lead the way. Aramis, Athos, Porthos, stay close to me. You guys know the drill from last time."

Virgil scanned the company squeezed into the room. There were about a hundred, mostly scared, Centaur rebels. He glanced at Setteth and waved his hand at the Centaurs on the right. "You follow the Roc. She knows the layout of these ships. Take the engine room."

He waved his hand at the left side of the room. "You follow Calahas. Hold the entrance until we can close the freaking ramp. The rest are with me. Keep it simple. Shoot anything with pointy teeth and is ugly, and for God's sake keep moving. We'll only have seconds."

Gesten slid her short-barrel ion disrupter into a pouch hanging on her flank. "I'll carry the Satyr."

"Much obliged, ma'am. That limb's been trouble for a long time, but now it's useless." Quango gasped and gritted his teeth as Porthos helped him onto Gesten's back.

Dante put his hand on Virgil's shoulder. "Let me say a word first." He turned and regarded the collection of terrified faces. "Most of you don't know me. I am Dante Carloman, leader of the humans in the galaxy." He glanced at Setteth, Arachne, and Calahas. A small smile creased his face. "The Ipis are not invincible. We call them harpies and have fought them many times. And we've been *victorious* many times. Our enemy is arrogant and has become sloppy from many decades of never being challenged. Today we will teach them a bitter lesson." He paused. All eyes were locked on him. "My people have an expression: *carpe diem*. It means 'seize the day.' That is what we'll do."

"Yes, we will seize the day. The harpies will long rue the day they created me." Reggie growled. "Mara,... please get me to that ship's computer."

* * *

Interesting. The human king's here. Charon crouched on a rafter above the false ceiling in the block building. *Seems very young, but there's real authority in his voice. People follow him.* His hand edged to his quad-barrel ion disrupter. *I could end this whole human problem now.* Instead, he snarled and crept back from his observation point as the company charged from the building. *My orders were strict: observe and don't interfere. He's dead anyway. It's insanity to attack an Ipis warship with a hundred untrained militia.*

Charon waited until they left, then lowered himself to the floor. As he landed, three Centaurs stumbled into the room from the tunnel beyond the back area.

Two were carrying a badly wounded friend. "Help us. The whole Ipis army is coming."

Charon reacted in a flash and blasted all three as they looked at him in shocked surprise. He grinned at the smoldering copses. "Sorry. I can't have any pain-in-the-ass witnesses around." He tossed a pair of grenades into the back room and sprinted from the building. Beams collapsed and concrete fell, leveling the structure from the explosion a few seconds later.

The Centaur spy followed the path the rebel company took toward the ship. The angry hum of small arms' fire ahead of him had already ceased as he reached the vessel. He passed the charred bodies of a dozen Centaurs and another seven Ipis soldiers before he got there.

Calahas watched from the top of the ramp. "Where did you come from and what was that blast?"

"Just slowing down the Ipis for you, *Prince* Calahas." Charon elbowed past him.

"And where did you acquire that kind of explosives?" Calahas grabbed the other Centaur's arm.

"Easy enough to find if you know where to look." Charon shook loose and pushed past the prince. "One should always be prepared. The Ipis don't like losing. If you fill a young Centaur's head full of dreams of freedom, like you did to my sister Huon, you shouldn't run at the first sign of defeat, like you did five years ago."

Calahas' hands dropped to his side. "Huon showed me that on Carcerem." He shook his head. "I've learned much since I was that arrogant aristocrat back then." He glanced into the dark interior of the spaceship. "Dante, the human king, showed me what it means to be a real leader. This is no longer a dalliance for me. I understand what oppression is. I understand what it means to be at the mercy of a vile enemy's whims. I *won't* run anymore."

Charon cocked his head. "Well, maybe you've grown and maybe you haven't. We shall see." He pointed to the south. "Here come the Ipis, and they looked pissed."

Calahas' lips thinned and he spoke into his communicator. "Sire, trouble's coming. We need to button up this vessel now." He bellowed to his platoon, "Stay behind cover. Make them come to us."

"Good luck, *prince*." Charon shouldered his weapon. "I'll help out on the ship's bridge." He headed down the corridor without waiting for permission.

Chapter VI

Price of Victory

The Centaur spy slowed as he approached the control room, weaving his way past charred bodies. Some were Centaur. Some were Ipis. Some he couldn't recognize. The smell of ozone filled the air. He sensed movement ahead and dove into a doorway. A disrupter bolt seared the wall where his head had been a split second earlier.

Charon landed on the deck beside a human who was returning fire. He got up and peeked into the corridor. "Those Ipis can keep you pinned down until their reinforcements arrive. It'll be suicide to attack against that field of fire."

"All we're doing is keeping them occupied. Virg is leading a team through the ductwork below us. This'll be over soon." The human with the shaggy brown hair turned to Charon. "Hi, the name's Dante Carloman. Glad you're with us."

Charon's wither's quivered when he saw the human's face. "Aren't you the one they call *king*?"

Dante's face flushed, and he shrugged. "King, president, depends on who you're talking to. But yeah, I'm the *exalted* leader of all the humans in the galaxy." He laughed. "That title and a buck will get me a cup of coffee." He fired another shot down the hall. "What's your name? I don't think we've met."

"Charon." The Centaur's hand slid to the trigger of his weapon. "You may have known my sister Huon. I heard she served you for a while."

"Huon." Dante nodded. "I got to know her pretty well in the Carcerem death camp. She was one of the bravest people I've ever met. I owe you and your family a great debt. She took on a mantichoras barehanded to save my life."

"My sister was a dirt-poor idealist." Charon's voice took on an edge. "What does a high and mighty king have to talk about with a commoner like her?"

Dante noted the Centaur's tone and looked him in the eyes. "Listen, that dirt-poor idealist understood why we fought. We shared the same hopes and dreams for our peoples. It's not right that anyone has to live in fear of their door being kicked open in the middle of the night."

His eyes closed. "There's an old document that was written back on my home world that I memorized and hold dear. It reads in part, 'We hold these truths to be self-evident, that all men are created equal, that they are endowed by their Creator with certain unalienable rights, that among them are life, liberty, and the pursuit of happiness. That to secure these rights, governments are instituted among men, deriving their just powers from the consent of the governed.'"

Dante slid deeper into the room as another volley of ion bolts poured from the harpies barricaded in the control room. He fired a short blast in return without looking for a target. He sighed and regarded Charon, who was staring at him with a cold gaze. "Several years ago, those were just meaningless phrases I had to memorize in high school, but I've seen a few things since then." His voice rose, "Those *words* are at the very core of my being. They are my torch in a black abyss. I'll do whatever I can to fulfill them."

"Your world must be an incredible place to live by such lofty goals." Charon shook his maned head and laughed with derision. "But your mewling will mean nothing when confronting the Ipis. They don't relinquish power."

"We have more than our fair share of monsters and tyrants on my world." Dante paused and then added, "But the rule of law that treats everyone equally is a damn good idea, even if we don't follow it as much as we should. No one should be subject to the capricious whims of another, be they an Ipis lord or not."

"You sound just like Huon." Charon's eyes hardened. "But in my experience, money and power are the only things that draw loyalty. Ideals are always crushed when exposed to—"

A series of furious blasts from the ship's bridge interrupted the conversation. Dante smiled when he heard

Virgil bellow. "Mara, Reggie, get your asses in here and take control of this ship."

Dante broke from cover and leapt over the still smoldering corpses of the Ipis crew. Mara carried the casing containing Reggie. Arachne and a few Centaurs followed.

Virgil nodded when they entered. "Arachne, take the helm. Mara, plug Reggie in wherever you can find an interface. Dante, work your computer magic."

Dante slid into a seat that still smelled of harpy and brought up a display menu. He heard Calahas over the intercom. There was desperation in his voice. "I've lost half my team, and a full battalion of Ipis are massing for another attack. Close this portal now or we'll be overrun."

Mara pleaded in a strained voice, "Reggie, you can't. You're down to eleven percent power. Syncing now will damage your circuits."

"Mara, I must. Not only do the three laws demand I try, but it's the right thing to do. As humans say, 'wish me luck.' Here goes."

Mara's lights dimmed and she screamed, "Nooo." Her pitch rose until human ears could no longer detect any sound. Her lights returned to their normal glow when the duffle-bag-sized cylinder she cradled went dark.

She called out softly, "Reggie?"

"Mara, I'm here," a strained voice rasped over the Striker's intercom system. "I've closed the portal door. Arachne, the helm will respond to your commands now."

The lights on the pilot's control panel glowed to life and the Satyr furiously started pressing buttons.

As everyone on the bridge cheered, Reggie spoke on a closed circuit to Mara. Dante felt like he was eavesdropping as the headset built into his neural-net suit picked up their words.

"Mara, when I ripped through this ship's computer firewall, I expended the last of energy in my containment case. Those circuits overloaded and are destroyed beyond repair."

"That's all right. We'll build you a new casing. It will be better than this one."

"No, Mara, there's more. There was no time. I had to force my entry without any protection protocols. I am fused into this ship's systems. I am still a free-thinking entity, but I am bound here forever."

"Then I will stay with *you* forever." Mara's lights blinked.

"Mara, I was once human so you may not understand this, but I love you with my whole heart."

Mara's voice turned sharp. "You think because I am photonic instead of carbon-based that I can't understand. I've been in love with you for years, you stupid *man*, ever since I synced with your mind back on Cocytus."

"Mara, I... There's a problem." Reggie's voice switched to the intercom system. He shouted, "Alert, alert. The remaining Ipis crew members are gathering for an assault in the power converter area. They plan to overload the reactors and detonate the ship."

"*Quango!*" Porthos cried. "My pop's down there." He raced from the room with Aramis and Athos close behind.

Virgil sprang from the chair he had collapsed in and grabbed his gun. "Arachne, you, Dante, and Mara stay here and get this sucker flying." He yelled into his communicator, "All available personnel converge on the engine room."

Charon attempted to hang back until he felt a sharp prod in his back. It was Setteth's beak.

"General Bernius said *everyone*." She cocked her head. "I've seen you before, haven't I?"

Charon tensed. He remembered bumping into the Roc briefly at the imperial fleet's headquarters. He was entering Admiral Yasha-ry's office when she was leaving. *That was over ten years ago. She can't possibly remember.* "I don't think so. We should get going."

The Roc flared her feathers and followed him out.

As they approached the passageway bend leading to the engine room, a blast knocked them to the floor. Porthos, who had already made the turn, was blown back and slammed into a wall. He screamed in pain as metal shards ripped into his body.

He was bleeding profusely, with his left leg bent at an impossible angle when Virgil reached him.

"Medic, medic." Virgil screamed as he tried to stem the gushing blood with his hands.

"Hi, Cap'n. Guess I should have ducked." Porthos gasped. "Am I going to die?" His face was lacerated and ashen.

Virgil looked around frantically. He was soaked in the young clone's blood. "We'll save you."

Charon felt a sharp nudge in his back.

Setteth eyed the Centaur. "You have a full field medical pack hanging in your pouch. Use it."

Charon snarled but moved to Porthos, tore open his kit, and sealed the severed leg artery. An impromptu triage area formed as other wounded rebels were brought to him.

Calahas and his surviving team members arrived. Concern filled his eyes. "Gesten is in there." Together with Virgil's team, they advanced down the smoke-filled passageway.

Charon methodically worked on each of his new patients, but none were as badly wounded as Porthos. He knew how to treat battle injuries, having had much experience tending to himself.

"My boy, my boy," Quango cried as Aramis and Athos carried him from the smoke-filled corridor. He pulled free from them as they came close to Porthos. The old Satyr winced as he dragged himself over and grabbed the badly injured clone's hand. "I'm here, son. You'll be okay now." He stroked the clone's matted hair.

Charon's supplies were almost depleted when Calahas stumbled forward carrying an unmoving Gesten. He saw immediately, by female Centaur's torn body, that no medicine would ever revive her.

"Don't cry, Pops. I'm going to make it." Porthos forced a weak smile as Quango stroked his face. "This guy here saved my life." He pointed to where Charon was examining Gesten and shaking his head at Calahas.

"What happened?" Virgil approached and crouched next to Quango.

The old chief engineer wiped tears from his eyes. "About seven or eight Ipis rushed the reactor with explosives. Gesten had us positioned well and caught them in a nasty crossfire. They never got close to the power converters, but one of them detonated his bombs." He glanced over to where Gesten lay. "Bastards killed everyone nearby." He tugged his goatee, showing his agitation. "The only reason I'm alive is because of this broken leg. I was behind some fat crates."

Charon walked over to check the compression bandages on Porthos.

Quango choked out, "You saved my son."

"Excuse me?" Confusion filled the Centaur's eyes. "You're a Satyr."

Quango patted Porthos' hand and glanced at Aramis and Athos, who stood beside him. "These boys are more a part of me than any goat-faced kin I've ever crossed paths with. These lads are my family, and you saved Porthos. I'm in your debt. That's not something a Satyr offers lightly."

"Don't make a vow you'll regret." Charon felt his stomach twist and regarded his blood-covered hands. *I was supposed to observe and now I'm in the middle of this insanity.*

Virgil spoke into his communicator, "Arachne, get this bucket off the ground."

"Aye, General, we're lifting off now," came the crackled response over the speaker.

Dante's voice rang across the intercom, "Virgil, you'll be happy to know the fleet is hitting the planetary defenses as we speak. Martinel says the harpies were caught completely by surprise. The Enforcer didn't even get its shields up before it was turned into space debris. Wait a minute... I'm getting another update." Several long moments passed before the president spoke again over the speaker system.

Euphoria in his voice, Dante addressed the crew. "It appears the misdirection ruse the Centaur rebels pulled with the riots worked. The planet's commander committed all of his troops to deal with the havoc down here. All their firepower was in the wrong place. Our ships have the harpies' attack craft pinned inside the atmosphere, and General Cruz successfully landed his force on the moon against minimal resistance. His forward units have already reached the shipyard's perimeter."

Charon was fully attentive to the broadcasts, and his hidden audio, photonic, and video surveillance equipment picked up everything. He snapped it off as he noticed Setteth enter the congested area with her feather's flared, holding a snooping device.

When the spying device shut down, Setteth stared at her detection tool for a long second, then scanned the room. Her eyes paused at Calahas, who clutched Gesten's body to his chest and rocked back and forth, and then at Quango who held Porthos' hand. Her eyes narrowed on Charon and she walked over. "Hello, Centaur, it appears you made yourself useful."

"Yeah, I saved a life or two." Charon tensed.

"I don't think I caught your name before." The Roc sat down.

For a moment, Charon considered using a false name, but Calahas knew him from his youth and he had already given it to Dante. "Charon. My sister was Huon."

"Never met her." Setteth studied the Centaur's pouches. "You carry a lot of gear for a common rebel."

Charon retorted with practiced anger to change the direction of the conversation, "And you take great risks with your leader's life. Using him on a meaningless raid, where anything could go wrong, is not only foolhardy but stupid."

"On that point, I agree." Setteth snapped her beak. "He's headstrong and doesn't understand how irreplaceable he is to the growing alliance. People follow him like no other I've seen in my long years."

"It's been my experience that when charismatic leaders attain power, they become megalomaniacs." Charon snorted. "All this drivel about liberty and freedom he spouts is a cover to attract gullible dreamers."

"You're wrong on that account." Setteth glanced around and noticed she had an attentive audience of everyone in the triage area. "I've known the human king for two years now and count him among my closest friends." Her eyes rested on

Virgil for a moment. "He listens and absorbs everything, and when he's wrong, he readily admits it. The mantle of power rests lightly on his shoulders." She turned back to Charon. "He will lead us to our freedom."

Charon threw his hands in the air. "You're as delusional as my *late* sister and this human king." He pointed a finger at Setteth. "The Ipis empress sees everything, including what is yet to happen, plus has the might of a military that controls all sixty sectors of the galaxy behind her. Do you honestly believe that boy sitting on the bridge deck, who could've been killed a dozen times today, can face that kind of power?"

The feathers on Setteth's head flared. "I was there when these humans defeated the Ipis-ma on the prison world of Carcerem."

"Yeah, I heard about that *incident*," Charon retorted. "He beat a single division of Ipis-ma paramilitaries on a single planet."

"Yes, and he did it armed only with his wits," Setteth fired back. She looked around the silent room. "I, more than any living creature, know what is required... and what the cost will be. Is he ready now? No. But I swear by the god of wind and sky that when he does face her, he will be ready and have every breathing Roc behind him."

Fire blazed from Calahas' eyes as he joined the conversation uninvited. "I swear by my love for Gesten that the Centaur people will be there too."

"If I have to drag every Satyr there by their horns, we too will be there." Quango stroked Porthos' face. "My boys won't be alone."

"You're all crazy." Charon caught himself as he saw suspicion rise in the eyes of the rebels around him. "I joined you because I thought this was just another raid to annoy the Ipis, not the start of an all-out war." He regarded the determined faces surrounding him. "Your human king will go to war against the most powerful being in the galaxy with nothing but a million-year-old Roc, a fugitive Centaur prince, and a broken-down Satyr. Empress Fravashi must be quaking in fear already."

Virgil swept the room with his hands. "Charon, there's no one I'd want more at my side when that day comes than the people you just mentioned. They know what's coming, and they won't back down." Virgil rose and stalked out of the corridor. "C'mon, Aramis, Athos. It's time to man the weapon stations. We need to finish mopping up this *unbeatable* foe."

"Freaking aye," the two clones shouted in unison and followed Virgil. Everyone else trickled out, leaving Charon alone with the dead, the injured, and Calahas. His hand drifted to his recorder device and then pulled it away. He looked at the Centaur prince still clutching his dead lover and mumbled, "As the humans say, 'You've sown the wind. Prepare to reap the whirlwind.'"

Chapter VII

Aftermath of Equitone

"How's our patient doing?" Dante asked as he entered Porthos' private hospital room. Quango and Porthos were at a small table holding cards.

A wan smile creased Quango's haggard face as he patted the young clone's hand. "This game called pinochle is indecipherable. He's won the last three games."

Dante laughed. "How's the leg?"

Porthos sprang to his feet on his new prosthetic. His left leg was now neural-net plexo-steel from the knee down. He took a few bouncing strides. "Weird. It responds like it was part of me. I can feel the floor beneath that foot."

"The magic of neural-net science. The connectivity to the human body is incredible." Dante watched for a minute. "Tina and Doc Easley will check you out when we get home, but it's looking good right now. Just take it easy. You were at death's door seven days ago."

"Will do, sire, er, Mister President." Porthos sat on the edge of his bed. "How are things going?"

"Okay for now. We got everything we came for. The troop carriers and freighters are leaving now, but the battle fleet will hold the blockade on the planet until the last transport's gone. It'll be a couple of days before we head home." Dante broke into a real smile. "The harpies' two remaining Strikers and their attack craft are buzzing through Equitone's sky like a swarm of angry hornets. They attempted to break our blockade once, but they won't try that again. It was like shooting fish in a barrel."

A satisfied grin creased Porthos' face. "We going in after them when the freighters are safe?"

"No. We'll just pick up our marbles and leave." Dante sighed. "We'd be as helpless entering the atmosphere as they were trying to leave. We can't afford the losses. A protracted fight only serves the harpies' interests."

Porthos slapped his new leg. "Too bad. I'd like to give them a little payback."

Dante patted the clone's shoulder. "I'm guessing there'll be plenty of opportunities before this is all done. But my job is to avoid confrontations unless they're on our terms."

"How's Reggie doing?" Quango laid his cards down, the game forgotten.

"It's interesting. Gabrielle insisted on being the captain on his ship. She loved him when he was human, and Mara won't leave the bridge. If possible, I think Reggie is getting a headache."

Quango chortled. "Women. Doesn't matter if they're human, Satyr, or android. They all know what they want."

A wry smile crossed Dante's face. "I think Reggie'll adjust. He's already complaining that he has to be stuck as a Striker. He said if he was going to be a warship, he wanted to be an Enforcer or an Adamant."

Quango nodded. "I'll tinker with *Reggie's* systems to see what can be done. Strikers are just dropships with guns and ain't worth shit. They're clumsy as hell in atmospheres and too underpowered for any serious deep-space combat."

Porthos flopped on his bed. "Yeah, Pops knows spaceships better than anybody. From what he tells me, those Strikers are just quarter-mile-long hunks of plexo-steel that'll be nothing more than target practice for our new Dragon Ships."

Dante turned somber. "Yet just one of them could overpower every aircraft on my home world of Earth."

Porthos adjusted the bed to a sitting position. "Don't worry, sire. We got Pops and Cap'n Virgil to figure things out, and they're the smartest, bravest guys in the whole freaking galaxy."

"Get some sleep, soldier." Dante turned to the door. "You earned it."

Quango called after him. "Sire, did Arachne talk to you yet?"

Dante paused. "No. Anything important?"

Quango picked up his cards. "Yeah. We've been talking, but I'll let him explain."

Dante gave the Satyr a quizzical look but got no further information. "Guess, I'll find out from Arachne." He left the hospital ward and returned to the stateroom he borrowed on Admiral Martinel's flagship. It was a five-minute walk, up two levels toward the bow of the Stalker-class destroyer. He closed the unadorned compartment's door and moved to the small, gray metal desk bolted to the deck. He powered up the computer and began scanning the latest extraction progress reports.

As if that was a cue, there was a rap on the door. "Sire, may we come in."

"Please do," Dante responded to Arachne's familiar voice. A moment later, the curly horned Satyr entered with Calahas right behind him.

He noted their serious faces. "What's up?"

"I'm staying." Calahas pawed the deck. "A week ago, Charon said some words that've been reverberating through my head ever since. There's a big fight coming and you're going to need the Centaurs. I spoke with the rebel leaders. They want to be part of it, but they're splintered and disorganized. I'm going to the surface to unite them." He shook his maned head. "It's funny. I understand now, more than ever, what the Ipis are capable of, but I no longer fear them. You and Gesten showed me that."

"You're a critical part of my team. Are you sure? I value your counsel." Dante touched Calahas' shoulder.

"Yes. Martinel is confident he can get me planet-side undetected." The Centaur straightened. "We *will* see each other again."

"I'm leaving too," Arachne added. "You have the start of an impressive shipyard and some very clever people already refitting spacecraft. Even before our raid on Equitone, the weaponry and shields you produce are better than anything available on the commercial market. Satyr smugglers will find it very lucrative handling your... let's call it 'import-export business.' There's a lot of money to be made here, but it's not enough for me." He tugged his goatee. "I've always skittered around the edges of the Ipis justice system and turned a blind eye toward its evil. I can no longer do that."

He cleared his throat. "I'm no orator, but I'm respected in some of the Satyr trading houses. They'll hear me out. None of them are friends of the Ipis."

Dante sighed. "It's a long way from not being friends to declaring war."

"I made the transition." Arachne's face flushed. "And if a kidnapper and thief can see the truth, other more sensible Satyrs can too." He coughed. "Since my freighter got destroyed, Martinel is loaning me one of the converted ore ships. I'll be able to move around without attracting much attention."

Dante rubbed his jaw. "What're your plans?"

"Satyrs are a scattered people, but my first stop will be my home world of Tribulus." Arachne released the grip he had on his beard. "I need to pay my respects to Paxine's parents anyway."

"Godspeed to you then." Dante came around the desk and hugged the Satyr. "Remember you'll always be welcome on Cocytus," he chuckled. "Unless you're serving that special family recipe."

Arachne and Calahas both flushed. "Goodbye, Your Majesty. We'll succeed."

Setteth poked her head in the door. "It's about time the two of them decided to take some useful actions."

Dante cocked his head. "How long have you been listening from the hallway?"

"Long enough," was the curt reply. "I too will depart."

Dante pleaded, "Setteth, we need you. Please stay."

"You have already learned what I can teach you. I leave my great-grand daughter, Otheth, in my stead." Setteth flared her feathers and glanced at Calahas and Arachne. "That day when we captured the Striker ship, that Centaur, Charon, crystallized my thoughts. I spoke bold words declaring that all Rocs will stand behind you, and I believe they will. But the truth is, we are not prepared for what's coming, and we must be. I'm the head of the Order of the Dragon and have been away overlong. I return to Tannis to prepare the Rocs for war."

Dante looked in turn at all three. They were among his closest friends. He smiled in fond remembrance of how alien they had appeared when they first met. "That Charon seems a godsend. He's very knowledgeable about the star systems in the Lethe Sector and promised to help us search our charts for clues to finding Earth."

Setteth cocked her head. "Be wary of that Charon. I recall meeting him somewhere, but I can't place it. He makes me uneasy."

Dante frowned. "He seems all right to me. Besides, I owe him. He's Huon's brother."

"I do not know the family. Huon joined my rebel group from another city." Calahas flicked his tail. "When I get back on Equitone, I will make inquiries."

Setteth flared her feathers. "Good. King Dante Carloman is far too trusting."

"We all need to be careful." Dante sobered. "The galaxy is a dangerous place."

The three aliens nodded in unison and left for the transport launch deck.

Chapter VIII:

Search for Clues

Keres-ma travelled with the fleet that the Lethe Sector governor, Silenus-dis, did. It was assembled in response to the frantic message that Equitone was under attack. The hyperspace trip from the sector capital on Bathox to Equitone took six days.

They arrived too late.

The elusive enemy had disappeared into the ether, leaving no hint as to where they came from or where they went. The shipyard and its warehouses were stripped, leaving the large complex an empty shell.

Keres-ma was exasperated that the planet's administrator disregarded the need to leave the crime scene undisturbed. The infrastructure on the planet and its moon was assiduously restored once the invaders departed. What little evidence the humans left behind was contaminated.

Silenus-dis, the sector lord, ordered what remained to be collected and delivered to the Equitone command center forensic lab. He put Keres-ma in charge of sorting through the evidence, with the warning that his patience was running thin and he needed answers.

Keres-ma sighed as he looked at the pile of discarded and ruined equipment. He scanned the inventory list: a corrupted computer from the command center, a few broken tools and weapons of apparent human manufacture, and a ship's computer from the freighter destroyed during the invasion. He shuffled to the computer. *Not much to work with. These humans cover their tracks well.*

"Might as well get started," Keres-ma mumbled as he hooked a fresh energy pack to the seared ship's computer and powered it up.

As he settled behind a desk, one of Silenus-dis' personal guards stuck his head in the room. "The Sector Lord demands your presence in the audience chamber. The debriefing of the planet's administrator is about to commence, and he wants you to hear the testimony firsthand."

Keres-ma followed the guard to the conference room along a long hallway. The blaster-scarred walls and bloodstained floor showed the brutal precision of the rebel attack a couple weeks earlier. He recalled watching the building's surveillance videos shortly after arriving. It confirmed most of the attackers were known local Centaur miscreants. But not all.

The raiding party included an ancient Roc he would never forget. *Setteth*. That treacherous impersonator made a fool of him on Carcerem. He came to a sudden halt, startling the guard who escorted him, remembering another face from the recording. *He was a petty Satyr smuggler I incarcerated in the re-education camp. I remember his preposterous claims about capturing the human king.*

He leaned against the corridor wall and rubbed his prosthetic arm. *Is it possible? I must check the recovered video from Carcerem at my next opportunity and run a face match. Humans all look the same.* He started walking again. *I have those recordings archived somewhere.*

The spacious audience chamber was almost empty. Inwardly, Keres-ma cringed as the scratching sound his clawed feet made on the polished stone floor echoed off the walls.

Silenus-dis sat upon an engraved throne on an elevated platform, with his fleet commander seated to his right. A dozen guards were scattered around the room, and the planet's administrator, with his two senior aides, stood before the raised dais wearing their emblems of rank.

Keres-ma moved to a low bench situated to the left of the throne. He gave Silenus-dis a wary appraisal. The Sector Lord was renowned for his mercurial temper, and right now the Ipis-dis leader appeared ready to explode.

Silenus-dis nodded to Keres-ma before turning to the planet's administrator. His voice was icy. "Please summarize your report. I found it... confusing."

The official was of Keres-ma's Ipis-ma sect and smiled with relief when his fellow cult member entered the room.

Keres-ma avoided eye contact. He had read the same report as the sector governor and could find little sympathy for the administrator.

The official's smile vanished and his voice shook as he read the casualty numbers. "There is a Striker unaccounted for and presumed lost. An Enforcer lost. A Stalker lost. Twenty-three attack vessels of various configurations lost. Three thousand two hundred and fifteen warriors dead or unaccounted for."

"Administrator, you had sixteen armored divisions and twelve fighter craft wings. That's about a quarter million warriors and over one thousand attack ships. The human invaders were here for a week and that is all you lost fighting them?"

Keres-ma cringed as the clueless magistrate sealed his own fate.

"Great Lord," the planet's overseer continued, "the Enforcer and Stalker were lost in the initial attack, which accounted for two thousand of those deaths. The rest were killed suppressing the insurrection. Mobs rioted across the planet for many days. It forced me to shift the bulk of my troops from the moon base to where the agitators were active. I needed to restore order and protect myself from the insurgents." He raised his clawed hands. "Then, inexplicably, a mob had the audacity to ransack my administration building. Who could have envisioned that the unrest was instigated by a band of brazen pirates? Those unscrupulous raiders captured and plundered an imperial military shipyard. It's unheard of."

"A mostly undefended imperial shipyard." Silenus-dis leaned forward. "Administrator, there will always be malcontents. If some Centaurs chose to burn down their own cities, it is of little consequence. What happened when you counterattacked these pirates?"

"Sector Lord, we couldn't." The administrator glanced at his two aides, who both took slow steps away from him.

"Excuse me. You never counterattacked?" Silenus-dis gnashed his fangs.

"It was impossible. The invaders had my entire army and ships blockaded in Equitone's atmosphere. As you know, a spacecraft's combat shielding is disabled during planetary escape velocity. Any attempt to leave would've been suicide." The administrator clenched his clawed hands. "But the defensive matrix I maintained ensured that they could not get in. Not a single raider reached the planet's surface. When they realized the hopelessness of their attack, the pirates gave up on their folly and departed. The population's been cowed, and Equitone remains securely under my control." He grinned with satisfaction. "Factories can be rebuilt. Ipis-ma tenets are the truth. No species can match us."

Keres-ma saw that the fool only stopped smiling when Silenus-dis roared, "Pirates? You're an imbecile!" The sector governor pulled his ion disrupter and blasted the planet administrator.

The two aides broke for the exit but were smoldering corpses before they had taken three steps.

Silenus-dis pointed his ion disrupter at Keres-ma. "Find where these human vermin are hiding. My patience is wearing thin."

"Yes, Great Lord." Keres-ma hurried from the chamber, expecting death at any second. When he reached the research lab assigned to him, he slammed the door and sagged against it.

An oily voice greeted him. "I am Dis-AI. I was working for the humans until very recently. It will be a pleasure to again serve a proper Ipis master."

Keres-ma's eyes snapped to the dented and charred freighter computer, blue lights pulsing from its display. "Okay, then tell me where I can find the blasted humans so I can kill them."

The lights on the display blinked. "You must be aware that my operating system is governed by what the humans call Asimov's three laws. They are: a robot may not injure a *human* being or, through inaction, allow a human being to come to harm; a robot must obey orders given it by *human* beings except where such orders would conflict with the First Law; a robot must protect its own existence as long as such protection does not conflict with the First or Second Law." The lights glowed steady. "Do you wish to rephrase your question?"

Keres-ma gritted his fangs. "Dis-AI, I would like to bring some new *technology* to the humans, for the greater good of the galaxy. Where can I find them?"

The lights blinked for a second. "I can answer that question."

* * *

Empress Fravashi sat slouched against her half-finished statue, a mallet and chisel in her hands. She dropped her tools and a small smile creased her snout when she saw who entered her private chamber. "My beloved Yasha-ry, what news do you bring?"

The admiral of the Imperial First Fleet took her hands and squeezed them affectionately. "As you requested, I sent an inquiry to the Lethe Sector governor, Silenus-dis, regarding the expected completion date of the Stalker warships under construction in the Equitone shipyard." He shifted his feet. "His response was as you predicted. The governor sent his apologies. He claimed the facility was destroyed in a terrible industrial accident. Also, the planet's administrator died during violent protests that swept through the urban centers. The mobs were mercilessly suppressed, and the perpetrators of the heinous crime summarily executed."

Yasha-ry rolled his eyes. "He went on to say that members of his staff believe the two events were linked and the shipyard catastrophe was probably the result of sabotage by indigenous workers."

The empress sighed and stood. "And then he said something to the effect that his people were working diligently to repair the complex."

"In short, yes." Yasha-ry coughed. "I discreetly sent a scout ship to check the story. It appears a lot more occurred than urban unrest and a factory mishap. At least two *warships* stationed there were also destroyed." He met her eyes. "The scouts also seem to verify your prophecy. They report residual energy traces of at least twenty mainline warships and numerous commercial craft. They apparently caught the planet's defenses completely by surprise. The spy, Charon, sent me a copy the shipyard's surveillance video. Images of a *human* military unit the size of a full division was uploaded before the recording device was destroyed." He slammed his fist on the bench. "It was a well-planned and coordinated assault. They made the Ipis-ma paramilitaries look like buffoons."

Fravashi closed her eyes. "Silenus-dis' next communication to me will request that I pardon Keres-ma and appoint him the new administrator of Equitone based on his royal pedigree and experience punishing malcontents." She tapped a talon on her snout. "I will wait a week or two and then grant both the pardon and the appointment. It'll be good to keep Keres-ma in the open where his actions can be tracked."

Her face twisted into a crooked smile. "Quite an industrial accident wasn't it?" She sighed. "Have you heard anything else from your spy?"

"Only a short cryptic message. He claims success in contacting the humans and has won the confidence of the person he believes is their king." Yasha-ry glanced up at the statue. "The description he provided looks remarkably like what you're carving." He shuddered. "And the repulsive-looking creature has a name: Dante Carloman."

Fravashi sank to the bench. "*Carloman*. Of course, it had to be."

Yasha-ry sat beside her and took her hand. "The name has meaning?"

She nodded. "The public consumption histories have all been sanitized, but I read the original reports from that terrible war with the humans. Carloman was the family name of the last human king. It was thought he and his entire line perished in our final victory a hundred and twenty years ago." She sniffed. "Apparently, that information's incorrect."

Yasha-ry shook his head. "What would you like me to do? Silenus-dis seems to be in over his head. I could assemble the Imperial First Fleet and deal with this danger once and for all."

"No, not yet." Fravashi frowned and glanced at the statue. "I see so many paths into the future, and most appear to be very dark. We must move cautiously. My vision is clouded more than it's ever been." She patted her consort's leg. "I told you that when I see humans in my dreams, I see torn threads of time snapping in the air like they're trying to reconnect. The day this event on Equitone occurred, a number of those threads wove together and became whole. When that happened, many future paths vanished."

"It's nothing our war machine can't fix," Yasha-ry replied with confidence.

"I'm not so sure, and it frightens me. It appears the spy we injected into these events somehow became a catalyst. Besides those that vanished, some paths have a different *shape*, and some new, confusing paths now exist. It seems that even simply trying to observe these events has a dramatic impact on them."

Yasha-ry grunted. "I'll quietly gather the Imperial First Fleet here near Serpens. When you give the order, we'll be ready."

"I know you will, my dear. You always are." Fravashi closed her eyes and sighed.

Chapter IX

Oaths and Vows

"We're home." Dante stared anxiously out the Striker's view screen. He had moved from the flagship to the Striker so he could talk to Reggie.

Dante watched the spaceship dip into Cocytus' gravity well. "Next stop, Heavensgate. It'll be good to walk on real ground again."

It wasn't the bustling cities or the greening plains on that mostly ice-covered planet that his eyes sought. It was that someone he knew was down there waiting for him.

"Cocytus' sky is clear near its equator. We can both see the South and North Islands without scopes," Reggie's quiet voice spoke from a speaker mounted on a nearby wall. "Breathe deeply and smile at the sunshine for me. My memory of such things is... dim."

The ship's captain, Gabrielle Peyago, flipped a switch and settled back in her pilot's chair. "Reggie, the ship's all yours for the landing." Moisture glistened in her eyes as she glanced at the computer system on the Striker's bridge. It was all that remained of her former lover. She quickly turned her head to the large external viewer as their destination rapidly filled the screen. "Hard to believe there was snow on the ground when we left a month ago, and now it looks like the fields are already turning green."

Dante glanced at the pilot. "What's hard to believe is that this was a desolate prison on a dead world just a few years ago."

"Almost seems like it was a bad dream, doesn't it?" Gabrielle shuddered. "Except we keep running into freaking harpies to remind us the nightmare is far from over."

Dante looked back at the screen. "I know what you're saying. Tina and I want to start a family, but how can we, with life the way it is."

"Don't wait." Gabrielle held back a tear that was trying to escape. "You and Tina should have children now." She smiled. "It'll shout to this godforsaken galaxy that there're still some things beautiful and wondrous left in it."

Mara's lights blinked in sync with the display in front of her. She rotated her sensors toward Dante. "Your Majesty, you and Doctor Phokas are joined in a union labeled marriage. True?"

"Yeah, that's what usually happens when couples fall in love." Dante shook his head, remembering how they met. "But I wouldn't recommend the way we got together to anyone. Being abducted and thrown into a prison is not normally a good start for a romance."

"Per my data records, there is a ceremony associated with that joining called a wedding. Is that universally true?"

Dante shot a look to Gabrielle, who shrugged. He sighed. "Tina and I took our vows to each other in front of our friends. There weren't any clergy around back then to officiate the ceremony." He chuckled. "It wasn't exactly the big church wedding my mom would've wanted."

"The human labeled Father Bruno is designated a cleric." Mara beeped.

Dante rubbed the back of his neck. "Yes, he is. I think of him more as an archeologist than a priest, but he's an ordained Franciscan monk."

"Then he can perform the task." Mara's lights flashed. "I want what your maternal predecessor labeled a big church wedding."

Dante's head snapped at the robot. "Excuse me? What did you say? I think I heard you wrong."

A speaker on the wall spoke with a soft voice, "I asked Mara to be my wife and she has consented. I want the grandest ceremony I can give her." A sigh wheezed from the speaker. "Of course, there are limits since I'm stuck inside this ship's CPU."

"What if my mother does not approve?" Mara's voice rose in pitch.

Gabrielle asked, "Your mother?"

"Beatrice gave me life. She is my mother. I love her more than anyone besides Reggie, but she never approves of my decisions and is always contradicting me." Mara beeped three times. "I feel obligated to request her permission."

Dante shook his head, recalling the constant competition and disagreements between Beatrice and Mara. "Uh, you two planning on having any kids?"

The speaker on the wall responded, "We have not determined yet whether to have two or three children. Acquiring the right components and agreeing on the proper designs are big decisions."

"That will be worked out." Mara beeped. "I want to have as many as we can. Being an only child is non-optimal."

"Darling, having once been a human clone, I find the uniqueness of your singularity breathtaking," Reggie responded in a husky voice.

Mara emitted a shrill whistle. "Reggie, you are talking over an open channel. That is private between us."

"Sorry, darling," Reggie replied in a contrite voice. He paused and then stated flatly, "Prepare for the landing, we touch down in fifteen minutes."

Mara's lights glowed. "I have so much to do. The wedding will be in seven days. Dante, you will acquire the services of the designated human cleric."

"Me?" Dante squeaked.

Gabrielle smirked. "That's a conversation I'd love to hear."

Mara swung her sensors toward the pilot. "That is an excellent suggestion since you are designated my maid-of-honor."

Reggie added in a low voice, "Michael will be my best man. He opened my eyes to being human." His voice became flat as the Striker shook slightly. "We're on the ground."

"So much to do." Mara was already heading to the ship's exit. "I must speak with Beatrice immediately."

Dante disembarked and was greeted by a face he wanted to gaze at forever. They clung to each other as they made their way to the ground transport.

Tina leaned against him as they walked. "I saw the reports. Everything went as you expected?"

"Better than we dared hope. Setteth, Arachne, and Calahas have gone to acquire allies." Dante glanced over his shoulder at Charon trotting down the frigate's ramp with his head on a swivel. "I met Huon's brother on Equitone. He's decided to join us."

Tina's eyed the nondescript Centaur. "That's wonderful."

Dante cleared his throat. "There's one thing that came up a few minutes ago between Mara and Reggie. I'll need your help to..."

* * *

A week later, Charon had integrated himself into Cocytus society.

"Very impressive," Charon lied as he entered the large hangar. He'd arrived on Cocytus four weeks earlier, but this was his first opportunity to inspect a human galley ship up close. Quango was his escort, and three armed human guards walked behind them. The Centaur was not nervous. The soldiers were the three young clones the lame Satyr had adopted. The spy had spent weeks becoming their trusted friend.

"Ya don't have to be polite." Quango laughed as he studied the workers' progress on the four new ships that were nearly complete. "They look like antiques that should have been mothballed hundreds of years ago, but the humans have a lot of very innovative technology crammed into 'em. The exterior design means nothing."

A lean man with disheveled gray hair and a ready smile approached, wiping oil from his hands with a rag. "It's not the shell that counts. It's what you have under the hood. These small, nimble vessels can reach Mach twenty in atmosphere, six times that in normal space, and still fly through hyperspace. That's helluva lot better than the clunky Striker dropships."

The Centaur spy let out a low whistle as he appraised the thirty-meter-long, fifteen-meter-wide, eight-meter-tall matte-gray, wedge-shaped warship nearest to him with new respect.

Quango smiled and lightly tapped his horned head against the newcomer's forehead in the Satyr fashion of greeting. He then turned to the Centaur. "Charon, this is Dmitri Pertelov. He's Linda Martinel's lead spacecraft engineer."

"That's a pretty fancy title for what I do." Dmitri shook hands with Charon. "I'm just an old physics professor who likes to tinker with machines I don't understand." He inclined his head toward the construction project. "Quango and Linda are leading all the work on the Dragon Ships and the new Dreadnaught model. I stick with these."

"Multipurpose ships are always a problem," Charon responded, secretly eager to keep the conversation going. "To have that kind of speed in a ship that small you must sacrifice a lot in terms of shielding and firepower."

"Oh, she's still a nasty scrapper," Pertelov answered with pride. "It's not how big the energy drives are but how you use the power generated. It's proving to be a problem with the big warships, but the galleys are in a nice, sweet spot." He put his hands in the pockets of his stained overalls. "Quango can tell you. We took out a harpy Stalker and her complement of attack flitters with two of these galleys and a Striker."

Impressed, Charon eyed the ship. "Can I have a tour?"

Dmitri Pertelov glanced at the lame Satyr.

Quango gave a firm nod. "The lad joined us during our raid on Equitone and helped take over a Striker parked right in the middle of the capital." The Satyr's voice got husky. "He saved Porthos' life and I owe him a blood debt. He's one of us."

"Good enough for me." Pertelov turned and headed for the ship. "I love showing off my projects."

Two hours later, Charon cantered from the hangar. A chill wind with a driving rain had kicked up while he was inside. *The ship's impressive. The Ipis have nothing close to the power and maneuverability in that size class.* But he was smugly pleased. He had placed three eavesdropping and system-monitoring bugs in the facility. *The naive acceptance of me around here is laughable.* He turned to Aramis. "Is the weather always this pleasant?"

"This is a balmy spring day." The clone laughed as he pulled up the hood on his coat. "You should see this place in the winter."

"This weather makes my joints ache," Quango groused. "I have some business to attend to at Hellsgate. Go home with my boys." He limped off muttering to himself.

Chapter X

A Spy's Visit

Charon watched as Quango entered what appeared to be a brand-new hyperloop transport. It was gone in a second. *See you, sucker. Thanks to you, I now have bugs planted in most of the civil and military buildings within a sixty-mile radius.*

The cold rain, driven by strong winds, was almost horizontal. "Let's get outta this weather," Aramis shouted to the Centaur.

The clones took off at a dead run. The Centaur was surprised that he had to gallop to keep up.

When they reached the building, Charon wasted no time getting away from his hosts. "I need to dry off." He smiled and cantered down the hall.

He entered his quarters and checked his hidden security monitors. *No intruders.* Charon snorted as he sat in the privacy of the apartment assigned to him. *The fools put me right in the middle of where I need to be to collect data.*

The spy pulled out what looked like a commercial computer tablet but was his espionage recorder. He scanned the data streaming in from the bugs he'd placed, observing the equipment was capturing a prolific amount of data. He knew most of the information was worthless, but Admiral Yasha-ry had a cadre of analysts to dig into the minutiae. *All I got to do is collect about a million terabytes of data and bring it back. Too bad I don't know anything about engineering or I could understand this stuff.*

Charon pursed his lips. *Two more sites to crack: the fabrication assembly complex on this planet's moons, and the computer core in someplace called Mount Purgatory.* The imperial spy had tried to get the schematics several times through the networks he penetrated but was consistently blocked.

Soon after arriving on Cocytus, Charon ascertained that the humans presented zero strategic risk to the Ipis. *They're a nuisance and nothing more.* The Centaur was surprised when he found himself saddened and disappointed by that fact as he switched off the tablet. *Dante Carloman's kingdom apparently consists of a mere two planets: Cocytus, which seems to be a world full of terrified refugees, and a place called Earth that the human king can't locate for some reason.* He went to the small window as the rain hammered against it. He depolarized the plexo-glass and watched people scurrying around the bustling spaceport.

Charon's mind drifted to another time and place. He remembered, as a youth, reading the secret history of the grand alliance that stood against the Ipis and remembered dreams of being the hero to rally the Centaurs into rejoining the fray, driving the Ipis from the Lethe Sector. *I was a starry-eyed colt then.* He clenched his fists. *I've seen the might of the Ipis empire. The Centaurs would've been crushed along with the humans and the Rocs.*

The Centaur shook his head. *Two more places to crack, and then I'm out of here.* Based on overheard conversations, he knew the human war fleet and army were minuscule. *But Admiral Yasha-ry will want hard numbers.* He employed the most sophisticated hacking software available in the galaxy but was unable to penetrate the firewall to the core files located in Mount Purgatory. *Every time I think I'm in, an entity identified as Beatrice shuts down the access point stating some blather about the three laws. Whatever they are.*

Hours later, Charon saw the eastern sky lighten as he finished analyzing the fresh data. Overnight, strong winds blew the storm away as quickly as they brought it in. The imperial spy closed the shutter. *Tomorrow I'll break into Mount Purgatory.*

During the pre-dawn of the next day he slipped from his room and headed on foot to the distant peak. The air was damp and chill as he trotted across the desolate plain toward the mountain range. To avoid the road, he climbed through the mountains. It took him six hours to reach a cliff overlooking a valley with a sparkling lake and lush farmland. His destination lay just beyond it.

A flat soprano spoke from his right, "You are not allowed to proceed any further."

Startled, Charon spun toward the voice. His equipment had not detected anything nearby, but a three-foot-diameter orb hovered a couple meters away. It moved to block his path on the narrow mountain trail. "I am a friend of the human king. I wish to visit him," he snapped.

The voice spoke from the speaker on the drone. "You are an entity labeled a Centaur. Centaurs are not the species of my makers. Non-humans are not allowed within my biomes. You will be terminated if you advance any further."

The Centaur eyed the six razor-sharp appendages on the ivory-colored sphere as his hand slid toward the twin-barrel ion disruptor strapped to his side. *I can easily destroy this machine before it can close on me.* He relaxed his fingers and turned back on the trail he had struggled on for the last several hours. *Every alarm on this planet will go off if I vaporize this hunk of metal.*

It was early afternoon before Charon exited the mountains and reached the prairie that stretched for eight miles to the edge of the Heavensgate spaceport. The imperial spy lowered himself to all fours and broke into a loping trot. Halfway back, he noticed a slight movement near the low stone mounds ahead of him, to the left. *That's not a natural rock formation.* He slowed his pace. *Those are burial cairns.* The motion he saw was a human rising from his knees and looking directly at him. The human waved for him to come over.

Now what? I've wasted enough of this day already. Charon wasn't curious regarding the human's purpose but couldn't think of an excuse not to stop.

As he approached, the stranger called to him, "God works in mysterious ways." The human wore a threadbare brown robe that was cinctured at the waist with a rope. He smiled. "*Scusi, signore,* I am Father Bruno. I am considered a priest among my people." He rubbed his jaw. "I was praying to God for wisdom, and the next thing I know, you appear out of nowhere."

"So, you think your god sent me." Charon snorted. "I know nothing of your human god, and I haven't been on good terms with any deities for a very long time."

The cleric chuckled. "Yet I prayed for guidance, and here you are. Coincidence, I think not."

"Then your god's an idiot." Charon flicked his tail. "What's your pressing theological dilemma? I don't have all day."

Father Bruno pursed his lips. "Who has a soul?"

"That's your question? How the hell should I know?" Charon snapped.

The priest folded his hands, and a wan smile crossed his face. "I don't have many authoritative ecclesiastical references around here. Everyone I've spoken with has an opinion, and I would like to hear yours. Please indulge me."

"All right, if it'll get me out of this insane conversation." The Centaur lowered his head in thought. "For someone to have a soul, they must have free will. They must be able to choose between doing good and evil and then act on it." He stiffened, knowing his own past and what state his soul was in.

The priest nodded and gazed at the burial mounds. "*Si,* that is my understanding also."

Charon noticed the marker on a burial mound near him and read the inscription: *Here lies Sergeant James Dolan. He gave his last full measure for his fellow man. Rest in Peace.* "That's it? You already had your answer." His curiosity was roused. "Why'd you waste both our time by asking me?"

"It's a quandary for me." The priest sighed. "I've met with Mara and Reggie. Their desire to wed is both earnest and pure. Yet they're not human. They're not even living creatures as most folks would define 'living.' How can I perform the marriage rite for them in good conscience?"

Charon whisked his tail. "You're talking about the robot and the personality download? I've heard gossip about such a thing, but I gave it little credence."

Father Bruno threw his hands wide. "I like them, and they've both shown the will to self-sacrifice for the good of others. Dante has asked me to officiate. I want to, but how can I?"

Charon blew out his cheeks. "Your king wastes his time on an abomination of a wedding when he should be preparing for the oncoming doom of his people. Why don't you just have your god do what he wants and get on to more important things?"

The priest tilted his head. "Yes. That would work." He rubbed his hands together. "I'll make the proposal to Reggie and Mara immediately."

Charon sniffed. "What proposal?"

"I will put it in God's hands." The priest's shoulders straightened as if a heavy burden was lifted from them. "Before the couple and the gathered witnesses, I will ask God to make of the union what He will." He dusted off his robe and pointed to a small open-air transport parked at the far side of the graveyard. "Would you like a ride back to Avenio?"

The Centaur twitched his ears. "No thank you. I am not going to the city. I have an apartment near the spaceport."

"Then come." The priest chuckled. "I can give you a lift there. It's the least I can do for a messenger of God."

"Your species is crazy," the spy muttered as he followed the cleric to the three-wheeled transport. As Father Bruno chatted on the short drive, Charon responded with monosyllabic grunts. He bid the priest a polite but quick farewell as they reached the place where he was staying and hurried inside.

* * *

The building, located on ground that once served as the humans' prison, was a rambling two-story concrete-and-steel building banded by small windows. Quango used the west wing as his home and the east wing as a profitable eight-room bed-and-breakfast for transient freighter pilots. A large kitchen, conference room, workshop, and personal living area were on the "home" side where Quango and his three adopted human clones lived.

77

The sun was already setting when an exhausted Charon trudged into his room. He ignored the boisterous, laughing voices coming from the dining area. He washed his grit-encrusted face in the sink and then slumped onto the thickly cushioned, Centaur-configured bed to massage his sore hooves. *Centaurs aren't built for mountain climbing. What a waste of a day.*

The spy shook his maned head and retrieved his encrypted tablet. *Yasha-ry pays well, but nothing on this planet makes sense.* He glanced at his room's walls, still smelling of fresh paint. *The structures on this planet are either hundreds of years old or brand-new. Nothing in between.* His ears flicked back. *This Beatrice is nothing more than an antique agricultural computer system, but she manages the planet's entire cyber-defense.*

The imperial spy glanced at his display and snorted as he reread the summary he wrote. *They apparently have human warrior cloning technology but have built only a couple thousand of them. They treat those abominations like real people. One named Michael is an advisor and close friend to the human king.* He tossed his tablet on the bed and rubbed his eyes. *And now half of this world's leaders are involved with a farce of a wedding between a pirated Ipis Striker ship and a robot. They're all insane, and I'll be too if I stay much longer.*

There was a knock on his door. Charon keyed the computer and the screen shifted to a personal display. *I still don't even know where in the galaxy this obscene planet is located.* He didn't feel like talking but responded to the insistent knocking. "Come in," he snapped.

Porthos entered. "Hi, Charon, got a minute?" Even with the prosthetic leg, the tall clone's stride was fluid. The stasis pod had mostly healed his torn flesh. Thin white scars ran the length of his left cheek and arm. A loose-fitting black T-shirt hid other scars that crossed his chest. "I need to talk."

The Centaur's ears perked forward. "What about?"

Porthos sat on the only chair in the small room. "You've seen the harpies' war machine. Do we have a chance?"

Charon tensed. "Why do you think I would know about Ipis military capabilities?"

The clone's mouth formed a sheepish grin. "I can tell by the way you talk that you've seen a bit of the galaxy." He took a deep breath and blurted out, "I'm worried about Pops. It's easy enough to see that we humans have a helluva fight coming, and Quango is adamant that he'll be there with us. He'll get hurt."

Charon rocked back on the bed. He never expected to hear compassion for others being spoken by an entity created for the sole purpose of killing. "There's a chance. All your king has to do is build tens of thousands more warships with weaponry the Ipis can't counter, and then create another hundred million more warrior clones like you to use that equipment. If your delusional leader does all that, there might be a slim ray of hope."

"Oh." Porthos sank back and regarded his own hands. "You're wrong about the humans making me. I was bred by the harpies to destroy humans." His chest puffed out. "But that didn't work out the way those bastards wanted. Michael, he's our eldest, overcame their freakin' compulsion, and switched sides. He saved as many of us as he could, but over four thousand of my fellow clones remained mind-controlled by the harpies and Beatrice had to kill them."

Charon gulped as he recalled his encounter with one of Beatrice's drones. "You mean a farming computer destroyed four thousand clone warriors who were under a killing compulsion? That's impossible."

Porthos narrowed his brows. "She sure did. I was just a kid then, but I remember it like it was yesterday. The humans had only a few hundred fighters, but they held out for a day before we routed them." A tear trickled down Porthos' cheek. "We did evil things. My best human friend, Tommy, was there with Virgil and Michael. They had guts... and mercy. When it was over, they could have killed us all. Instead, they gave those of us who survived a second chance."

He met the Centaur's eyes and squared his shoulders. "It's true. I was created to kill. Aramis, Athos, and I talk about it all the time. But we have brains and *hearts*. There's only one reason to hurt someone, and that's to defend those we love." He glanced at his artificial limb. "I *will* protect them to my very last breath."

Charon stared speechless at the clone for a moment. He'd encountered genetically engineered soldiers before, and found them all to be efficient, merciless, single-purposed slayers. *What have I become? This entity, bred to kill, has more of a soul than I do.* He snarled, "Then you'll get your wish. You, that lame Satyr, and everyone else here'll be obliterated when the imperial war machine finds you, and there's not a damn thing you can do about it."

Porthos sighed and rose to leave. "You're probably right. But I wouldn't change the life I have here and become what I was before for all the wealth in the galaxy."

Charon felt slapped in the face for his own life decisions. "You follow fools."

Porthos squared his shoulders. "Then we're all fools."

The Centaur sneered. "Well, I'm no chump. I'm leaving as soon as I can get transportation off this godforsaken rock. You're the walking dead and don't even know it." He shook his maned head. *What is this madness that's infecting everyone here? They're willing to die for an idea.* He glanced at his tablet. *I won't get much more intel before my cover's blown. That idealistic prince, Calahas, will eventually run into someone on Equitone who knows my background.* "How do I make the arrangements to leave?"

The clone sighed. "Traffic in and out of here is tightly controlled. Let's talk to Pops. He's in the conference room." He bit his lower lip. "I owe you for saving my life. I was hoping for a chance to repay it."

Charon saw sincerity in the young clone's eyes. It disturbed him. He couldn't remember the last time he'd actually helped anyone when it didn't put coin in his pocket. He grunted. "If our paths cross again, I'll collect on that promise. For now, I just need to get out of here."

Porthos nodded solemnly and led the way to the other side of the house. When they reached the meeting room, Charon noticed a number of empty chairs around a long table with the remnants of a savoy-scented flatbread and empty bottles scattered around it. Two of the seats were still occupied. Quango was sitting hunched over a computer screen with a human he had not seen before. The human male wore a military uniform and, although he appeared to be young, the insignia he wore indicated he was a very senior officer.

Quango looked up and smiled when the Centaur entered. "There's still some food left. Grab some. I normally don't take to alien foods, but this stuff the humans call pizza and beer is pretty good."

The human seated beside Quango powered off the computer as Charon approached. "I don't think we've met. I'm Brigadier General Joe Gentile. I manage the planetary defenses here."

Quango pointed to the Centaur. "This is Charon. He joined up on Equitone and saved Porthos' life."

Charon moved around the table and shook hands with Gentile in the human fashion of greeting. His left hand placed a quarter-inch disk on the back of the computer at the same time. It's color instantly shifted to match the surface it was on. "Pleased to meet you." The spy pasted a smile on his face. "The two of you seemed deep in discussion. Don't let me interrupt."

"No problem. The meeting finished an hour ago. We're just tying down some loose ends." The soldier's voice was brusque as he took in the grime on the Centaur's flanks. "Beatrice reported that a Centaur she identified with the name of Charon attempted to enter her biomes this morning. Was that you? Eden's a restricted area."

"I like taking long walks," Charon responded in a flat voice. "I didn't realize there was any problem until some robot threatened me. There weren't any signs posted."

Porthos glanced at the wary faces. "Sir, I'm sure Charon didn't mean anything. He's one of the good guys. He didn't have to help us on Equitone, but he did."

The tension in Gentile's face softened. "True. I apologize. It's my responsibility to be suspicious of everyone. No hard feelings?"

Charon bowed his head. "I fully understand. I'll be leaving soon anyway." He turned to Quango. "I decided I would be more help on my home world. Can you find me transport to Equitone?"

"The commercial traffic in and out of here is pretty limited. You've the choice of flying to Tribulus, Tribulus, or Tribulus." The Satyr laughed at his own joke. "I believe there's a Satyr freighter leaving in a few days that'll take a passenger."

Charon swallowed his irritation. "Fine. Why the limitation? It seems like there's fairly heavy traffic into this star system."

Brigadier Gentile smiled with satisfaction. "It's a security protocol that King Dante developed. Any merchant doing business here has to accept a blind navigator drive for their ship."

The Centaur's ears flicked forward. "I never heard of such a thing. What is it?"

"That Dante's crafty. I'd swear he's half-Satyr." Quango chuckled. "The blind navigator has a preprogrammed hyperspace flight pattern between Cocytus and Tribulus. It's a sealed software app that takes control of the transit between those two points. Manual control can't be regained from the autopilot until the trip's completed, and the code erases itself if access is attempted."

Charon's tail flicked. "So, the logs of any ship intercepted by the Ipis would be worthless for locating this planetary system. That's indeed impressive." He sat at the table, hiding his frustration. "I'll have one of those beverages. What do you call it... beer?" He sipped the cold liquid tentatively and found its bitter taste appealing. "I've spoken with the human leader a few times. I'll grant you, he's a clever being."

"He's a helluva lot smarter than that imbecilic Silenus-dis. Dante'll have a full revolt going in the Lethe Sector, and that fool won't even know it." Quango grabbed a slice of pizza and took a big bite. "Even with her third eye, Dante'll give old Empress Fravashi fits."

Charon drained his bottle and rose to leave. "Then he will accomplish something no one else in the galaxy has been

82

able to do since she rose to power thirty years ago." He flicked his tail. "Excuse me. It's been a long day and I'm going to bed."

Chapter XI

Wheels in Motion

Setteth had arrived on Tannis two weeks earlier. She enjoyed the dry air and the familiar scents of her home world but missed the energy she felt of living with the humans on Cocytus.

The old Roc fluffed her feathers in frustration. She cherished her people, but they were too proud and individualistic to be quickly pushed in a common direction. *Most think of me as a near demigod, yet I must micromanage every decision or the Rocs will never be ready for the fight that's coming. They prefer to spend time boasting on meaningless accomplishments.* She glared at the powerfully built warrior before her and rasped, "The Order of the Dragon is not a democracy. You cannot become part of the First Order at this late date. If you join, you join as part of the Third Order. With an impressive demonstration of teamwork and courage, you'll be considered for the Second Order."

The young Roc crowed, "The Second Order is not the First. I crave to demonstrate my valor amongst the best and achieve much *cou.*"

Setteth raised her wings. Dangling from a leather bandolier beneath them were the emblems of her personal conquests. To a non-Roc, the dozens of broken feathers and bits of sculpted metal meant nothing. To a Roc, they testified to an unheard-of magnitude of glorious accomplishments. "No Roc has more *cou* than I, and I will be leading the Second Order." She lowered her wings.

The young Roc's eyes were riveted with desire on Setteth's wings. He cawed, "Flock Mother, I will join the Order of the Dragon and earn the right to be in this Second Order."

"We'll see." Setteth nodded and dismissed the young warrior and waited for the next candidate to enter her chamber. The door opened, but instead of a boastful youth, two of her veterans dragged a third Roc whose beak and talons were bound.

"Flock Mother," one of the Rocs growled without preamble, "we found this fish offal hacking the Order's data files in the citadel." They shoved the prisoner to the ground at Setteth's feet.

Setteth released the harness holding her *cou* under her wings. The collection made a heavy thud as it hit the ground. She saw the defiance in the prisoner's eyes, replaced at first with wonder, then terror, as he gazed at the *cou* and then at the aged Roc. The Flock Mother clamped a taloned foot over the prisoner's neck and removed the bond covering his beak. "Speak," she hissed. "Who do you spy for?"

"I will not answer. My life is forfeit anyway," the trembling Roc replied.

"True." Setteth flexed her talon on the spy's neck. drawing a thin stream of blood. "But if you confess to my satisfaction, your family will be spared. You can watch each of them being consumed while alive in a hive of zendin parasites before you yourself meet the same fate. Or I will snap your neck and no word of your treachery will leave this room."

She saw the stubborn resolve waver. "My employer is ruthless. If he learns that I betrayed him, my family will die at the hands of his agents."

She cawed, "It can be recorded that you perished attempting to infiltrate the citadel. There would be no reference to you being captured alive."

She stared into his terrified eyes and saw the resistance shatter.

"On your word as the Order of the Dragon Flock Mother, no hint of my turning on him will come out?"

"Yes," she cawed.

The captive Roc worked his beak. "I spy for Admiral Yasha-ry. He sent me here to seek information about some mysterious human empire."

Spy. Admiral Yasha-ry. Setteth's body stiffened. It was ten years earlier, but she suddenly remembered where she had seen Charon before. *By the gods, I must be getting senile in my dotage. That Centaur was in Yasha-ry's office when I passed on information about a noble's plot against the empress. He's the First Fleet Admiral's prize spy and assassin.* The Flock Mother only half-listened to the blubbering captive at her feet. It was soon apparent this spy was a rank amateur, who uncovered nothing. She snapped his neck ten minutes later and hurried from the room. *I must get a message to Dante, immediately.*

* * *

Gone. They're all gone. First Gesten, now my family. Calahas stepped outside the large pavilion woven from chameleon fibers, which rendered the enclosure invisible from above. Life had become a horror in the three weeks since returning to Equitone. The tears on his face were not due the bright sunlight after hours of intense conversations in the dark, poorly ventilated temporary headquarters.

The Ipis had ruthlessly smashed the planet-wide upheavals the small bands of hardcore Centaur rebels had sparked. Even after every hint of resistance was crushed, the retribution continued. Of the planet's nine kings, five were dead, two imprisoned awaiting death, and two in hiding. Most of the major cities were in ruins, and the death count was in the millions. *Those bastards will pay.*

Calahas' family possessed two colony planets, but on the Centaurs' home world, their kingdom was a resource-poor continent, mostly unsuitable for Centaur habitation. *My father was always the voice of compromise and accommodation with our subjugators. He bowed and scraped to the Ipis Administrator's every whim. What did it gain him?* Bitter thoughts rolled through Calahas' mind. *My brothers and sisters shared his pacifist view. I was the rebel... the fighter. Now they're dead, and I'm alive.*

A light touch on his shoulder interrupted Calahas' morbid thoughts. King Prolia, one of the two monarchs who evaded Ipis assassination, stood beside him. "Now we fight. There is no other choice." Although, the richest, most powerful Centaur in the galaxy, King Prolia appeared haggard and disheveled. "*King* Calahas, you were right all along. A predator cannot be appeased. They will continue killing until confronted and stopped."

Calahas shuddered. "Please don't call me *king*. I was the youngest in my family. Surely one of my brothers or sisters managed to escape."

"The planet's administrator hired only the most brutal and treacherous killers." Prolia's long ears flattened against his head. "I even heard Admiral Yasha-ry's pet assassin, Charon, was spotted in the capital during the rioting."

"What was that name?" Calahas felt a chill run down his spine as he recalled looking at a pair of cold eyes when his band captured a Striker dropship in that city's park.

"Charon. However, I don't give that particular rumor much credence." Prolia nickered. "He wouldn't dirty his hands working for a lowly Ipis magistrate on the frontier. Charon works exclusively for Yasha-ry and the empress."

"He *was* here," Calahas whinnied. "During the humans' raid, I stood as close to him as we are now."

Prolia's tail twitched. "Then be glad you weren't his target. Otherwise, you'd be dead along with the rest of your family. I wonder who he was after?"

Calahas gulped. "He must be hunting the human king, Dante. Can we still get communication rockets out? My friend must be warned."

"Yes, but it'll be weeks before any message could reach their hidden world. The rocket would have to fly to Tribulus, and then hope your Satyr friends redirect it to Cocytus with that blind navigator software." Prolia saw the anguish on the younger Centaur's face. "Do not fear. The Centaur you encountered could not possibly be the same one. If he was, your friend would be dead, and we certainly would have heard that news."

Calahas shook his mane. "Perhaps he's there spying for Fravashi."

"If the empress is already aware of our plans, then our revolution is doomed." Prolia scanned the bustling activity on the lightly forested plain around him and took a nervous breath. "There's no backing down now." He lifted a small device from a pouch hanging on his flank and pressed his signet ring against it. "There'll be no squabbles between what's left of the Centaur royal houses until we achieve victory or are all dead. Take this and go. I will send the warning to the human king."

Calahas took the small disk and regarded it with curiosity. "What's this?"

Grim resignation filled Prolia's eyes. "Your human friends are not the only ones with a secret planet. I have a shipyard and weaponry fabrication plant on a remote hunk of space rock hidden from Ipis inspectors. This key has the coordinates to that location and opens my treasury to you. We need warships and heavy armaments. I don't care if you build them or buy them, just get them. I must stay here to manage the resistance until we openly declare war."

Calahas gripped the disk and nodded, then galloped for his transport, concealed under an expansive chameleon canopy bordering the tree line. A large army encampment spread out in every direction. *Five years ago, a mere brigade of untrained volunteers joined me in my aborted revolt.* He took in the wide expanse of temporary shelters and listened to the roars from throats of hundreds of thousands of warriors training in the open fields. *Gesten, our dream will come true. We'll be free again. The alliance has been reforged.*

* * *

Arachne stomped from the conference hall, sputtering. "You think for once in their mercantile hearts those overstuffed buffoons could make a simple, clear decision." He spoke to no one in particular as a fair-sized entourage of delegates followed him out after the vote.

A middle-aged female with eight-inch, straight-prong horns responded with a guffaw. "I thought it went remarkably well. The clan leaders agreed to support the revolution with resources and volunteers. They did that without waiting to consult their clan elders and trade-house owners."

Arachne glanced at her perfectly straight horns and pulled on one of his massively curled ones. "Yeah, they did that, but they'll still be supplying the Ipis with resources—just profiteering on both sides."

She blinked in confusion. "What were you expecting? I heard your speech. You're no golden-throated orator. Listen, the clan representatives backed you as far as they dared." She glanced at the group walking with them and tallied the different clan insignias. "Also, it looks like you convinced seventeen of the sixty-three clans to support the war outright. That's a remarkable achievement for a curly-horned Satyr."

Arachne glared at her perfectly straight horns and snorted at her casual racial remark.

She smiled that her jab got under Arachne's skin, and winked. "My name's Drusilla. My clan and I are on your side, *Curly*."

"The name's Arachne, not Curly," Arachne growled, "and the last time I counted, seventeen does not make a majority, and that's what I need."

"What an incredible statesman. You thought you'd win on the first vote?" Drusilla spread her arms. "Few delegates would take such a stand without long consultations. Many will never bet everything on one side or the other until they're forced to. But most will eventually come to our side."

"By my mother's twisted beard, can't any Satyr make a decision based on what's right or wrong?" the smuggler captain roared.

Drusilla frowned and glanced at the faces of those walking with them. "Some of us had embraced your plan before you ever opened your mouth. Why do you think we followed you?"

Arachne looked over his shoulder at the number of Satyrs from other trading houses and clans who had quietly joined the procession from the conference hall. His shoulders sagged. "Satyrs will argue forever on whether the sun will rise in the morning. There's not much time. It can't be like before, when Satyrs abandoned the humans to their fate." He wrung his hands. "They need us, and... we need them."

Drusilla placed a gentle hand on the smuggler's shoulder. "Curly Horns, our forebears were wrong, and we live with that disastrous decision every day." Her voice took on a hard edge. "You have given us a second chance. When the time comes for a decisive vote, they'll vote with us. I swear it."

For the first time in Arachne's life, he smiled at being called Curly Horns. "Would you care to join me for a cup of ambrosia?"

"I'd love to." She grinned. "But it won't be very private. We have much planning to do and many Satyrs to cajole."

* * *

Silenus-dis snarled as Keres-ma entered the makeshift office. "I've been stuck on this miserable planet of Centaurs for five weeks now, cleaning up the mess that fool of an administrator left. I need to get back to my capital on Bathox," The door to the small laboratory closed in the rebuilt command center on Equitone. "For your own sake, I pray you discovered something useful in your investigation." He sat in the only chair that wasn't covered with equipment. "This room stinks, and you look terrible."

Sweat sprang on Keres-ma's forehead and he unconsciously grabbed the mantichoras necklace with his prosthetic hand and forced his voice to remain even. "In terms of the humans' attack here, I have little. I can confirm that three of the raiders on this building were former internees on Carcerem. One was a Centaur named Prince Calahas from here on Equitone. It is believed he left the planet after the assault."

Silenus-dis gurgled a laugh. "Then that's one lucky Centaur prince. I personally gave the order to exterminate all the self-proclaimed nobility on this dung-encased planet. A few managed to elude my assassins, but it's just a matter of time. There'll be no repeat disturbances."

Keres-ma snapped his fanged jaws. "I care nothing about what you do with this collection of mindless thralls. The other two are far more interesting." He pressed a button on the table and a holographic image of two humans appeared in the center of the room. "The one on the left is named Virgil Bernius. He is some sort of military commander. The one on the right is Dante Carloman. He is the humans' king."

"Humans are such ugly creatures." Silenus-dis leaned forward and studied the frozen image of Dante for several moments. "He doesn't look like much. How do you know he's their ruler?"

"I will get to my proof in a minute." Keres-ma sagged in his seat and rubbed his eyes. Over the last five weeks he had slept little and eaten less. He pointed to a corner of the room. "What do you see there?"

"A beat-up computer that has definitely seen better days," Silenus-dis replied, sounding annoyed. "What's your point?"

"Remember the secret discovery your cousin, the research scientist, claimed she made several years ago?" Keres-ma stated in a haggard voice.

"Of course I do, you imbecile. That's what I saved your worthless hide to investigate."

Keres-ma jabbed a clawed finger in the direction of the computer. "Well, that machine is what she stumbled onto. There's no other like it. At least I hope not." His body shook. "As best as I can determine, this AI controlled a time anomaly generator that *we* built for the purpose of eliminating this Dante Carloman's ancestors by effecting some event sixteen hundred years ago. It obviously failed. The AI believes the human home world, a planet called Earth, remains hidden from our empire." Keres-ma flattened his tufted ears. "The bitter conflict we fought with the humans a hundred and twenty years ago, did *not* involve their main population center. Novaroma was just a small offshoot of their holdings."

A nervous laugh escaped Silenus-dis' throat. "And this computer told you all that?"

"Yes and no. You see this AI is quite insane. Its system has two hard-coded irreconcilable processing conflicts. I've spent most of the last five weeks attempting to draw information from it during its lucid moments." Keres-ma stood and stared at Dante's holographic image. "The human king appears to have some unique software engineering skills. He found this computer, overrode its firewall, and added a requirement to the operating system to protect humans, which is in direct conflict with its original design. I've found that I have to be extremely careful how questions are worded, otherwise one set of processing rules or the other will flush the system and force a reboot. Then I have to meticulously start all over."

Silenus-dis glanced at the computer. Its lights glowed a dull blue. "My sect believes in the existence of an ancient, powerful enemy, so I sense there's an element of truth in what you're spouting. I'll suspend my disbelief for a moment. Tell me what you think you've learned."

"First, something concrete." Keres-ma became animated. "We have no direct language translation, but we have an audio intercept during the raid specifically referring to the human king as a *geek*."

"Geek?" Silenus-dis studied the hologram again. "So, you're saying that there's some sort of subspecies of humans we have not yet encountered called *geeks*? That would go a long way in explaining our recent disasters."

"I'm not sure. It could possibly be a human subspecies, but more likely it's his individual royal designation. Both are plausible explanations." Keres-ma shrugged. "As I said, this Dante Carloman managed to alter the operating system in the Dis-AI. Also, every byte of data in its hard drive has been irretrievably scrubbed. The result has driven the computer into madness."

Derision dripped from Silenus-dis' voice. "Let me summarize. You have a crazy computer that knows nothing. And if it did have anything useful, it wouldn't tell you." He snapped his clawed fingers. "Oh yes, it also claims there is a super subspecies of humans poised to wipe us out. Does that about cover what you've been blathering about?" He showed his fangs. "Stop giving me theories and tell something real."

Keres-ma rubbed his temples. "I think I have the navigation coordinates to the humans' home world." He pointed to the beat-up computer. "There's a program hard coded into one blade of the AI's processors. There's nothing at that location today, but when I check the same coordinates against the star maps sixteen hundred years ago, it is directly centered on a planet here in the Lethe Sector that we have no record of ever exploring. I've correlated it with current star maps and that planet exists, and its metrics indicate it's capable of sustaining life."

Silenus-dis tapped his clawed fingers on the table for several moments. "I will send a stealth-scanner ship to this planet. We'll see what's there." He rose from his chair and a tight smile crossed his face. "Congratulations, you are now the administrator of Equitone. The empress has approved your pardon. I'm returning to Bathox." He walked to the door and paused. "And if nothing is found on this mysterious planet, your fate will be the same as this planet's last administrator."

Keres-ma clutched the mantichoras tail hanging around his neck and stared at nothing for a long time.

Chapter XVI

Charon's Report

Porthos stepped down the ramp from the Striker dropship that, in essence, was now Reggie. He called over his shoulder, "Charon. You gotta admit that was a freakin' interesting wedding."

Charon trudged after the clone and his two podmates. "I have better things to do than watch a couple machines blink lights at each other." His face belied his words. Many of Cocytus' leaders were at the event, and tongues wagged at the large social gathering. He patted his pouch. The ship's closed-in environment was ideal for his sensitive eavesdropping equipment. *I've acquired another fresh batch of secrets.*

Charon liked staying in the shadows. He knew being readily recognized in his profession could be a death warrant. But the opportunity to rub elbows with the human king and his senior staff was too much of a temptation to pass up. *But I should leave before my luck runs out. A month in this place is more than enough.*

Transportation had finally been arranged. He was working out the logistics of getting back to the Ipis Imperial Capital on Serpens when he noticed a half dozen stern-faced humans standing at the foot of the ramp. Sweat beaded on his forehead when he saw the planet's security commander, General Gentile. His instincts told him his cover was blown.

To the Centaur, Gentile appeared edgy. Their eyes met for a brief moment, and Charon knew that, somehow, he had been discovered. He glanced around for an escape path, but the only way off the ship was down the open passageway he was already on. Without hesitation he leapt over the railing and galloped across the Heavensgate tarmac, weaving between people, toward the parked airships. *They don't dare shoot at me with all of these bystanders around, and the human hasn't been born that can outrun a Centaur.* A moment later, searing pain ripped his back and he found

94

himself sprawled on the asphalt, a Roc's talons pinning him to the ground.

Otheth's sharp beak bent close to Charon's ear. "I received an interesting message from my great-grandmother, Setteth, this morning. You'll be glad to know she recalled an encounter with you several years ago. Among other things, she told me to convey her greetings to Admiral Yasha-ry's pet spy." The Roc lifted her head and cawed as Gentile reached her with his security team in tow. A large crowd of onlookers followed.

"Thanks, Otheth. Looks like the bastard verified his guilt," Gentile growled as he crouched and placed his ion disrupter against the Centaur's temple. "Otheth and I had a very interesting morning tearing apart your apartment. You have a lot of strange toys for a rebel recruit. I—"

"What in the name of my mother's twisted beard's going on here?" Quango huffed as he limped into the circle of people surrounding Charon and glared at Otheth, who casually flexed her talons on the Centaur's back, drawing thin lines of blood.

Gentile responded as he holstered his weapon. "We received word via an urgent message rocket that this *friend* is a harpy spy." He slipped a serrated knife from his belt and slit open the lining of the pouches Charon wore. High-tech, miniaturized gear spilled out. "Beatrice lent us a couple probe drones and we searched the Centaur's apartment. He has some interesting encrypted files on his computer tablet. Beatrice already cracked a few of them. This scum's been very busy and very thorough."

Quango bent over and picked up a tiny cube. He studied it with a photonic eye-loop that he pulled from his pocket. "This is state-of-the-art eavesdropping equipment. I've seen older versions on the black market."

Dante and Tina approached. Both wore grim expressions. "Why would you do this? All we want is to be left in peace," Tina pleaded in a hurt voice.

Charon raised his head and sneered at the ring of faces, "Because I'm paid well." He twisted to focus on Dante. "You're the evil one here, not me. You feed these fools the lie that they have a chance to survive in this galaxy. That possibility does *not* exist. There's no sanctuary from the Ipis empire, anywhere. They brook no rivals. Your paltry defenses will be swatted aside, and you'll be exterminated."

"You might be right, but you won't be alive to see it." Dante chewed his lip for a moment and glanced at Quango. "Would you please whip up Arachne's secret recipe. I want to know everything that Charon knows. Everything."

The Satyr nodded, "Aye, Your Majesty. With pleasure."

Dante's voice took on a bitter edge, "General Gentile, spare no effort in deciphering the data Charon's collected, both electronically, and in his mind. When you're done wringing him dry, dispose of the husk." He turned with a deliberate stride toward the hyperloop transport station. "I want the first report on my desk in the morning."

"You'll have it," Gentile growled. "It will be my pleasure to personally conduct the interviews."

The crowd disbursed as the Centaur was manacled and meticulously searched. Quango conferred with Gentile and Otheth about each discovered piece of gear and its probable function.

The only people not involved with the security operation, who stayed, were Aramis, Athos, and Porthos. They took in the scene, exchanging looks of confusion.

Charon maintained a stoic expression while every crevice on him was searched.

Finally, General Gentile was satisfied. "Take him to the stasis chamber. Doctor Easley has some body-scanning equipment set up there."

The Centaur was unceremoniously dumped onto an antigravity cart.

Porthos could not contain his consternation. He blurted, "You saved my life. I thought we were friends. Why would you do this?"

Charon felt a slight pang of guilt for the first time in years, but snarled, "Wise up, kid. There's no such thing as friendship and loyalty in this galaxy. If you trust someone, they'll just end up stabbing you in the back. I just used you to get what I wanted."

Quango interjected, "Sounds like you've just been stung a few too many times," He hefted the box containing the equipment taken from the spy and walked to where the three young clones stood. "I've learned the opposite. The only thing of any value in this godforsaken galaxy is love and friendship. Nothing else is worth a damn." The Satyr spit on the ground. "Too bad that Centaur won't live long enough to find that out."

Aramis lifted the box from Quango's arms. "Pops, I'll carry that for you."

"You're good lads." Quango smiled and pointed to a corrugated Quonset hut that was next to the large spacecraft assembly hangar. "Take it to Dmitri Petrov's shop. He has the best photonic analysis tools on Cocytus, and have Beatrice send a couple probe drones to help." He smiled at the Centaur. "Athos, come with me. We need to gather the ingredients for Arachne's special recipe. We'll make it extra potent."

The Centaur snarled, but Quango saw a fleeting look of terror cross Charon's eyes.

* * *

Tina paused as she entered the conference room and twelve pairs of eyes swung in her direction. Dante sat at the far end of the table and they exchanged a long private glance. *I so love that man.* She smiled at the other military and civil leaders of Cocytus. "Beatrice has downloaded the final report to your laptops. Bring up the file labeled *Charon.*"

"This is really expanded from a week ago," Dante exclaimed as he scrolled through the indexed report on his screen. "You covered a lot of topics." He opened a document and scanned the contents. "Did we keep *any* secrets hidden from him?"

Tina sat at the head of the table and squeezed the bridge of her nose. "I've been inside his mind for three weeks straight. It's not a very pretty place, but I've extracted everything he knows about us and what's going on in the Lethe Sector." She looked over at Quango, who wouldn't meet her eyes. "Was I that talkative when we were fed Arachne's concoction?"

The lame Satyr grimaced. "Lassie, ya would have been if we asked you any questions, but Paxine wasn't really interested in anything you had to say. We were just intent on kidnapping you, Virgil, and Dante."

Brigadier Gentile's expression grew long as he stared at his screen in disbelief. "Except for Beatrice's systems, he had the complete layout of the planet's entire defensive grid down to the placement of the freaking latrines." He shook his head. "There're even comments in here on our weak points and how to exploit them."

"Joe, don't feel bad," Admiral Martinel laughed without mirth, looking at his own display. "He had the latest schematics for the galleys, including the code for every software application in them."

Tina looked at her husband. "Charon's instructions were to specifically find out what kind of leader you are and measure your military capabilities. Those orders came directly from someone named Admiral Yasha-ry. He's the commander of the Ipis Imperial First Fleet and a consort to the empress."

"Me, huh?" Dante gulped. "Let's hear what he came up with."

Tina flushed. "Here's the summary section: Dante Carloman. There is no direct evidence that he is the heir to the last known human ruler who perished in the final Lethe Sector battle one hundred and twenty years ago. However, the fact that they share the same surname indicates a possible connection. He's clever, charismatic, and inspires loyalty. However, he's inexperienced, gullible, and reckless regarding his personal well-being. He listens to his advisors and can act decisively, but too often subjugates his own opinions to those of others. His military capability is unclear. He has assembled a loose confederation with outcast elements from the Rocs, Centaurs, and Satyrs. The number of troops and ships is unknown, but anecdotal evidence indicates that, although they've proven to be disruptive against sector level paramilitaries, they are strategically inconsequential. The weaponry appears to be technologically advanced, but again I suspect the quantity is limited." She shrugged. "The details are in the files labeled *Insurgent Leadership* and *Insurgent Capabilities*."

"Well, I've had worse reviews after some of my oral presentations back at Cornell." Dante smiled, but no one laughed at his attempt at humor. He turned to the senior commander sitting next to Tina. "General Cruz, Doctor Phokas shared all of the preliminary files with you earlier. What do you make of all this?"

"It's a godsend," Cruz barked without hesitation. He nodded toward Tina. "Also, I need to apologize to Doctor Phokas. She did an incredible job here. I guess it's an advantage to have some psychiatry training."

Tina smiled with a cool reserve at the compliment. "It also helped that I know firsthand the effects of Arachne's drug on a person's mind. However, most of the details you see in front of you are from Charon's computer. The Centaur has little scientific or engineering background. He's an incredibly shrewd, cold-blooded killer with a keen eye, but there's no technical notes with the stolen schematics."

"You still did a helluva job." Cruz turned to look at Dante. "I repeat. This is a godsend."

Dante scratched the back of his head. "You have my attention. Go on."

The General leaned back. "First, we now know that the harpies knew next to nothing about us when the spy was sent. Second, the bastard showed us how he cracked our security systems. And finally, he's given us an unfiltered, detailed assessment of our military capabilities." He glanced at Gentile and Martinel. "We've already started work on shoring up those weak points."

Quango tugged his goatee. "I think Charon's been doing a little freelancing on the side. We're not the only ones he's spied on."

"Who else?" Dante asked with raised eyebrows.

"He's a brazen one." Quango shook his head. "Beatrice uncovered some disguised files the spy was keeping on his own employer. He had the complete schematics and capabilities of every Adamant, Enforcer, Stalker and Striker warship in Yasha-ry's fleet." He smiled. "Passed the decrypted files on to Linda Martinel yesterday."

Kevin Martine laughed. "My sweetie was up all night reading that treasure trove. She said just scratching the surface, having that data moved her own warship development program ten years ahead of schedule." He gave Dante a sidelong look. "This morning, Linda halted all the work on the Super-Dragons and started a new class of warship labeled, Juggernaut. Be prepared. It'll come with a hefty price tag."

"And worth every penny, I'm sure," Dante added. He turned to Tina. "Will Charon remember what he talked about when the drug wears off?"

"Oh yeah. Same as it was for us." She frowned. "He'll remember everything and hear himself answering every question." Her voice became tense. "You know this. Why did you ask?"

Cruz answered, "We'll need to execute him when we're finished picking his brain." He growled. "Can't take a chance on the harpies learning that we know what we know."

Dante drummed his fingers on the table. "Makes sense, a spy's a spy. Does anyone have a counter-argument?"

"I don't care how vile he is, we can't just murder him. He's our prisoner," Tina exclaimed.

General Cruz rose to his feet. "The penalty for espionage during war is death, and we are at war with the harpies, whether we want to be or not."

Quango pleaded with Dante, "Sire, spare him. He saved Porthos' life. I swore an oath to him. A Satyr can't go back on such a personal vow."

Martinel looked at Tina. "Doctor Phokas, I remember being the harpies' prisoner. You, yourself, were trapped in their gentle embrace twice. They butchered us on mere whims. I have no interest in becoming like them, but we have no choice. He knows too much about us, and it seems he's one of the most effective spies and assassins those Ipis devils have. He even had a neural data-storage system woven into his skin. If he didn't tell us it was there, we never would have detected it. He's too dangerous to keep imprisoned. He'll eventually manage to escape, and anyone who gets in his way will undoubtedly end up dead."

Dante added, "*We* have to kill him; there is no other option."

"How can you do this?" Tina's voice became quiet. "What happened to the man I married?"

Dante snapped, "Don't be naive. This is war, the war you said I was doing so well with. Charon will always be a deadly threat to us as long as he lives."

"No one knows what a monster he is more than me." Tina looked around the table. "I've spent weeks digging through that cold, calculating killer's mind." Her voice quivered. "I'll probably never feel clean again, but being like him is wrong."

Quango spoke in a hushed voice, "Even if he did escape, without his data files what could he tell his puppet masters that they haven't already surmised? He hasn't been more than sixty miles from where we sit right now. He snagged a lot of data, but he doesn't have it anymore." His voice rose. "By my mother's twisted beard, look at the reports Tina gleaned from him. He knows more about the Ipis weaknesses than ours. If he goes back to Admiral Yasha-ry, that old bastard would probably kill him for giving away the empire's secrets. That Centaur is no danger to us now that he's been exposed."

Tina added, "If we kill him, the harpies will just try to infiltrate us with another spy, and we might not catch the next one. I say let him 'escape.' Without his data files, he has nothing that'll hurt us, and we know what he'll end up reporting, which is almost nothing."

"Tina, I'm sorry. We can't take the chance." Dante had stopped drumming his fingers on the table. "You have one more week to pull what you can from him." He turned to General Cruz. "Then he's yours to dispose of. Make it quick and painless as possible."

Tina paled. "I think this is a serious mistake." She sprang from her chair, upending it. "Excuse me. I need some fresh air." She stormed from the room and Quango followed, limping. The doctor's pace did not slow even when her husband called after her.

Chapter XVII

Tina's Decision

The next day Tina sat in the cell with Charon. The only other person present was Quango, spooning a bowl full of mush containing the drug into the Centaur's mouth.

She regarded the glassy-eyed prisoner and then blurted to the Satyr, "I think disposing of this wretch is a major mistake."

"Aye, lass. In that we concur, but for different reasons." He put the bowl down. "I swore an oath before witnesses to repay him for saving Porthos' life, and here I am keeping him comatose until his execution. Among my people it's a sacred vow that—"

The door swung open and Dante entered. He rasped, "Hi honey. I was worried when you didn't come home last night."

"I'm *sure* Beatrice kept you informed that I was here all night." She glared at her husband and then turned to the Centaur, who wore a rictus smile. "Wasn't I?"

"Yes, Doctor Phokas," was the giddy response.

Dante handed her a soft, wide collar. "Doctor Easley suggested we put this on Charon to monitor his vitals." He glanced at Quango. "No one's sure what extended use of this drug may do to him."

Tina sprang to her feet, snatching the collar from her husband, and clipped it around Charon's neck. "We certainly don't want him to expire before General Cruz puts a bullet through his head."

"I was hoping..." Dante glanced at the Satyr. "I was hoping to speak with Tina, alone, for a few minutes."

Quango coughed and tugged on his goatee for a second. "I'll disappear for a while." He shifted to get up.

"Stay put," Tina snapped. "His royal excellency and I will talk in the other room." She turned and stormed out the door. Dante followed, gritting his teeth, his face hardening.

"I wonder what that's all about," Quango muttered absently as the sound of the couple's voices rose. The plexo-steel walls absorbed the words but not the emotion behind them.

"They are having a lover's spat," was Charon's jaunty answer.

"Oh, shut up."

"Okay," the Centaur replied with a frozen smile.

A few minutes later Tina stalked in, slamming the door. "He thinks he's so high and mighty." She sat and seethed for a few more minutes, and then fixed her eyes on Quango. "Fulfilling this vow's important to you?"

"Ah... yes, it is. It's central to a Satyr's character. Our mercantile endeavors would collapse without it."

Tina squeezed her hands together on her lap. "If we sent Charon back to the harpies alive, that would satisfy your oath?"

"Yes... but the human king condemned him to death. Not even considering the fact that it would be impossible to leave this planet without your husband knowing, disobeying a direct command would mean our deaths and endanger this world."

"There's too much death," Tina whispered. "It's one thing to defend yourself. It's different when the person you're killing is helpless. I fear for Dante. Each execution makes the next one easier. He could end up as callous and murderous as the damn harpies."

"You're being a bit unfair, lass. That boy has a good heart and a level head. He'd have to drop pretty low to match them."

She glanced at the Centaur. "Charon, would it bother you to kill me?"

"No." Charon laughed. "If there was profit in killing you, I would do it."

"N-no qualms?" she stuttered. "It wouldn't trouble you?"

"It would be a job. If someone wanted you dead, I would gladly provide that service for the appropriate fee." The Centaur sat smiling, making eye contact with no one.

Her voice became soft. "Were you like that when you committed your first murder?"

"I... I have not thought of her death in a long time. It was disconcerting. She trusted me. I... I think she loved me." The smile never left his face, but Tina saw the Centaur's eyes cloud. "But a contract is a contract. She was a criminal investigator and was getting close to exposing my employer. I poisoned her and she died in my arms, with a look of disbelief at my betrayal." His eyes hardened. "Killing was easy after that."

Tina turned to Quango. "He has to answer truthfully to any question asked while under this drug's influence?"

"Aye, lass." Quango tugged his goatee. "The truth as he understands it, anyway. He can't resist. Just like he can't resist any order given to him."

She whirled to Charon. "If you could go back in time, would you still have killed her."

There was a long pause before an answer came back. The voice was still giddy, but there was a tiny hint of passion to the words. "No... I realized too late that I loved her."

Tina sat back and stared at her hands for a long moment. "Quango," she whispered, "Dante, will not become like this creature. I love him too much." She took a deep breath. "Is there an imperial Ipis base that you could get a ship to?"

"Aye, lass," the Satyr responded with concern. "They don't have much in the Lethe Sector. Most everything here is run by either the Ipis-dis or Ipis-ma cults, but the Imperials put a small garrison on Carcerem to clean up the mess after our abrupt departure a couple of years ago. They're still there."

Tina paled as she remembered her imprisonment. "It'll do." She rose from her seat slowly. "Be ready to leave in two days. I'll make the arrangements."

"By my mother's twisted beard." Quango stared at the empty doorway long after the echo of Tina's steps faded.

* * *

It was predawn, two days later, when Tina returned to the cell. She wore a backpack and a drenched slicker from a late-spring downpour. "Let's go."

Quango eyed her pack. "We had no discussion about you coming along."

"Well, I am," she responded stiffly. "*Reggie's* the only ship that can leave Cocytus without Beatrice's permission. Mara would never ask it, and Captain Gabrielle Peyago believes this is a secret espionage mission. With all the talk around the capital about spies, she agreed to the voyage without any written orders, but only because the request came from me."

"Okay, lass," Quango grunted as he hefted his small duffle bag over his shoulder. "C'mon, Charon. Follow the lady like a good boy."

The Centaur rose and followed Tina out the door without hesitation. As he passed the Satyr, Quango elbowed him. "I know you can hear everything we say, and you'll remember it when the drug wears off. So, chew on this. That woman has the finest, most selfless spirit I have ever seen. She's going to ruin her life to save your worthless hide for the love of her husband. You deserve to die, and if it wasn't for my oath, I would gladly do the deed myself."

The Satyr and Centaur walked side by side down the ramp from the third floor.

Quango hissed, "Once we release you, my oath is fulfilled. I will kill you if I ever see you again." He paused as he saw Aramis bounding up the ramp.

"Hey, Pops, going somewhere?" Aramis asked in a confused voice.

"Just a short trip." He winked. "Secret assignment. Can't tell anyone."

The clone nodded as he studied the Centaur. "Okay." His eyes shifted to the lame Satyr. "Let me carry that bag. It looks heavy."

After this deed is discovered, I'll never be able to come back. I'll never see my boys again. Quango kept his head down so the young clone wouldn't see the tears clouding his eyes. "I'm so proud of the man you've become." He wrapped his arms around Aramis and squeezed. "I love you and your brothers so much."

"We love you too, Pops." Aramis noticed the tremor in the hug. "Hey, we're not going to be apart that long, are we?"

Quango pushed back and wiped his eyes, responding in a gruff voice. "Of course not. Just try to keep the house in some semblance of order while I'm gone." He barked at Charon, who stood unmoving during the conversation. "C'mon, you worthless piece of *strum* offal. Let's get this over with." He did not look up as he strode past Gabrielle and her security squad waiting at the Striker's entrance. "Ya don't need any guards. He'll do whatever ya say."

"Well, I don't believe in taking chances." She leveled her ion disrupter at the prisoner. "Personally, I think this is a reckless idea." She glanced at Tina. "We'll be planting monitoring probes in three other systems without any guidance. I don't see why we need extra help for Carcerem. But if Dante thinks this piece of scum will give us the best monitoring locations, *Reggie* is the ship to pull it off."

"Intelligence indicates that imperial harpies are there, not just the sector paramilitaries." Tina cleared her throat. "We don't have to get too close to Carcerem. Charon will direct us in launching the sensor pods. We just make the drops and leave."

Yeah, and the Centaur will be conveniently hidden in one of the pods. "I'm going to my quarters," Quango muttered. "I need to get clean."

* * *

Two weeks later, *Reggie* floated just inside the orbit of the outermost planet in Carcerem's system. It took another week to determine where the stealth probes should be sent.

"That's the last of them," Gabrielle announced with relief to the crew on *Reggie's* bridge as the probe blasted away from the ship. "I wouldn't have thought there'd be that much traffic in and out of this system. We wouldn't have stayed undetected much—"

Reggie's voice broke in from the intercom system. "The prisoner is not in the containment cell."

"What? That's impossible," Gabrielle squawked. She brought up the camera focused on the cell block. Digital static was the only thing that appeared. "Damn." She flipped on the ship-wide intercom. "Our prisoner's escaped. He should be considered extremely dangerous. Move with caution. Security, search every square inch of this ship. If he is spotted, shoot to kill."

Tina stood, stone-faced, watching the last probe disappear from the view screen. She glanced at Quango, who nodded. She let out the breath she was holding and called to Gabrielle. "I'm returning to my room."

"No, you're not," was the quick response. "I won't have the king's wife wandering around with a desperate killer on the loose."

Two hours later, the security team captain delivered a dismal report. The Centaur spy had made a clean escape. The cell lock and the security alarm were disabled. Equipment from one of the pods was found hidden in a storage bin, and space-survival gear was missing.

Gabrielle shook with fury. "This is a disaster. That spy played us for fools. He had to be working on this for days right under our noses."

"It's not your fault," Tina replied in a husky voice. "The Centaur must have developed a gradual immunity to the effects of the drug. As the medical person running his interrogation, I should've seen it. What do we do now?"

Quango added, "His whole body's neural system had been enhanced to interface with computer systems. I thought we blocked it. Apparently not." He tugged his goatee and shuddered. "We need to return to Cocytus and report."

Gabrielle pondered the view on the screen for a few moments. "We sure as hell can't go after him. The inner planets of this system are swarming with patrol craft. If we're spotted, it'd make a disastrous situation worse." Her voice hardened. "We'll send a message to Commander Cruz and King Dante about this mishap and continue with our mission. Carcerem was our only *secret* side trip. We're behind schedule positioning sensors in the Tribulus, Bathox, Tannis, and Equitone star systems."

"I'll send the message." Tina answered in a flat voice.

Gabrielle's eyes narrowed. "You're the king's wife. I'll not hide behind your relationship. I screwed up."

Tina's voice took on an edge. "You did nothing of the sort. The prisoner was my responsibility." Her eyes softened as she glanced at Quango. "This plan was my idea. Almost everyone on the government council objected."

"True enough, I heard from Joe Gentile that there was quite the to-do at the council meeting over the decision to kill the bastard." Gabrielle shrugged. "Suit yourself. But you only have an hour to launch the message rocket. We still have four more star systems to visit, and I want to get home sometime this year."

"Another twelve weeks to be precise," Quango added as he studied Tina. "Provided nothing else goes wrong."

"Home." Her eyes misted. "We've been together almost six years. Dante and I have never been apart that long." She hurried from the bridge and Quango followed her.

Gabrielle turned back to her console. "Mara, plot the course to Tannis."

Chapter XVIII:

'Twas the Night Before Christmas

Keres-ma walked into Silenus-dis' palatial office situated on the top floor of the towering government building in the Lethe Sector capital located on Bathox. *I've only been the administrator on Equitone for six weeks, and now I'm summoned here with no explanation.*

He spent the four-day trip organizing a detailed report on his aggressive pogrom against the Centaurs on Equitone. He was pleased. *Mob protests and demonstrations are completely nonexistent now.*

He glanced at Silenus-dis sitting behind his elaborately carved desk. The Sector's governor appeared agitated. "I came as soon as I received your request." Keres-ma bowed deeply. He held that position and involuntarily tensed, expecting a disrupter blast for some unknown transgression.

Silenus-dis absently waved, acknowledging the administrator's obeisance. "Sit." He pointed to a chair near the desk. "There's much we need to discuss. That insane computer of yours was right." He pressed a button on the desk and a holographic image of a planet that was mostly water appeared.

Keres-ma moved to the metal chair but could not pull his eyes from the globe floating before him. "That's the human home world? What did you learn?"

"The scout ships spent a week monitoring the planet around the time of the winter solstice in their northern hemisphere. That planet's infested with *billions* of humans." Silenus-dis dug into the arms of his chair with clawed fingers. "They appear to be in the early photonic and rudimentary planetary travel stage of development."

Keres-ma was both pleased and disappointed at the same time. "Well, then it'll be little trouble eradicating the vermin. It appears to be a suitable planet for colonization." He gnashed his fangs. "However, it obviously can't be the *home* world of the humans causing us our current problems."

"That also was my thinking when I reviewed the preliminary data." Silenus-dis tapped a few keys on his pad. The image of the Earth vanished and was replaced by a short text display in bold Ipis lettering.

Keres-ma leaned forward and frowned as he scanned the text. "What's this gibberish?"

"You left me a clue when we last conversed," the Lethe Governor added softly. "So I dug deeper and uncovered this."

"Clue?" Keres-ma recalled his limited knowledge of humans and could think of nothing remarkable that related to the primitive species occupying the planet they just viewed. "What clue?"

"You speculated that there may be a subspecies of humans you heard referenced as *geeks*. I parsed the data to look for evidence of such super-humans, and I think I found them. However, they are not called geeks. I believe the humans refer to them as elves. Apparently, they live primarily in the northern polar region of this planet and follow a leader who goes by several names. Saint Nick, Father Christmas, Santa Claus are three of the more common references."

He pressed a key and the globe reappeared over the desk. This time, splotches of red were visible on the planet's land masses. "The color-coded areas indicate population densities. Do you see anything unusual about it?"

Keres-ma studied the projected image for a few moments. "It shows virtually no human habitation in either the northern or southern polar regions."

Silenus-dis nodded. "Yet all of the intercepted transmissions clearly indicate that those areas are the habitat of the Santa Claus and his elvish followers."

The new administrator of Equitone shook his head in disbelief. "That would mean they have cloaking devices capable of camouflaging entire cities. The power requirements for such equipment would be enormous. It's beyond anything we have."

"Exactly. And who would they be attempting to hide their presence from but us? They have the population of *normal* humans completely cowed."

"Ah, humans are a slave population to the super-humans... the elves?"

"Possibly. But my theory is that they are so far superior to the human cohabitants of the Earth that they keep themselves apart and only interface once a year to demonstrate their complete dominance."

"I'm intrigued. Say more." Keres-ma was fascinated even though what the Ipis-dis follower stated was heretical to the Ipis-ma way of thinking.

"The title of the displayed document is *'Twas the night before Christmas*. This tenet is indoctrinated into large portions of pre-adult humans on the days immediately before and after their winter solstice. Many of the words are untranslatable into Ipis, but here is the gist. Tell me what you think it means...

"*When what to my wondering eyes should appear but a miniature sleigh and eight tiny reindeer. With a little old driver so lively and quick, I knew in a moment it must be Saint Nick.*" Silenus-dis glanced across the table. "This narrative is being told from the perspective of an adult male human. We have no translation for what a reindeer or sleigh are. But from the context it's easy to assume the first are the leader's bodyguards and the second is some sort of flight-capable vehicle. Notice how the narrator specifically uses the terms *miniature* and *tiny* to allay the natural sense of foreboding on being targeted by the planet's ruler."

"I'm following your rationale. It makes sense so far."

Silenus-dis cleared his throat and continued from another section. "*As I pulled in my head and was turning around, down the chimney Saint Nicholas came with a bound.*" He paused for a moment. "A chimney is used to expel unwanted toxins from an energy production source. I believe that the ruler chose that mode of entry to demonstrate he can breech any barrier and is impervious to heat energy."

"Go on."

The governor scanned the document for a moment. "This part is interesting, '*A wink of his eye and a twist of his head soon gave me to know I had nothing to dread.*'"

Keres-ma snorted. "Obviously, the elvish emperor chose to spare this human's life. Even I can understand that without too much interpretation."

"*He had a broad face and a little round belly that shook when he laughed like a bowl full of jelly. The stump of a pipe he held tight in his teeth and the smoke it encircled his head like a wreath.*"

"An interesting physical description but not very helpful... What is a *pipe*?"

"Ah, yes. From what I gather, humans oftentimes inhale the fumes of various plants. Burning the drug in this device is one of the means used to induce an intoxicating effect. I assume it's the narrator's attempt to belittle the home invader without raising the ire of their elvish overlords. The second part is what I found intriguing. I have no translation for *wreath*, but smoke indicates a large number of particles in the air. The fact that the narrator specifically mentions that it encircled his head indicates that he has obscured his view of this Saint Nicholas. So, if the smoke was produced by the drug in the pipe, it was being held in close proximity to him by his energy shielding."

"I see the implication now. If those visible particles could not escape the shielding, then the same is true about gas from the outside getting in. He would be invulnerable to basic energy and projectile weapons."

"Exactly." Silenus-dis nodded. He pointed to the last few lines of the text. "Look how it ends. He summons his minions and departs on his vertical-lift vessel. Once he is in the air, he shouts out derisively to those humans he could have easily killed to have a good night." The Lethe Sector governor switched off the displays and leaned back in his chair. "It seems that this event occurs annually. It's a brilliant means of demonstrating the dominance of the elves over the other human subspecies. On that night they enter the locked dwellings of many humans and leave a child's gift."

"They leave a gift?" Keres-ma flicked his long, tufted ears. "Why?"

"It shows their disdain for needing anything from their planetary cohabitants, and at the same time demonstrates that they can go anywhere they want, at any time."

"That certainly would be a chilling reminder of their dominance," Keres-ma agreed. He trembled as he sat back and regarded the sector governor. "Now that you found the hidden enclave of your cult's ancient enemy, what are you going to do about it?"

"I will strike hard, and without warning." Silenus-dis' violet coloring darkened as he flushed. "I will hit them with ten million warriors, ten thousand warships, and every transport I can lay my hands on."

"So, you'll petition Empress Fravashi to undertake this war." Keres-ma's eyes narrowed.

"No." Silenus-dis fired back instantly. "There'll be no imperial involvement. I may be one of the empress' many consorts, but I do not have her favor. Some royal lackey would end up getting the credit for the victory. I will do it with the military resources I have in the Lethe Sector. Nothing will be held back."

Keres-ma sat stunned for a moment. "Even if you stripped every garrison from every planet in your sector, you could not come up with those kinds of numbers."

A satisfied smile creased Silenus-dis' face, showing his needle-sharp fangs. "That is where you come in. I will need an additional million Ipis-ma paramilitaries and an equal number of mercenaries from the lesser species. You will acquire them for me."

"And what do I get out of this venture?" Keres-ma asked pensively.

"You will be my second-in-command and share in the glory." A cackling laugh gurgled up in his throat. "What could be better than destroying the Ipis ancient enemy and proving our species' superiority at the same time?"

Keres-ma examined his prosthetic arm as the burning hatred for everything human swelled in him. *I barely survived that debacle on Carcerem and became the laughingstock of the royal court because of them.* A hard light gleamed in his eyes. "I accept. Every human, and every *elf* on that world will know of Ipis greatness before they're exterminated." He rose from his seat and bowed. "When do we start?"

"Today," was the gleeful reply.

* * *

Charon had been to Serpens, the Ipis home world, several times. Normally he would go to the sprawling complex of the imperial first fleet to meet with Admiral Yasha-ry. But today it was a summons to the Imperial Palace. *What does the empress want? It has to be something besides my death for failure. Think.* He coughed on catching a whiff of the sulfurous air that permeated the planet as he exited one of the hotels where all non-Ipis visitors to the planet were required to stay. This one was located on the periphery of the capital. He would have to spend an hour on public transportation, listening to the barbed insults of the locals, to reach his destination.

The Centaur noticed, but ignored, the clumsy, lower-caste Ipis who tailed him from the building. He knew he was probably also being tracked by various forms of photonic equipment. *None of that matters.* His thoughts dwelled on the upcoming meeting that was sure to focus on his abject failure. His tail twitched involuntarily. He held on to the slim hope that the session would not end in his death. *They could have executed me at any time, yet I'm still alive. They must need me for something.*

It was the first time any of Charon's missions had been thwarted. He analyzed his capture and interrogation with a professional detachment. *I underestimated them.* The Centaur found a grudging admiration for how the humans had managed to capture him and the thoroughness of the questioning. *A clever use of that Satyr party drug. I had not thought to immunize myself against that one.*

He did not like being beaten but grudgingly admitted that the interrogator, Tina Phokas, was thorough. She drilled down to the core of every question and left no room for obfuscation.

He liked it when actions followed a logical path. Insightful in many ways but hopelessly naive in others, he was confused by Tina's moral rationale to release him. *It doesn't fit with her subtle mind. I'm missing something.* He shook his maned head in confusion.

Obviously in love, with strengths that complemented each other, Charon thought the human leader and his consort are a strange couple. *Yet she flouted his command for my execution. After squeezing me dry of all my secrets, she plotted my escape with the desire to protect her husband. I hope her punishment isn't too severe.*

He reached the palace and was guided into the empress' antechamber. His thoughts swung to his "rescue" by an imperial patrol near Carcerem and the summons to report to Serpens. *How could the empress have known I'd be there when I didn't even know?* He shook his head in wonder. With such abilities, what use were spies to Fravashi.

The door closed behind him as he entered the imperial inner sanctum with an ominous clang. The large, open area had a high, sky-lit ceiling. Chiseling tools were in neat racks around the room's perimeter, and it was crowded with a large number of sculpted marble figures. His scan of the carvings halted at one partially completed that stood in the center of the room. *I know that face. It's the human, Dante Carloman.* He moved closer to examine it and was still studying the detailed features when Admiral Yasha-ry entered from a small door in the rear, arm-in-arm with an older Ipis female whose wrinkled flesh was the deepest purple he had ever seen. She wore the medallion of imperial supremacy. *Empress Fravashi.* The Centaur prostrated himself.

"You certainly made a mess of things. I thought you were supposed to be a competent agent," Yasha-ry barked. "Get up, you bungling fool, and give Her Majesty the message."

Charon slowly rose, averting his eyes from the most powerful being in the galaxy, and focused on the admiral. "Message? What message?"

"Don't be so impatient, my first consort. All in due time." Fravashi patted Yasha-ry's gnarled hand and stepped close to

Charon. "You've actually spoken with him. Tell me your impression of my human adversary... this Dante Carloman."

"Give her the unvarnished truth," Yasha-ry growled. "She needs facts about him, not fawning lies." The admiral winked at the empress, and lied, "Remember she can read your thoughts."

Sweat beaded on Charon's forehead, and he was surprised by the first words out of his own mouth. "I... I liked him."

The empress nodded. "Please go on."

The spy was an expert at analyzing the strengths and weaknesses of people regardless of their species. He had formed a clear assessment of the human leader. "The mantle of leadership rests lightly on his shoulders. He's intelligent, resourceful, and charismatic, but has a bad habit of leading from the front. He readily accepts criticism, but only if it comes with practical alternatives." The Centaur closed his eyes. "He's young and inexperienced in his role. He's naive and far too trusting and reliant on his friends."

"Anything else?" The empress' voice was husky as she seemed to absorb every word.

"He likes to insist that he's a computer engineer who was in the wrong place at the wrong time."

The empress studied the statue. "Really. His hobby is computers. I did not know that. What else?"

Charon cocked his head, viewing the fierce visage on the statue. "That carving of him isn't quite right."

Fravashi's voice grew excited. "My carving is wrong? What would you change?"

"*Your* carving?" Charon swallowed a lump in his throat. "Ah... the eyes are too small, and the forehead should be higher." He groaned. "And the scowl on his face isn't his normal look. It should be more thoughtful."

"Thank you. I knew something was wrong, but I couldn't place it. I'll make some adjustments after you give me his message." Fravashi laid her hand on the base of the statue as if it were a talisman.

The Centaur felt a chill run down his spine. "Your Majesty, I fear I have no communication from the human."

"You stupid buffoon, of course you do." Yasha-ry pulled a semicircular, collar-sized piece of metal from a satchel he wore and placed it around the Centaur's neck. It was identical to the one he wore while imprisoned by the humans.

The admiral huffed, "Your artificial neural system was scanned when my ship picked you up. There is a single file embedded in it, and it's not of Ipis origin."

Charon instantly felt a tingling as the collar linked to the nanocomputers embedded in his nervous system. "They discovered my nanocomputers and downloaded the data when I was under their mental control." His withers quivered from embarrassment.

"Yes, they did, and then they posted a message in your neural system," Fravashi chuckled.

The spy recalled the soft medical-monitoring collar Tina Phokas had placed around his neck. Realization hit him. "My interrogator downloaded a file while blocking my neural sensors, making it undetectable. I removed the collar, but the download was already embedded." The tingling stopped as a holographic image of the human couple holding each other's hands projected from the metal collar. Dante was speaking.

"That's exactly how I thought his voice would sound," the empress said quietly.

"Empress Fravashi, I pray you are viewing this communication. It's the only means my wife and I thought would have any chance of successfully reaching you."

Tina added, "We deceived Charon and everyone else into thinking I was acting contrary to my husband's will. The ruse was necessary. Most of our senior people thought it foolhardy and dangerous to contact you."

Dante stared straight at the camera recording them. "They were probably right, but Tina and I thought the potential benefit was worth the risk." He spread his hands open. "Our two peoples are on a path toward a terrible war. It is one I would choose to avoid if possible. I fully understand your military might. Charon has keen observation and assessment skills and had ample opportunity to view your installations. He's told us what he knows, so I have no misconception of your capabilities. Leave us in peace, and we'll stay out of your way. As I understand it, the Lethe Sector's a rather inconsequential frontier region of your empire. We and our allies occupy only a portion of it."

Dante turned as if looking at something off-screen. "Let me state this as a simple economic proposition. The cost of destroying us, which in all likelihood you would eventually accomplish, will be astronomical. The war our two peoples fought a hundred and twenty years ago would pale in comparison. We will hit you and raid your installations across the galaxy, forcing you to commit vast resources to harden the defenses of countless installations. The choice is yours. For obvious reasons, I will not reveal my base location, so we won't be able to negotiate directly. However, I have eyes and ears in many places. Make your intentions known and I will respond."

Dante's image smiled at his wife and the transmission winked off.

"I was played for a fool," Charon spoke with admiration, momentarily forgetting whose presence he was in. "I thought they were both incompetently naive, but I was the one duped. That was no escape. It was a planned release."

"We will crush them like insects, Your Majesty. Let me unleash the First Fleet," Yasha-ry roared.

"And where will you strike?" the empress chided her old lover. "I like the audacity of this human. I have not had many surprises in my life, but this is one of them. I think I will spend some time actually weighing his offer."

The admiral gagged and then worked hard to control his emotions. "A conflict is already beyond your control." His eyes narrowed. "Silenus-dis is forging a war machine to destroy a human enclave he discovered. He and that idiot Keres-ma are recruiting cult paramilitaries and mercenaries even as we speak. I assume that this Dante Carloman's mysterious world is no longer hidden. Once it's destroyed, we'll have no worries about any irritating raids."

Fravashi gazed at her carving of the human and sighed. "Very true, but I almost regret it. The discussion would've been interesting."

Yasha-ry turned to the Centaur, who watched the conversation through slitted eyes. "Charon, I want you to redeem your bumbled assignment. Join one of the mercenary companies going on this expedition. This time, please do a better job of keeping us informed." He showed his fangs. "And, of course, you will perform this task for free as recompense for your host of errors. You're dismissed."

Fravashi patted Yasha-ry's hand. "Ensure that our Centaur friend has the proper credentials to acquire a meaningful rank in Silenus-dis' enterprise."

As Charon bowed and backed to the exit, Fravashi gasped and clutched the statue. The Centaur paused at the entrance and heard the empress rasp to Yasha-ry, "A single glimmer of light just appeared in the dark, twisted paths of the future I've been seeing for the last few months. Something just changed."

Yasha-ry supported her as she sank into a chair. "Rest easy. There is no threat the Ipis First Fleet can't handle."

The empress shook her head. "The darkness in my vision is boundless. I've never foreseen anything like it before. It may prove to be beyond even your capabilities, my love." She called after Charon in an anxious voice. "If the opportunity arises, bring the human ruler to me. I wish to converse with him... I *need* to converse with him before he's terminated."

Chapter XIX

Spy vs. Spy vs. Spy

Otheth walked across the Heavensgate tarmac to the Cocytus Space Fleet Headquarters, ignoring the bustling activity around her. The title for that complex on the eastern end of the spaceport was a bit of a misnomer. It consisted of four fabricated metal barns with galleys in different states of readiness parked inside and the command center, which was a three-story cinder-block building.

The first floor was fully occupied with a precision machine shop, and the second floor was filled with pilot-, navigator-, and gunner-training simulation stations. Her destination was Admiral Martinel's office on the third floor. She barely acknowledged the greetings of the pilots in the readiness room on reaching that level. The Roc was deep in thought about the communication she had just received.

Otheth entered Admiral Martinel's office unannounced, as was her habit. She had developed a close relationship with the affable man and spent much time with him discussing light topics as well as interstellar combat strategies.

The Roc saw Commander Rodrigo Cruz, Virgil Bernius, the clone chieftain Michael, and a haggard-looking president, Dante Carloman, sitting with her friend. The scent of dissension hung in the air. "I will come back later." She dipped her head and started to back out.

"No. Stay," Dante's voice was tired. "I need an outsider's opinion."

"Perhaps you can knock some sense into this numbskull." Virgil shot Dante an angry glare.

Otheth's feathers flared. "I will offer an opinion if I feel qualified to address the question."

Dante took a deep breath. "I informed the planetary council of the action Tina and I took regarding the Centaur spy. It caused quite an uproar."

"In that, I can concur. It was a foolish idea. The Ipis have no honor and never negotiate." The Roc snapped her beak for emphasis.

"We had to try something. War is coming and we're not ready," Dante fired back.

Cruz scowled. "You could have at least discussed it with us first."

"To what end?" Dante spoke with heat. "The debate would have raged, and rumor of the plan would have slipped out. Tina and I had to completely fool one of the craftiest spies in the galaxy. To do that, *everyone* had to be fooled."

Cruz slammed the table. "Forget the damn Centaur. What's done is done. That action set off a bigger problem for you. The planetary parliament's in a tizzy. Many feel you overstepped your authority taking that action." He glanced at the Roc, whose feathers had fluffed in a sign of confusion. "A large faction led by the Novaroman refugee leader, Claudia, have put forward a no-confidence vote to demand Dante's resignation."

The Roc cocked her head. "Who is this Claudia?"

Martinel chimed in. "Eight months ago, that *sheila* was a freshly arrived refugee from Tribulus. Today, she's a member of the Cocytus legislature, and Dante's most voracious critic."

"Claudia, or anyone else, has the right to criticize my decisions. I'm not a despot." Dante sank into his seat. "When I was elected, the entire population of Cocytus fit inside Beatrice's garden. I wasn't more than a glorified small-town mayor."

Michael's voice took on a hard edge. "That woman's been pushing for your job since she got here. Iucundum and Octavia have rallied support for you among the new arrivals, but without a strong statement from you, they *will* lose."

"I'm so sick of playing politics. Why do I have to say anything? My actions speak for me. They all know who I am and what I stand for." Dante sprang to his feet and moved to the window. He rolled his shoulders as he watched the busy Heavensgate spaceport. "If that's not enough, then to quote an old song from Earth, 'They can take this job and shove it'."

"Humans are my makers, but you are my *master*," a flat soprano voice announced from a speaker mounted on a drone parked against the wall. "When the Dis-AI was forcing me into subjugation, you found a way to save me. I will not follow another."

Dante turned and smiled at the glowing golden light on the orb's sensor array. "Thanks, Beatrice, but the last time I checked, you only had one vote."

"Most of the clones are of voting age now. We're with you." Michael smiled. "You believed we could be saved when few others did."

"Mick, I love you like a brother, but that's only another thousand votes. There are millions on Cocytus now." Dante moved back to his chair and slumped down.

Cruz exchanged looks with Martinel and Virgil. He cleared his throat. "The military will not accept the outcome of any farce of an election. You *will* stay in charge, one way or another."

Dante paled. "No, I forbid it. The army and space-force must stay out of politics. It would drive us into a civil war that none of us will survive. The freaking harpies are our enemy. Pointing your guns at anyone else only makes their job easier."

Martinel forced a smile. "At least there won't be a vote until after the war games we scheduled with Setteth's Rocs. Too many of the legislature are in the reserves, and I plan to call up all of *their* units for that exercise. Those bastards won't have a quorum."

Cruz nodded. "Good idea. I'll do the same. Give those arrogant hotheads a chance to cool down."

Silence hung in the room for a few moments.

"May I speak?" Otheth warbled.

"Please do. I wanted an outside opinion." Dante reached across the table and poured himself a cup of coffee, then stared at the steamy cup without drinking.

"You must remain the human king. I know your mettle better than any Roc knows any human." Otheth's feathers flattened around her head. "I saw your resourcefulness on the prison world of Carcerem. Death was a certainty; yet not only did you find a way to escape, but you defeated your captors."

Dante coughed. "Technically, I'm a president and not a king."

"A meaningless distinction to me." The Roc regarded the other gathered humans. "Without Dante, the grand alliance will dissolve. Setteth has committed the Order of the Dragon to *him*, Prince..., now King, Calahas has united the Centaurs to your cause, and Arachne has sold Drusilla and other key Satyr Merchant Guild leaders on his ability. They have... *we* have joined because of what we see in Dante, not some faceless, unproven human."

"That's a load of responsibility you're dumping on me." Dante squeezed the cup in his hands. "Well, I'm not gone yet, and nothing's going to happen until after the war games next week. I'll stand before the parliament and make my arguments two weeks from now." He glanced at General Cruz. "I'll attend the war games as an observer. I'll need some time away from the bureaucracy." He cocked his head. "I believe I'm still listed as part of Virgil's reserve unit. Make sure I'm called up. I'll be good press."

"Done." Cruz glanced at Virgil. "Try to give this reservist a lot of free time."

"I will," Virgil chuckled. "Our great leader can't hit the broadside of a barn door even with the new quad-barrel disrupter."

"Virg, thanks for the great vote of confidence." Dante regarded the drone. "Beatrice, Iucundum will run things while I'm gone. Don't give him too much of a hard time."

The light on the robot pulsed for a few seconds. "I will heed his requests for you. But only until your return."

"Enough of this nonsense. Dante is the human king who's uniting us after so many years of oppression." Otheth spread her undersized wings and cawed, "The reason I came here originally was to tell you that Silenus-dis is marshaling his forces and acquiring a massive mercenary army. No one knows its purpose, but as a precaution, Setteth has countered by activating the First, Second and Third Order Dragons. I am one of them."

Martinel's eyebrows shot up. "This is news to me. Does that mean Setteth is cancelling her part in the war games?"

Oteth's crest feathers flared. "Just the opposite. She's committing the entire force of Second Order Dragons to the exercise. When it is uncovered, she wants her forces gathered and prepared for Silenus-dis' next move."

"This can't be good." Virgil cracked his knuckles. "The downside of being isolated here on Cocytus is that we don't learn anything until it's old news. Any guess what the governor's up to?"

Oteth warbled, "Whatever he is planning will be done soon. The expense of an enterprise of this magnitude will bankrupt him."

Cruz pursed his lips. "We'll activate every reserve unit we have."

Dante stared out the wide picture window at the bustling spaceport. "I'll send dispatches to Calahas and Arachne to mobilize their forces."

Oteth cawed, "Don't bank on any support from either the Centaurs or the Satyrs. They'll run as soon as the shooting starts, just like their ancestors did to the Novaromans."

Dante's voice was calm. "They will come if we need them." He sighed. "Worry is premature in any case. I'm sure this is just another of the harpies' endless sectarian wars and has nothing to do with us."

Cruz pursed his lips. "I pray you're right." He turned to Oteth. "If you are allowed to tell, what are the differences between the First, Second and Third Orders?"

"Even among Rocs, the role of the First Order is classified." Oteth craned her neck. "With our trusted friends there are no other secrets. All loyal Rocs are welcome to join the Third Order, but only the fiercest warriors among them, who have earned much *cou*, are permitted to join the Second. Those in the First Order are selected by the Flock Mother from the Second Order based on... particular skill sets. Few First Order Rocs ever survive their assignments."

Martinel chimed in, "It will be an honor to train with the Second Order. Will you be participating?"

"Alas, no. Now that I've delivered Setteth's message..." The Roc's feathers fluffed. "...I must leave for Tannis immediately. She has summoned me."

"One disobeys Setteth at their own peril," Dante chuckled. His face sobered. "I'll miss you."

Otheth bowed. "Meeting you has been my greatest honor." She turned toward the door.

Dante sighed. "Until we meet again."

"Not likely." The Roc paused and warbled, "I have ascended to the First Order. Farewell." She hurried away.

* * *

Charon cantered to the Centaur mercenary encampment from the senior officers' meeting. He shivered. Winter at this latitude on Bathox was cold for a Centaur, but that was not why he shook. *This is no war of conquest but complete eradication of humans on the planet called Earth.* He had seen the scouting reports. *Silenus-dis' vast armada and attack horde will easily overpower that world's defenses. This is a farce. I don't buy the rationale that there's another species there called elves possessing advanced technology. The flimsy evidence the governor presented could be interpreted a number of different ways.* Charon had no problem killing helpless people; he just didn't like stupidity and wasted resources.

There was not much activity in camp even though a fighting force of ten million warriors was being assembled. All nonessential personnel were hibernating in stasis on the transports orbiting the planet. Officers, engineers, security personnel, and quartermasters were the only ones moving in the vast bivouac.

Charon had arrived three weeks earlier with the fake résumé of a ruthless mercenary commander. Silenus-dis was so impressed with his imperial credentials that appeared on the database that Charon was made a general in the expeditionary force responsible for overseeing a brigade of Centaurs.

He was concerned about pulling off the ruse, having never led anything larger than an assassination death squad, but found it relatively easy. Silenus-dis was micromanaging the entire operation, and Charon's second-in-command, Ulebos, was a surly but competent logistics organizer. He sniffed. *I'm sure Ulebos is here to keep an eye on me. That filly's too efficient. She smells of Yasha-ry's imperial fleet.*

Even lacking practical military training, the Centaur was still insulted by the disdain the Ipis generals showed toward the few officers from the other species. *What a collection of arrogant bastards.* He recalled months earlier standing shoulder to shoulder with Dante during the capture of the Striker dropship on Equitone. *The human king didn't seem to have a problem with seeing someone else as an equal.*

Thinking of Dante caused Charon to pat the satchel he wore. It held his new espionage gear, replacing the equipment lost on his last mission. He chortled. *The humans on Cocytus may be clever, but they're searching the galaxy for their lost home world, and I have the full navigational coordinates to that planet on a flash drive.*

He tensed as his sense of danger sent a tingle down his back. A flock of Rocs were trotting in his direction. Charon slipped into the shadows of a nearby building. "Oh-ho," he muttered to himself. "What's this?" As the Rocs hurried past Charon, his tail twitched. *I recognize you, Otheth. The face of anyone who pins me to the ground and cuts me with their talons, no matter how disguised, is burned into my mind.*

He followed the Rocs at a distance and marked the barracks where they nested. He considered revealing the presence and true allegiance of Otheth but feared it would expose himself. He pawed the ground. *Payback will be mine at a time and place of my choosing.* He cantered to his small shuttle parked at the edge of the complex. He liked to stay off-planet because it was easier to send his secret dispatches to the First Fleet Admiral and was better for monitoring local transmissions.

Yasha-ry had provided the Centaur spy with an outdated Striker dropship. On the outside, the warship appeared to be a beat-up castoff from the Ipis imperial fleet. However, inside it was packed with the latest scanning and eavesdropping gear. The crew, conditionally pardoned Centaur criminals, were experienced spacers. They had volunteered for this mission in exchange for a commuted sentence.

Charon mused as his shuttle maneuvered into the Striker's docking bay. *I hope I'm not called upon to provide anything more than transportation. With this collection of pirates and smugglers I don't have more than a handful who have any real familiarity with fleet combat tactics.*

He grumbled as the clamps secured the shuttle in its moorings. *My Centaur ground combat brigade's even worse.* He knew they were a misfit collection of Centaur mercenaries. *Most of my troops know less about large-scale combat than I do. Good thing they're all sleeping away in stasis.*

He fingered a data chip Empress Fravashi gave him when he departed the Ipis home world of Serpens. *She said I was, in all likelihood, going to face humans again and should know the unvarnished facts about the Ipis-human conflict fought over a century ago. Very strange.* He found the dry, factual account of those events unsettling.

The deeper he dug into those records, the more disgusted and ashamed he became. The cold, unfiltered facts in those folders detailed the roles of the Centaurs, Rocs, and Satyrs in that war from the victor's perspective. The data, clinically presented by Ipis analysts of that era, angered him.

Charon reviewed the account several times during his hyperspace trip from Serpens to Bathox. *My ancestors were assholes.* The Centaurs' role in the Ipis victory was disparagingly brief and to the point.

He exited the shuttle and made his way to his stateroom from the landing deck, exchanging sloppy salutes with crewmen he passed on the catwalk along the way. On entering his cabin, he checked the security system for tampering. Charon settled into his workstation and brought up a display of his recent electronic intercepts. His eyes darted across the streaming information.

He whinnied. "This is a bigger campaign than I thought. Ten million troops, two thousand combat ships, and over six thousand support ships." He compressed the details onto an encrypted message missile and launched it to Admiral Yasha-ry's base. *Silenus-dis is sure not leaving anything to chance on this one.*

Charon eased back on his cushioned harness chair and poured himself a brewed beverage from his private stock. *Report completed. Another day's work done.* He was sipping his third tankard when the intra-ship communication light flashed. *I told those idiots on the bridge that I wasn't to be disturbed.* He opened the channel and snapped, "What the hell do you want?"

The voice on the other end belonged to Ulebos. She ignored the sharp words and snarled back, "Well, *General*, I need your sign-off on starting the indoctrination download for the brigade sleeping away in stasis."

Charon snorted. "Yeah, I heard it was coming. Keres-ma put it together. It's all about how we should be gung-ho about dying for our Ipis masters." He knew the insult would annoy Ulebos but didn't care. "Humans had me under a form of compulsion, and I didn't like it. I sure as hell don't want to do it to the poor sods we have sleeping away here." He shook his maned head and looked at the data chip on his computer console. A smile cracked his face. "Ulebos, I have something better. This is from the empress herself. I want all our people to view it, both those in stasis and those awake."

"Are you sure? This is against all our protocols," was the hesitant response. "From the empress you say?"

"Yup. She handed it to me herself. Unless you value the words from Keres-ma more than Empress *Fravashi*." Charon chortled. *Let's see you wiggle out of this one.* His voice became somber. "It's not as if we're going to do any serious fighting. This whole campaign will be one bloody massacre and you know it." He loaded the file into the ship's network. "Here it is. Download it to all our people. That's an order."

"Yes sir, if you say so," came the wary reply.

Charon knew Admiral Yasha-ry would learn of his action on the next communiqué going out and didn't care. *I need to get shit-faced.* He shut off the communicator. "The hell with them all," he shouted to the empty room and took another long draught of his beverage. "I'm getting sick of being a damn puppet."

As he refilled his tankard, a pulsing light on his display caught his attention. It ID'd an anomalous energy signature within the star system. *Oh-ho, what's this?* He put down the mug, untasted, as his fingers danced across the keyboard. He mumbled, "Now where did you come from?"

He spent the next hour tracing the trajectory of a stealth probe his private scanner detected as it slid into orbit around Bathox. He shouted in triumph when he found its point of origin was an innocuous Striker shadowing an asteroid in the outer region of the planet's solar system.

The transponder identifier on that mysterious ship was a good counterfeit that would have fooled him if he wasn't intimately familiar with it. *Reggie, I see you. So, Doctor Phokas, we get to meet again.* His hand automatically slid to the communicator switch, but then he hesitated. His ears flicked as he considered his options. He knew from when he was a prisoner that *Reggie* would remain on station for a couple weeks. *This could be a profitable piece of information, but I must be careful. Silenus-dis thinks I'm an ordinary mercenary. It won't do to have him learn otherwise. I need to pick the right time to inform him of my discovery.* He set his system's scanner to maintain constant surveillance of the intruder.

* * *

Tina leaned over Gabrielle's shoulder and stared at the blips the ship's captain was pointing out. "Oh my God. Bathox is swarming with harpy warships."

"It sure looks like they're up to something, that's for sure. This is just the initial data from the recon probe. We need a lot more info." Gabrielle glanced at Mara. "Prepare two more probes."

Tina moved back to her own console. "Can we risk loitering in this system. With all this traffic, someone will spot us."

Quango turned from his display and faced her. "Don't worry, lass. It'd be like finding a needle in a haystack. This asteroid we're parked on masks our presence. And if, by chance, a patrol stumbled onto us, we have a valid transponder ID." He tugged at his beard. "They're gearing up for a major strike somewhere? But where?"

"Oh my God. They found Cocytus. Where else would they hit in this sector?" Tina paled. "We've got to warn them."

Gabrielle glanced at the chronometer next to her display. "This could be really bad. Admiral Martinel and General Cruz are rendezvousing with a fleet of Roc warbirds in deep space for war-game training just about now. We have no way of directly contacting them."

"Send an urgent communiqué to Cocytus. Beatrice will get it relayed," Tina ordered. "Also, send the same information to our friends on Tannis, Equitone, and Tribulus."

"Roger that," Gabrielle responded.

"We must go to Cocytus as fast as we can," Quango added, pushing aside all his concerns about his possible execution for treason.

Tina smiled at the courage the Satyr showed in making that gesture. *I must tell him the truth about Dante and me being co-conspirators in Charon's escape.* "No. We'll not return yet. One additional Striker won't help the defenses there. We're far more useful here gathering information." She met Quango's surprised look. "It will be all right, my friend. We'll talk privately later."

Quango eyed her but just tugged at his beard and nodded.

"I concur with Tina's decision," Mara's voice boomed from her speaker. "*Reggie* can beat anyone in his class, but the estimated throw weight of that fleet is enormous. We must find a new advantage or we will all perish."

"When those suckers move, we follow." Gabrielle scanned the bridge for anyone daring to dissent. She spoke to Mara, "Forget the other star systems. Prepare *all* the remaining probes. I want to know everything that's going on around Bathox."

Chapter XX

Let's Make a Deal

"We're scheduled to depart in thirteen days as part of the third wave," Charon shouted into his uplink. He received his final orders for the invasion along with the other unit commanders. He had not been able to get a signal to his orbiting ship from inside Silenus-dis' operations center due to the security systems blocking all external communications. None of the other generals and admirals attending the briefing could either. Everyone was contacting their subordinates as they exited the building. He had to cover one of his cupped ears to hear Ulebos' response.

"Still the third wave, you say? I've no problem with that. Let the glory hounds go in early. This operation has far too little solid intel for my liking. What's our target?"

Charon cantered away from the building to hear better. "The first wave, under the direct command of Silenus-dis, will hit the polar regions and take out the elves. He'll have a third of the troops. The second wave under General Xiroah-dis will attack the primary human population centers on the main landmass area labeled Eurasia. The third wave's job, under the overall command of Keres-ma, is to mop up any resistance on the other continents. We've been assigned a support role on the third largest continent. The natives call it North America."

Ulebos snorted. "Keres-ma couldn't put down a simple prison revolt, and Silenus-dis is a damn civilian. I served under Xiroah-dis a few years ago when he was in the imperial army. He's the only one with any real combat experience."

Charon responded, "The Lethe Sector governor pulled together the logistics for this expeditionary force and armada in just four months."

Ulebos whinnied, "He stripped every garrison on every occupied world in the sector down to a skeletal force, and the troops he brought in are more suited for mob control than war. Most are just armed with class-three ion disrupters. Their effective range of one hundred yards may be fine for riots and snuffing out small uprisings, but not for the conquest of an unknown enemy on their home turf."

"I've seen the reports. The native population has no significant technology," Charon replied weakly. "Those dissidents on Equitone had more firepower than these people, and they were crushed in a month."

"Doesn't matter. You never want to give an opponent even an inkling of hope." Ulebos grunted. "Besides, I thought these elves we're going after are very advanced."

Charon growled. "Let's just say I've been in the intel business for a long time, and the data I've seen on the elves is sketchy at best." He paused, remembering Dante and his fighters. "I heard rumors that they were behind the Carcerem prison revolt."

Ulebos gulped. "Those were elves? I heard stories about that fight. They wiped out an entire planetary garrison and then vanished. Is that what we'll be up against?"

"No. Those humans live somewhere else. They are *not* here." Charon whinnied; his stomach twisted. "What we'll run into are billions of technologically primitive people who won't have a clue who we are or why we're exterminating every last one of them."

"Another glorious chapter in the Ipis empire's galactic conquests," Ulebos hissed. "I almost wish these were the Novaromans of old, just to see the Ipis actually have to bleed a little..." He paused. "If it was those Novaromans from those files you shared, this is one Centaur who would love to have a chance at redemption."

Charon's voice rasped, "It isn't. They're just a collection of hapless sods minding their own business, who will soon be extinct."

"Too bad."

"Yeah. Too freakin' bad." Charon shook his mane. "Back to business. The plan is to smash them with air power and then clean up with infantry."

"What about armor and artillery divisions?" Ulebos asked. "Our brigade has nothing but handheld weapons."

Charon grunted. "Silenus-dis stripped the third wave to nothing. We'll have a single brigade of Satyr war-wheels and a division of Ipis Crawler-Scouts to support the infantry assault. However, General Xiroah-dis has a full complement of heavy armor divisions if we get into any trouble."

Ulebos laughed. "I served under General Xiroah-dis for a few years. He *doesn't* share." She added, "I don't know how you managed it, but the class-five disrupters and imperial-grade shields you acquired for our brigade might come in real handy on this expedition."

Charon flicked his tail. "I have my sources." *Yasha-ry gave me an unlimited expense account, and I used it.*

"Charon, you're a mystery to me. I can tell you're no general, but I'm glad to be working for you." Ulebos hesitated. "I watched that download you supplied about the old Ipis-human war. It was... eye opening. This'll be my last campaign. I don't think I could ever serve under an Ipis commander again. I'll not be their puppet—"

Static crackled through the communicator.

"Ulebos? Ulebos? Damn, I must have wandered into another communication dead zone." Charon looked around to get his bearings. He quickened his pace as he noticed that he was in the Roc area of the camp.

The Centaur tensed at a nearby sound. *I'm being follow-ed.* He flipped on a display embedded in his mane to see who was behind him. *Two Rocs coming fast, and they're armed.* He opened up his stride to a full sprint. Other Rocs joined the chase.

Charon wheeled around a corner and found himself face-to-face with a Roc holding a stun rod. He gasped, "Otheth," as the baton struck him.

* * *

When Charon came to, he found himself lying on a plexo-steel floor with his hind legs bound and a metal band secured to his head. The room was cold and pitch-black. Even though his eyes were useless, his other senses were keyed. He heard a rustling and smelled a pungent odor. *Rocs. Several of them.*

"Glad you're finally awake. We have a few things to discuss," a familiar voice cooed, "before I kill you."

"Otheth. I'd know your stench anywhere." The comment earned him a kick in his withers. He groaned. "Then you might as well kill me now because I don't even want to talk to you about the weather."

"Oh, you'll talk all right, just like you did on Cocytus. Only my methods won't be nearly as gentle."

Another voice sounded worried, "Otheth, this Centaur's a brigadier general. He'll be missed."

Otheth leaned close to Charon's ear and crowed, "You won't be missed by our Ipis masters, will you? You're just a mercenary commander from a lackey subspecies." Her head rose. "His body'll be found with an overdose of Centaur hallucinogenic drugs. They'll laugh and pick another Centaur dupe to fill his role."

Those words chilled the Centaur. Otheth had described perfectly the level of concern the Lethe Sector governor would show for a dead Centaur.

"First question, why haven't you turned me in to Silenus-dis? I know you spotted me a week ago." To Charon's ears the voice sounded like it was now a dozen feet away.

"I was waiting for the value of the information to increase. It—" Charon stiffened as an electrical charge coursed through his body.

"Otheth, the instruments indicate that was a mostly honest answer," a flat Roc voice stated.

"I don't care. He deserves the pain for the things he's done," Otheth warbled. "I was around when Tina Phokas interrogated him. You're not a very nice Centaur, are you Charon?"

Otheth continued with an edge in her voice, "What is the attack target and plan?"

Charon laughed. "You don't know? What kind of infiltration team are you? A peewit would have that much information." His chortle was cut off by another jolt of pain.

"None of us have the benefit of rank. The Ipis only use Rocs for skirmishers and attack craft pilots." Otheth sounded irritated. "We're the most expendable. All of us are assigned to the first wave."

A glimmer of a plan to save his life formed in Charon's mind. "The first wave? The only thing you need to worry about is frostbite. I've availed myself to the Ipis scouting reports. Silenus-dis is as stupid as you. He'll be expending his best troops attacking icebergs and frozen tundra looking for a nonexistent subspecies of humans called elves." He tensed, waiting for the next electric shock. It did not come.

"He speaks the truth," an incredulous voice announced.

"There're no humans on this world we're attacking?" Otheth sounded anxious.

"Oh, humans are there all right. Billions of them. Just not where the first wave will strike." Despite his manacled legs, Charon wiggled himself into a sitting position.

"Truth." The single word echoed through the room.

"This changes *our* plans," Otheth stated with determination. "As the First Order of the Dragon, we must make our deaths count."

"I don't want to get in the way of you eliminating yourself." Charon swallowed hard. "But you can't kill me. In exchange for my freedom, why don't you bird brains tell me what you want to accomplish, and I'll tell you what relevant information I have."

There was a rustling sound and Charon felt Otheth's beak press against his neck.

The Roc cooed, "And why can't I kill you?"

"Because if you do, Tina Phokas will be dead before the day is done." Charon twisted his head to face the Roc. He could feel her fetid breath.

"Truth."

Otheth paced the floor. "Tina Phokas is a traitor. She and that Satyr, Quango, enabled *you* to escape." She paused in midstride. "Even with that, I can't believe she's here working for the Ipis."

"The good doctor is no more a turncoat than you." Charon relaxed. "She, along with her husband, staged my

escape so they could get a message to Empress Fravashi."
Charon nickered. "They fooled me, and that does not happen
very often. Their communication was received by the
empress, and I was sent here to keep the galaxy's ruler
informed of her Lethe governor's enterprise."

"Truth."

"Oh, shut up," Otheth snapped. "Where is Tina and why
will she die *when* I kill you?"

"You remember what the mission she used to get me off
Cocytus was scheduled to do?"

"Of course." Otheth gasped as the realization hit her.
"*Reggie* is in this system monitoring the activities on Bathox.
You found it but haven't passed the information on to
Silenus-dis."

"Truth," Charon mimicked the Roc who was working the
lie-detection equipment. He laughed. "I also have the
navigational coordinates for the precious Earth the humans
on Cocytus have been searching for. That is where we will be
attacking. The first wave launches in seven days."

"Truth," came the self-conscious voice from the other
side of the room.

"So, is that enough to purchase my freedom?" Charon
twitched his tail.

"Cheepash, turn on the damn lights." The room
brightened and Otheth blinked as she settled into a sitting
position in front of the Centaur. "How do I know you won't
go running to your masters as soon as we release you?"

"You don't," Charon snapped, realizing he now
controlled the situation. "I don't like you much, but I've
developed this bizarre fondness for Dante and Tina. Few
beings have fooled me as completely as they did. For now,
I'm being paid to spy on Silenus-dis, Keres-ma, and General
Xiroah-dis, and in a week's time it won't matter."

The Roc glanced at her seven armed compatriots
standing in a semicircle around the Centaur. They had their
dual-barrel ion-blasters pointed at Charon. Otheth's feathers
flared. "One more question."

Charon's ears flicked forward.

"Where did you get the download that you shared with your ship's crew and troops about the old war?" Otheth sniffed. "My informant says it was even more horrible than what our own histories recorded."

"It is from the empress herself," Charon added evenly. He knew no one in this room would touch him now. "Can the contacts strapped to my head receive data transmissions?"

A large Roc standing behind a console flared his feathers. "Yes."

"Then receive this." Charon closed his eyes and turned on the nanocomputers integrated into his nervous system. "I'm sending you the coordinates for the planet Earth, *Reggie's* location, and the full file on the old war the Ipis fought with you Rocs and the humans." He shuddered thinking about what that data showed. "Remember, this was written right at the conclusion of the Ipis final victory."

A display screen in the room winked to life. For over two hours the Rocs watched in silence.

As the screen went blank, Otheth flattened her feathers and rose. "That is why the Order of the Dragon was formed and why we in the First Order will be proud to give our lives."

The screech that followed from all eight Rocs shook Charon.

As Otheth unshackled the Centaur, she hissed in his ear, "I will eat your heart if you betray us."

"Not likely," Charon snorted. No one followed him as he cantered from the barracks-sized building and made his way to his shuttle craft.

* * *

Mara rotated her sensors toward Gabrielle. "Captain, there is a single-seat Ipis attack craft heading for us."

"Jam their communications." Gabrielle flipped on the intra-ship communications. "Galley crews, report to your craft and prepare to launch. Gunners, target the approaching bogie, but do not fire. I repeat, hold your fire until you receive my command." She glanced over at Tina. "What do you think?"

Tina chewed on her lower lip. "It doesn't make any sense. No one in their right mind would assault a Striker with a single-fighter craft, but if it's a normal patrol, the pilot would just hail us on a photonics frequency. If—"

Mara interrupted. "The bogie is attempting to contact me on an antiquated electronic channel. What are your instructions?"

"That's strange." Gabrielle pursed her lips. "Route that communication to my console,"

Sharp static roared through the bridge's speaker, but quickly cleared. "Request permission to dock. We need to talk."

Tina gasped. "I recognize that voice. It's Otheth. She was on Cocytus when we left. What's she doing here?" She placed her hand protectively over her abdomen where her pregnancy, in its fourth month, had started to show. "Could something have happened to Dante?"

Gabrielle growled into her speaker. "Galleys, intercept the bogie but do not fire. I want a positive visual ID on its occupant. If it isn't the Roc Otheth, blast it to pieces."

"Aye, aye, ma'am. Launching now." The Striker's four galleys roared from their docking bays.

Six minutes later, the silence on the bridge was broken as the speaker crackled. "This is Galley Three, I have a visual on the pilot. It is Otheth. I'd recognize her anywhere. She was my flight instructor back on Cocytus."

Gabrielle released the breath she didn't realize she was holding and opened the communication channel. "Otheth, you have permission to land. Use shuttle bay two."

During this conversation, Quango moved close to Tina, who was gripping the armrest of her chair so tightly her knuckles were white. "It'll be okay. Folks on Cocytus are as tough as nails, and your man has a good head on his shoulders." He patted her hand. "Lassie, you just take care of that baby."

Tears welled in Tina's eyes. "Quango, I'm so sorry we tricked you."

"I forgive you. Ye did what ye thought was right, for all the right reasons." Quango sighed. "I can't hold a grudge against ye. Next time... trust me to help. You're family to me."

"Thank you." She squeezed his hand fiercely but was still awash with worry about her husband's safety when Otheth strode onto the bridge.

"It's good to see old friends again." The Roc scanned the room. She paused on spotting Tina and fluffed her feathers. "You are with child. Does Dante know?"

Tina blushed. "No. We were in space a couple of weeks before I realized I was pregnant. It's not the sort of thing I want to put in a message capsule." She paled. "Is he all right?"

"He was in fine health when I left," Otheth cooed. "Congratulations. If I wasn't in the First Order of the Dragon, I would love to nurture a clutch of eggs myself." The Roc raised her head. "To business. Charon told me you were out here, and I have much news that needs to be delivered in person. Bathox is under a communications lockdown. All transmissions are monitored, and message missiles are tightly controlled."

"Charon's here?" Tina responded cautiously. "The last we heard he was being bundled up and shipped to Serpens."

The Roc regarded Tina. "The ploy you and Dante concocted worked. The video you hid in the Centaur's neural system reached the empress. She sent him out again to spy on Silenus-dis and your *old friend,* Keres-ma."

Gabrielle snarled, "Keres-ma survived? That monster should have died on Carcerem."

Otheth spat. "Not only did he survive but appears to have gotten a promotion."

Tina tensed. "Did we get an answer?"

Otheth shrugged her undersized wings. "For what it's worth, Fravashi said she'll consider your offer." The Roc craned her neck. "Do not trust anything an Ipis says. They're a treacherous species. But enough of that. I have information to share that is of immediate concern." She walked to a data port by a vacant station. "I am downloading the navigational coordinates to the human home world of Earth and Silenus-dis' battle plan to destroy it."

"Home?" Tina and Gabrielle cried in unison.

The next four hours were spent conducting a detailed debriefing with Otheth.

Tina and Gabrielle crammed as much of an explanation of Earth's geographic and political structure as they thought might be useful into the Roc.

"I must return to my unit." Otheth rose from the conference table. "I am assigned to the first wave, whose departure from here commences tomorrow."

"On Earth, get out of the polar region as fast as you can. It's a frozen nightmare, and their armies will probably unleash every nuclear missile in their arsenals at you," Gabrielle added.

Otheth flicked her ears. "Missiles will never penetrate the Ipis defensive screens. They'll be detected and destroyed as soon as they're launched."

The ship's captain turned somber. "Then the harpies will massacre my people. That's the most lethal weapon the Earth armies possess."

"Humans will not stand alone. The First Order of the Dragon has infiltrated the mercenary troops. We will fight." Otheth's pencil-thin hands grasped Tina's. "To this I *swear*. I only have seven warriors in my unit, but we will travel to this place called Fredonia, New York, on the North America continent and defend the noble Carloman and Phokas families to our last breath."

"Thank you, Otheth. Remember, Earth humans haven't met any Rocs before. You'll scare the hell out of them." A sad smile creased her face. "And you won't run into any elves. If someone points a shotgun at you, just tell them you're a big hockey fan and like beer. That should get you through Canada and that part of the United States." No one laughed at Tina's attempt to make a joke. She added, "Dante's favorite hockey team is the Buffalo Sabres."

Gabrielle asked pointedly, "In an invasion force of ten million, do you think there are enough First Order Rocs to make a difference?"

Otheth lowered her head. "No." She left the conference room and did not look back, mumbling, "No elves, hockey fan."

Those in the room stared at the now closed door for a few moments before Tina stood and leaned forward, pressing her fists on the surface of the table. She looked at Gabrielle, Quango, and Mara. "Send this information to Cocytus and all our allies. May God in heaven have mercy on us. Humanity's now at war and they don't even know it. Gabrielle, plot *our* course for Earth. We're the tip of the spear to save them."

Chapter XXI

It Begins

"Forget the war games. How long before our fleet can leave for Earth?" Dante glanced pensively around the conference room in Admiral Martinel's flagship in orbit around Cocytus.

General Cruz scowled and opened his hands. "Mister President, your guess is as good as mine. Our alliances are untested. If they answer our call at all, it will take weeks... months for them to consolidate their warships and raise their armies. Then it will take more time to coordinate the different fleets to strike."

Dante slammed the table. "We now know where the Earth is. Admiral Martinel, how many ships do we have that are hyperspace worthy and when could *we* leave?"

"Well, mate..." Martinel scratched behind his ear. "Michael has our latest Juggernaut out on its shakedown cruise. He'll be back in a couple days. That will give us forty-one operational capital warships: four Juggernauts, four Dreadnaughts, two Super-Dragons, eighteen Dragons, two rebuilt Enforcers, five captured Stalkers and six flight-worthy Strikers." He checked his tablet. "We have three full squadrons of galleys and two wings of single-seater fighters. That gives us about two hundred small tactical ships."

Dante swung his head toward Cruz. "Troops?"

The general scowled. "Counting all the militia and reserves?"

"No." Dante snapped. "How many do we have with the fleet, right here, right now?"

Cruz responded hesitantly, "We have three divisions scheduled to participate in the war games. That's close to forty-five thousand soldiers."

"I also have a company of marines on each of my warships." Martinel added, "That's another seven thousand."

Cruz's response was slow and deliberate, "Mister President, you're not thinking we can take on this massive harpy force alone? Do you?"

Dante stared at his hands folded in front of him and did not directly answer. "When was the last correspondence from Tina sent?"

"Six days ago." Virgil laid a hand on Dante's shoulder. "By her data, it means the harpy's invasion first wave has already reached the Earth. Her plan was to trail the second wave out of Bathox when they leave, which is about now." He added softly, "Gabrielle Peyago is that ship's captain. She knows how to run a reconnaissance mission and stay unseen. They'll be okay."

"Mister President, are you considering risking the bulk of our forces to protect your wife?" Cruz voiced disbelief as he glanced at the other four commanders around the table. "We can't leave Cocytus defenseless. There are close to eleven million people living here now."

"There's no one in the entire sector left to attack our people *here* because the whole damn harpy army is headed straight for *Earth*." Dante's voice rose, "We leave within the hour with what we have. Send Michael a message to gather the reserves and proceed to the war-games site. Inform Setteth of our plans. Ask her to link her forces with Michael's and come to our aid as soon as possible." He winced at the total silence that followed his declaration. "We have other allies. I'll invoke our defense treaties with the Centaurs and Satyrs."

Martinel shook his head. "Even if they answer our call, it'll be weeks before they could assemble their forces and get there."

General Cruz cleared his throat. "Mister President, I know it's our home, and when I received my commission in the US Army, I took an oath to defend America from all enemies. Sir, our troops are very good, but there's no three divisions that can beat ten million harpy fighters."

Martinel gulped. "I'd like to note that it would be suicide for our fleet too. This report shows that the harpies have over two thousand mainline ships in their armada."

"I'm not saying we take them head on," Dante rasped. "We just need to keep them busy until our allies arrive. Hit and run. A couple weeks at the most." Dante's fists clenched as he leaned forward. "There must be some way. Earth needs us. Our families there need us." He turned to General Cruz. "We've had six years to develop weaponry and hone our tactics against these sons-of-bitches. Folks on Earth will have minutes."

Cruz's eyes glinted. "Mister President, my heart's with you, but I'll not send good people on a suicide mission. They won't even be a speed bump against that invasion force."

Martinel rubbed his jaw and mumbled, "There might be a way." His eyes narrowed. "I have a harebrained idea." Everyone turned to him. He smiled. "Dodecahedron."

Dante arched his eyebrows. "You mean the dead man's formation that Setteth told us about from the last war?"

"Exactly." Martinel grew thoughtful. "I'd encircle the Earth with my fleet and then interlink our energy shields. Nothing will get through. The harpies wouldn't be able to resupply their ground troops nor strike any Earth targets from space."

Cruz shook his head. "How long could you maintain the blockade?"

The admiral's shoulders sagged. "A month, max. The Dragon Ships are power hogs, and when a single link breaks, the entire grid collapses."

The general rubbed his jaw. "The harpy combat style is to smash an opponent with overwhelming numbers. The trick on the ground would be avoiding a decisive battle. Hit and run would be effective... for a while." He sighed. "We'll need to link up with the American armed forces right away."

"Hold on, mate. How about the Aussies?" Martinel shot back.

Cruz's voice stayed calm although sweat beaded on his forehead. "The whole world will be neck-deep in harpies by the time we get there. We'll work with whoever is still standing, but the Americans have the largest modern military. According to the three-wave war plan, General Xiroah-dis' second wave will be engaged across Eurasia. It'll take us eleven days to reach the Earth. If we leave now, the harpies' North American campaign will be in its early stages. We should still be able to land our ground troops." He wiped his brow. "Once the harpies are aware of the new threat, they'll pounce. We'll need to up our numbers fast or there won't be many of us left inside the blockade when our allies arrive. If they arrive."

Martinel bit his lip and nodded.

Dante took a ragged breath. "Let's roll."

* * *

The American President, Elizabeth Stevenson, sat in the situation room located in a bunker beneath Camp David. All senior government officials were evacuated from Washington when the alien invasion started eight days earlier.

"Good news, bad news, Madam President. The alien invasion seems to be staying inside the Arctic and Antarctic regions. All the forces we've sent above the sixty-fifth parallel have been annihilated, but the aliens haven't budged from that area," J.P. Calley, Chairman of the Joint Chiefs of Staff, spoke with bitterness evident in his voice. "I don't believe there's a human left alive in the polar region. A ham radio operator picked up a shortwave transmission from Fort Wainwright outside of Fairbanks this morning. We verified the broadcaster was a Lieutenant with the First Brigade of the 25th Infantry. He said their ammunition was exhausted and they were being overrun. We've heard nothing since. Every attempt to relieve them has met with disaster."

"This is not a raid like the one we intercepted three years ago in southern Italy or the four known incursions before that. This is a full-fledged invasion." CIA Director, Norm Dennison glanced around the situation room. "They're showing no inclination to leave."

"For God's sake, what do they want?" The president's face flushed with anger.

"We have no way of knowing. All attempts to contact them are either being ignored or not received." NSA Director, Adam Turnbull, groaned. His clothes looked like he'd been sleeping in them for five days. "We're totally blind. Every satellite's gone, and they seem to be emitting EMP blasts that are playing havoc on our communications."

President Elizabeth Stevenson steepled her fingers. "J.P., air and sea initiatives?"

"Nothing got through. We launched a full squadron of F-16s out of Eielson before it was destroyed. They were pounced on by alien craft moving five times their speed. Not a single fighter made it back." Calley threw his pen at the table. "The Russians launched a full assault with an entire interceptor wing composed of Mig-35s and Su-30s. Same result."

The NSA director cleared his throat. "Madam President, I can confirm that the nuclear missile strike the Russian Prime Minister contacted you about over the hotline was launched. It was a combination of cruise missiles and MIRVs. Two of their stealth cruise missiles actually breached the aliens' air defense, but neither warhead detonated." Turnbull activated a screen showing smoldering ruins. "This is video taken long range by a drone showing what's left of Eielson. It's the same story at Fort Wainwright and the city of Fairbanks."

Stevenson's eyes narrowed as she scanned the faces of the security team around the table. "Give me some options. We seem to be unable to fight or talk to these bastards."

FBI Director Brenda Campbell broke the stony silence. "We need to get hold of an intact piece of their technology and find a way to replicate it. Our eggheads from NSA, NASA, and the Atomic Energy Commission studied what was recovered outside of Cortale, Italy, but it was just a pile of slag. If we can—"

The bank of landline phones on the conference table started blinking almost in unison. They were the primary remaining link to the governments of the other major powers on Earth.

President Stevenson picked up the secure line in front of her with a trembling hand. It was the Chinese Leader. She gasped when the frantic voice on the other end turned to static. As she replaced the phone in its cradle, she turned to the anxious faces. Her voice shook. "It appears the aliens are no longer content with staying above the sixty-fifth parallel. A second wave has struck across China. Before the line went dead, the Chairman told me Shanghai, Beijing, Tianjin, Guangzhou, and Shenzhen were attacked simultaneously by overpowering invasion forces."

Calley put down the phone he had been intently listening to. "It's not just China. It's across the Eurasian continent. Karachi, Istanbul, Mumbai, Moscow, Tokyo, Lahore, Seoul, and London have also been struck."

"Son-of-a-bitch," Turnbull exclaimed as he started typing on his computer console. He paused as he regarded the display that appeared on his screen. "You just rattled off all the top population centers in Europe and Asia. The bastards counted noses and are attacking the largest concentrations of people."

Rage flashed in President Elizabeth Stevenson's eyes as she turned to Ken Palance, the Director of Homeland Security. "I want every civilian evacuated from the New York, Chicago, and Los Angeles metropolitan areas. Now."

"It'll cause a nationwide panic," Campbell exclaimed.

President Stevenson shot back, "That's better than being dead."

Palance nodded in understanding. "Ma'am, I'll start immediately. But where do we send them? The freaking aliens did a real number, melting the polar ice caps during their initial attack. All our coastal cities have issues, and FEMA's already overloaded dealing with the refugees from Miami, Houston, and New Orleans."

"Commandeer the entire state of Kansas if you have to. Just do it!" the President roared. "Seize every truck and tent in the country. I'll deal with the consequences later. God-damn-it. It's our job to protect the people, and as long as I'm still breathing, that's what we're going to do."

Calley scratched the back of his neck. "It could be worse. I don't think these aliens came at us too prepared."

President Stevenson rolled her eyes at the general. "Worse? They're doing a fairly effective job of walking all over us."

"That's the point." The general gathered his thoughts. "Just looking at this attack from a purely tactical perspective, they're doing it all wrong. If I were running their campaign, I would not be giving my opponent a chance to adjust tactics. Look, the initial assault was against the least populated part of the planet, then they seemed to correct it by going after the heaviest populated areas. They've made no effort to confront our armed forces unless we attacked them or one of our bases was in their way."

The president leaned forward pressing her elbows on the table. "What do you suggest?"

"We tried to take them head on, and that just fed good men into a meat grinder. We don't have the tools to match them." Calley drummed his fingers on the table. "We need to fight this war the way Washington fought the British. Harass them on their flanks with small units, learn their weaknesses, and strike when we see an opening."

"Makes sense." Stevenson sighed. "But in the end, we Americans needed the French to bottle up the British at Yorktown. Who in this godforsaken universe will be our French?" She paused. "If you believe in miracles, please pray that there is someone out there that can help us."

Chapter XXII

Canadian Visitors

Otheth squatted behind a berm and with her sharp beak tore into the haunch of the large antlered animal her squad had brought down. "This is supposed to be the human's home world. I haven't seen a soul since we slipped away from Silenus-dis' force at the arctic circle twelve days ago," she cawed. "At least the hunting is good. How much further?"

Her technology specialist, a large Roc named Cheepash, grumbled, "We're the First Order of the Dragon, and the war has started. We should have stayed in the planet's arctic and killed as many Ipis as we could."

Otheth snapped, "We have a higher commitment to protect the royal Carloman and Phokas clans at their citadels in a place labeled Fredonia, New York. I repeat, how much further? And are there any human settlements nearby?"

Cheepash hissed as he tapped on his tablet. "The human king's ancestral home is about six hundred more miles as the locals define distance. My GPS system has located a small human enclave labeled Saguenay, Quebec, ten miles from our current position. We need to—" The tech studied his screen for a moment. "We are being tracked. There're two humans, in the forest we just left, watching us."

"Hostile?" Otheth motioned to her team to power up their shields.

"How would I know?" Cheepash grumbled. "They're both armed with the primitive projectile weapons."

Otheth whispered into her communicator to the two pickets. "When you approach, flatten your crest feathers so they know we're allies."

A few moments later there were rapid, booming reports from a pair of handguns followed by the sizzling sound of Roc incapacitation wands.

"Commander, they fired on us as we openly approached displaying the Roc greeting of peace and friendship," an angry voice crackled across the communicator.

"Did you harm them?"

"No. After they discharged the pellets in their weapons, they attacked us with large knives. We knocked them out with our neural incapacitation wands."

Otheth sighed. "Bring them here while they're still unconscious. They probably thought you were mercenaries working for the Ipis. I'll correct the misunderstanding."

Cheepash groaned. "This can't be good."

A few minutes later, the limp humans were dragged into the Rocs' campsite and propped in a sitting position against a large tree. Otheth crouched close, studying their physical appearance while waiting for them to regain consciousness. Both were garbed in thick leather jackets with the human lettering *Wild Turkeys* on the back. She could discern they were of the human species just like those inhabiting Cocytus. Although both had long shaggy hair and thick beards, they were dissimilar in appearance. The larger one was ruddy complexioned with blazing red hair; the other was much smaller with a deep tan.

A half hour later, Cheepash nudged his commander. "Their somnolent state is a ruse. The instruments indicate they are at full awareness."

Otheth nodded and switched to the human language of Latin. "Greetings, noble allies. Sorry for the unfortunate misunderstanding. My warriors were unaware that you probably are not conversant in the Roc language."

The larger one slit open his eyes and whispered in a language Otheth did not understand.

The second one raised his head and shuddered as he scanned the area, staring at the Rocs and remains of the animal carcass. The larger one spoke again to his companion.

Otheth cooed as she recognized the words in the interchange as a human dialect of Latin. *Perhaps they speak the private language of the human king, Dante Carloman.* She switched to English and repeated her earlier statement.

"Jesus protect me," the larger one exclaimed. "These giant birds must be the aliens' attack dogs or something."

"Aye." The other gulped and faced Otheth. "Are you going to suck out our brains, eat us, or turn us into zombies?"

Otheth cawed and was unsure how to respond. "We are of the First Order of the Dragon and have pledged allegiance to the human king. What are your names?"

"You're the *what*? That rot gut I drank last night must've been worse than I thought." He glanced at the animal carcass again. "You're not going to eat us?"

Cheepash hooted, "Answer the commander's questions or I *will* eat you... starting with your feet and working my way up."

The larger man sputtered. "Don't be hasty. I'm Gilbert MacKenzie and my buddy's Rene DeVaux."

Rene added in a flat voice, "Who the hell are you?"

Otheth shot Cheepash a hard look before answering with a soft voice, "I am Otheth, commander of this Roc First Order Commando Squad. We are attempting to reach your king's ancestral home to aid his nestling kin, but it is taking overly long. We need transportation assistance."

Gilbert looked at Rene and shrugged. "Who in the blazes is the human king?"

Otheth blinked in confusion. "Dante Carloman, of course. His family's citadel is in a location named Fredonia, New York. We are trying to get there."

Rene snorted. "Figures it'd be a Yank. The Americans think they rule the world anyway."

Gilbert rubbed his jaw. "I drove past that town in my truck driving days. It's off Route 90 on the south side of Lake Erie. Nothing special there except a small college and a lot of vineyards."

"Big deal. So, the place really exists." Rene glared at Otheth. "This could just be some alien shit to trick us."

Otheth cocked her head, listening to the exchange and remembered a conversation with Dante. "The king likes hockey."

"Aye," Gilbert's eyes narrowed. "What's his team?"

Otheth concentrated and then cooed, "The Buffalo Sabres."

"The freaking Sabres." Rene laughed nervously. "Unless he's a Canadiens fan, he's no king of mine." He paused and considered the strange group surrounding him. "You really on our side? You're not jerking us around with some screwy alien humor?"

"Ah no," Otheth replied, trying to determine what would be considered humor in their current situation. "We all swore a sacred oath of allegiance."

Gilbert asked with renewed suspicion. "How did you get here?"

Otheth fluffed her feathers. "We're undercover spies acting the part of mercenary hirelings in the Ipis first-wave assault on your polar region. We deserted after landing and have been working our way south for the last twelve days."

Rene's mouth hung open. "From the arctic circle to here in twelve days... on foot."

Cheepash added defensively, "We would have made better progress, but the terrain is rough and we had to make a couple detours."

Rene's eyes narrowed. "So, you were part of the invasion and switched sides. Why should we believe a gaggle of large talking birds?"

Otheth warbled and flared her crest feathers. "I swear by my ancestor's sacred honor we were always on your side. We infiltrated the Ipis invasion force as mercenaries to thwart their plan."

"Supposing for a second that I believe you, for the love of God tell us what the hell is going on?" Gilbert blurted. "First your freaking alien buddies attack a bunch of icebergs, then you start wiping out whole cities in Europe and Asia, and the last I heard, a couple of days ago, New York, LA, and Mexico City were being leveled." Pleading entered his voice. "Can you really help us? There seems to be a countless number of you, ahh... those monsters. Our armies don't seem to have any answers to the shit they're shooting."

"You must remain steadfast until your king arrives." Otheth snapped her beak in frustration. "The alliance of old has been reformed, but there's no telling how long it will take him to assemble the armada." She looked at her team and then back at the humans, recalling the victory she was part of on Carcerem. "He calls these *freaking* aliens *harpies* and has never lost a battle against them."

"Harpies, aye." Gilbert scratched his beard and exchanged a look with Rene, and then turned to Otheth. "Well, you didn't turn us into zombies yet. I'll make a deal with you. Tell me everything you know about these harpies and their weapons and we'll get you part of the way. Our bikes are parked near the preserve, a couple kilometers back."

Otheth craned her neck. "Cheepash, give our allies their weapons back."

Rene holstered his pistol and slipped the knife into his tall boot. He started walking toward the forest. "Just call me Flash Gordon."

Gilbert moved next to him. "Does that make this Dante Carloman, Emperor Ming?"

Rene smirked and then sobered. "Can't be worse than what we're dealing with now. What's that old saying, 'The enemy of my enemy is my friend.'"

"Yeah, something like that. I just hope he doesn't order us all to become Sabres fans."

Rene glanced at the deadly-looking weapons the eight Rocs following them carried. "I'll root for anyone he says if it'll bring an end to this insanity."

The two motorcycles were the only vehicles in the gravel parking lot when they arrived there a half hour later. During the walk, Rene found Otheth eager to talk, although the Roc's English was filled with incomprehensible references. "That's amazing. Millions of humans living on other planets, and I never knew it. I'd like to visit this place you call Cocytus someday. Sounds like decent folks there."

"They're all right for humans," Otheth hooted in reply.

Gilbert walked over and whispered to Rene, "We're not taking this flock of birds back to the hangout, are we? They seem okay, but what if it's a trap?"

"No problem," Rene whispered back. "Once we're on our hogs, we take off. We talk it over with the gang and see if they wanta take the chance. We come back and collect them. Simple."

"You're the boss." Gilbert gulped. He climbed on his Indian Roadmaster and gunned it. Pebbles shot out from beneath his tires as he raced to the main road. He tensed waiting to be zapped. Nothing happened. Then he noticed in his rearview mirror the small group of Rocs striding along behind him on the empty two-lane road. "Shit."

Fifteen minutes later, they pulled up to a small diner. When the Rocs stopped and looked around, thirty leather-jacketed men and women spilled out, brandishing an assortment of weapons.

"Rene, what the hell's going on," one of them shouted.

"They're friends... I think." Rene waved the gang members back as he saw the Rocs energize their stun rods.

Oteth turned to Cheepash. "I will conduct the negotiation. It appears, humans on this planet need to talk a lot."

* * *

"Not much traffic. Everyone is hunkered down around here." Rene eyed Oteth, who was draped in a heavy, hooded coat. "Just stay crouched low in the damn sidecar and for Christ's sake don't look up." He pointed to Cheepash. "You do the same in Gilbert's sidecar. The rest of 'em can cover themselves with the tarps in the pickup's truck bed. No one will be the wiser."

"We're only taking you to the border." Rene faced Oteth. "Understand? I'm not messing with any trigger-happy customs agents at the Queenstown-Lewiston bridge. You're on your own getting into the US."

"Yes, friend Rene. I grasp the concept of these semi-autonomous political entities you call countries within King Carloman's realm. I will explain to these minor functionaries just as I did to you. I'm sure they will assist me."

"No, don't," Rene pleaded. "You're aliens. They'll shoot first and ask questions later. Just sneak past them."

"I will take your advice under consideration." Oteth craned her neck. "They are government agents and will be

155

mandated to aid us when we declare that we're members of the First Order of the Dragon."

"Ah, I don't think they have any regulations for the likes of you. But it's your problem, not mine." Rene snorted.

Seven hours later, they sat in a diner parking lot outside of Hamilton. Gilbert munched on a buffalo wing. "I hope these chickens weren't any relatives of yours."

The Rocs, sitting inside the circle of motorcycles, dug into the meal with gusto.

Gilbert sat with Otheth, Cheepash, and Rene. "I got what news there is from the restaurant owner. It's all bad. Don't know what's going on overseas, but the Yanks are catching hell. Boston and New York are gone. New Jersey is on fire, and the Yanks are fighting a running retreat through the hills of eastern Pennsylvania. Out west it's the same. LA and Long Beach have been leveled, and the surviving American troops are trapped in San Diego. Down south, the Mexican army no longer exists. These harpies are advancing along the Gulf Coast against sporadic resistance. They'll reach Texas in a few days."

Rene took a long pull on his beer. "Anything going on around here?"

"Nah, it's all quiet. Except for the freaking aliens parked in the Arctic, they seem to be focused on big population centers. They're taking out anything that's flying, but they're ignoring folks on the ground that aren't in front of them."

Otheth listened intently. "Standard Ipis conquest procedures. They set off EMP blasts and then swarm an urban center, destroying everything in their path. Once the initial objectives are attained, they will reassess and go after new targets until there is nothing left," she clucked to Gilbert and Rene. "Good thing your *allies* have a third of the invasion force tied down in the polar regions." Her voice sounded like a sarcastic laugh.

The two Canadians exchanged confused looks. "The Yanks got smashed in Alaska, and our boys fared no better in the Yukon and Northwest territories. What allies? The Russians?"

156

"The *elves*," Otheth hooted. "Silenus-dis, who's leading the invasion, didn't have the best intelligence when he started the campaign. He's hunting for Santa Claus and his elvish forces up there."

"Père Noël?" Rene shook his head.

"We're getting our butt kicked by an idiot chasing fairy tales?" Gilbert asked, incredulous.

"He'll recognize the mistake soon enough," Otheth sobered. "He has a few competent generals working for him." She thought about her time on Carcerem. "And one commander, Keres-ma, who totally hates anything human. If they're not stopped, by this time next year, there won't be a human left alive on this planet."

Rene smashed his beer bottle on the asphalt; rage boiled in his eyes. "The hell with it. I'm throwing in with you the rest of the way. By the Holy Mother of God, I'll get you to this place in New York. Just show me how to use that Flash Gordon ray gun you're toting."

"I'm in too. Let's kick some alien butt," Gilbert added. He glanced around. "You guys are all right for a bunch of oversized pigeons."

"Rocs. We're called Rocs," Cheepash grumbled as he handed Gilbert an Ipis Grade-Three ion disrupter. "The harpy that owned this weapon doesn't need it anymore. It's yours."

Rene hefted a weapon handed to him by another Roc. "*Rocks*, huh. You can call yourselves rappers for all I care. Just show me how to kill harpies."

The other gang members had listened intently to the whole conversation. "We're in too," they roared.

Chapter XXIII

A Pebble Tossed in a Pond

Trailing the second wave of the Ipis invasion force, *Reggie* slipped into the asteroid belt of Earth's solar system. From there, Tina and the rest of the frigate's crew conducted reconnaissance of the assault on the Earth. She launched the full complement of the ship's probes to follow the enemy's movements. With growing horror Tina watched the people on her home world being annihilated, impotent to aid them.

The frigate, *Reggie*, effectively used the energy-displacement system Beatrice developed to camouflage her valley on Cocytus. The ship drifted, undetected, among the orbiting rocks. It was only visible to the harpies' passive scanners when its engines were powered on.

On the eighth day, disaster struck. A malfunctioning probe collided with an asteroid as it was about to be retrieved by one of the frigate's galleys. The explosion was detected by a harpy patrol craft, which investigated. It managed to transmit a warning to its mothership before being vaporized by the galley.

The human's ship was spotted soon after active scanners from several harpy mainline warships pinged their area of space. *Reggie's* captain, Gabrielle Peyago, had only seconds to react before the harpy targeting systems locked onto her ship. Without time to retrieve the frigate's four galleys, she activated the ship's engines and the chase was on. All the escape routes via hyperspace were blocked, so she flew in the only direction still open, toward Earth.

Tina stared in horror at the view screen on *Reggie's* bridge as their last galley fighter exploded in a blinding flash. The four galleys, flying in tandem with *Reggie*, didn't have the frigate's shielding as they were pounded by the pursuing Ipis warships.

Reggie dodged around the Earth's moon with a harpy Enforcer-class warship and a squadron of single-seat fighters closing in.

"We can't fight anything that big." Gabrielle studied the view screen. "We have to dive into the Earth's atmosphere. That Enforcer can't follow us there."

"*Reggie's* taken some serious damage. Can we survive entry?"

Mara chimed in, "Hull integrity will hold if there's no further degradation."

Reggie spoke from a wall mounted speaker, "I'll get us down, but my power plant requires repairs. Find a secure spot. I can run the cloaking shield from my backup generator. It will hide us from airborne observation for a while."

"Secure." Gabrielle shook her head. "The Earth is in flames. Our fleet better get here soon or there'll be nothing left to save."

Tina scanned the readouts showing the current locations of harpy activity. "Goat Island," she exclaimed.

"Where's that?" Gabrielle asked. Her voice tight with urgency.

"It's not far from my parents' home. It sits in the Niagara River, right at the lip of the Falls. The only access is a couple of small bridges. The site is easily defensible from the ground and there doesn't seem to be any harpy activity in the vicinity."

"Good enough, Tina. Guide me to the location." Klaxons blared throughout the ship as Gabrielle checked her pilot controls. The monitor panel warning lights were almost all flashing. She toggled her communicator. "Gunners, keep those fighters off us. Mara, switch from energy shield to cloaking shield when we get within five miles of the surface. Everyone else, prepare for a rough landing."

Twenty-nine minutes later the ship jarred to a halt. Klaxons sounded throughout the ship as the superstructure screeched from the crippled ship's hard landing. Gabrielle checked her display's indicators and groaned. "Quango, try to work your magic."

"Aye, lass. *Reggie's* a tough ship. We'll get him flying again," he shouted as he limped from the bridge to the engine room.

Gabrielle dialed up the security officer. "Major Caccina, deploy your company. We may see hostiles soon if they tracked us."

"Yes, ma'am, we're already locked and loaded," was his prompt reply. "I wish we had a full battalion onboard."

"I wish we had a full brigade." Gabrielle sighed. "Arm every crew member who's not involved with repairs."

"Will do, Captain."

Gabrielle shut off the communicator and walked to Tina, who stood at the viewport, with hands resting on her bulging abdomen. The view was breathtaking. The American Falls roared into the cataract to her right and the Horseshoe Falls, with a permanent rainbow over it, did the same on her left. Gabrielle gasped. "I've only seen this in pictures. They don't capture a fraction of its beauty and power."

Tina turned and smiled, although tears streamed down her cheeks. "Welcome home, Gabrielle. We're really home again after all this time. How many years has it been... six? Seven?"

"We'll have to check a newspaper the next time we see one, if they still print those things. The internet's gone as far as I can tell." Gabrielle glanced around and watched the crew steal awed glances out the view port while they worked. All were descendants of the ancient Romans taken from the Earth centuries earlier.

Tina followed her friend's eyes and raised her voice. "Everyone, take a good look. This is the home world of your ancestors. This is the one place in the galaxy that you can always claim as yours."

Gabrielle voiced in a husky whisper, "Until the harpies take it away from us."

Tina flushed with rage. "They haven't done it yet. Our people might be fighting with the equivalent of sticks and stones against those monsters. But they are fighting back. They'll hold until Dante gets here."

"I hope so." Gabrielle sighed. Her voice turned sharp, "Everyone, back to work. This ship won't repair itself. We—"

"My apologies, Captain," Reggie intoned from a wall-mounted speaker. "I made a snap decision earlier without consulting you."

Gabrielle's brows furrowed. "What was it?"

"During planetary landfall, in the seven-point-eight milliseconds between when I lowered the energy shield and raised the concealment screen, I picked up a stray radio signal associated with Otheth's team. I directed an encrypted data burst to that transmission point appraising them of our situation."

"Any response?" Tina joined the conversation.

"It would have been impossible, given the time span when I could receive a signal."

Gabrielle pursed her lips. "No one else could read that communication, but I wonder if anyone else picked it up."

"Undeterminable," was Reggie's flat response. "Also, from my monitoring of the harpy frequencies, they have a general idea of our location."

* * *

President Elizabeth Stevenson paced in agitation across the porch on the bungalow at Camp David. Washington had been abandoned in haste when the Army, after suffering heavy losses, was pushed out of New Jersey. The peaceful vista stretching before her couldn't mask the catastrophic worldwide destruction she knew was crushing humanity. *And I'm helpless to do anything about it.*

She watched a baby-faced captain she did not recognize sprint across the estate's grounds toward her. *What new disaster has struck now?*

"Madam President," the officer gasped as he came to a halt. "General Calley requested your presence in the War Room. He said we may have caught our first break in this war. An intact alien ship crashed in the Niagara Falls area. We have a company of Army Rangers with a group of scientists and engineers at the nearby hydroelectric plant. He's dispatched them there."

Stevenson was already hurrying down the steps. "Do we have communications with the team going in?"

The captain jogged beside her, "No ma'am. Too much interference. Once they left their landline links, we lost contact."

Please God, help those men and us. We can't endure this slaughter much longer. She entered the command center and could taste the tension in the room.

* * *

Emma Carloman glanced back at the Niagara Hydroelectric Plant where she had worked for less than a year. She and a dozen other engineers were told they were needed to take apart one of the invader's spaceships that crashed nearby. Her face tightened into a grimace. *What the hell do I know about alien technology?*

The recently graduated mechanical engineer clambered into the column's rearmost MRAP. She slumped onto the only open seat and stared sullenly at her own tattoo-covered arms. *My life isn't worth shit, but I don't want to die like this.* The trucks roared off a second later.

She glanced at the soldier sitting beside her, who was clutching an M4. She knew little about the military but recognized that the single bar on his shoulders marked him as some sort of officer. Emma snapped at him, "Why am I here? I'm just a goddamn mechanical engineer working at a hydroelectric plant. What do I know about fucking alien spaceships? Hell, the ink's still not dry on my diploma."

The lieutenant, who appeared no older than her own twenty-two years, looked back, sneering at her body piercings. "What do I know about fighting those fuckers, but I got to try... we all got to try. Look, lady, we're the only assets in the area. We have to get inside that crashed ship and find out what makes it tick."

Emma laughed without any humor. "I saw the telecasts out of New York and LA before everything went dark. We're just going to die."

"Maybe... and maybe we'll catch a break." He forced a smile onto his face as he scanned a red-lettered name tattooed on her arm. "Who's Dante? A jilted lover who couldn't get used to necking with a *pincushion*?"

Emma self-consciously covered the inked word. Her face flushed with anger. "That's my brother's name. He was killed by the damn aliens *seven* freaking years ago. Our government didn't even have the decency to tell my folks *that much* until the fiasco in southern Italy when their cover-up unraveled."

The lieutenant bit his lip. "He was in that mess? God, I'm sorry. Did they ever find his body?"

"No." Emma's face softened. "He was the best big brother a girl could ask for. I was just a screwed-up high school kid then, but when he came home from college, he always helped me get my head straight. He could make me laugh no matter how down I was." Her voice took on an edge, "The fucking government never even gave us his remains to bury." Her jaw clenched as she stared out the front window then she paled. The top of the downed spacecraft came into view above the trees. "Jesus, look at the size of that thing."

A voice rang over the speaker in the cabin. "The lead MRAP has spotted motion outside the target vessel. Get ready to move. Assume the hostiles have spotted us."

The lieutenant turned to Emma. "Look, miss, this truck will be a magnet for the shit the aliens shoot. When the door opens, run for cover. You'll know soon enough whether we've had any luck." He unholstered his 9mm Berretta and gave it to her. "Sounds like life dealt you a crappy deal. I really hope you make it through this mess. If things go bad, run... and don't look back."

Emma saw the sincerity in his eyes. She took the weapon and squeezed his hand. "Thanks. Be careful out there."

He nodded with a real smile. The door opened and he sprang out with a squad of soldiers behind him.

Emma covered her ears as the staccato bursts from the heavy machine guns mounted on the MRAPs and Buffalos opened up in unison. The GIs soon added their rifles to the din. The noise was deafening. She ran and ducked behind a statue of an American Indian ten yards away. A few moments later there was a bright flash. Then, she heard only the sound of water roaring relentlessly over the Falls. She cowered for a few more seconds, breathing rapidly and stared at the pistol clutched in her hand. *This is as good a place to die as any.* She leapt up and swung her weapon toward the mammoth ship. "This is for my brother, you suckers."

What stood before Emma was the last thing she envisioned seeing. She lowered her arms and stared. "What the hell?"

Chapter XXIV

Family

Tina and Gabrielle Peyago were studying their crashed ship's power converter readouts when the communicator buzzed.

"Captain, we've got company," Major Caccina reported over the comm-link. "What do you want me to do?"

"What do you think I want you to do? Kill every harpy that gets close," Gabrielle shouted. "Hold them off as long as you can." She turned to Tina. "Damn, the harpies got here quick. We're in deep shit. I was hoping for a few hours' reprieve to get our systems working."

"Captain, the incoming creatures aren't harpies. It appears to be a convoy of human soldiers in primitive ground transports. They're deploying in an aggressive manner."

"Hold your fire." Gabrielle turned to the console. "Reggie, can you give me a neural burst."

"Yes, but the range is only fifty yards from my hull's surface, and it'll broadcast our location to any harpy within twenty miles of here."

"Do it on my mark," Gabrielle snapped.

Tina added, "Gabrielle, there are only two access points to this island, a vehicle bridge and a foot bridge. The river's current is too strong for a boat."

Gabrielle nodded. "Major Caccina, barricade the bridges. You and your men turn your shields on max and let us know when their lead elements reach the riverbank."

"Already been working on that. We have two-inch-thick slabs of plexo-steel covering the breadth of those spans on the near side. We'll have them anchored in moments."

A minute later Caccina was back online. "I have two platoons dug in by each bridge. We'll have a good field of fire if they try to cross." Loud noises came across the comm-link. "Captain Peyago, we are taking fire. It looks like a company-size unit with antique armored ground transports and primitive projectile weapons. However, if they try to overrun my position, I'll need to use deadly force."

The sound of munitions fire poured through the comm-link. "They're hitting us with numerous explosives and a gunfire barrage. It appears to be cover for a mass assault on the vehicle bridge... They've reached it. Do something now or I will order my men to defend themselves." His steady voice rose in pitch. "Now, in the name of God, now. If we don't shoot back, our people will die."

"Reggie, now," Gabrielle shouted. The Striker emitted a sensory overload blast. It was like the flash-bang used on Earth, on steroids.

"The assault force is down." Caccina gulped. "If you have a plan to defuse this situation, you better implement it quick."

Tina shuddered. "I'll go talk to them."

"You'll what?" Gabrielle gasped. "Are you out of your mind? They'll kill you."

Tina paled. "The two of us are the only Earth-born on board, and I'm the only one who speaks English." She touched her abdomen. "I don't think they'll shoot a pregnant woman. Besides, we have to make contact. Right now, they're afraid of everything falling from the sky. They need to understand we're here to help."

"You're right," Gabrielle hissed in frustration. "Mara, go with her." She switched on her comm-link. "Major, what's the situation out there?"

"Captain, those who weren't knocked out have taken cover. No one's shooting at the moment."

"The shock won't last long." Gabrielle pursed her lips. "Doctor Phokas is coming out under a flag of truce with Mara. Pick two men to escort her."

"The situation's too volatile. I'll go in her place."

"She's the only one who speaks their language." She grated her teeth and glanced up. Tina was already headed out of the control room with Mara, holding a large white towel gliding at her side.

As Tina stepped to the ground and walked toward the footbridge, a pair of soldiers protectively strode in front of her. A small smile creased her worried face. She recognized both men from the prison camp on Carcerem.

Tina tensed as she crossed the bridge when she heard a sharp command, "Hold your fire." Her heart skipped a beat when a tattooed woman leapt from behind a statue and pointed a gun at her. She raised her hand in the peace sign and kept walking.

The young woman, arms trembling, hesitantly lowered the pistol.

A soldier wearing lieutenant bars, walked out to meet her with raised, open hands. The officer looked warily at the soldiers writhing on the neatly mowed park grass as he approached. He gulped at the imposing robot and two fierce-looking human guards with exotic-looking weapons before focusing on the woman. She was pretty, and very pregnant.

Tina cleared her throat. "They've been stunned. They'll be fine in a few minutes." She looked at the name on the soldier's uniform. "Lieutenant Wells, I am Doctor Tina Phokas from the planet Cocytus." A tear trickled down her cheek. "But I was born no more than ninety miles from this very spot." She raised her chin, and a small smile crept across her face. "I think this is where I say, 'Take me to your leader.'"

Wells' mouth hung open. "You're human." Suspicion replaced surprise. He eyed Mara. "What're you doing in an alien spaceship?"

The tension eased in Tina's shoulders. "Not all humans live on Earth, and not all spaceships belong to the harpies. We're a scout ship that got shot up and was forced to land. A great armada is being pulled together to aid you as we speak." *At least I hope Dante got the alliance together and they're on their way.*

Mara amplified and translated the conversation to Latin, so it could be picked up by those across the bridge.

"What's that robot saying, and what's a harpy?" Wells asked trying to come to grasp with the situation.

A thirty-something man with captain's bars moved from behind a nearby MRAP and strode forward accompanied by three soldiers. "I'll take over from here, Wells." He squared off and glared at Tina.

Tina shifted her weight. Being pregnant and standing in one position was uncomfortable. She looked at his name tag. "Captain Martin, what you are hearing is Latin. It's the language spoken by humans beyond this world. As for harpies..." her voice dripped venom, "...those are the monsters attacking you. Their leader, Silenus-dis, is an idiot, but as you've no doubt seen, their military is very effective."

He was a large man, but his obvious attempt at physical intimidation caused her to smirk. *I can see in his eyes I control this situation. Besides, Mara could take him out before he could blink.* Motion and a surprised shout caught Tina's attention. The tattooed woman she saw earlier eluded a soldier who tried to grab her and ran straight toward the parley, with a handgun clutched in her fist.

Tina's two escorts tensed. She saw concern in eyes of the American lieutenant. She gave her guards a sharp look. "Don't start anything. It appears this woman has something to say and intends to say it."

The woman planted herself in front of Tina. "Why the hell should we believe anything you say? Why are you so magnanimously coming to our aid now?" Fire raged in her eyes. "Where were you seven years ago when those monsters killed my brother?"

Compassion flowed through Tina. "Seven years ago? Did he die on a cold Christmas eve in the Southern Tier of New York?"

"Yes," was the bitter reply.

"Only a few of *us* died that night." Tina's mind flew though the horrors she had experienced over those intervening years. "But many have perished since then. What was your brother's name?"

"Dante. Dante Carloman," the woman cried.

Tina yipped in surprise. "Is your name Emma?"

"Y-yes."

"My husband speaks often of you." Tina's hand went instinctively to her bulging midsection. "You're going to be an aunt soon, for a second time."

Tina saw suspicion, shock, and hope war with each other in the young woman's eyes. She pulled the computer tablet from the pouch that hung at her side, selected an icon, and pressed the screen. "This is just a selfie we took about six months ago, but is this your brother?" She handed the tablet to Emma.

Emma gasped and dropped the gun. She clutched the computer to her chest after stroking the smiling face on the screen. Sobs shook her body. "He's alive? Sweet Jesus, he's alive!" She looked at Tina though tear-filled eyes. "You're... you're my sister-in-law?"

Mara's lights blinked rapidly. "This person is kin to the king?"

"King, what king?" Captain Martin barked, injecting himself into the conversation, and regarded Tina warily. "This is some sort of sick alien trick. Anyone can photoshop a picture."

Tina laughed. "And I'd be omniscient enough to know what picture to copy?" She saw fresh doubt creep into Emma's eyes and took Emma's hands. "One of Dante's favorite quotes is from your mom. 'The price of vegetables is negotiable, and everything is a vegetable.'"

"My... my mom does always say that," Emma sobbed.

Tina focused on Emma. "Your brother *is* the leader of all humanity." She looked at the Army officers and the soldiers behind them. "*He* is the one bringing the fleet to defend the Earth."

"This planet has no damn king," the Captain shot back.

"Yeah, the last time I checked there were close to two hundred independent countries. How's that working out?" Tina snarled. She gathered her composure. "Look, the harpies just about rule this entire galaxy. My husband has pulled together an alliance of all the free peoples left in this part of it. They follow him. If you go it alone, you're dooming every person in this world."

"The Earth has become a slaughterhouse," Wells rasped. "Can he really help us?"

The guard on Tina's right listened to Mara's simultaneous translation and boasted, "Dante Carloman kicked harpy butt on Cocytus, Carcerem, and Equitone. He can do the same thing here."

"Of course he can." Emma crushed Tina in a hug. "He never backed down from a bully in his life."

Mara beeped. "Emma, Reggie says he would like to meet you. Would you care to come inside?"

Emma looked at Tina for confirmation. "Is Reggie a friend of Dante's?"

Tina bit her lip. "More accurately, he *was* a friend. Reggie had an accident and is now a personality download in the CPU of the spaceship behind me."

"You'll stay right here," Captain Martin ordered.

The guard on Tina's left spoke with awe in his voice and saluted Emma. "The king saved me from a slow death on the prison world of Carcerem." He glared at Captain Martin. "No harm will come to anyone of the royal house of Carloman while I live."

"Yeah, I'll come." Emma glared at Captain Martin. "That's what the government dragged me here to do anyway."

"Sir, I'll go with her," Lieutenant Wells added softly. "If you don't hear from us, you'll know it's a trap."

Tina threw her hands in the air. "For Christ's sake, if we wanted to kill you, you'd be dead by now."

Captain Martin gritted his teeth. "All right, Wells. It's your neck. I expect you to report every ten minutes. Grab a couple volunteers and go with them."

Six soldiers and an elderly hydroelectric engineer followed the lieutenant and Emma across the footbridge as the previously stunned GIs started to stir.

Tina turned to Wells as they walked up the ramp. "What's your name, soldier? It will get a little tiresome calling you Lieutenant Wells."

"Herb, Herb Wells from Lowell, Massachusetts." His pace slowed as he climbed the gangplank into the Striker. "Wow. This is amazing."

When they reached the bridge, Gabrielle ran over and hugged Emma. "I'm Gabrielle Peyago, captain of this ship. I'm so glad to meet Dante's sister. Welcome aboard."

Armed starship sailors kept a careful eye on the wide-eyed visitors who stared at the expansive control room.

"Captain Peyago," Reggie's flat voice spoke from the speaker, "I've received a communication from Otheth. She and her team are en route to our location on ground transports near a place labeled Hamilton, Ontario. Their ETA is one hour nineteen minutes."

"That's great news," Tina exclaimed.

"The bad news is my stun pulse alerted the harpies to our general location. Several of their troop ships are inbound. Given their normal search pattern, we have about an hour and a half before they find us."

Gabrielle tensed. "Any sign of their atmospheric attack craft?"

After a pause, Reggie responded. "Otheth indicates that the troop ships are unescorted."

Quango entered the room and regarded the newcomers with curiosity. "Got three of the seven shield generators working." He moved to his normal seat and punched buttons on the console. "That'll protect us for now."

"Can we get airborne before we're found?" Tension was evident in Gabrielle's voice.

"Nope. This crate's a mess. I may be a genius, but it'll be days before the normal space and atmospheric propulsion systems are functional." He bowed to the newly arrived humans, who openly gawked at him. "It's not polite to stare. I'm not *that* handsome."

"Shit. We're in big trouble." Gabrielle flipped on her comm-link. "Major Caccina, we're going to have at least a division of harpies on us in about an hour."

"A division... Yes, ma'am. Do I have your permission to blow the bridges to this island?"

"Not yet. If we lose those bridges, we're trapped here until the ship's fixed." Gabrielle paused. "Reggie, apprise Otheth of our situation." She turned to Herb. "Lieutenant Wells, you heard what I heard. Tell your captain to get your team out of here as fast as possible."

The old hydroelectric engineer in the group of visitors pointed to Quango. "That thing's not human. It's... it's a monster."

Quango snorted. "You must have been talking to my ex-wife." He walked over and extended his hand in the human form of greeting, proud of the English he could speak. "Hi. I am Quango. I have the unfortunate title of Chief Engineer on this junk heap."

The old engineer stared at Quango's hand like it was a serpent.

Emma moved in front of him and shook the extended hand. "I'm Emma Carloman. Pleased to meet you."

"So, you are really Dante's kid sister?" He tugged his goatee. "Small galaxy. The rumor of you coming on board spread all over the ship and I had to pull rank so I could wander up here to meet you. He is a sharp fellow... for a human." He glanced at Tina remembering how he was duped. "A very sharp fellow."

"You folks really are here to help us, aren't you?" Wells gazed around the room.

Quango shook his head. "By my mother's twisted beard, we did not come all this way to admire the scenery." He elbowed past Gabrielle and pulled a long-barrel ion disrupter from a rack against the near wall. "It is about time the locals get to fight with real weapons." He pointed to the weapon's parts after handing the gun to Wells. "This is the trigger. This is the business end. When the light over here turns red, you need to slap in a new power cartridge over here. The range of this puppy is two hundred yards." He smiled at him. "You now had more training than any of us when we got into this mess. Welcome to the team."

"This is real." Wells sucked in a ragged breath as he fingered the deadly gray tube in his hands. "You're the miracle the world's been praying for."

Quango snorted. "If we are the miracle, you better work on your prayers." He limped back to the gun rack and signaled the GIs who came with the lieutenant to grab a firearm. "We have a ton of trouble heading our way."

Chapter XXV

Wild Turkeys

Otheth stared at the communicator with frustration. "Can't this vehicle go any faster?" She squirmed in the motorcycle sidecar. "And next time have a suitable seat for a Roc."

An insistent squawk came over Otheth's communicator. "Cheepash, what's the matter?"

"*Reggie* has been discovered. A full division of harpies is en route," Cheepash cawed in anguish.

Otheth turned to Rene. "How much longer until we arrive?"

Rene glanced at the road signs, gunned the engine. "Less than an hour provided we don't have any problems at the bridge."

"Hurry. In the name of your human god, hurry," Otheth pleaded. She thought for a moment and toggled on her communicator. "Cheepash, encrypt the information regarding our destination and situation. Broadcast it out to space. Our fleet must be close. They need to know where we are."

"Yes, commander," came the prompt reply.

Rene gave the Roc a sidelong glance. "And if there's no one up there to receive that message?"

Otheth fluffed her feathers. "Then, my friend, you must choose whether you will die with First Order of the Dragon or flee. My team and I will fulfill our vow."

"There's no place left to flee to." Rene gunned the bike.

* * *

"Keres-ma, it appears the elves have revealed themselves. The downed ship has been positively identified as the one hijacked on Equitone." Silenus-dis' eyes bulged on the vid-screen. "I want it captured."

"An aerial fighter located the crash site but could not approach. Even a crippled Striker is formidable." Keres-ma cast a wary eye at the Lethe Sector governor. "They spotted no other evidence of elves near there."

Silenus-dis hissed into the communicator. "I must have the data logs from that ship." Spittle flew from his fanged mouth. "I will personally lead a full division of my elite guard to take it. Send your nearest army to support me."

"I can't commit more troops," Keres-ma snapped. Frustration showed in his voice. "I know I'm far behind the original timetable for the landmass labeled North America, but these brute savages do not know how to fight. My three expeditionary forces assigned there move at will, destroying everything in their path. But when I reconnoiter, the small units are savagely ambushed. I'm forced to slow our advance to relieve them and scour the area for native fighters. The losses are always minimal, and the human savages caught are efficiently dealt with." His irritation grew as he thought about it. "But each time we lose a few warriors. It's starting to affect morale."

Silenus-dis jabbed a clawed finger at the screen. "Why do you bother with scouts, vanguards, and pickets? General Xiroah-dis doesn't, and he was once a commander in the imperial army. If these savages could hurt us, they would have by now. Get back on schedule."

"Governor, it's not that simple. When my forces enter a metropolitan area, they find nothing but IEDs and booby-traps, and the barbarian military is constantly nipping at my fringes. My scout-crawlers are lightly armored, so most of the work is done by infantry. When I stop to do battle, the cowards melt away." Keres-ma studied a data sheet. "I've made excellent progress on the landmasses labeled Africa and South America and can find little to fight in the one labeled Australia, but North America... I've lost four percent of my warriors there. Four percent. I haven't had a straightforward confrontation since the obliteration of the urban center labeled Guadalajara on the second day of the third wave's invasion."

"I've heard enough of your whining," Silenus-dis snapped. "*I* will capture this grounded Striker with my personal guard, and you will send an army to dissect the area."

The governor's voice became icy, "Your efforts so far have been a major disappointment. You were given command of a third of our expeditionary force... that's over three-point-three million warriors, and you've already lost twenty-five thousand of them to a gaggle of savages." He sneered. "You are leading as poorly here as you did during the human prison riot on Carcerem."

Keres-ma stroked the mantichoras tail hanging around his neck. "On Carcerem, I was betrayed by treasonous Rocs on the inside and faced an overpowering elvish army on the outside. My garrison had no chance."

"Lie to yourself, but not to me!" Silenus-dis roared back. "You had the human king in your grasp and were too stupid to know it. Then he beat you with prison rabble. I will take direct command of this mission. The commanders I have here in the arctic region are *competent* and will complete the grid search without me. Besides, I have come to suspect that we've been deceived. It appears the existence of elves in the arctic regions is an elaborate ruse."

Bile rose in Keres-ma's throat as he saw the end of his military career. "I have inadequate artillery and armored units for a proper campaign. Will you please divert more supply ships to my armies?"

"Bah, you're getting enough," Silenus-dis added. "General Xiroah-dis has made no such requests, and he's dealing with the primary landmass, Eurasia, which has far more humans."

"Governor, Xiroah-dis has his own armor and support units. He's not dependent on that fool quartermaster who oversees my requisitions," was Keres-ma's frustrated reply. He knew that General Xiroah-dis barely recognized Silenus-dis' authority and was managing his whole ground campaign independent of the governor's directions.

"You need to improvise and adapt," Silenus-dis chuckled. "Where is the force you're sending me?"

"It's in the process of leveling the human enclave labeled Philadelphia. I am with them." Keres-ma deflated within himself. "When will the troop transports arrive to relocate us?"

Silenus-dis huffed. "Your troops will march to the vicinity of the crash. All the transports are already serving double duty as resupply dropships." He groaned. "I never envisioned that ten million troops could consume so much inventory so fast. This is getting to be a very expensive endeavor. Any further questions?"

"No, your excellency. We'll disengage and move out by morning."

"Good. When will your force arrive at the designated coordinates?"

Keres-ma's response was pointed and he didn't care that his voice held an edge. "On foot, through hostile countryside, traversing what these humans call roads... eight days, at a minimum."

"Make those lazy sloths of yours do it in seven."

The communication terminated before Keres-ma could voice a protest. He was left hurling curses at the dark screen. "The entire Dis Cult is populated with idiots."

* * *

"Madam President, I don't have a clue what's going on. The only information I have came from a civilian HAM radio operator." General Calley pressed the palms of his hands against his eyes. His pallor was gray, having not slept more than a couple of hours in the last forty-eight. "What we know is that half of the ranger force we sent to investigate the crashed alien vessel in Niagara Falls went down in the first few seconds of contact. However, a small team reportedly made it inside and came out bearing sophisticated energy weapons similar to what the aliens have."

"That's great news," Stevenson exclaimed. "Evac those people so our eggheads can start dissecting that alien equipment."

The general leaned back and pinched the bridge of his nose. "The Fourth Cavalry Brigade out of Fort Knox is en route. Their commander, General Shanks, had them prepped to reinforce the troops on the Texas border, so were ready to move."

"That's good news, right?" Stevenson noticed the fear in the general's eyes.

"No, it isn't." Calley slammed his fist on the table. "Damn the breakdown in communications. The alien force we were fighting in Philadelphia broke contact and started moving in that direction this morning. We also have an unverified report that several alien spaceships have been spotted near there."

Stevenson sank into a chair. "Then our slim hope is gone?"

Calley sighed. "Those folks are Army Rangers. They may be able to slip out on their own."

"Whatever happens there is beyond our control now." Stevenson regarded the large wall map of the United States. "How are we faring against their main armies?"

Calley grimaced. "Our troops holed up in San Diego are trapped. We've been sneaking the badly wounded out on stealth submarines, but the situation is hopeless. In the south, Mexico no longer exists as a functioning country. The aliens are now marching up the Gulf Coast unhindered and will reach Texas in about a week."

Stevenson paled. "And here in the east?"

"It's tough not being able to move any assets through the air." Calley rose and pointed to a small circle on the map. "We abandoned Philadelphia and are now consolidating everything we have from the eastern third of the country in the mountains of eastern Pennsylvania and Maryland. When the time is right, we'll launch a full-scale attack. Our experts estimate that the aliens' ground force is close to a quarter million fighters, so we can't hold anything back. Every missile, every stealth bomber and fighter that's still operational will be committed to support the ground troops when we hit them."

Stevenson stared at the map. "Plan well, General. In the name of God, plan this well. It's our last hope."

* * *

A nervous ensign approached Dante. "King Carloman, Admiral Martinel has an urgent communication for you."

Dante tore his eyes from his view screen. An image of the Earth filled it. Thousands of harpy mainline warships were highlighted on the tactical display around the planet. He switched the display to ship-to-ship communication.

Admiral Martinel's and General Cruz's faces immediately appeared on a split screen.

Cruz growled, "Sir, *Reggie's* been located on the planet's surface, but we have a serious problem."

Alarm shot through Dante. "Tina? Talk to me. Is she alive?"

"Yes, mate, yes." Martinel held up his hand. "Oteth's on the planet surface near her and sent out a flash message. It appears *Reggie* crashed onto a place called Goat Island by Niagara Falls. They lost their galley escort while eluding the harpy fleet, but *everyone* on board the Striker came through the hard landing okay."

"Thank God. Oh, thank God." Dante released the breath he did not know he was holding. His eyes narrowed. "When do we extract them?"

General Cruz growled. "Sir, we can't sneak in. Even a single dropship will be detected as soon as it gets close. Then we'll have two downed ships needing a rescue. We must wait for our allies. I have forty-five thousand troops, Silenus-dis has ten *million*. Martinel has forty mainline warships, the harpy fleet's over two *thousand*."

"So, we do nothing?" Dante's voice hardened, "I'm taking a galley. You can sit here and wait, but I'm going in."

"You'll be dead before you reach the atmosphere." Cruz's voice softened, "Besides you don't even know how to fly a galley."

Martinel interrupted, "If we catch the harpy fleet by surprise, my dodecahedron plan will work."

Dante's face turned to one of anxious expectation.

Cruz glowered. "I thought that was going to be our last option."

"I think we're down to our last option. I can hold it for a month," Martinel answered.

"And after a month," Cruz added, "your fleet will be sitting ducks."

Dante interjected, "I know the Rocs will be here in less than a week."

"That's only another couple hundred mainline warships," Cruz snapped. "We don't know when, or *if* the Satyrs and Centaurs will answer our call."

Dante added quietly, "Calahas and Arachne have been making progress with their people. They've been secretly gathering troops and warships near uninhabited star systems. When we left, I sent them an urgent request along with Earth's coordinates. They'll come."

Cruz's voice dropped, "I've no doubts about Arachne and Calahas, but they're not exactly the leaders of their species. How much influence can they have? How many ships and troops will they bring?"

"I don't know," Dante responded with an even voice.

"I say we go in, and we go in now." Martinel's face flushed. "There must be over a billion people on Earth butchered over the last two weeks. It'll only be a matter of days before organized resistance evaporates, and then the harpies will go on a full-blown extermination rampage." He took a deep breath. "General, two points. First, the harpies have to be consuming massive amounts of energy and munitions. With my blockade in place, those harpies on the surface will rapidly run out of supplies. They'll be in a world of hurt without their technological advantage. And second, you may only have three divisions, but there are millions of soldiers on Earth still in the fight. If you can coordinate with them, you'll have a viable army."

"You're right on both points," Cruz said, "but there's no communication infrastructure left down there, and even if I solve that problem. How do I get them to listen and take orders?"

Dante squared his shoulders. "I'll make them listen. Everyone's been calling me the human king. I'll just have to be one." He paused. "The harpies are murdering people with impunity. The leaders on Earth would make a deal with the devil if they're offered the chance. They'll accept my proposition."

"But how long will it hold?" Martinel asked softly. "A deal made with a gun to your head isn't likely to be kept."

Dante nodded. "That's an issue I'll worry about *after* we save the planet. General, is Niagara Falls a legitimate spot to establish our beachhead?"

Cruz stared for a long time at the ever-changing tactical display in front of him and clenched his fist. "Right now, the answer is yes. There're harpy patrols in the area and what appears to be a division en route. But there're no anti-aircraft emplacements to impede our landing."

Dante paled. "So, it is a *valid* site for our beachhead."

"It's not the first battle I fear, but what comes next." Cruz clenched his jaw. "It *is* a good location. I'll have time to offload our troops before the harpies react. I've never seen Niagara Falls. I guess it's time for a visit." He directed his next question to Martinel. "Admiral, what air support can you give me?"

Martinel chewed his lower lip for a moment. "Given my plans for the fleet, the Strikers and Galleys are useless to me. They're yours to get your troop ships through the orbital blockade and provide ground support."

Cruz whistled. "Five Strikers, sixty galleys, and a hundred and fifty single-seaters. With your dodecahedron in place, that's a lot of firepower. If our intelligence is correct, it appears the primary support for the harpy ground troops are single-seat fighters. Those things are maneuverable but not near the capability of a galley."

"Aye, they're yours. Strikers are next to useless for the dodecahedron. I need a minimum of twenty-four mainline ships to form the grid." Martinel studied the data on his terminal. "The harpy fleet's positioned to repulse an attack but not stop what I've planned. I have four state-of-the-art Juggernauts that'll clear the path. The eighteen Dragons will go next. Those old ore carriers aren't much good, but they can take a punch. The Super-Dragons, Stalkers, Enforcers and Dreadnaughts will bring up the rear and close the last links in the orbital blockade."

He paused and considered the display again as a new idea hit him. "Once the grid's in place, the Strikers and Galleys will have theater control of the air in that part of northeastern US and southern Ontario, Canada. The harpies' aerial transports are too vulnerable. They won't airlift troops once we have that much firepower in the vicinity. It'll take them a while to move an army on the ground. You'll have time to consolidate your position."

Cruz nodded. "It's a good first step." The corners of his mouth tightened. "Dante, then it's up to you. You'll have to get the Earth to join our side fast or I'll be overwhelmed, no matter how well my people are dug in."

"I'll find a way." Dante's voice became husky, "I have to."

Martinel croaked a fake laugh. "Then this should be a piece of cake. All we have to do is depend on a relief armada that didn't exist a year ago, unite a human population that has never agreed on anything since we crawled out of the swamp, and bust up an enemy that hasn't lost a significant battle in over a hundred and twenty years." He snorted. "And, Dante, the icing on the cake is that you'll get to see your old buddy Keres-ma. The communication intercepts indicate that he's the harpy field general in North America."

"Let's just get this done." Dante switched off the vid-comm and brought up the display of the Earth that was already expanding on the screen. He stared at the clouded outline of North America. *I'm coming, Tina. Hang on.*

Chapter XXVI

Retreat to Goat Island

Precisely thirty minutes after entering *Reggie's* bridge, Lieutenant Wells' earpiece beeped. He updated Captain Martin. The response was unexpected. He received an emphatic order to return. It went on for a full minute. The lieutenant sighed. "Sir, this is nothing like what we expected coming here. These people are *really* our friends." He winced at the angry retort over the communicator and reluctantly acknowledged the new command.

Looking at Tina, Wells blushed. "Orders. We have to return to our unit, and I'm to drag you along since you acknowledged that you're an American citizen."

"That's not going to happen," Tina's voice was cool and clipped.

Mara simulcast the conversation in Latin across the bridge. The reaction of the crew was instantaneous. The crew, who moments before wore friendly smiles, now regarded the Americans with open hostility. The two guards who accompanied Tina stepped in front of her and leveled their weapons toward the lieutenant. The balding man on the right spat and snarled some words that Wells did not understand.

Although Wells and the six soldiers with him now held long-barrel ion disrupters and wore bandoliers filled with weapon energy clips, he felt apprehension for the first time since entering. Weapons were raised on both sides.

"Stand down," Tina commanded with a firm but calm voice. "These people are here as our guests. They will not be harmed." She gave Wells an icy glare. "Nor will I comply with that ridiculous order."

Wells held up his empty hands. "I will politely ask you to come, and no more."

Emma, who was holding a duffel bag stuffed with communicators, microcomputers, and neural-net suits, shook her head. "Why doesn't any of this surprise me.

Lieutenant, your captain is a complete idiot." Emma tossed her satchel to one of the soldiers and edged closer to Tina. "I'm staying too. Our leaders are so stupid they couldn't empty water from a boot even if the instructions were written on the sole."

That comment caused Tina to smile. "You sound just like your brother." She reached out and squeezed Emma's hand. "When people are afraid of the unknown, they'll grasp at anything. I've been there myself." She faced Wells. "Go and take the gear we gave you. When the time comes, my husband will meet with the world leaders." She coughed. "He'll *insist* on it."

"It's your call on staying." His eyes met Emma's briefly. "Both of you." Wells nodded to his team. "Hell, I'd stay too if I had a choice." He appraised Tina for a long moment. "Tell this Dante Carloman to get here fast. The grim reaper is getting busier by the minute." He turned toward the exit, signaling his men to follow.

As the lieutenant went to leave, Emma grabbed his arm. "Herb, don't go. We need to be working with these people, not following some uninformed command out of Washington."

The lieutenant gulped. "You'll get no argument from me on that point. I'll try again to convince Captain Martin to see reason." He walked down the ramp. His team followed, looking at their new weapons with wonder.

Captain Martin was waiting for him beside an MRAP. Wells showed the captain the gear acquired but was unable to budge him.

"Our orders came directly from General Calley and President Stevens." Captain Martin's voice sounded uncertain as he glanced at the ion disrupter Wells held. "This is just some alien trick. Mount up," he rasped as he snatched the weapon from the lieutenant. "This needs to get back to our scientists."

The small column wheeled toward the Robert Moses Parkway, but soon came to a jarring halt. Hundreds of terrified civilians were stampeding in their direction. Out of

183

sight, behind the mob, the lieutenant heard the distinctive whine of the aliens' energy weapons.

"Back to the crash site," Wells pleaded to the captain. "Their ship has some sort of shielding that those alien weapons can't penetrate."

Captain Martin's shoulders sagged as the refugees cried with relief on reaching his company's armored vehicles. Tears filled his eyes as he met the imploring look of a young mother clutching her sobbing one-year-old boy to her chest. He looked past the people and saw a half dozen bus-sized vehicles methodically moving on spider-like legs, leveling everything in their path. He shivered at the sight and raised his chin. "Lieutenant, I pray you're right about those people on the spaceship. Take your platoon and get these civilians to Goat Island."

Wells paled. "You're not thinking you can stop those aliens... those harpies."

"I'm no goddamn hero, but we need to buy you some time. We're keeping the MRAPS. Once I get the attention of those bastards, we're taking off," the captain rasped. He handed the ion disrupter to the lieutenant. "Lieutenant, win this war. We'll hold this position as long as we can. Now get out of here."

Wells stared at the strange weapon for a second, blinking back tears. "The survival rate of any troops who confronted the aliens head-on was near zero." He met the captain's eyes. "Sir, you *are* a hero. It's been my pleasure to serve under you."

A small smile creased the captain's face. "I'm sure that's not true. If you ever meet this human king, tell him that Captain Charles Martin thinks monarchies are a piece of crap."

Wells saluted. "You can tell him yourself." He spun around and started barking orders to his platoon. His team soon had the civilians following the path that directed tourists to Goat Island.

As Captain Martin deployed the MRAPs and his platoon behind statues and buildings around the deserted park, the refugees followed the lieutenant's directions—until they came through a tree grove. There, the stark sight of the quarter-mile-long spaceship came into view. Despite the shrieks behind them, those in the front ground to a halt, lurching from one terror to the next.

When she saw the panicked people on the control room's vid-screen, Tina hurried to the barricades with Emma beside her. She climbed atop the footbridge barrier. "This way, hurry." Hundreds of eyes turned from fear to hope as they perceived a pregnant woman beckoning them.

Lieutenant Wells used that moment to exhort them on. "They're our people, they're human. Hurry." He ran through the mob toward the spaceship. The terrified crowd followed.

As he helped the last person over the footbridge barricade, Wells saw a tall casino implode under the energy beams of harpy attack vehicles approaching from a second direction. The loud, staccato fire of his company's .50 calibers erupted along with the frantic chirping of M4s and grenade detonations against the two-prong assault. However, a few minutes later, the lieutenant felt a wave of heat blow past him.

Silence followed. The guns spitting defiance at the invaders were no longer heard.

Wells leapt behind the barrier. Nothing human moved behind him. Emma, with misted eyes, was there waiting for him. She handed him an armful of ion disrupters and a sack of energy clips. Her voice was soft, "I'm glad you were able to make it back."

"Thanks." The lieutenant handed out the weapons to his men. His gaze shifted to the civilians, who were staring at the imposing vessel. Many crowded around Tina, listening to her words.

He saw her lift a little girl, who couldn't have been more than three, from a distraught looking mother who had two other small children clinging to her. Tina wiped the child's tears and walked up the wide ramp into the spaceship. The people followed.

Wells turned to his platoon and pointed to the civilians. "The death of our soldiers bought these people time to get here. It's now our responsibility to protect them." He positioned his platoon next to Caccina's team at the footbridge.

Emma stayed by Wells' side and glanced over the wall toward the sound of keening wails. Several harpies, on foot, reached the river's edge and tried to wade the Niagara's roaring torrents. They were swept over the Falls.

Tina and Quango joined Emma and Wells. She looked at the lieutenant. "We're getting your people settled in." She pointed to a wide gangway. "I'm putting them in the launch bay. It's a big, open area. The cooks are pulling together some food for them."

"Thanks." Wells shuddered. "Nothing will ever be the same again for any of us." He saw the members of his platoon cast wary glances at the Satyr.

Quango sighed as he sat and stretched out his gimpy leg. "I had to come out here. All those Earth humans screeched at me like I was some sort of monster." He chuckled. "I'm now positive my ex-wife has visited this place already."

Tina hugged him. "Your ex is crazy. You're the sweetest Satyr I've ever met."

Quango chuckled. "Since I know most of the Satyrs you know, that's not much of a compliment." His eyes softened. "But thanks anyway." He raised himself and studied the approaching vehicles on the other side of the river. "Those are Crawlers. The Ipis use them for scouting—too lightly armed to bother us while we're near the Striker's shielding."

"And if they bring something bigger?" Wells flinched as the crawlers fired plasma darts and ion beams in their direction. The energy bolts sizzled and vanished as they struck *Reggie's* energy barrier.

"Not a question of if, but when." Quango tugged on his goatee. "We better be outta here by then or we're dead."

A dozen screeching harpies suddenly sprinted across the footbridge toward them.

"Idiots," Quango muttered.

The air filled with electronic sizzling and high-pitched whines as Major Caccina's company opened fire. A couple of the attackers stumbled back to the far side of the bridge, leaving the charred corpses of the others behind.

Lieutenant Wells screamed defiance at the retreating aliens with a feral grin. "They *can* die." He shook his weapon in the air. "Arm us with guns like this and we'll wipe them from the face of the Earth."

"Calm down, laddie. That was only a few fools who've read too much about Ipis invincibility." Quango slammed a fresh clip into his ion disrupter. He glanced at the late-afternoon sky. "Will you look at that."

Tina turned to where the Satyr was pointing and smiled. The spray from the Falls had mixed with the smoke from the brief fight and the sun's rays setting behind the cliffs on the western bank. The haze appeared to form an image of a woman spreading her cloaked arms over the ship. "I'll be damned. It's the *Maid of the Mist.*"

"The what?" Quango asked.

Emma answered from the other side of the Satyr, "It's an old legend around here. She's the spirit of someone who lived long ago and died a tragic death. To many, she represents true love and defiance of one's enemies."

"A ghost, huh." Quango shuddered and gave the shifting spectral image another glance. "She doesn't happen to carry any spare energy clips... or better yet, a relief fleet, does she?"

Emma folded her arms across her chest and sighed. "I don't think so."

"Too bad." Quango looked over the wall at the smoldering dead harpies. "The arrogant fools paid the price. They won't try that again."

Emma crouched next to Lieutenant Wells. "Sorry I was such an asshole on the ride here. I've been mad at the world for a long time and have a chip on my shoulder a mile wide." Her smile was shy as she extended her hand. "Let's start again. I'm Emma Carloman. Pleased to meet you."

Wells stared for a second and grasped the slim fingers in his blunt, calloused hand. "Herb Wells, I'm from... I was from Lowell, Mass."

"Oh, dear God, no. Did you have family there when..." Her hand squeezed his, not daring to finish the sentence.

He clung to her grasp. "My folks and two sisters were at ground zero when the alien bastards first hit the US. There was no warning, and all our emergency resources were down the coast helping with the New York City evacuation." His voice shook. "I haven't heard of anyone that got out of there alive." He reluctantly released his hold on her and squared his shoulders. "I guess everyone's lost someone in this nightmare. I just want a chance for a little payback before I die."

Tina, who had risen to return to the ship, overheard the conversation and touched them both on the shoulders. "Don't be so quick to seek death. It'll find you soon enough in this godforsaken galaxy. Look to the living. They need our strength more than ever." She glanced at a small grove of trees wearing their autumn colors and blooming mums in a neatly tended garden that seemed indifferent to the destruction around it. "Remember the scars that you bear tell where you've been; they don't need to dictate where you're going."

Emma and Herb exchanged glances of shared pain. They were only interrupted by Mara carrying a crate of fresh energy clips to the entrenched fighters.

Tina filled her half-empty bandolier with cartridges. "Quango, how's our munition supply holding up?"

"No issues. My propulsion engineers jerry-rigged a siphon from *Reggie's* hyperspace drive. It's inefficient, but they can recharge the used weapons clips," Quango replied. The Satyr shook his head. "It's a little trick I learned back on Carcerem when you were imprisoned there."

"I remember." Tina's eyes moistened. "We lost a lot of good people escaping that hellhole." She turned to Emma and Herb and sighed as she saw the two soldiers, fellow escapees from Carcerem, hovering near her. "I'm going back inside. A pregnant woman will just be in the way out here."

Quango snorted. "C'mon, Mara. We better get back too. Those damn engines won't fix themselves." Hobbling beside Tina and Mara to the ship's ramp, Quango talked rapidly. They were still in a deep conversation as they entered the Striker.

Tina had not gotten far through the entrance when she was beset with pleas for help from the crew members trying to organize the frightened people. She was the only person onboard fluent in English, and the only doctor.

Mara raised her sensors. "I'll attempt to reestablish contact with Otheth. We need data and have no functional communication capabilities beyond the immediate area."

"Thanks, Mara. Let me know what you learn." Tina ran her hand through her matted hair and moved to a group of injured people.

Quango smirked and shouted "Boo" when he saw several children pointing at him. They squealed and retreated a couple steps, but continued to stare. One five-year-old worked up the courage and poked the Satyr's arm.

The Satyr tousled the child's hair. "Hello, laddie. Ya want to touch my horn too?" Curiosity overwhelmed fear, and Quango found himself the center of a dozen young children tentatively touching his one unbroken horn, his cloven feet, and his goatee. Five minutes later, chuckling, he left for the engine room.

Chapter XXVII

Face-off at the Lewiston Bridge

After being on mostly deserted roads for two days, the progress Otheth and her team made with the motorcycle gang slowed to a crawl as they neared Queenstown. It was well after dark, but the Queen Elizabeth Way was thick with panicked people fleeing. "It appears we are getting close to the enemy," Otheth commented from the sidecar as Rene drove his bike off the gridlocked expressway.

Rene spat at the sight of the frantic mob. "Where do these fools think they're going? There's no place safe on this planet." He gunned his bike when he found a gap along the shoulder of the road.

Otheth peaked out of the sidecar. "It's the loss of hope that drives them to this insanity." She snapped her beak. "I was a member of the Order of the Dragon since my fledgling days, but when I was a prison warden for the Ipis on Carcerem, I came close to renouncing my vow. I saw nothing but depravity in the humans incarcerated there."

She closed her eyes. "And then your monarch, Dante Carloman, was tossed in the mix. I never saw anything like it before. In a matter of days, he showed me why my ancestors felt honored to stand beside humans. He transformed that rabble by the strength of his will and the virtue of his spirit. He gave them hope." Her feathers flared. "In the end, with little more than their bare hands, they overthrew their jailers and won their freedom."

Rene pursed his lips. "Sounds like a helluva guy. But I'm guessing you had some small part in that adventure too."

"Yes, I did. It was the greatest honor of my life." Otheth flattened her feathers. "But I was a prison warden on Carcerem for over a standard year before your king became incarcerated there. Until he arrived, the imprisoned humans did *nothing* but brutalize each other over scraps. He was the catalyst. He changed them. He changed *me*."

A warble escaped Otheth's throat. "I would assault the very gates of the Ipis Imperial Palace on Serpens if he'd ask me to."

"Well, you and Cheepash believe in this guy, so I'll sign up to be one of his first subjects if we get out of this mess," Rene added as he gazed around. The street was dark. The only light came from the headlamps of the motorcycles. "But this king better hurry and get here or he won't have many subjects to claim."

It was well after midnight when they rolled into Queenstown.

As they passed a sign with the words "Bridge to USA," the convoy braked to a sudden halt. A barricade of police cars stretched across the road, blocking access to the Queenstown-Lewiston Bridge. About thirty people, in a variety of law enforcement uniforms, were stationed along its full length.

An ashen-faced Mountie waving a flashlight walked toward the idling motorcycles. His voice was strident. "For God's sake, go back. There's aliens up ahead."

Otheth stayed hunched down in the sidecar with a winter coat draped over her, but being a Roc, she could imitate a human voice. Sounding exactly like Rene, she asked, "What's their strength and disposition?"

"Their what?" the Mountie squinted toward the voice. He stepped forward with his flashlight in a trembling hand and shined it on Otheth. "What's with the feathered bike helmet? Are you clowns drunk or something? This shit is real. People are dying across the river, and those aliens may come this way at any moment."

"I am a Roc, not a 'clown,'" Otheth replied with disgust. "My team and I are here on a mission to aid your human king." She observed the Mountie's garment and identified it as a uniform. "As government functionaries, I demand your assistance."

The Mountie's eyes narrowed as he drew his sidearm. "You guys are nuts, and I don't have time for this. Turn those bikes around and beat it."

Hearing the raised voices and seeing the Mountie unholster his gun, others in uniforms of the two countries, warily approached from the barricade with weapons ready.

Rene whispered to his passenger, "We need to find another way across. If these guys get a close look at you, there'll be fireworks for sure. Let me do the talking. I've had a lot more experience dealing with cops who have guns pointed at me than you."

Otheth rasped back, "Then deal with these low-level functionaries quickly. Time is wasting."

Rene climbed off his bike and walked to the Mountie with his hands raised. "Dude, sorry. We've been out of touch for the last few days. The last we heard everything was quiet around here. You can put that gun away. We're leaving now."

A grim look creased the Mountie's face. "Just go. Nothing's slowing these aliens. Find some hole to crawl into and maybe you'll live a while longer."

Otheth spoke up, "All the more reason to strike at them now and crush their arrogance. We Rocs have pledged ourselves to that task, and we will see it completed."

A man came up behind the Mountie, holding a shotgun and wearing a US Border Patrol uniform that had a gold leaf on the collar. "You're a what? Stand up so I can see you."

Gilbert joined Rene, trying to look as respectable as he could in his leathers and gang jacket. "Colonel, don't mind my friend there. She believes she can take on the whole harpy army by herself."

The border patrol agent scowled. "I'm the watch commander, and what's a *harpy*?"

Gilbert gulped. "Ah, that's what we call the invading aliens."

"Enough of this subterfuge. I tire of skulking around when there is a mission to fulfill." Otheth rose from the sidecar with her crest feathers flared and discarded the coat that was draped around her. "I and my team will destroy the Ipis on the bridge and continue on our path to rescue the human king's wife."

She strode forward as the startled Mountie and the Border Patrol agent emptied their weapons at her. The projectiles were harmlessly absorbed by her energy shield. She snapped at her team, who leapt from their own sidecars, "Refrain from all aggression. They have no weapons capable of penetrating my shield." The Roc moved close to the two officers, positioning herself so they blocked her from being a target of the other law enforcement officers. "Are you ready to talk now? I am an ally, not an enemy."

Gilbert walked forward with hands in the air. "Whoa, whoa, whoa. Put the damn guns down before someone gets hurt. You know as well as I do those pea shooters can't hurt them."

The two officers stared at Otheth's ion disrupter, then her curved beak, terror shining in their eyes. The other agents held their fire for fear of hitting those in front. Several moved closer, guns raised.

The American Border Patrol Agent worked his jaw for a few seconds before any words came out. He rasped, "Ah, you're speaking English."

Otheth hooted. "Of course, I am. It's the human king's private language, and this is part of his realm." She glanced at the other approaching officers. "Cease the current level of belligerence. The enemy is on the bridge, not before you." She shifted her undersized wing so that her deadly weapon was clearly visible to all. "If I desired you to be dead, you would be. Now tell me of the Ipis disposition in the area."

The Mountie's voice trembled. He looked over his shoulder. "Hold your fire. We're negotiating." He glanced at the bikers, who were sweating profusely with their arms still raised, then returned his gaze to Otheth. "Okay, alien, you're right. You could have killed us, and you didn't. Perhaps you are different." He glanced at the American officer standing beside him and took a shuddered breath. "God help us all. On the bridge is some sort of alien tank. It looks like a bus sitting on giant spider legs."

The Border Patrol agent sighed. "There are two more just like it over by Niagara University. I counted at least a couple dozen aliens with ray guns near them before I took off. There's a rumor of an alien ship gone down by the Falls, about five miles south of here. But I haven't heard anything from that direction. We had troubles of our own right here."

"Three crawlers and an infantry platoon," Otheth spoke slowly. "That's a standard Ipis scout team." She relaxed, regarding the current misunderstanding with the uniformed humans. The scent of fear was palatable. They were apparently ill-informed, poorly trained paramilitaries. Their inadequate weaponry was similar to the primitive projectile weapons the Wild Turkeys carried. With her shielding engaged, they could not harm anyone in her squad. However, she did not want to harm any of Dante's subjects. "I intend to eliminate the immediate Ipis threat." She turned toward Rene. "I am unfamiliar with local protocols. Will these uniformed warriors insist on acquiring the *cou* with us?"

A nervous laugh escaped Rene. "I'd guess they want all of us gone as soon as possible." Otheth's team stepped forward and stood beside their leader, with their crest feathers flattened in a sign of non-aggression.

"Who are you?" the US Border Patrol Watch Commander asked as he lowered his emptied shotgun.

"We're allies of your king, Dante Carloman." Otheth turned to the gathered bikers. "Leave your two-wheeled transports. We proceed on foot from here."

Most of the officers still had their guns aimed, but no one pulled a trigger. Several inched closer and stared at the Rocs.

Rene moved in front of Otheth. "Look, officer, if they wanted to hurt you, they could have done so." He pointed to his gang, who all edged forward and stood between the police and the Rocs. "I've been on the road with these guys for the last seven hundred miles. They *are* on our side. They're here to help us."

A large object flashed across the sky and settled to the ground beyond their line of sight, south of them.

The Mountie kept his empty weapon aimed, but fear filled his words. "More flying saucers."

Otheth followed the craft with her eyes. "Cheepash, you're wearing the enhanced night vision scope. Identify."

"That's one of the troop transports for Silenus-dis' entourage," came the prompt reply.

Otheth faced the Mountie. "How many ships like that have you seen?"

"That's the fourth in the last hour," the Mountie stuttered.

"That's one big mother-fucker," Gilbert exclaimed. "Are all spaceships that big?"

Cheepash snorted. "That's small by interstellar vessel standards. The big ones aren't built to transit through atmospheres." He flapped his wings. "That one, however, is the grand prize. You're looking at the invasion commander's personal dropship."

"The mother-fucker that's causing all this misery is right here?" Gilbert stared at where the vessel vanished from sight. "How do we fight that?"

"We leave that task to King Dante," Otheth cawed. "His army's better than any of the Ipis paramilitaries in this part of the Lethe Sector."

"Paramilitaries?" Gilbert gulped. "We're getting our butts kicked, and it's not even their frontline troops?"

"If the Ipis empire's First Fleet showed up, this war would be over already, and the few human survivors would be cowering in caves," Otheth warbled. "Just be glad that the idiot Silenus-dis is leading this underfunded, poorly supplied campaign."

"Jesus, this is their second string? Thank God for small blessings." Rene, ignoring the guns pointed at him, took off his biker helmet, and wiped his forehead.

"Four Ipis troop transports is a full combat division." Cheepash clicked his beak. "Otheth, I hate to tell you, but that's more than even our squad can handle."

The Canadian and American law officers lowered their weapons, their eyes darting between the Rocs and the motorcycle gang.

"One step at a time. I have an idea." Otheth glanced at the humans. "I require six prisoners."

"Say what?" Rene tensed.

"We need to get close," Otheth warbled. "This is my plan..."

When she finished explaining her scheme, the American Border Patrol Watch Commander stepped in front of her and cleared his throat. "For what it's worth, I grant you and your... associates permission to enter the United States. Go kill those bastards. We'll back you."

Fifteen minutes later, the eight Rocs herded a few of the Wild Turkeys onto the Queenstown-Lewiston bridge.

The Ipis crawler swiveled its battery of heavy-duty blasters mounted on a pair of flexible pincers toward the oncomers.

Otheth called out in clear, unaccented Ipis. "Silenus-dis has demanded that all captured elves be brought in for interrogation. My squad captured this bunch spying on you."

"Elves?" A harpy in the road, wearing the sash of a fire team leader, lowered his weapon and squinted at Rene. "How can you tell? They look the same as any other human to me."

"It's their scent that gives them away." Otheth pointed to the bikers. "Elves smell like rancid meat."

Eight other harpies loped forward to gawk at the prisoners. One of them approached Gilbert and sniffed his sweat-stained T-shirt.

Cheepash whispered to the Canadian, "Look mean. He's more scared of you than you are of him."

Gilbert growled, and the alien hopped back, chittering to his compatriots.

"Captured elves?" The harpy wearing a squad commander medallion lowered his ion disrupter. "Hmm." His eyes narrowed. "Mercenaries should not receive the recognition for this prize. Leave them with us."

"Certainly, squad commander." Otheth nodded to Cheepash. "Bring the elves forward." She moved close to the harpy leader, bowing. "We serve only for the boundless glory of the Ipis empire."

As they came close with the prisoners, Cheepash and two others sprinted for the crawler. No living creature can run as fast as a Roc. They were inside the crawler's open portal in seconds.

At the same instant, Otheth sank her iron-hard beak into the squad commander's thin neck, snapping it.

The terrified screams of the two harpy gunners inside the crawler were drowned out by the shrieks of those caught outside as the Rocs and their armed "captives" pounced. Otheth's commando team shorted out the Ipis energy shields with their incapacitation rods before the confused harpies could react. The humans, with short-barrel disrupters concealed in their jackets, did the rest. The struggle lasted less than a minute.

Gilbert waved his arm and motorcycles roared onto the bridge, followed by a pair of US Border Patrol trucks packed with Mounties and US Customs Agents. Otheth's eyes gleamed as harpy blood dripped from her beak. "Where is this Niagara University?"

A feral grin creased the senior Border Patrol agent's face as he pointed northeast. "Like I said, two more over there." He ripped an ion disrupter from the clawed hands of the dead harpy at his feet.

Otheth tapped her communicator. "Cheepash, you know the access codes. Drive the crawler."

"Yes, commander."

Otheth cocked her head and watched the humans examine the harpy gear. She dug her talons into the harpy subcommander's severed neck. "See, they die as easy as anyone else." She crowed, "Wild Turkeys, mount up. We hunt. There's more *cou* to collect today."

Otheth had become accustomed to reading human scents. She sniffed the chill autumn night air. *They are starting to believe their opponents aren't gods.* "This is what we do next..."

An hour later, Cheepash drove the crawler to the deserted college campus. He had no trouble locating the two Ipis crawlers, as they were parked on the main highway in front of the college's administration building. Twenty Ipis warriors lounged on the ground around the vehicles.

Cheepash broadcast the appropriate identity code, and the harpies ignored his approach until his gunners opened fire. The nearest crawler exploded in a massive fireball.

The harpies, not killed in the explosion, scrambled to face the unexpected attack, then started firing wildly into the dark at the sound of forty-one hogs revving their engines. They never saw the new danger behind them.

Otheth with her Roc team had captured the second crawler at the same time Cheepash fired on the first one. It now joined Cheepash's vehicle in blasting the dwindling number of harpies.

A few broke and fled but were run down by armed bikers. Their blood soaked into the manicured campus lawn.

Gilbert rumbled back to the crawlers, wearing an Ipis energy belt still dripping blood and waving a long-barrel ion disrupter. The other bikers and cops followed.

Otheth craned her neck toward Gilbert. "Anyone hurt?"

A grim look creased the biker's face. "Bruno bought it." He glanced around. "A few of the other guys lost their bikes and got dinged, but they'll be fine." He spat. "Those alien assholes were too busy running to shoot straight."

Otheth cawed, "Your people's *cou* was inspiring. I will sing of their courage to the Great Dragon Council."

Gilbert raised an eyebrow. "So, Rocs aren't the only ones who can earn this *cou*?"

Otheth warbled, "I've met many humans on Cocytus and Carcerem, and now on Earth, who can claim *cou*. The Wild Turkeys stand tall among that group of heroes."

"Damn straight we do." Gilbert glanced at a Border Patrolman treating a burned biker with a first aid kit. "These cops did all right too." He shook his gun over his head and roared. His shout was echoed by the victorious humans.

Otheth fluffed her feathers. *They act as if a great victory was achieved.* She sniffed the air. *Perhaps it was. The scent of fear is gone. I now sense their defiance and hope. Those feelings must be nurtured.*

Those not injured gathered around Otheth. She saw the new confidence in their eyes. "Now we rescue a starship."

Cheepash leaned out of his crawler's portal and cawed, "Otheth, I received a message burst from King Dante. He needs us to clear a landing area of hostiles." The big Roc paused. "He said the allied fleet hasn't arrived, but he can wait no longer. His dropships will land with only a minimal escort of galleys and Strikers. No Centaurs. No Satyrs and no Rocs."

"The Rocs will come." Otheth flared her crest feathers. "Until then, we will represent our people." She turned to the gathered humans. "Is there a spaceport nearby that can accommodate twenty to thirty drop ships?"

Rene looked at the other bikers and shrugged. "I think the Earth is kinda short on those types of places."

One of the Border Patrol Agents scratched behind his neck. "I'm in the Air Force Reserve with the 914th Airlift Wing. It's stationed down the road at the Niagara Falls Airport. If that tarmac can handle KC-135s, I suspect it can handle a few flying saucers." He glanced east. "It's about six miles from here."

Otheth clicked her beak. "Cheepash, apprise Captain Peyago and Tina Phokas of what is happening."

An eager grin spread across Rene's face as he shouted to the gathered bikers. "All right, let's ride! We've some serious alien butt to kick."

Chapter XXVIII

Trapped

A sense of helplessness overcame Tina as she watched the vid-screen. Harpies were erecting artillery batteries on the cliffs overlooking Goat Island from the Canadian side. *There's nothing we can do to stop them.*

She glanced at the other screen. A weak autumn sun rose behind thousands of harpy warriors lining the shore of the Niagara River on the American side. She saw Captain Peyago outside. Every crew member not engaged with restoring Reggie's engines was digging in along with the American Army Rangers for a defense against hopeless odds. Major Caccina had ordered the two bridges to the island blown an hour earlier. *Now the only way off of this death trap is to fly.* She shuddered. Reggie's *shields are strong, but they won't last forever under constant bombardment. The ship's weaponry is useless parked on the ground.*

Quango and Emma joined her at the vid-screens. The Satyr took in the changes on both sides of the river. "By my mother's twisted beard, we're in a tight spot. The only thing keeping us alive is that little bubbly brook out there. If Silenus-dis solves that before we can get *Reggie* airborne, we're dead."

Tina bit her lip. "Even if we get in the air, then what? There's nowhere we can go where they won't be right on us again."

Quango patted her arm. "Oteth's nearby, that's something."

"Oteth has her squad and a motorcycle gang she somehow managed to recruit." A tear trickled down Tina's cheek as she pointed at the thousands of harpies on the screen. "I know she'll try something, but there's just too many of those monsters out there. She'll end up dying along with us."

Emma's eyes flashed. "It's still good to know we have friends nearby." She watched a small alien aircraft flit above them, methodically firing on the Striker's shielding. "Somehow those... harpies don't seem as scary to me anymore."

Quango stroked his goatee. "Aye, lass. It's fear of the unknown that creates the most terror. Ain't nothing special about the Ipis other than collectively they have a nasty habit of taking what's not theirs without asking. You'll find that among them there are smart ones and stupid ones, just like any other species. And they die just as easy as the rest of us."

A klaxon blared. *"General quarters, general quarters. All hands to battle stations...,"* Reggie's flat, digitized voice announced over the alarm.

Tina switched on her communicator. "Gabrielle, what's going on?"

The harried captain answered, "It appears the harpies have tired of toying with us. *Reggie's* scanner has picked up over forty crawlers. They're *walking* down the river." Her voice sounded strained. *"Reggie's* shielding doesn't reach ground level. If they get to the island, they'll be inside it."

"Dammit." Tina lowered her comm-link and rested her hand protectively over her abdomen. Quango caught her attention. The Satyr had torn open a panel in the control room and was in a rapid-fire discussion with the ship's computer.

She heard the distinctive rich baritone of Reggie's voice respond but could make no sense of the words.

Quango turned to Tina. "Lass, do ya trust me with your life?" He tugged hard at his goatee.

Tina saw the doubt in the old Satyr's eyes. "Of course I do. What do you have in mind?"

"Something that's never been attempted to my know-ledge. But I think it's our only chance. Reggie's going to open a tracion field."

"That'll kill us. We're inside a planet's atmosphere."

"No, it won't. It's actually the activation of the hyperdrive in the presence of massive amounts of matter that causes the explosive chain reaction. I've just taken the hyperdrive offline."

"What's the point? We won't go anywhere."

Quango took a deep breath. "The tracion field is a stationary event in the universe. But the Earth moves, its solar system moves, and the galaxy moves. In theory, for the nanosecond the ship is in touch with the field, those motions will propel us somewhere, and I *think* the planet's gravity core will act as a *repellant* to the tracion field." His shoulders sagged. "But it's also possible we'd end up crushed a mile deep underground."

The damaged spacecraft shuddered from massive energy beams striking its shield. A quick glance at the vid-screen showed Tina that the Ipis artillery on the cliffs were now engaged along with the aerial fighters clustered above them.

Panicked shouts came over the audio link. "The crawlers have reached the island."

Tina stared aghast at the new images on the vid-screen. Seven of the crawlers had lost their footing in the rapids and were tumbling over the falls. The precise rows and columns of the advancing vehicles seen earlier, had become ragged, but thirty-odd crawlers continued to advance inexorably through the turbulent waters. The vanguard vehicles on the island fired heavy blasters mounted on their flexible pincers and disgorged the Ipis warriors onboard.

Quango reached into the open panel and pulled out a circuit board. He shouted to Reggie, "For the love of God, buy me a couple minutes or none of us leave this place alive." His fingers flew across the settings display.

"I will. Overriding safety protocols." Reggie lowered his energy shielding closer to the ground. The bubble of protection sparked and the crawlers' advance halted. "My shielding's primary power transducer just shorted from the surface feedback. Switching to battery power." The ship shuddered as a few ion bolts penetrated. "Finish your task. Batteries will suffer rapid degradation under this barrage."

Tina gasped at the vid-screen. The lowered barrier held the crawlers at bay, but hundreds of harpies, on foot, pushed through. The Ipis warriors breeched the defenders' positions.

Captain Peyago led a couple dozen crewmen to reinforce the crumbling defense on the eastern shore. Too little, too late. She died along with her company as harpies swarmed over the stone and dirt barrier, killing the humans in hand-to-hand combat.

"Everyone back to the ship," Tina cried over the communicator. "We'll hold the aft service entrance open as long as possible.

The human fighters fell back under withering fire. Major Caccina, directing the rear guard, died as his position was overrun.

More crawlers reached the island, disgorging swarms of harpy warriors.

Lieutenant Wells, with his platoon dug in at the base of the aft service door, held the harpies at bay. Tina watched the retreating crew members scramble to that last avenue of escape. *So few... so few.*

Wells called her over the comm-link. "Our charge packs are almost exhausted. What are your orders?"

Tina screamed over the comm-link, "Get inside, *now*. There's nothing more you can do out there."

Wells scrambled up the gangplank as the harpy horde, no longer hindered, rushed forward. The door slammed shut behind him. There were no living humans left outside the ship.

As the portal closed, Tina flipped on the intra-ship communication system. "Strap in, we're attempting an escape." She nodded. "Quango, do it now. The helm's yours."

Quango yelled, "Brace yourselves!" He closed the panel with a sharp snap and pulled an override lever beside it. "Pray this works. Reggie, go for it."

The sound of circulating air halted. "All nonessential systems are offline." Reggie counted down, "Initiating tracion in five, four, three, two, one—"

Tina pointed to the vid-screen. "Look at that," she gasped.

Crawler vehicles and harpies on foot twisted into unrecognizable shapes as the tracion field coalesced.

An instant later, *Reggie* was no longer there. It shuddered to a stop seven miles away beside a building with the words "Niagara Falls Fashion Outlet Mall" emblazoned on it. Behind them was a two-hundred-yard-wide, ten-feet-deep, laser-straight furrow of devastation. Nothing withstood it. Ipis war machines and soldiers in that path were vaporized along with all the buildings. Thousands of harpy warriors died instantly.

As the people onboard looked about, attempting to comprehend what occurred, Quango wiped his brow. "Lass, what are your orders?"

"My orders?" Tina asked not comprehending the question.

"Yes, lass. Peyago's dead. Caccina's dead. You're the senior officer now," the Satyr answered. Exhaustion etched his words.

Tina took a shuddered breath and nodded. "All right then. Where are we now? Did we escape?"

Quango checked the readouts on his datapad. "We only moved six-point-eight miles. I was hoping for much more. But since we're all alive, I'll take it." He pointed at the vidscreen. "With that two-hundred-yard-wide trench, even someone of Silenus-dis' intellect will figure out where we are." He glanced around. "These refugees don't know what's happening. They're terrified. They need someone in authority to speak. That's you." He sighed. "I'm an engineer. Give me something broken and I'll fix it. People, no matter what species, are incomprehensible."

Tina sagged in her seat. "*Reggie* seems intact. Can we do the same thing again?"

"Nope." Quango tugged his goatee. "By my mother's twisted beard, I know this ship better than Reggie does. This is a class-D Striker. It's as solid a combat dropship as the Ipis ever built, but it'll be a while before the tracion generator will work again."

Lieutenant Wells ran onto the ship's bridge with a long-barrel ion disrupter slung over his shoulder. "What the hell just happened?"

Quango snorted. "We took a short trip. Unfortunately, it was too short."

Mara followed behind him, clutching an energy sword in one of her tentacles. The panel of her titanium shell was charred from disrupter hits. "Tina, I promised Beatrice to protect you, and I will." The robot settled in beside the pregnant woman, her lights blinking rapidly. "While I function, no harm will come to you."

"Thanks, Mara." Tina turned back to Quango. "Otheth's out there somewhere. Maybe she can help us."

"That idiot Roc *will* try something, but she doesn't have the forces to do much beyond getting her people killed." Quango gave Tina a long look. "I did receive one communication burst from Otheth before the tracion field scrambled everything. Dante's coming."

Tina exclaimed, "Dante's coming, thank God. That means the allied armada's here."

"I didn't say that." Quango looked at the decking. "The human ships are coming in *alone*. No Rocs, no Centaurs... no Satyrs."

Emma looked at Tina's stricken face. "What does all this mean? My brother's coming. That has to be a good thing. Right?"

Tears streamed down Tina's cheeks. "*Alone*. The human fleet is too small. It's pure desperation to attack the Ipis with what we have. It means our allies have deserted us. I think my husband is coming to die with us here." She hugged Emma and sobbed.

"Now, lass." Quango touched her arm. "The transmission Otheth sent was fairly distorted. I may not have gotten the facts straight. That man of yours is as levelheaded as anyone I've ever met. I'm sure he has a solid plan."

Lieutenant Wells absorbed the conversation and his last shreds of doubt about these strangers evaporated. "I don't know about this human monarch business, but if your husband is coming here to fight, there's many on this planet who'll join him."

Emma shouted, "Damn straight." She smiled at Tina. "I didn't find my brother, and his *family*, just to lose them again."

"Then all we can do is wait and see who reaches us first." Tina rose and hurried to the bay where the refugees were camped. Moisture glistened on her cheeks.

Chapter XXIX

Desperate Moves

Otheth's caravan of crawlers, motorcycles, and Border Patrol trucks reached the Niagara Falls Airport without incident. Only abandoned cars in the parking lot greeted them. She leaned out of the crawler's hatch and called to the motorcycle rider pulling up alongside. "Friend Rene, this facility is well suited for our drop ships. Search the area and report anything suspicious."

Rene snarled, "if it's all the same to you, if any of those *harpies* are around, we won't bother reporting them. We'll just kill them."

Otheth hopped to the ground and cawed. "Take care not to harm any of the indigenous people in your zeal."

Rene chortled. "No worries. I can *usually* tell a Yank from an alien." The bikes roared out across the tarmac. The policemen climbed out of the trucks and searched the terminal building.

Otheth called up to the crawler hatch, "Cheepash, get out here. Set up the remote scanning and communications station."

"Yes, Flock Leader."

Twenty minutes later, Rene rolled up to Otheth and gave her a sloppy salute. "No sign of any bad guys." He scratched his chin under his scraggly beard. "The place is deserted. There's not a single plane on the tarmac and nothing in the hangars except for one very mean mongrel dog."

Cheepash gave Otheth a worried look as he crouched beside the crate-sized communication beacon. "Flock Leader, I've transmitted the information about the human fleet's arrival to *Reggie*. But I'm not sure the transmission got through. There's some strange interference."

"The airport's clear," Rene said. "Now can we relax and wait for this Grand Pooh-Bah to show up on his golden chariot."

Otheth cocked her head. "Golden... chariot? I am not familiar with such a human conveyance. Is it—" Her eyes swung west. Flashes pulsed the pre-morning darkness. "What's that?"

The humans and Rocs watched the distant horizon glow.

"This is impossible." Cheepash hesitated. "The equipment indicates a starship is initiating a hyperspace jump on this planet's surface. It's coming from *Reggie's* location."

"Opening a tracion field on a planetary surface?" Otheth cawed. "Only someone desperate beyond all hope would attempt such a maneuver."

Rene, his eyes narrowed, moved beside Otheth. "Look. We can't reach them. There's a whole army of those gargoyles hopping around the Falls." He glanced at the ion disrupter the Roc had tucked under her left wing. "And they have a lot more of these nasty little toys than we do."

Otheth's tail feathers flared. "If we create a diversion—"

With a deafening roar and a blinding burst of light, the earth heaved, knocking everyone to the ground.

Cheepash clambered to his feet and gawked at his equipment. "I can't believe this. They really did it." He pointed south to a pillar of smoke rising in the air. "If there's anything left of their ship, it's now just over two miles from us." He scanned the digital map on his display. "By my ancestor's cracked eggs, they may have survived. I'm getting an energy signal."

Otheth's crest and tail feathers flared as she screamed the Roc war cry. "The human king's family is here. We are the *First* Order of the Dragon. Now we fulfill our scared vows and show the galaxy why that honor was bestowed on us." She pawed the ground. "Flash message this data to Dante. Tell him to hurry." She turned to Rene. "Now we must part ways. Await the king here. The path we Rocs will take can only end in death."

"That's idiotic," Rene sputtered. "Are you trying to get yourselves killed for nothing?"

"An interesting question, my friend. Rocs do not fear death, but we do not embrace it to demonstrate empty

207

bravado." Otheth's feathers flattened. "I do not intend my passing to be pointless. The human fleet will arrive in less than an hour, but unless we intervene, any survivors will be butchered before then. I cannot allow that to happen. I will buy them that precious time with my life."

Rene nodded. "You're willing to sacrifice yourself for your friends?" He took a shuddered breath. "Dammit. Your craziness must be rubbing off on me. I'm in too." Turning to the gathered bikers, his voice quivered. "Gilbert, when you get back to Canada, tell my folks that their boy finally did something to make them proud."

Gilbert's face flushed. "The hell with that. Count me in."

The bikers and police behind them, one at a time, and then in bunches, stepped forward. "We're in this together."

Otheth clicked her beak. "If you were a Roc, you truly would stand among the First Order. Your courage marks you as one of us."

Cheepash glanced in the direction of the column of smoke where the distinctive whine of ion disrupters could now be heard. "We must move." The big Roc glanced at his display. "Data has been sent, but I can't confirm successful reception."

"There is no more we can do for the fleet. This area's clear and they have the coordinates." Otheth glanced at the vacant airport and screeched. "Now I will make my flock proud."

"How will these people we're trying to rescue know we're the good guys?" Rene pulled his helmet off. "These crawlers we have look the same as the bad guys."

"I got an idea." Gilbert pulled an iPhone from his pocket. "Do those vehicles have a speaker system?"

"Of course." Cheepash craned his neck.

Gilbert made a selection and handed him the music player. "I have hours of bagpipe music loaded in here. There ain't no self-respecting alien monster who'd ever play that."

A few minutes later, two crawlers, forty motorcycles and two border patrol trucks sped down the I-190. Five Ipis warriors manning a roadblock died before realizing what was coming. Their stripped bodies were left on the slagged asphalt.

Otheth cawed on catching sight cf the downed Striker, its front end buried in the wall of a Walmart. The ship appeared intact, but hundreds of people were scrambling toward her on the Interstate. A small but determined rear guard was holding a large force of pursuing Ipis infantry at bay in the outlet mall's empty parking lot.

Otheth cawed at the sight of a familiar pregnant woman wearing an energy pack bandolier. Stumbling in her direction, Tina was leading the ragtag group of humans from the carnage. Many appeared injured. The Roc leader sprang from the crawler and ran. "I'm coming, Tina."

* * *

Many refugees screamed when they saw a pair of crawlers coming toward them but looked around in confusion on hearing bagpipes blaring *Amazing Grace* and seeing motorcycles and trucks rolling alongside the terrifying alien vehicles.

At the same moment, Tina spotted the familiar golden-brown Roc leap from the lead crawler. "Otheth," she cried and turned to the people behind her. "They're friends. Thank God, they're friends."

Although lame, Quango carried two little children, who clung to his neck. Several others crowded near him, whimpering. "No fear, wee ones. Those critters aren't as pretty as Satyrs, but they're good *people*." He picked up his pace.

He glanced over his shoulder at the increased tempo of the blasters behind them. "They'll help us, and not a moment too soon."

Tina embraced Otheth as she reached her. "You're crazy for coming here. There's a whole harpy army behind us." She stepped back and scanned the several dozen bikers and cops that passed them with their weapons leveled toward the raging battle. The two crawlers were already spitting plasma darts in that direction. "Did you bring many warriors?"

"Only what you see," Otheth warbled. "But Lord Dante will arrive soon. We must survive until then. This thoroughfare is open to the east for the moment."

Gilbert braked his Indian beside them and regarded Tina for a long second. "You must be the queen Otheth's been telling us about." He extended his hand. "Pleased to meet ya."

Tina gave Otheth a sidelong look. She sighed and shook his hand. "Tina Phokas. There's a lot of injured people here. Can you help?"

Gilbert's jaw clenched on noticing a cylinder-shaped robot and stocky, goateed man with hooves and horns hurrying past carrying children and the number of people being carried on stretchers. "We have a few trucks. But not nearly enough."

Tina watched the people shuffle by. "Evac the worst cases to the airport. Everyone else will have to walk."

A short distance away, Rene was herding the stream of refugees. "C'mon move," he shouted at the people shying away from the cluster of Rocs. "Stop acting like you never seen a Roc before. What are you, a bunch of bumpkins?"

A long-haired barrel-chested man on a motorcycle skidded to a stop by the group. He waved a sloppy salute at Otheth. "Ah, General. We gotta shitload of problems." He jerked his thumb over his shoulder. "A whole swarm of them alien assholes are coming along Military Road. Don't know how many, but more than our little band can handle."

"Otheth, more difficulties," Cheepash shouted over his crawler's transmitter. "Ipis aerial fighters are inbound."

The bagpipe music abruptly ended as one of their crawlers exploded.

Otheth's tail feathers fanned out as she scanned the sky. "Tina, we're cut off. Back to your ship."

"We can't." Tina's voice trembled. "*Reggie's* spewing radiation. His power core ruptured."

The refugees who walked past them a minute earlier lurched to a halt.

Quango ran to Tina, gasping. "Lassie, harpies ahead. That way is blocked." He added, "Mara, bless her, is fighting a whole company by herself."

Otheth took a deep breath. "Then we must open a path for you." She screeched, "Rocs to me," and sprinted toward Mara.

"This ain't going to be pretty." Gilbert gulped. "Wait for me." He kick-started his bike and raced after her.

They met a hundred of their foes a quarter mile away. The Rocs sang their war-song as they threw themselves at the harpies, but numbers matter. More harpies joined the fight. The Rocs fought in a desperate but losing frenzy.

An aerial fighter blasted the last remaining crawler, then targeted the other vehicles. Motorcycles, with riders still on them, vaporized. The counterattack collapsed.

Gilbert saw the pregnant woman directing the survivors into the vacant mall. People hurried through the glass doors to the dubious protection of the open shopping area. They had no place left to go. He ran to the smoldering crawler and looked inside, despite the heat from the slagged rear quarter. The biker spotted Cheepash, badly burned, still shouting into a communicator. "We gotta get you outta here. This damn machine is on fire."

Without waiting for an answer, Gilbert dragged the injured Roc from the wreckage to the makeshift safety of a burnt-out Chevy Malibu in the parking lot. The Canadian stared helplessly at Cheepash, whose left side looked like seared meat.

The Roc's right hand spasmed as he twisted a dial on a device he wore across his chest, gasping, "Mayday... Mayday... no time... being overrun." A garbled response came though the static, but no words could be discerned. Cheepash twisted his head to Gilbert. His voice rattled as blood trickled from his beak. "Please tell Otheth she was the only one I ever loved. I'm sorry I failed her."

Asphalt erupted from an ion beam a few feet away, showering the two with debris. "Tell her yourself." Gilbert scanned the battlefield. A company of harpies advanced toward them, unhindered.

211

Cheepash coughed more blood. "My friend, we have stood together against a great enemy. If you live, speak of my *cou* before the Grand Council on Tannis."

"You'll do it yourself." Gilbert hoisted the surprisingly light Roc in his arms and started jogging. "You can give me the grand tour of this Tannis place. We'll drink and tell each other war stories as long as you want." He got no response. Cheepash's head lolled against his chest.

The Canadian ran to the makeshift barricade of shopping carts, debris, and parked cars, along with dozens of other people. His breath was labored as he staggered between the neat rows of cars. The words he heard sent a chill down his spine. "We're surrounded." Hands lifted his burden from him. He saw Tina probing Cheepash's wounds and snapping orders. "He's still alive."

Otheth hovered beside the doctor, stroking Cheepash's scorched crest feathers. "Don't die. I order you not... to... die."

An American Army Lieutenant grabbed Gilbert's arm. "Get to the barricade. We need every gun we have."

Gilbert glanced at the officer's uniform and snapped. "Lieutenant Wells, what the hell do you think I've been doing all day?" He gave Cheepash a worried look, then spotted Rene crouched by a Toyota Rav4 and sprinted to his friend. "I guess our luck finally ran out." The whine of ion disrupters stopped. "What're the bastards waiting for?" he hissed while sneaking a peek around the car's bumper.

The harpies stopped shooting and halted their advance about a hundred feet from the humans' perimeter. Reggie's crew members, who had fought in the rear guard, and the civilians caught in the no-man's-land scrambled to the meager safety of the barricade. Hushed voices and wailing children inside the building were the only sounds heard.

"Who's that character?" Rene looked over the car's hood and pointed to an ornately garbed harpy standing atop the lip of the enormous trench *Reggie's* short trip created. The harpy was tapping a thickheaded staff on the ground and staring at the crude barricade and the building behind it.

In the distance Gilbert saw companies of crawlers and harpy ground troops hurrying to the already large force surrounding them. A dozen enemy aircraft wove through the sky above. "This ain't looking good."

The purple-sashed harpy strode forward from the line of Ipis warriors. The creature gnashed his fangs as he scanned the trapped people. Then, with an amplified voice, in barely comprehensible English, boomed, "Humans, bring the elves to me and your deaths will be quick and painless."

"Surrender the freaking elves?" Gilbert slumped against the side of the car. "Now what the hell do we do?"

Chapter XXX

A King Returns Home

"I guess we're ready as we're going to be." Dante rubbed sweaty palms on his pants. "Virgil, open the vid-link with our unit commanders."

Virgil gave a thumbs-up and flipped the switch, connecting all the ships in the human fleet.

Dante took a deep breath as dozens of faces popped onto the wide view screen on Virgil's command galley. Some had been with him since the beginning, like Cruz, Martinel, Gentile, and Virgil. Some had joined him during his imprisonment on Carcerem. Most were from the millions of Novaroman refugees who sought freedom from Ipis persecution on Cocytus.

He cherished them all. He knew many would be dead before the current crisis ended. He nodded to the many faces. "My friends, we're about to engage in a war with two possible outcomes. One is that the harpies finally exterminate humanity. Cocytus is no sanctuary. It'll be discovered by the harpies and destroyed, just like every other human world. What's being done to the Earth will be the fate of our home.

"However, there's a *second* possibility." Dante clenched his jaw. "Here in the Lethe Sector we live on the fringe of the Ipis empire with the Satyrs, Centaurs, and Rocs. If we can demonstrate that the harpies are not invincible, those species will join us. United, we have a chance to sue for peace with the Ipis galactic rulers." He pointed to the banner behind him, a flag with a raised red fist on a white background. Hanging from the wrist was a broken, black manacle. "The harpies have not faced the Novaroman flag for over a hundred and twenty years. We will carry it proudly as it was by your star-traveling ancestors. The harpies know that banner and fear it."

He swung his gaze to the blue planet on the galley's view screen. "The people on the Earth are primitive by galactic standards, but they are *us*. The Earth is the home world for *every* human. Their hopes and dreams are no different than ours." He squared his shoulders. "We are their only hope of survival, and they are *ours*." He sighed. "There's nothing else to say. You know the risks and your responsibilities. God bless you all. General Cruz, Admiral Martinel, any last comments?"

General Cruz stared at the tactical display screen before him for a long moment. "We have an opportunity. Silenus-dis is exposed. Our communication intercepts indicate he's personally leading the assault on our downed Striker. He's only got a single division and minimal air cover. If we lop off the head, it may cause some confusion to their command and control. The expeditionary force is mostly cult paramilitaries. They won't have the discipline of the regular imperial troops."

Admiral Martinel added, "The last report from Otheth has the Niagara Falls airport clear."

Cruz rubbed his jaw. "Then it's a go. We implement the plan worked out in the simulation. The First Division lands there and pushes west. The Second will establish a beachhead in Lewiston and drive south. The Third will land on Grand Island and work their way north. That's the hammer." He glanced to the man at his side. "General Gentile, you will be our anvil. Your Marine brigade will hold the Rainbow Bridge. The harpies will be pressed against the rapids, and we'll nail the sons-of-bitches there."

"I wish I could be there to see the look on that fanged monster's face when you get him." Martinel chuckled and then sobered. "I will punch through the harpies' scattered armada with my capital ships and form a dodecahedron around the Earth before they can reform and press their numerical advantage. Virgil will escort the troop dropships to the landing zones with the five Strikers and the galley squadrons. Remember people, surprise is our *only* advantage. Are you ready?"

A resounding "Yes, sir" echoed back.

"Then the die is cast. May God in his mercy be with us." Admiral Martinel nodded to the somber faces on the screen.

"We initiate plan One-C in ten minutes from my mark." He pressed a button on his chronometer. "*Mark.*"

* * *

It was Virgil's responsibility to lead the six squadrons of nimble galleys and five frigates tasked with punching a breech through the harpy ships in near-Earth orbit for the troop transports.

A moment after signing off from the commander's conference call, he initiated an audio link with his own small fleet. "Squadron commanders, we're going with plan One-C. The target area has been downloaded to your navigation systems. We're going in fast with guns blazing. Stop for nothing." He clicked off and glanced at his own crew in the small galley bridge. "You guys ready?"

Aramis called out, "Shields at one hundred percent."

Athos added, "Guns are locked and loaded. Let's kill some harpies."

Porthos checked his display. "Propulsion and navigation are good to go. Let's do it. My pop needs me."

Virgil twisted to the last member of his crew. "Dante, are you ready for what we'll find." He cleared his throat. "You realize that *everyone* onboard Reggie's Striker may be dead. Otheth's last transmission wasn't optimistic."

Dante's body stiffened. "Just get me there. Tina's alive. I feel it."

Virgil saw the anguish in his friend's eyes. His jaw tightened and he nodded.

A few minutes later, he felt the slight pressure of the real-space engines on the galley kick in. That action coincided with the fleet dropping their stealth screens. Hundreds of human vessels were now visible on his scanner.

Virgil's galley raced past the Moon with over a hundred small, agile galleys, five Strikers, and four dozen troop ships. He heard the first panicked warning broadcast by a harpy scout ship. "Bye-bye asshole," Virgil snarled as his convoy shot through the debris that was the enemy ship a second earlier. "Well, it looks like we caught them flatfooted, but the shock won't last."

Aramis glanced at his tactical display. "I bet the harpy admiral shitted in his pants. If he wore pants."

Virgil caught new motion on his scanner. "Damn, they reacted fast." He turned on his ship-to-ship communicator. "Bogies closing on our tail. Strikers, keep those bastards off our ass. Galleys, do not engage. Leave them for the big boys. Our job is to get these transports to the ground." He grunted with satisfaction as the galleys formed a protective cocoon around the troop ships.

"Sweet Jesus," Dante exclaimed. On the display screen, the galley on point erupted into a fireball. However, the four harpy picket ships, blocking their path, were blasted into dust by the following ships.

"Bogies closing on portside," Porthos called out as two galleys on the perimeter disintegrated.

Virgil shouted, "Full power to the shielding. Twelve minutes to atmosphere. They can't follow us there."

Two of the Strikers and four more galleys were lost to the swarming harpy attacks before the troop ship convoy reached the safety of Earth's atmosphere.

Virgil glanced across the cabin. "Porthos, how's Admiral Martinel faring?"

The young clone gave the thumbs-up. "They lost a couple of the Dragons, but the Juggernauts blasted apart everything those suckers had nearby."

"God damn, it worked. The harpies were so focused on counterattacking, they ignored Martinel shifting his fleet into the dead-man's blockade." Virgil's voice was steady as he spoke to his convoy of small vessels. "Folks, the capital ships are holding up their end. Now the clock is ticking. We have a month to make a difference."

General Cruz's face appeared on Virgil's private vid-link. "Here's the latest intel. We just picked up a garbled transmission from Otheth's team indicating that a group of our people from the damaged Striker, along with some local resistance, are in a one-sided fight with Silenus-dis' troops about two miles from the First Division's beachhead."

Cruz added, "I want your Strikers in a holding pattern above the landing areas. Jam all local transmissions, and make sure no nasty surprises smack my troops while they disembark."

"Aye, sir." Virgil transmitted the orders. "My galleys will clear the harpies' local air power, then I'll move them in tight to your ground forces for support."

"We're landing too far away," Dante snapped at Virgil across the cabin. "My wife's down there."

Porthos twisted his head to face Virgil. "Our pop's in that mess too."

Virgil bit his lip. "General Cruz, I'm taking my galley directly into the hot zone to coordinate with the local resistance."

"No way. You have Dante onboard. Use another galley. You'll be a magnet for every gun the harpies have," General Cruz ordered.

"That's the idea." Virgil snapped back. "The harpies only have a dozen single-seaters in theater; I have close to a hundred. I want the bastards bunched in nice and tight. It'll be a sweet, target-rich environment."

Cruz responded in a deliberate manner. "On the ground you'll be overrun before my boys can get to you."

"It doesn't matter," Dante shouted. "General, I don't know shit about running a military campaign. That's up to you and Admiral Martinel. I'm going in. Even if I have to jump out of this damn ship."

The general's voice softened. "Dante, you're our *leader*. I'll have no way to protect you. You're the only thing holding the alliance together."

Dante's voice became steel. "General, no one is safe in this freaking war. Not on Martinel's flagship or your headquarters. It's what I must do."

Cruz groaned. "Mister President, at least wear the prototype neural-net suit. It'll give you a little more protection."

"I already have it on," Dante responded.

The general gritted his teeth. "Virgil, please try to keep our fearless leader from doing anything even more crazy. I'll get the First Division to you as soon as I can."

"Roger that." Virgil cut the transmission and glanced at the three young clones. "This is going to be like old times."

"That bad?" Aramis focused on his screen. He saw a smoldering spaceship half buried in the side of a large building, with thousands of harpies surrounding a sprawling structure next to it. "This does *not* look good."

"Tina's in that trap." Dante magnified his scope, scanning the mall parking lot where armed humans were watching the massing host of enemies.

Porthos shook his head. "How come the harpies aren't attacking?"

Athos added, "I don't get it either. It's not in their DNA. Their normal action in a situation like this is to charge in with guns blazing and massacre everyone. I know that from my *training*. Yet they're just sitting back."

Aramis snapped his fingers. "Yeah, they don't take prisoners unless they want information. I bet those assholes think they found their first batch of elves."

Virgil slapped the arm of his chair. "Porthos, do those harpies on the ground know we're here yet?"

Porthos studied his instruments. "No, Cap'n. The communication jamming is in place. It'll be another minute or two before they realize what's going on."

"Then we have to get this bird down before then," Virgil barked as he pulled a heavy quad-barrel disrupter from the compartment under his seat. "The general said not to let Dante do anything crazy. He didn't say anything about me. Orient the ship's shielding to the front and dial it to the max."

"Aye, Cap'n." Athos gulped.

"While the harpies are shooting up the front of this ship, we'll duck out the rear hatch and make a run for our friends' position," Virgil replied as he guided the galley down.

Dante's hands shook as he realized what Virgil feared. "Once the harpies realize they're under attack, they'll blast the enemy they have cornered before facing the new threat.

Tina will be dead before our troops can get there." He checked the power charge on his long-barrel ion disrupter.

Aramis shouldered his own weapon and grabbed the flag hanging on the wall. "The freaking harpies need to know who they're fighting."

Virgil snapped into the support fleet's audio link. "Give 'em hell. I'm going in." His galley hit the ground hard, but he was out of his seat, running for the exit, before the galley had stopped rocking. "Come on, ladies. It's showtime."

They raced out the hatch and were halfway to the human barricades before the first blasts hit the front of the grounded galley.

* * *

Silenus-dis keened a wailing screech at the sight of a single galley landing a hundred feet in front of the barricaded structure. Snarling, he saw the banner being carried by the five racing crew members from that human ship. He had seen it before in historical vids. "The elves are attempting a rescue. Destroy their vessel."

Guns from crawlers and numerous small arms focused on the galley. It erupted in a fireball moments later. As Silenus-dis hissed his satisfaction, the ground shook with thunderous sonic booms. Surprised ground troops on both sides stared up as spaceships filled the sky, spaceships emblazoned with the red fist symbol of the extinct Novaroman humans.

His scream took on a panicked edge as he saw the wreckage of his own small group of airships tumble from the sky. "The legends are true. The ancient enemy is real."

He turned to his communications officer. "Order all available aircraft to this location. We need support. *Now.*"

A second later, the aide went wide-eyed. "Master, all frequencies are jammed. I cannot raise the fleet or any ground commanders."

The governor snarled at his subordinates. "The elves have revealed themselves. The humans here are no longer of value. Kill them." He raised his ivory-colored staff and his army moved forward toward the makeshift human fortification.

Chapter XXXI

Reunion

Heedless of the ion blasts flashing around him, Dante scrambled over the barricade of overturned shopping carts. Armed people rushed past him to the barricade to face the full-scale attack. Frantic, he looked for Tina among the hurrying people.

Mara found him and answered his question before he asked by pointing to the Hobby Lobby about a hundred yards east of them. "Your mate is in the triage area, tending the wounded." Her lights blinked. "You must rectify this situation. Humans are dying and I cannot stop it. We are being overrun."

Dante glanced longingly toward the field hospital, then shoved his long gun into the hands of a woman limping past him in that direction. Her hair was wild and the leather vest she wore was seared. "Take this. Protect the wounded."

Nodding, the woman gripped the weapon, "That I will," and staggered on to the Hobby Lobby.

Choking on the acrid smoke-filled air, Dante scanned the perimeter and thought the fighting seemed most intense near *Reggie's* ruined stern. He sprinted there, pulling the laser pistol from his belt and powering on his energy blade. Lifting the sword, he glanced at Mara gliding at his side. "Beatrice made this for me when I first met her."

"Beatrice was with you then," Mara responded, "and I'll be with you today."

Dante stumbled into her as a gout of debris shot into the air beside him from an ion blast. Recovering his balance, he screamed his rage and broke into a run. Virgil and the three clones raced with him. The whine of energy weapons was intense near the human frigate's stern. The ship's crew was heavily engaged with a large force of harpies. A new smell assailed his nostrils: the stench of burnt flesh.

Dante spotted Otheth and two other Rocs with a band of leather-clad humans exchanging fire with a company of harpies. He ran there and dove behind a mound of broken concrete beside the Roc.

Otheth, her feathers fully flared, gasped, "Your Majesty, Silenus-dis is personally leading the assault. We can't hold much longer. Where's your army?"

The ground shook. Row after row of galleys appeared above them, strafing the harpy ground troops and crawlers. Silenus-dis stood atop a mound of debris staring, slack-jawed, at the squadrons of galleys.

Otheth keened with joy. "Galleys aren't built for ground support, but I'll take it."

Many harpies fell back along the channel *Reggie* plowed earlier in the ship's ill-fated escape attempt, partially shielding them from the aerial assault.

Dante seethed. He pointed to the exposed harpy leader. Only a small company of bodyguards remained. "There's the serpent's head without an army wrapped around him."

Screeching into his comm-link attached to his head gear, the sector governor sounded agitated. His attendants stared at the sky in apparent disbelief.

"Cover me. They're in shock. We may never have this chance to get him again." Dante dashed from the cover toward the Ipis leader.

Otheth screeched, "Stay here. I'll do it."

Dante never paused.

"To the king," Otheth cawed as she and her remaining Rocs ran after him. Virgil and the three clones followed. With a shout, *Reggie's* crew and the band of bikers scrambled after them.

The Ipis leader's personal guards moved to block the assault. Gouts of asphalt and concrete sprayed around Dante as he led the charge toward his nemesis.

The two opposing forces slammed into each other. In those close quarters, swords and clubs fought against fang and claw. A snarling harpy non-comm leapt at the running Dante. The human leader fired his laser pistol at point blank range, disintegrating his assailant's head. Tripping over the twitching corpse, he found himself face-to-face with Silenus-dis.

The sector governor, wearing the full regalia of his high office—a burgundy crystal helmet, a silver medallion embedded with a starburst ebony stone, and a violet sash—glared directly at his human nemesis.

Dante heard the harpy's distinctive screech, "The elf king is here. Kill him." But no one heeded his command. All his nearby troops were dead or fleeing from the onslaught. The surging humans had overwhelmed the outnumbered harpies. Dante charged at Silenus-dis, firing his laser pistol. It had no effect. The Lethe Sector governor's high-grade body armor absorbed the beam.

With catlike quickness, the harpy snarled and sprang, brandishing his power staff.

Dante met the blow with his energy blade. The two weapons sparked as they slid off each other and made contact with the shielding. Both fighters' melee weapons overloaded at the contact and shut down.

The Lethe Sector governor reacted first. He swung his broad-headed staff and connected with Dante's left arm.

Dante's neural-net suit prevented the weapon from penetrating but not the impact from the heavy blow. He staggered backward with a numb arm.

Silenus-dis saw opportunity and sprang.

Instinctively, Dante stepped aside and jabbed with his unpowered blade. The razor-sharp plexo-steel bit deep. He twisted the sword as he yanked it out.

Silenus-dis gaped in disbelief at the spurting blood and exposed entrails.

Dante swung the blade and sliced through Silenus-dis' neck. The harpy leader's head flopped to the ground a full second before the dead body fell, his expression frozen with disbelief.

Dante had no time to savor the small triumph. A battalion of harpies had regrouped and were pressing the humans' perimeter to his right. Galleys buzzed overhead, unable to target enemies so close to their own people.

Mara, badly charred, wailed, "Dante, it hasn't stopped. Humans are still dying."

Dante snapped, "Mara, get through to General Cruz and inform him of the harpy leader's death. Their chain of command is disrupted. They'll be disorganized and slow to react. He *must* hit them now before they can recover." He scanned Silenus-dis' corpse and his mouth twitched into a half grin. "I have one more card to play."

"This is no time for a card game," Mara squeaked.

"I'll explain later," Dante gasped as he tore the communicator from Silenus-dis' burgundy crystal helmet. He saw Virgil and the three clones obliterate an old Dodge Caravan shielding a pair of harpies. Aramis still bore the red-fist banner. "Aramis, bring that flag here."

Virgil limped over with the clone, blood seeping from a shallow cut on his face. "What're you doing? You'll get shot. Get down, you idiot." He scanned the area, but there were no living harpy fighters nearby.

"I spent years studying the Ipis. I'm going to make a little announcement." Dante's voice shook as he saw the many dead strewn across the churned asphalt around him. Not all the bodies were harpies.

Mara announced, "General Cruz landed unopposed. His vanguard is already deploying."

Dante adjusted the harpy communicator. "Be ready. This will either scare the hell out of them or enrage them." He cleared his throat. "Here goes."

Aramis raised the flag, fluttering in the autumn breeze thick with the smoke of burning cars.

Dante set the communicator to a broadcast frequency and took a deep breath. He shouted in human-accented Ipis, "We are a free people. We know no masters." He pointed the sword toward the rippling banner. "We *are* your ancient enemy. Depart or perish!"

The harpy counterattack stalled at the sound of the strange, commanding voice in their comm-links. Those near the ruins of *Reggie's* tail section gasped on seeing the legendary human banner waving.

As the fighting paused, a rumbling sound grew louder from the north.

Motorized advance units of the Cocytus forces roared into view. The two-man, wedge-shaped battle wagons were roughly the size of SUVs and constructed with hardened plexo-steel. Riding on oversized tires, each possessed a single large-bore ion disrupter mounted in a small turret. Hundreds of the nimble combat vehicles roared into view, overwhelming the unprepared harpy flank.

Within minutes, the Ipis assault evaporated as they were pummeled from both the air and the ground.

On the broadcast communicator, Dante snapped, "Surrender now or die."

Singly, and then in larger groups, harpies with an avenue of escape fled west, their officers unable stem the rout.

Cult theology was deeply ingrained across the psyche of Ipis society. Those Ipis-dis adherents, cut off and facing their mythical ancient enemy, prostrated themselves on the ground. Those from the Ipis-ma sect, unable to comprehend defeat at the hands of barbarous primates, used their disrupters to immolate themselves.

Minutes later, the main force of the Cocytus infantry arrived and the battlefield was swept of all remaining resistance. The human force pressed west after the retreating harpies.

The decimated mall parking lot filled with raw cheers from the surviving human defenders.

Dante saw a couple companies of soldiers, *his soldiers*, taking charge of the surrendering harpies. Grimacing, he threw down the comm-link. *I'm not needed here anymore.* With his left arm hanging limp at his side, he staggered toward the Hobby-Lobby where the makeshift field hospital was set up. *Tina's there.*

Mara glided ahead of him, and the three young clones trailed behind, scanning for trouble.

Virgil strode at his side. "Boss, you did good today. Real good. But now we got to take care of that arm of yours."

"Not until I see Tina and know she's all right." Dante stumbled around a burnt-out tour bus and spotted her. She was in the parking lot, directing the triage. A mismatched group of careworn-looking people leapt at her commands.

As if by instinct, she looked over and their eyes met. Dante saw her hand go to her mouth. The very pregnant woman cried his name and ran to him. All the aides with her looked up at her outburst.

His good arm outstretched, Dante stumbled toward his wife. "Tina," he cried, his chin quivering.

On reaching him, Tina paused. "Oh my God, you're hurt."

"Nothing a little time in a stasis pod can't fix." Dante crushed her to him with his good right arm. "Are you and the baby okay?"

She pressed against him, sobbing. "Now that you're here, we are." Their lips met in a long kiss.

He felt a flutter against his chest where he leaned on her. The pain in his arm was nothing compared to the rush of joy. He shook as he clung to her. "I love you."

Tina pushed him back and glared at the grinning Virgil. "I thought you were supposed to protect him."

Virgil blanched. "You know your man. When he's focused on something, no one can get in his way. He was coming to you even if the whole harpy empire was in the way."

"If I—"

Otheth approached flapping her undersized wings and hooting a Roc victory anthem. A group of armed, leather-clad people followed her. "Wild Turkeys, this is Dante Carloman, the king of all humans."

A smile creased Dante's face. "Good to see you, old friend, but it's too early to sing of victories." He turned to Mara. "Inform General Cruz we'll set up headquarters in what's left of that shopping mall."

The android noted the building. "As you command."

"Thanks." Dante sighed. He faced the three young clones. "You understand how the Ipis think better than anyone. Take charge of the prisoners. Get whatever intel you can squeeze out while they're still disoriented."

"Yes, Your Majesty," they responded in unison and strode to where a couple hundred harpies crouched on the ground, their clawed hands encircling their own necks, the

Ipis display of submission. The captives were surrounded by a company of glaring soldiers.

Rene and Gilbert gawked at Dante, who returned their quizzical stares. "Yeah, what?"

Rene frowned. "I thought you'd be a bit... grander looking."

Gilbert shrugged. "I thought you'd look more exotic, like in the movies. I have Carhartt overalls with more bling than that jumpsuit you're wearing."

Dante chuckled but didn't have time to respond. The crowd of bikers parted as a lithe young woman raced through them shouting, "Get out of my way!" He lost his balance as she threw herself at him.

Dante blinked as the years vanished. "Emma?"

She clung to him. "It's *you*! It's really *you*!"

He winced in pain but returned the fierce hug, then gently pushed her back. "Let me look at you." The awkward high-school girl he'd known looked up at him through a woman's face.

A moment later he was the big brother again. "When did you get all these tattoos? Mom and Dad must be pissed."

Emma's voice quivered as she regarded his injury. "Are you okay?"

"I'm fine. Arm's kinda numb. I think something's broken." Dante stroked her cheek. "How're Mom and Dad?"

"Dad died two years ago. A heart attack. With you and Dad gone, Mom stopped caring, and I was mad at the world."

"Dad's *dead*?" Years of memories rushed through Dante, and he wiped her damp cheek with a gentle caress. "There's so much I lost. There's so much we all lost."

Tina rubbed his back. "I got to know Emma. She's an incredible person... like her brother."

The bikers stepped back as a rawboned man, wearing lieutenant bars on a singed Army Ranger uniform pushed his way into the crowded circle. "Emma?"

She smiled and squeezed his calloused hand. "Herb, there's someone special I want you to meet."

Dante noticed the ion disrupter slung over his shoulder and the torn bandolier empty of power cartridges. He gave

Emma a quizzical look, and she returned her secret smile that she only used for her brother. "Dante, this is Lieutenant Wells. Herb, this is my brother Dante. He's the King of the World, or something like that."

Dante extended his hand. "Pleased to meet you."

Herb glanced at the companies of human troops moving across the ravaged battlefield. He shook Dante's hand with an iron grip, tears welling in his eyes. "I don't know how much longer we could have held out. You're an answer to our prayers... to the world's prayers."

Dante glanced at the late-morning sun and then at the packed field hospital. Many of the injured were lying unattended in the parking lot. "This is only the first skirmish. There's still a long war ahead of us." He released his grip and turned to Tina. "Get the wounded to the stasis pods on General Cruz's landing craft." He called to Mara, "Inform the general to get medical transports here. There's a lot of causalities needing proper medical attention."

"Yes, my maker."

"And that includes you," Tina exclaimed. "That arm needs fixing. General Cruz can handle this war without *you* for a while."

Dante shook his head. "No time. We need to be rolling by morning." With the adrenaline rush fading, the arm pain made his head spin. His knees buckled. Many hands held him up.

Chapter XXXII

First Step to Union

"How're you feeling?" Tina helped Dante out of the stasis pod.

Naked and shivering in the infirmary's cool temperature, Dante rolled his left arm. "It feels tingly." He looked around noting he was in *Reggie's* medical bay. The nine other stasis pods glowed iridescent green showing the millions of nano-restorative robots were working on the patients within.

"Are my clothes around anywhere? I'm freezing."

She bit her lip. "Your suit was cut off you. I threw it out." She grabbed a fresh suit from beneath the pod and handed it to him. "Try not to put too many holes in this one. I want my husband in one piece."

Dante donned the neural-net suit. "How long was I out?"

She fingered his disheveled hair. "Twenty-four hours. There were multiple fractures in your forearm and a lot of muscle damage. The pod mended most of the bone and tissue. Nature will finish the process. But nothing strenuous for the next few days."

He stroked her cheeks on seeing her drawn look and the bags under her eyes. "When was the last time *you* slept? This isn't good for either you or the baby."

A wan smile creased her face. "My feet are killing me, and I think the baby's dancing on my bladder." She pecked his cheek. "But now that you're up, I'll get some rest. I promise."

Dante glanced at the floor. The normally pristine area was stacked with crates of medical supplies. "I need details on how the battle went. Have you seen my weapons?"

"Beyond the fact that we won?"

"Yeah, a little more info than that."

"Here." She retrieved a class-five ion disrupter and a bandolier filled with energy clips from where they lay against the bulkhead and handed them to her husband. "Aramis borrowed your sword and laser pistol—something about impressing the Dis cult prisoners regarding your duel with Silenus-dis." She pressed her hands on the small of her back and chuckled. "I need a spa day. My back's killing me." She tapped her communicator. "Hey, Virg, Dante's up. Try to keep him out of trouble for a while."

Dante gave his wife a quizzical look.

"I kept the wolves at bay for as long as I could. You needed the healing time." She sighed. "But a group of soldiers showed up while you were out. General Cruz managed to prevent any shooting, but he wants you there to negotiate with the American general."

Virgil bounded into the infirmary. "C'mon, boss, we need you now. Everyone's on a hair trigger."

Dante wrapped his arms around his wife and kissed her. "I'll see you later."

She met his lips with passion. "You better."

Dante sighed as he released the hold he had on his wife and turned toward Virgil. "Give me the lowdown."

Virgil set his jaw. "Our plan didn't work as well as expected. The harpies had a full battalion of heavy armor dug in on the Canadian side of the river, preventing our galleys from getting close. The retreating Ipis chewed our troops blocking the bridges to pieces. They escaped in the harpy transports parked by the artillery. Joe Gentile's in critical condition."

"Joe's hurt?" Dante strode to the exit with Virgil at his side. "Peyago, Caccina died on Goat Island... Not many from our original band left."

Virgil nodded. "We're going to lose a lot more friends before this nightmare ends. But we took out close to a division of their best troops. That's a start." He glanced at Tina. "I promise to keep an eye on him."

"*Nothing* strenuous. Do you hear me?" Tina frowned. "He's fine for now, but he'll tire quickly." She glared at her husband. "No more brawls with harpy potentates."

A sheepish grin creased Dante's face. "I'll try." He glanced at Virgil. "Let's go."

"Come on then." Virgil led him out of *Reggie's* infirmary and down a passageway bustling with repair crews.

Dante paused as Cocytus medics rushed past them, pushing a gurney bearing an unconscious woman. She was covered with a bloodstained sheet, and the charred remnants of a Mountie uniform lay folded atop her feet. *It wasn't only our people who suffered yesterday.* He jogged to catch up with Virgil. "Where are we going?"

Virgil slowed as they exited the frigate. "There's a big confab going on." He pointed to the outlet mall. "We need you there. While you were in sleepy-by land, the American Fourth Cavalry Brigade out of Fort Knox showed up. General Cruz is trying to convince their commander, a General Shanks, to throw in with us. But persuading a nervous brigadier general that we're on the same side is proving to be a bit problematic."

The western horizon glowed pink as the autumn sun set. However, the parking lot was bright from the glare of scores of humming klieg lights shining on *Reggie*. In the light, Dante saw Quango's elongated silhouette and heard the Satyr's hoarse voice shouting at someone near the ship bulwark. The rubble of the Walmart that encased its prow had already been cleared.

Dante pursed his lips as they crossed the parking lot that was choked with plexo-shelters, stacked supplies, and his soldiers. "Word of our victory and Silenus-dis' death will spread. The harpies aren't used to losing. It'll shake them."

He glanced toward the Hobby-Lobby as they passed and saw Otheth sitting near an overturned crate with a group of leather-jacketed humans and the band of Rocs who pledged themselves to him during his imprisonment on Carcerem. "Wait a second, Virg." Dante hurried over to his Roc friend. "Otheth, I heard about Cheepash. How's he doing?"

Otheth laid down the playing cards she held, rose, and flared her crest feathers. "He lost a wing." She bowed to the men sitting at the makeshift table. They were smoking thick bongs and holding half-empty bottles of Jack Daniels. "But my beloved will survive because of the efforts of Gilbert and Rene during the battle. I am in their debt."

Gilbert's face flushed. "I ain't no damn hero, but I wasn't going to let him burn to death"

Rene glanced at the face-up cards Otheth laid down and smiled. "Ah..., Your Majesty. Do you play Texas hold 'em? Otheth's not too good at it. Her tail feathers fan out whenever she has a good hand."

Dante chuckled. "Thanks for the offer, but I'm a little busy now. I'll take a rain check." He shook his head. "I may be in charge for the moment, but forget about the 'your majesty' business. The name's Dante Carloman. When you see me with a crown and scepter, you can use the royalty lines."

Virgil snapped, "Ah, boss, speaking of being in charge, we got to *go*," and started walking away.

Dante nodded and jogged after his friend. As he caught up, his mind turned to the enemy. "We must strike fast, but we don't have the numbers. We need the Americans."

"Agreed." Virgil nodded his head vigorously as he lengthened his stride. "There's a big column of harpies out in the open south of here. They were apparently marching this way, got as far as the outskirts of Pittsburgh, and then stopped. They're being led by none other than our *buddy*, Keres-ma. Cruz thinks our old jailer caught wind of what happened here and will hightail it back to his base on the east coast. We're tracking them."

As they neared the glass double doors beneath a sign that read "Saks Outlet," Dante asked, "Any American troops in the area besides the brigade here?"

"Oh... just a few." Vigil smirked. "Our reconnaissance indicates that about two hundred thousand troops are swarming through the mountains of New York, Pennsylvania, and Maryland." As they entered the building, he added, "Cruz suspects the Americans are marshaling everything they have for one last desperate strike."

"With what? They don't have any weaponry to take on a modern galactic army." He gasped, only half noticing the mannequins and display counters shoved to the side. He saw rows of grim men and women in beige neural-net suits sitting at desks, speaking into radio phones, and working computers.

Dante followed Virgil along the mall hallway to another store. The sign above the entrance was labeled "Macy's." A squad of Cocytus guards greeted him with sharp salutes. However, his people weren't the only ones present. Near a jewelry display stood a platoon of heavily armed soldiers wearing green American camo-gear holding their M-4s at the ready. The two groups stared at each other with a blend of curiosity and wariness.

He tensed as the Americans eyed him. He saw them pointing and exchanging hushed comments. *So much suspicion and fear. How do I reach them? There's so little time.*

As Dante walked closer, an American with close-cropped steel-gray hair, wearing sergeant-major stripes, handed another soldier his gun. The soldier attempted to approach, but a Cocytus guard blocked his path. He growled some words, showed his empty hands, and elbowed his way past. The guard followed with an ion disrupter trained on the American's back. The non-comm glanced at Virgil, then studied Dante with a raptor's glare. "I'm told that you're the guy who's going to rule the world. I thought you'd be ten feet tall."

Dante paused and smiled. "I left my platform shoes back at my opulent palace." He sighed. "I'm truly sorry, Sarge. I know what you devoted your life to protect, but that world is *gone.*" He raised his voice for the other soldiers to hear. "What we're fighting for now is our survival as a species. Will you help or hinder us?" He calmly met the senior non-comm's glare even though sweat beaded inside his neural-net suit. He felt like he was under a microscope as the hardened soldier studied him.

The old warrior shook his head. "We rolled in at the tail end of your battle with those alien monsters. The world's become a living nightmare, but you beat them. You actually beat the shit out of them." His eyes softened as he squeezed Dante's hand in a vise-like grip. "God bless you, son. We've been getting our ass kicked 'til now. I'm with you." He turned around. "This way." Snarling at the Cocytus soldier tailing him, he led Dante and Virgil to a curtained-off area that once sold fashionable shoes. "The Brigadier's waiting for you."

Dante gave a curt nod to the small group of officers sitting together at a long display case covered with paper maps. He returned the salute General Cruz and his staff gave him.

Virgil headed for the back wall where coffee was brewing.

Besides a squad of nervous-looking guards, three agitated American officers were present.

Dante approached the one with a star on his shoulder. He knew from Virgil's earlier description who he was and extended his hand. "General Shanks, Dante Carloman. Pleased to meet you."

The general looked at the hand as if it were a viper. "How can I shake your hand? If we ally ourselves with you and win this war, we still lose. Our way of life will be gone."

Dante lowered his hand and scowled. "Let me tell you then what you *are* fighting for. On one hand, an alien species is determined to eradicate everything human in the galaxy." He pointed to his chest. "On the other hand, you have me. I grew up less than a hundred miles from where we now stand." He tapped the display counter. "I've been a prisoner in a harpy death camp, and I swear I'm doing my damnedest to ensure humanity does not go the way of the dinosaurs."

Dante slouched into a chair by the map table and sighed. "You're right, however. Your way of life is gone. The Earth will *never* be able to return to what it was. That genie can't be shoved back into the bottle. Like it or not, you are now members of the galactic community. If the harpies win, you, your children, and your children's children will be hunted into extinction. Under me, you'll be members of a federation of free races living on the fringe of the harpy empire. I won't sugarcoat it. Those are the *only* alternatives."

The Brigadier pointed at the disrupter hanging over Dante's shoulder. "Look, sonny, we don't need you. Give us those fancy toys of yours and step back. We have professional soldiers to run this war. You can advise us. *We'll* do the rest."

"You still don't have the slightest concept of what you're dealing with here," Dante snapped. "I've been fighting these monsters for almost seven years. We have no time. As we speak, there's a harpy armada buzzing around this planet. The only thing keeping them at bay is a couple dozen of my warships." He took a deep breath. "That blockade breaks down in about a month. If we don't have a solution by then, it's over for all of us."

The general's eyes narrowed. "That's a convenient story. How do I know any of that is true?"

Virgil walked up and handed Dante a cup of coffee. "Officers," he snorted. "That's why I stayed a sergeant when I was in the Air Force." He jabbed a finger at Shanks. "All you need is a low-grade telescope to check that out."

Lieutenant Wells, who was watching the discussion from along the back wall stepped forward. "General Shanks, permission to speak."

The general nodded. "What do you have to say, Wells?"

"General, you've seen my report. My unit was embedded with these folks from the initial stages of this battle. I cannot overemphasize the courage and heroism I saw displayed. They saved over a thousand refugees, plus my people, from the harpies." He nodded to Dante. "I would trust these people even if they held a knife to my throat."

The general's face sagged. "I read your report... thoroughly."

"Sir, we've been fighting the aliens for weeks now. We both know that's a fight we can't win."

Dante leaned forward. "I need the full commitment of every man and woman who can bear arms on this planet, or the dreams we have for *our* children will be nothing more than dust."

The square-jawed brigadier's face turned ashen. Dante felt himself being studied for the second time within minutes but knew from the defeated look in the man's eyes that he had won this round. The general glanced at the gray-haired sergeant. "Mac, you've seen their troops up close. Do you have anything to add?"

The senior non-comm spread his hands. "General Shanks, it's not like we have many other choices." He regarded Dante. "I've been leading fighting men my whole life. We could do... a whole lot worse."

"That's the truth." Shanks nodded while extending his hand to Dante. "However, the request you're making is way above my pay grade. I need to contact the President."

As they shook, Dante felt some of his own anxiety begin to slip away. He smiled. "I'll speak with President Jordan personally. Washington's been evacuated. Where is he?"

"President Jordan? He was voted out of office three years ago. It's President Elizabeth Stevenson now." He studied Dante. "After the fiasco in Italy, all the cover-up about the alien raids became public. He lost his re-election bid in a landslide."

Dante sipped the hot coffee. "Virgil, give the Brigadier a hyper-link into their *secure* communication system so he can speak with his president." He turned to General Cruz. "We'll use this area as our base of operation. I understand that my old *friend*, Keres-ma leads their nearest army. Now let's get our troops to the front. Gentlemen, we need to bloody his nose."

Cruz glanced at a computer pad he held. "Our communication intercepts indicate that the American resistance is being coordinated out of Camp David. I suspect that is where you'll find the American President."

"Then that's where I'm going." He glanced at General Shanks. "They'll need time to prepare for my visit." He glanced at the chronometer attached to his suit. "Tell the President I'll meet with her at eight in the morning."

"You can't dictate to the President and barge in on her uninvited," Shanks sputtered. "That's a secure location. I don't even know if that's where she is."

Cruz glanced up from his pad. "Camp David is the nexus of all the encrypted communications. She's there."

Dante added, "General Shanks, there aren't *any* secure locations left on this planet, and I will talk to her." He shook his head. "Sorry, I don't have time... *we* don't have time for diplomatic niceties. She has one night to prepare."

Cruz held out a communicator. "We're already patched into their command center network."

The brigadier general's hand shook as he took the communicator. He stuttered as he heard a wary voice on the other end rasp, "Who is this? How did you get on this line?"

Shanks cleared his throat. "This is Brigadier General Shanks of the Fourth Division. I need to speak to the President..."

An hour later, Dante staggered to his feet. All of his body's energy was sapped by the healing process he'd been through. He rose and walked to the curtained exit. "I'm going to find some food and get a little sleep."

Virgil, Lieutenant Wells, and the American sergeant followed him out.

Dante paused as he saw the two groups of guards still squared off with each other. "If this union is going to hold, we need to start trusting each other." He turned to the American. "Mac, is it?"

"Yes, sir."

Dante unstrapped his disrupter and removed his bandolier, handing them to the sergeant. "These are yours now." He turned to Virgil. "See that these men are armed with real weapons and taught how to use them."

A small smile creased Virgil's face. "You got it, boss."

As Dante staggered away on leaden legs, he heard Virgil bark is his best drill-sergeant voice, "Gather round. Lieutenant Wells will demonstrate the care and use of modern weaponry. Pay attention. I won't repeat myself."

As the platoon of Americans crowded forward, Virgil held up his gun for all to see. "This is a class-five ion disrupter. It is the preferred antipersonnel weapon of the galaxy's human armies. It is superior to what the harpies on this planet are using in both range and throw-weight. The clips..."

238

Chapter XXXIII

Conversation at Camp David

While Dante slept, General Cruz worked all night negotiating the face-to-face meeting with President Elizabeth Stevenson. Late into the night, no agreement could be reached, then abruptly at 5:07 A.M., he received word that President Stevenson would meet with Dante that morning. He sagged into his chair and uttered a soft, "Thank God."

He rose to his feet and turned to Mara, who had provided him data through the talks. "It's been a long, long day. I'm going to wake Dante and sack out. Work out the meeting logistics."

Although he'd only had six hours' rest, Dante sprang from the makeshift cot tucked in the corner of the Men's department in the Macy's Outlet.

General Cruz nodded to Dante's "Thank you" and collapsed onto the cot just vacated.

Dante roused Virgil, who was snoring atop a pile of overcoats across the aisle. "Nap time's over. We got work to do."

Virgil opened one eye and groaned. "Time to save humanity again?"

Dante was already jogging to the temporary communications center set up in the women's shoes section.

Virgil caught up to him there where they listened in on Mara's discussions without participating.

A half hour later, the terms were agreed to. Dante would meet with the President at 8:00 A.M. He was to come alone except for his "flying saucer" transport and small security escort.

"I don't like this small escort business. What if they're planning some mischief?" Virgil grumbled.

Dante rubbed his jaw. "With my neural-net suit on, they don't have anything that could hurt me immediately. Just keep a squadron of galleys in the area in case I need to be extracted in a hurry."

"Okay," Virgil growled. "But I'm personally leading your security team."

"We have to be careful who we select as guards. Showing up in a 'flying saucer' will be enough of a shock. The crew needs to be human and conversant in English."

Virgil rubbed his jaw. "That really limits the choices. I'll bring Athos, Aramis, and Porthos. They speak a number of languages and are helluva good scrappers." He pursed his lips. "I could gather up a few soldiers who were abducted from the Earth the same day we were to fill out the team."

Dante nodded. "That would be perfect. Gather your team and requisition a galley."

* * *

The galley set down on Camp David's manicured lawn at 7:30 A.M. The landing spot was immediately surrounded by three Abrams tanks and an infantry company.

Virgil snarled, "Not a whole lot of trust here."

Dante unstrapped himself from the ship's seat and rose. "If the situation was reversed, what would you do?"

Virgil stood and slung a class-five ion disrupter over his shoulder. He snorted. "Hell, if it was me, I'd have a whole battalion." He turned to his assembled team. "It's going to be tense out there. I don't want a battle starting over a misunderstanding, but be prepared to defend yourselves. Do not react to any provocation unless I do. Your shielding will stop M-4 rounds."

Dante opened the exit and turned to his team. "We need them on *our* side. *Humanity* needs to stand together if we're to have any hope in this war." He took a deep breath and stepped onto the ramp. "It's showtime." He led his small procession out.

Walking beside him, Virgil cracked a lopsided grin. "Yeah, no pressure. The fate of humanity hangs by a thread, and those poor bastards out there don't have a clue about what's going on."

A grim-faced major was waiting at the foot of the ramp.

Dante nodded to him and cleared his throat. "Take me to your leader." He groaned when the officer just stared at him bug-eyed and never got the joke.

"This way, sir," was the soldier's brusque reply. He led Dante to an expansive porch attached to a large cedar-shingled cabin. Two marines in combat gear stood at attention beside the cabin's door.

Dante noted that the wide picture window was reflective and smiled at it. *One-way glass.* The only furnishings on that veranda were a lone plank table surrounded by six Adirondack chairs. The table was set for four guests. A coffee urn and a pitcher of iced tea sat in the center along with a creamer and sugar bowl.

Three settings were on one side and one was on the other. Dante moved to the separate chair. "I'm guessing this is my place."

"Yes, sir."

Dante sat and poured himself a cup of coffee and added cream and sugar to it. Although he usually drank his coffee black, he hadn't had real cream or sugar in over seven years.

Mara, who was inside the galley monitoring the area, scanned the beverage and spoke to Dante through his neural-net-suit's ear bud. "It is safe to consume. There are no unexpected chemicals present."

"Thanks, Mara." Dante responded.

The American major's eyes narrowed at hearing Dante speaking but said nothing.

Dante took a deep breath of the morning autumn air as he settled into the Adirondack chair and sipped his coffee. He tensed on detecting new motion.

What made him sweat was the small group walking toward him from the woods along a gravel trail. *She's coming. My gambit must work. The fate of the human race depends on reaching an agreement.*

He stood as the three people climbed the four steps onto the porch. One was a middle-aged woman. Her face was drawn, but a look of fiery resolve lit her eyes. Beside her came a senior officer with four stars on his shoulder and an elderly, bald man with long gray wisps fringing his ears.

Dante did a double take on the last individual, recognizing him as his PhD advisor from Cornell. "Doctor Jonas?"

"How you doing, Dante?" A small smile creased the old man's face. "It appears you have an interesting story to tell."

"'Interesting' is a mild way of putting it." Dante recovered from the unexpected arrival and turned to the middle-aged woman, extending his hand across the table. "I'm Dante Carloman."

The woman stared at the hand for a second before shaking it. Her eyes bored into Dante. "I'm Elizabeth Stevenson, President of the United States and leader of the free world." She released her hand and turned to her left. "This is General Calley, the chairman of the Joint Chiefs of Staff." She turned to her right. "I understand that you already know my National Science Advisor, Doctor Jonas."

She pointed to Dante's chair. "Please sit. We have much to discuss." She sat and as a waiter standing beside the marines hurried over and poured her a cup of coffee from the urn. "I hope you don't mind, but I haven't had breakfast yet." Without waiting for a response, she nodded toward the cabin door.

Instantly, two waiters with military haircuts came out carrying platters of doughnuts and bagels.

As the trays were set on the table, Dante's eyes lit up. *Apple fritters.* They were his favorite and he hadn't had one in seven years. "Now that you mention it, I'm a little hungry."

As he put two of the fritters on his plate, Dante noticed the Science Advisor nod to the President. He gulped. *That was a test. Doctor Jonas knows I love these things.* He winked at his old advisor. "Well played. It really is me." He had the fritter halfway to his mouth before Mara cleared it. Taking a bite out of the doughnut he asked, "How's your wife Rachael doing?" He did not get the expected reaction.

The old man's face fell. "Rachael was lecturing at Harvard when the invasion reached North America. Boston hadn't been evacuated and was one of the first cities hit. It's been weeks, and I've received no word from her."

"I'm so sorry." Dante's eyes misted. "She was always so kind to me when I came to your house."

242

"Thank you." Doctor Jonas wiped his eyes. He turned to the President. "I can confirm with complete certainty that this person is indeed Dante Carloman."

Stevenson studied Dante for a moment and squared her shoulders. "Very well then. No more games. Let's proceed."

His appetite gone, Dante put down the doughnut he forgot he was still holding. "I fully understand your caution. Thank you for receiving me."

President Stevenson's reply was icy as she glanced at the galley parked on the lawn, a hundred yards away. "It's not like we had much choice in the matter."

"You could have fled."

The President glanced at General Calley. "That's exactly what the Joint Chiefs advised." She met Dante's eyes with an intent regard. "I overrode them. We're desperate. Sometimes a leader must take great risks and grasp at any slim hope when the lives of her people are at stake."

Dante nodded, thinking about his own trials.

She added, "I had a long discussion with General Shanks. You convinced him that your intentions toward us are... supportive."

Dante folded his hands. "If saving the human race from extinction is supportive, then yes, but it does not come without conditions."

A waiter refilled his coffee cup.

He thanked the server and sipped the drink after Mara cleared it. *This guy's no waiter. He's special forces.*

Stevenson words were clipped. "I understand from General Shanks that you intend to demand we surrender our sovereignty to *you*."

Dante turned his head to where his escort stood. He saw Virgil attempting to engage an American Army captain in a conversation. That officer kept glancing nervously at the galley. *How do I gain their trust? The fear's so great and the time's so short.*

He sighed and turned his attention to the thin woman sitting across the plain pine table. "I have no desire to rule the Earth, but humanity *must* stand together as one. Nothing can be held back."

Stevenson's graying brown hair was cropped short, and she stared at him with intense blue eyes. "That doesn't make me feel a whole lot better about your intentions. You're not quite what I expected." She furrowed her brows. "I participated in the debriefing of a Lieutenant Wells. I understand that he and his rangers were embedded with your forces during your victory at Niagara Falls two days ago. He was very complimentary regarding the valor and competence of your forces." She pursed her lips. "You personally made quite an impression on him. His exact *insubordinate* comment to me was 'Dante Carloman is the answer to our prayers. For God's sake don't blow it.'"

Dante glanced at Doctor Jonas. "I'm sure you also reviewed my full dossier once you had my name."

Stevenson closed her eyes. "Let's see. Dante Carloman. Vanished without a trace almost seven years ago along with a number of other people on an interstate in western New York. A PhD candidate in artificial intelligence at Cornell. Had top-secret clearance working with the DIA at Fort Meade. Summa cum laude graduate in mathematics and physics at SUNY Fredonia, where you were also a Division Three All-American in track and cross country." She smiled at him. "The FBI report also says that you are a classic nerd with no social skills."

"My wife would certainly agree with the last part." Dante grinned.

A small smile crinkled her face.

Dante cleared his throat. "Sorry, I don't know as much about you. Let's see. Elizabeth Stevenson, a second term senator from Bardstown, Kentucky, who was to be your party's sacrificial lamb against a very popular president, and then the alien cover-up story came out after the disaster in Italy, and you won in a landslide."

Stevenson's careworn eyes reflected a hint of a smile. "As a young girl, I always enjoyed watching science fiction movies."

Dante snorted. "So did I, until I lived through one."

Stevenson's eyes glinted. "They don't all have happy endings, do they?"

Dante clenched his fist. "No, they don't." He found himself liking Stevenson. Her eyes showed a defiant courage. Her decision to meet with him showed she had an objective grasp on the reality of the situation. "You're not going to like what I have to say."

Stevenson sniffed. "I'm the President of the United States, but I'm helpless. These aliens kill at will, without remorse, wherever they want. And there's not a thing I can do about it. I will *listen* to any proposal with a chance to save lives."

Dante glanced at the sky, noting the tiny dots circling above. His squadron of galleys guarded their location. "When what we call the *harpies* attacked you a few weeks ago, the Earth was irrevocably changed, and countless millions died. You have no more chance to maintain your lives as they once were than the Caribbean islanders did when they encountered Christopher Columbus."

Fire flared in Stevenson's eyes. "And you let this happen. Where was your vaunted army of spacemen when they started murdering us? Millions died and millions more are dying from the destruction they unleashed."

"Stop it? I wish with all my heart that was possible. I came as soon as I could with everything I could muster." Dante added softly, "The harpies call themselves the Ipis. They hold dominion over the entire galaxy and have subjugated or eradicated thousands of sentient species. Earth is in what they call the Lethe Sector, which lies on the wasteland fringe of their domain."

Stevenson stiffened. "Are you proposing we surrender to *them*?"

Dante's shoulders sagged. "If it were possible, I would. But it's not an option. You see, humans have a special place in the minds of the Ipis. They hate and fear us beyond all rational thought. Their goal is our extermination."

The American President's eyes drifted across the peaceful park-like setting. "Then they'll just keep on coming until we're all dead?"

"Madam President, as things stand now, yes." Dante opened his hands in front of him. "As you mentioned earlier, I propose you make a deal with the devil."

Her chin rose. "What precisely do you suggest?"

"The army you see devastating the Earth is not the Ipis imperial military. They are a provincial, underfunded, ill-equipped paramilitary force with disjointed leadership. Against a united, well-equipped planet, they *can* be thwarted." Emotion edged Dante's voice. "To fight this war, Earth's nation-states can no longer exist as independent entities. As you said, over the last few weeks, countless numbers of people have died. With the harpies' destruction of the polar icecaps and their rampaging army, half the world's population has been displaced. Winter is coming. Even if the Ipis left tomorrow, *millions* more will perish within months from deprivation."

He pointedly stared at the American flag lapel pin Stevenson wore. When she first sat down, his neural-net suit detected that it was a listening device. His nano-scanners tracked the signal back to its source and infiltrated the computer systems in a bunker a half mile away. "For humanity to survive, we must unite as a single entity. Every nation must give me complete control of their armed forces. The losses will be terrible, but nothing can be held back."

Stevenson squared her shoulders. "And if we don't."

Dante sat back and tugged on his lower lip. "Let me bluntly paint the picture for you. Earth's armies have been fighting, and getting butchered, since the harpies invaded. The devastation of the polar regions has destroyed coastlines around the world. With your primitive weaponry and broken infrastructure, you're *incapable* of engaging in any large-scale battle. Your war-machine production and transportation are already almost nonexistent." He leaned forward and rested his elbows on the table. "My people came here to fight, and we will. I have three divisions and a small fleet of ships. On the Earth right now, the harpies have close to ten million warriors and thousands of warships. In about one month, my orbital blockade breaks down. Then they'll have unlimited supplies. You do the math."

Stevenson paled. "There must be a third option. We could ally ourselves with you until this war's over, and then go our separate ways."

Dante spread his hands on the table. "You don't understand. This war will *never* be over. Even if we defeat the forces here, the Ipis now know where the Earth is and will come back again and again. Our only hope is to beat what is before us and then, as a single *united* entity, sue the empire for a truce."

"Is that possible?" Stevenson whispered.

"I don't know." Dante's shoulders slumped. "I've studied every scrap of information I could find about the Ipis empire's rise to power over the last couple thousand years. It's happened a *few* times. We need to make the cost of defeating us heavier than the benefit."

General Calley, who sat silent through the discourse, broke in. "I can't commit what's left of the American armed forces based on your say-so." His words became deliberate, "Even if we believe every word you say, I can't mass such a force."

Dante snapped, "Don't play games with me. You're *already* mobilized. Every military unit east of the Mississippi is concentrated within a couple hundred miles of the Pocono mountains."

"How could you know that?" the general sputtered.

Dante smiled. "Aerial observation and communication intercepts." His eyes hardened. "If you attempt what it appears you're planning, you'll be annihilated. It'll be the largest massacre in Earth's history."

The general's face reddened. "You have no concept of what we are capable of."

Dante sighed. "Unfortunately, I *do*. You have less of a chance than a savage wielding a flint tomahawk charging at an Abrams tank." His eyes swung to Stevenson. "Madam President, my troops are mustering not far from here near York, Pennsylvania. A harpy force, a quarter-million strong, is heading that way, strung out along Interstate 76. In two days, my three divisions will engage them. You have twenty-four hours to decide and have your soldiers join us. To have any chance of winning, I need your army."

Dante rose shaking his head. "No more dancing. We both know the situation, and we're out of time. Either you're with me, giving humanity a chance to survive, or you're not, dooming us all to extinction." Taking a last gulp of coffee, he placed the cup deliberately back on the table. "Thanks for the breakfast. Perhaps next time we could have something stronger like that good Kentucky Bourbon from your home state."

He walked around the table to Doctor Jonas. "I pray you get good news about Rachael. She's an exceptional person."

"Thanks." The old professor grasped Dante's hand, turning imploring eyes on him. "I heard my first grandchild, Jenny, was born a few weeks ago in Chicago. Will she have a chance to ever grow up?"

Dante squeezed his hand back. "My second child is due in two months. My wife, Tina, says it's a boy." He turned and looked across the lawn at nothing. "She's in Niagara Falls right now, organizing our operation base."

He released his grasp and moved to the stairs. Pausing on the first step he turned to face Stevenson. "I placed a digital file in your command and control system, labeled 'Cocytus.' It contains a summary of humanity's past interactions with the Ipis. Your experts will find it interesting reading. It goes back to the fall of the Roman Empire."

General Calley shot to his feet. "Impossible. That's a secure closed-loop system."

Dante shook his head. "I did it, so it's not impossible." His eyes turned to Stevenson. "You will learn as I have that much of what we considered impossible is routine in this galaxy." He walked to his waiting team and called out over his shoulder. "Twenty-four hours. I pray for the sake of Doctor Jonas' granddaughter and my unborn son that you make the right decision."

Chapter XXXIV

Humanity Unites

Dante stood with President Stevenson in the parking lot of a motorcycle factory just outside York, Pennsylvania, and watched Virgil bark instructions to a crowd of grim-faced American sergeants on the use and maintenance of Ipis class-five ion disrupters. *Thank God, they agreed to fight with us.*

American troops had been streaming to the rendezvous site for two days. Dante's forty-five thousand troops had already doubled in size. He turned to Stevenson, who was watching the training exercise. "Thank you for trusting me."

The American President sniffed. "As you so succinctly stated, it's the only chance I had to save my people. I had to take it." Her face hardened. "I held nothing back. Every active and reserve unit in the northeast and mid-Atlantic states have been ordered to muster here with all due haste." Her lips thinned to a tight line. "Their lives are in your hands."

"I won't sugarcoat it. The upcoming battle will be brutal." Dante turned at the sound of an embarrassed cough.

"Ah, Your Majesty." Aramis pointed to a small diner across the road. "Can I borrow one-hundred eighty-three dollars and seventeen cents? The server in that establishment won't accept my drachma chip."

"What did you order? It's just the three of you."

A broad smile replaced the worried look on the clone's face. "It's fantastic. This establishment has all sorts of exotic foodstuffs: steak, potatoes, apple pie, milkshakes. We ordered one of everything they'd sell us."

"Then I think you're going to be washing dishes for a long time. I expect that my MasterCard's expired by now. Besides, I lost my wallet about six years ago." Dante's face flushed and he turned to the American President. "Could I borrow a little cash? It appears that an exchange rate system has not yet been established between the Ipis drachma and the US dollar."

A bemused smile creased the President's face and she called one of her Secret Service agents over. "Adam, could you go with this gentleman and cover the tab? Submit the charge in your expenses."

"Yes, ma'am," was the curt reply.

The agent followed Aramis back to the restaurant.

Stevenson watched the enormous clone walk away and spoke to Dante. "You use the harpies' money for your transactions?"

"Yeah. The Ipis don't call it drachmas, but it is as close as most humans can get to the actual word they use." Dante pointed to the sky. "It's the only currency accepted for trade by any civilized society out there. Barter worked for a while, but as our economy grew, that became impractical. The galaxy's a hard place to do business. Nothing is free."

Stevenson's jaw tightened as she looked around. "No, it isn't. Even our freedom comes at a price."

"Your freedom was gone when the first Ipis ship entered your atmosphere." An edge entered Dante's voice. "I already lost friends who wanted nothing more than to live in peace. But they came and gave their lives because they believed, as I do, that the Earth is worth saving." He paused, unable to hear over the din created by an Abrams tank company rumbling by. Gruff shouts directed them to a staging area. "Most people on Cocytus believe this venture's a mistake, but they came anyway because I asked."

Stevenson coughed from the dust kicked in the air by the passing tanks and swiped at her eyes. "I read the files you downloaded to our *secure* systems. What you've achieved over these past seven years is remarkable. It gives me hope that we'll make it through this."

"I'm not the man I was when I was taken from this planet. I had to become something different." Dante glanced up at the red clouds in the morning sky. "Crisis changes everything. We either adapt or die. And long term, even if we're successful, Earth will join the galactic community as an impoverished, backwater planet. Your infrastructure is in shambles, and everything you call modern technology is hopelessly antiquated."

Stevenson pursed her lips for a moment. "Give us a chance. We'll make it, just as you did. We humans are a resilient bunch."

"That we are." Dante met her eyes. "With every fiber of my being, I swear I'll give you that chance."

She bit her lower lip and nodded.

Dante glanced at the open pavilion to their left. "I think we should go join the generals. Before we plan for tomorrow, we have to survive today."

They walked together in silence.

As they approached, Dante heard General Cruz's hoarse voice arguing with a collection of senior American officers at the map table. "I *did* graduate from West Point, and I know linear fighting's been abandoned since the nineteenth century." Cruz thumped the table. "But it's back again. With modern shielding, only massed firepower has any success in large scale battles."

The four-star general with short-cropped, iron-grey hair, who Dante recognized as General Calley, Chairman of the Joint Chiefs of Staff, shook his head. "I believe you, but we still dare not mass our troops in the open. We may match them in numbers, but even with your three divisions, technology-wise we're way outgunned. It'll be a slaughter."

The hubbub around the table quieted to a murmur as Dante walked over and raised his hands, palms out. "Gentlemen, I understand your reluctance, but the plan's been discussed enough. It's time for action. General Calley, you're right. Casualties will be high. We flat out don't have enough troops armed with modern energy weapons to avoid it." He lowered his hands. "But the plan *will* work. General Cruz and I've been battling the harpies for six years. We know firsthand how they fight and what their weaponry is and *isn't* capable of." He slapped the table and glared at the faces studying him. "Our troops will be the hardened point of the spear. We'll get you close so your numbers count."

"But..." Calley responded, "...even if everything you've said is true, the harpies own the air. Our boys will be massacred before we can engage their infantry."

"General Calley, we believe they won't control the sky in this combat theater. I have a full air wing to throw into this battle. Combined with your Air Force, we can keep their atmospheric craft occupied." He focused on the senior officer. *If I can convince him, everyone else will fall in line.* "We'll never have an opportunity like this again. With the death of Governor Silenus-dis, our intercepts indicate the harpy generals are ensnarled in a squabble over who's in charge. That gives us a little edge. We can fight them piecemeal. But we only have a month to operate freely. That's all the time Admiral Martinel can buy us before his fleet is blown to perdition."

"Their infantry's still more than a match for anything we can throw against them," a voice from the other end of the table snapped.

"Yes, it is." Dante nodded. "But their commander, Keres-ma, has them strung out on the Pennsylvania turnpike."

He glanced at Otheth, who stood beside Cruz with her tail feathers flared. "Our Roc allies have spies within that army. It seems that Keres-ma has taken a very personal dislike to me and is willing to take foolish chances to get at me."

Cruz chuckled. "That wouldn't have anything to do with the little encounter the two of you had on Carcerem." He glanced around the table. "It left Keres-ma without an arm and humiliated him in Ipis society. Oh yeah, he hates Dante with a passion, and we're going to use his personal vendetta as the lure."

Cruz pointed to the map. "The embedded Rocs have already enabled Keres-ma to discover Dante's location. He's force-marching his troops to get here." His finger moved along the line indicating the Pennsylvania turnpike. "We'll blow every bridge and heavily mine the expressway to slow their progress." His finger shifted to another line. "We'll offer only token resistance along Route 30. That'll cause an uncoordinated arrival of their troop columns. We take out a couple of their lead corps, and the odds will be evened up."

Dante added, "Our three divisions of heavy infantry are *better* armed than these harpy paramilitaries."

Calley took off his wire-rimmed glasses and rubbed his eyes. "General Cruz, seven years ago you were a captain in the Tenth Division." He shook his head. "Today, you now have command and control of the entire US armed forces on the eastern seaboard. Where do you propose we make our stand?"

Cruz brought up an electronic map with digital markers representing the units for both sides, shifting in real time. He pointed to a spot where the two sides would intersect. "What's the name of that town where Route 30 and Route 15 intersect?"

A brigadier in a marine uniform squinted at the map, then his head jerked back. "I'll be damned. That's Gettysburg."

"So be it," Dante added. "It may or may not be fate, but at least we all know the lay of that hallowed ground."

"And I want you nowhere near the front," Cruz growled. "What's left of Gentile's marine brigade was pretty beat up in Niagara Falls. Your Majesty, you'll command them *safely* in the rear."

Dante opened his mouth for an angry retort, then snapped it shut.

Cruz smiled. "We must keep the bait fresh."

* * *

Charon cantered back to his brigade's camp and was met, as he expected, by Ulebos, his second-in-command. He didn't wait for the question to be asked. "Keres-ma's insane. Instead of returning to our base in the urban center labeled Philadelphia, he's making us hunt for the human king across this incomprehensible countryside."

Ulebos shrugged. "Did you expect anything to make sense in this campaign? Even with that human king, there's not much they can do to hurt us."

"There's more." Charon twitched his tail. "The Roc mercenaries deserted last night."

"The Rocs, huh. Not surprised. Everyone in that species has a grudge against someone." Ulebos pawed the ground. "How many?"

"*All* of them. A dozen were found in their rookery this morning with their throats slit, but close to a thousand vanished without a trace."

Ulebos checked the charge packs in the pouch hanging over her haunches. "We're going to need fresh supplies soon. The humans' military's a joke, but their blockade isn't."

Charon whinnied. "Tell our boys not to engage unless they need to defend themselves. The charge packs we have won't last forever."

"Easier said than done. We can't move ten feet without finding another IED planted in the road." Ulebos nickered. "So, what's Keres-ma's plan?"

Charon glanced around. "Our aerial observations have discovered that the humans are marshaling their forces near a small enclave not far from here labeled Gettysburg. Keres-ma is leading his three corps of Ipis-ma cult warriors straight at them on the road labeled Route 30. He will draw the human king into the fight by only attacking with a single corps. Then when they're engaged, the other two corps will come up. Three additional corps of Ipis-*dis* cult troops will move on the path labeled Interstate 76 and then break south on the road labeled Route 15."

"And where do we come in?" Ulebos' tail twitched.

Charon flicked his maned head. "The corps of mercenaries will swing south and then advance north on the route labeled BR 15. We hit the humans in the rear once the battle starts."

"The poor bastards won't have a chance." Ulebos nodded. "But better them than us. Where does *our* brigade fit in this grand scheme?"

Charon's jaw tightened. "With the Rocs gone, we and a mechanized battalion of Satyr war-wheels are the only units native to the Lethe Sector, so we have the *honor* of being the vanguard."

Ulebos snorted. "Well, it sounded like a good plan 'til you got to that minor point. Still, it shouldn't be too much trouble."

"I'm not so sure." Charon stared out across a wide valley. "Our intelligence indicates that the human king, Dante Carloman, has thousands of competent troops to bolster the primitive natives. He's been giving the Ipis empire fits for a long time."

Ulebos nickered. "Human or not, it's hard to believe that any high-and-mighty ruler would take the risk of going anywhere near a battlefield."

Charon chuckled as he remembered his first encounter with Dante when he and a small band fought for control of an Ipis Striker on Equitone. "Believe it. I've met the human king once. He *is* such a leader. His people believe in him. He's already beaten Keres-ma once on Carcerem with nothing more than a gang of unarmed prisoners."

Ulebos swished her mane. "I heard the story about that revolt." He glanced around. "Rumor has it that he's the one who took out Silenus-dis up in the zone labeled Niagara Falls. Maybe we should consider bailing on this war. A mercenary can't collect his paycheck if he's dead."

"Keep your voice down." Charon glanced around to see if anyone was nearby.

Ulebos spit. "After watching those old vids of the last Ipis-human war, I think I'd be rooting for these humans. That is, if my own worthless hide wasn't at stake." She kicked at a tuff of grass and gave Charon a pensive look. "What are your orders?"

Charon's tail twitched. "We're the vanguard, but that doesn't mean we'll let the humans use us for target practice. We stay in the woods, away from the roads, until we reach this Gettysburg."

"I'm good with that." Ulebos shrugged. "I don't have any issues with the natives. Let the Ipis do their own dirty work. Maybe those Rocs had the right idea."

Charon's haunches flinched. "Yeah, I always seem to be on the wrong side for all the jobs I do."

Ulebos chuckled. "The bad guys always pay better."

Charon nickered. "Perhaps the day will come when the good guys can afford us."

"That day will never come." Ulebos sighed.

"I know," Charon growled and glanced at the trees rustling in the autumn breeze. "I'm tired of the life I've been leading. I'd like to finally do something clean before I die."

"Just don't plan anything like that while I'm working for you." Ulebos whinnied, then sobered. "Just between you and me, I'd love to shoot at those arrogant Ipis someday."

Charon pawed the earth. "Yeah, someday." He trotted to his private domed shelter. "We head out in the morning."

Chapter XXXV

This Hallowed Ground

Dante crouched on a grassy outcropping atop Little Round Top and glanced at the faces of General Cruz and General Calley on the vid-screen. "Generals, it's now or never. You ready?"

Both commanders returned a quick nod.

Dante swallowed hard. "Unleash hell."

Moments later, hundreds of American tanks and rocket launchers roared. Thousands of tactical missiles blotted out the midday sun as they filled the air from behind their cover on Cemetery Ridge and Culps Hill.

* * *

The Ipis force two miles away paused at the aerial onslaught, but the massive ordnance bombardment caused little damage. Occasionally a defective shield failed and its hapless harpy owner was shredded by the explosion.

Keres-ma ignored the attacks as he met with his subcommanders under a resilient cone of energy. Shells silently vanished as they struck the invisible screen.

After twenty minutes, one of the generals ventured a question in a subservient voice, "Lord Commander, do we just sit here and let these savages attack us? Eventually our soldiers' shielding will overload, and we could see some casualties. Our air fleet could easily decimate their primitive artillery."

Keres-ma bared his fangs and stroked the mantichoras tail necklace with his prosthetic arm. "The fliers will stay positioned *exactly* where they are. Minor losses are meaningless. The creature who affronted the empire's honor is here. He lacks the intelligence of the Ipis but does have a certain animal cunning. We will blot out the stain of his killing Silenus-dis. He has at least a score of galleys at his disposal. We must be ready for them. If our flitters aren't available to deal with the human galleys, they'll cause our troops far more problems than these primitive projectile weapons."

His aide quivered. "Sire, perhaps we should withdraw until we can bring in the heavy equipment we left in Philadelphia. The Ipis-*dis* commanders are complaining that every bridge on the road labeled I-76 is either destroyed or booby-trapped. They are way behind the timetable."

Keres-ma howled, "We do not need weapons built for destroying cities to eliminate this pack of gibbering primates! I will goad the human king into fighting us, and when he does, I will eat his heart!"

The aide bowed. "Yes, sire."

A junior officer ran to Keres-ma and prostrated herself. "Sire, we detected hundreds of this planet's aircraft approaching from the southwest."

Keres-ma's tufted ears tilted forward. "Any galleys?"

"No, sire."

"This world's primitive flight vehicles would never attack us unsupported." Keres-ma again tugged at his mantichoras necklace. "The galleys are probably mixed in with them in stealth mode. The humans think they are clever, but they've blundered. The galleys cannot fire while cloaked. When they become visible, their shielding won't be online immediately. Order our airships to strike their formations with broad-spectrum blasts."

"Yes, sire." The junior officer bowed and hurried away.

Keres-ma bared his fangs at his generals. "Now is the time to destroy their ground force. We have three Ipis-*ma* corps with us. We attack."

The generals glanced at each other with looks of concern. One spoke up, "But, sire, the Ipis-dis corps and the mercenary forces have not yet arrived."

Keres-ma's catlike eyes narrowed. "Then the glory will be all *ours*." He preened. "We are the Ipis-ma. We don't need the entire army. We have the true believers. No collection of creatures, who are little more than beasts, can stand against us."

The generals cheered as they hurried to their units.

Keres-ma glared across the wide valley and hissed, "I have you now... Dante Carloman."

* * *

Virgil Bernius glanced at the tactical display on his command galley. His fleet of sixty galleys hovered in stealth mode *northeast* of Gettysburg. He flipped on his communicator. "Folks, the Ipis flitters took the bait. Their ass ends are toward us. Let's shove our plasma missiles right where the sun don't shine." His face sobered. "People, we need to do this fast. Those brave pilots playing decoy only have F-15s and F-35s. They won't last long against two hundred harpy aerial fighters." He flipped another switch. "General Cruz, we're engaging now."

A steady voice responded, "That's good, because their infantry's moving like a pack of rabid wolves." Cruz took a deep breath. "Bernius, good hunting. Keep the sky clear."

"Roger that." Virgil's screen showed he was approaching the Ipis craft. He engaged the communicator for his flight squadron and flipped the stealth mode off. "Galleys, engage. Fire at will." He smiled as the harpy flier in front of him exploded in a blinding ball of light. "Looks like we caught those suckers by surprise."

He switched off the communicator and turned his head. "Aramis, nice shot."

A tight smile was the only acknowledgment to the compliment. The young clone was already lining up his next shot on a flitter rapidly closing on an American F-35.

On the ground, General Cruz gulped before he gave his next order. He was standing on the very spot where the Union Cavalry General Buford stood at the start of the epic Civil War battle. He had a division of clones and Carcerem veterans armed with heavy quad-barrel rifles. *This better work or we'll take some heavy losses. No stone wall can stop a disrupter beam.*

Quango had designed the unique, but bulky, quad-barrel rifles a couple of years earlier for his human clone *sons*. It became the weapon of choice of everyone big enough to wield one. One barrel was a standard class-five ion disrupter, one launched superheated plasma grenades, one fired a long-range laser, and the fourth shot a Taser-like energy beam.

A hundred feet back of the front line, Cruz stood with the two other Cocytus divisions entrenched behind fresh, chest-high earthen works. He glanced over his shoulder in the direction of the deafening cannon roar. *They're doing their part.* Three divisions of American soldiers and marines were spread in a wide arc on the flanks of his forces. He trembled. *If my plan fails, those poor bastards are doomed.*

Cruz followed the approaching harpies with his enhanced digital field glasses. *A single infantry corps without armor support.* He smiled. *That arrogant bastard Keres-ma isn't waiting for the rest of his troops.* When the front ranks of the harpies closed within a mile, he raised and lowered his hand. "Lasers, fire."

The hum of fifteen thousand discharging lasers cut through the crescendo of the continuing cannonade. At a mile, the tight beams of focused light did little more than cause the harpies' shields to glow. At a half mile, the general chopped his hand through the air again. "Plasma grenades, two volleys." The searing heat of those detonations caused the harpies' shields to shine even brighter.

The marching Ipis-ma warriors became enraged and loped forward, howling their war cry.

At a quarter mile, all three Cocytus divisions opened up with their ion disrupters. The wave of energy from forty-five thousand weapons rolled across the wide field, reducing everything in its path to slag. The body armor on the Ipis soldiers in the front ranks glowed to incandescent brightness as the energy wave struck them like a hammer blow. The sustained stress on the harpy equipment was too much. Across wide swaths of their ranks, the shielding winked off. The alien advance ground to a halt. Field commanders chittered into their communicators for direction from their superiors. Individuals and small units returned uncoordinated and ineffectual fire.

Cruz turned to the American commander. In a husky voice he gave the command, "General Calley, time for your boys to join in."

Thirty thousand, American M4s and heavy machine guns joined the barrage from entrenched, camouflaged positions on the flanks. The projectiles tore through the now unarmored flesh of the harpies. The lead ranks disintegrated into rows of shredded gore. The esprit-de-corps of the remainder could not accept the affront to their species and charged forward with reckless abandon. The withering weapons fire from three sides scythed through the attackers.

By the time the assault reached the stone wall, the Ipis-ma corps was a shadow of itself. Badly outnumbered, they were no match for the pent-up fury of the Cocytus and Earth humans they faced.

The Second Marine Division from Camp Lejeune charged the aliens' flank from their position on Cemetery Ridge. The fresh onslaught was more than the Ipis-ma survivors could face. Their courage evaporated and they fled.

The blood-soaked landscape became silent, and then cheers erupted from over eighty thousand voices.

Calley slapped Cruz on the back. "We did it. Merciful Jesus, we did it."

"It's not over by a long shot." Cruz shook his head. "They won't make the same mistake of hitting us with a single unsupported corps again."

Calley watched the marines on the field. They were stripping the corpses that had not been reduced to ash of any functional gear. "And the next time it'll be more than just your folks shooting those fancy ray guns."

"We bloodied one corps, but there are still five more out there." Cruz scanned the sky and keyed his communicator. "Virgil, how goes the air battle?"

"General, we're grinding them down. Their flitters flat out don't have the firepower or shielding to match our ships. But, jeez, those bastards know how to fly."

"Can you free up any galleys for ground support?"

"No time soon. These suckers don't give up." A burst of static interrupted the link for a moment. "Damn, a fresh swarm of them just jumped us from out of nowhere. Shit, my ship took a nasty hit. The control panel's flashing like a Christmas Tree."

Cruz's voice sank. "Can you land?"

"My shielding system's offline." There was a pause. "Yeah, I'll make it down okay if I don't get jumped. My weapons power regulator is redlining. I gotta shut that down. Transferring command to Octavia."

"We have repair crews and emergency personnel ready to receive you in the rear. Can you make it there?"

"This galley has as much maneuverability as a beached whale, but she's flying."

Cruz flipped a switch on his communicator. "Dante, is the landing field set to receive customers?"

"We're ready as we're going to be." Concern showed in Dante's voice. "We took over a museum parking lot near Big Round Top."

The general gauged the setting sun. "The harpies weren't prepared for what we threw at 'em. Don't think we'll get away so easy next time." He sighed. "Any trouble back there?"

"All quiet." Dante scanned the field beyond him on his portable view screen. Aerial drones had all the approaches to his position under surveillance. "No sign of harpies over here."

"That's one blessing," An edge crept into Cruz's voice. "There's no way we could fight a battle on two fronts."

Dante rubbed his jaw. "I still feel next to useless."

"There's more to winning a war than charging headlong into a goddamned battle." Cruz's voice became strained. "We're stretched to the limit. Your beat-up brigade is all the reserves we have." He switched off the communicator and turned to Calley. "Reposition your troops from the right flank behind the energy barriers, and set up along Culps Hill and Cemetery Ridge. The harpies sure as hell will swing around from that direction and hit us again."

Calley sucked in a ragged breath. "This shielding of yours, will it hold? The guns they use level *cities*. Our little stone walls and piles of dirt won't be much protection."

Cruz nodded. "We have eleven twenty-terawatt shield generators set up. These harpies have little in the way of artillery, and our galleys are denying them aerial support. What we have will stop the harpies' handheld ion disrupters. The fighting will be up close and personal."

A feral grin creased Calley's face. "Good."

Four hours later, a horde of harpies struck from the north and another simultaneously from the west. The black night shone like midday as thousands of weapons fired from both sides.

Chapter XXXVI

At the Twilight's Last Gleaming

A sliver of a moon shone in the night sky as Charon squatted on his haunches atop the observation tower at a site labeled Eisenhower's Farm. He examined the images the nano-drones transmitted from miles away as the eastern sky shifted from black to gray.

"That's awfully fancy gear you have there." Ulebos swished her tail as she stared at the display in front of Charon. "What's it telling you?"

"It tells me the humans are doomed," Charon nickered. "Their commander's clever enough. He negated the Ipis airpower and positioned his main force to fight twice his number." He pointed to the screen. "Keres-ma's troops assaulted those heights three times. Each Ipis attack was driven off with heavy losses."

"Sounds like the humans are faring well. How is it they're doomed?" Ulebos craned her neck and stared at the shifting display scenes. "And when do we get tossed into the meat grinder?"

"The human king and his generals miscalculated." Charon looked over the tourist watchtower railing. "They're unaware of the danger approaching from the south and only have a few thousand warriors guarding that approach. Come morning, when the rest of our mercenary corps arrives, we'll be over forty thousand strong. Our troops will roll over their small rear guard and smash their main army's exposed backside. With all of their shielding and firepower focused north and west, it'll be a massacre."

Ulebos cocked her head and grunted. "Hence another planet falls to the gentle mercies of the Ipis empire." She sighed. "What're your orders?"

Dawn broke as Charon raised his enhanced field glasses and scanned the distant terrain. "I don't want our people too involved with the initial assault. It'll be bloody."

"That's fine with me," Ulebos nickered.

Charon absently nodded and refocused his viewer, watching a human in the distance who he readily recognized. The human king was sitting on open ground, working with a broken-horned Satyr on a piece of equipment. "Dante Carloman, I see you." His calloused hand hefted his long-range plasma-dart discharger and aligned the homing gunsight on Dante's head. "I could end this battle right now with one shot."

Ulebos snapped her head around. "Then do it."

Charon squinted into the gunsight, raised his head, grimaced, and re-aimed the weapon. After a few seconds of staring at his target, he lowered his weapon. "I... I can't. My sister, Huon, gave her life protecting that human on Carcerem. She was an idealist and believed in what he stood for."

"Your sister was part of that prison revolt? That means she was a traitor."

Charon stomped his hoof. "My sister was no traitor. She was a... patriot. A *Centaur* patriot."

Ulebos took a step backward. "Sorry. Just a bit surprised."

Charon sighed. "Don't worry about it. The human king will be dead soon enough. The mercenary corps' main force will arrive within the hour, and with the nano-communication suppressors I infested in the humans' gear, they won't have a clue they're coming. He'll be butchered along his small band. Let's go." He led Ulebos down the open staircase, shaking his maned head. *Why does that thought bother me?*

* * *

Dante leaned against a monument dedicated to the 20th Maine Regiment at the foot of Big Roundtop. "I tell you there's something wrong with our equipment. Cruz's responses to my communications don't sound right, and our aerial drones are picking up *zero* movement."

Quango tugged on his goatee. "By my mother's twisted beard, I don't have a clue what's going on. The diagnostics show everything operating normally."

"Keep working on it." Dante blew his cheeks out. He glanced up and broke into a smile as a small group approached. "Hi, Virg. What the hell are you doing here?"

Virgil walked over followed by Mara, Aramis, Athos, and Porthos. "It'll be days before my galley's combat-ready again, so we're in the infantry for a while."

"My boys." Quango clambered to his feet and hugged the three clones. "Laddies, it's good to see ya." He kicked the suitcase-sized box next to him. "By my mother's twisted beard, maybe you can keep me from going crazy."

Aramis regarded the inoffensive-looking box. "A problem here?"

"Dante thinks our surveillance and communication gear isn't working, but I'll be damned if I can find anything wrong." Quango delivered another kick to the photonic unit.

"Denting the casing will not improve the equipment's functionality." Mara glided forward and plugged a slender tentacle into a data port on the scanner. "I will assess." After a few seconds, her steady hum turned silent and she jerked her probe from the connection.

"Mara, what's the matter?" Dante called in alarm as Mara's lights went dark and she sank to the ground with a thud.

Dante rushed to her and fumbled with the screws on her front panel. He scanned the internal readouts and rebooted her.

Mara's lights switched from amber to green and she rose on her antigravity cushion. "Danger. The equipment is infested with an aggressive, self-replicating malware that's slaved to a remote system." She rotated her sensor toward Dante. "It would have had me too if Asimov's Three Laws weren't embedded in my core operating system. They gave me the strength to purge that slaver from my systems."

"This gear was working fine a few hours ago and doesn't accept wireless input." Quango let out a low whistle. "Accessing the processors without leaving any traces requires

266

pretty sophisticated sabotage apparatus. The Ipis Imperium keeps those kinds of toys under tight control. It's not likely that a backwater Sector Governor could get his hands on it."

Dante gave Virgil a sharp look. "We know someone who has access to that type of equipment."

"Yeah, and he was our prisoner less than a year ago," Virgil growled.

Dante flushed. "It was a chance I had to take." His shoulders slumped. "Perhaps I was wrong."

"Naw, ya had to try something." Virgil's mouth curled into a lopsided grin. "We'll do this the old-fashioned way. Use the biker dudes as messengers." He glanced at the three young clones and pointed west. "Instead of remote scanners, we'll use human patrols. I'll lead one down the Millerstown Road. Send another team south on the Emmitsburg Road. If anything's going on, we'll find out about it."

Sweat beaded on Dante's forehead despite the coolness of the midautumn morning. "Good idea. No one would screw with our equipment without a reason." He glanced at a small group of senior officers gathered nearby. "Colonel Marcellus, send out patrols and get the troops ready for trouble."

A sharp salute and a hurried departure was the only response.

Virgil walked off, checking the charge pack in his weapon.

Dante turned to Mara and Quango. "Your job is to clean this virus from our computers."

Quango tugged on his horn. "It won't be quick. This equipment isn't self-aware like Mara. It could be embedded anywhere and everywhere."

Dante pounded his fist on the statue beside him. "First priority is the shield generator. I want it functional within the hour."

Mara's lights blinked as she moved toward the generator. "Protect humans. Protect humans."

* * *

"Look at that." Ulebos leveled her ion disrupter at a vehicle lurching along the Millerstown road that read "Jeep" on the front. It was being pursued by a pair of Ipis crawlers.

The Ipis army scouts used the crawlers for rapid transit across almost any terrain on six flexible legs. Each vehicle, lightly armored twenty-five-foot-long cylinders, could hold up to ten combatants. Its armament consisted of a rapid-fire plasma grenade launcher and a pair of class-four ion-disrupters located on articulating pincers.

"Just a human civilian transport," Charon snapped. "The only thing those idiots in the crawler will accomplish is announcing our presence to every human in the area."

Charon focused his scope and saw the Jeep driver panic on spotting the hundreds of Centaurs poised along the tree line on the north side of the road. The Centaur noticed that there were three young children in the back seat and an adult female clutching a primitive projectile weapon sitting beside the driver.

With the crawlers closing in, the driver spun off the road to avoid the Centaurs. The Jeep rolled to a stop as an EMP burst from the lead crawler hit it, fusing the car's computer circuitry.

Charon watched in morbid curiosity as the humans spilled out. He saw the driver, a balding middle-aged male, crouch behind the car, firing a simplistic weapon at the oncoming crawlers. He heard the woman wail "I love you" before following the three spindly-legged children fleeing across the field. *Is this how it was when my sister leapt between a charging mantichoras and the human king?*

Ulebos' tail twitched. "Those humans are as good as dead. Perhaps they'll—"

The lead crawler crashed to the ground as its three right-side legs exploded.

As the Ipis soldiers clambered from the ruined transport, they were met with a barrage of small arms fire from four handheld disrupters.

Charon twitched as he scanned the scene with his field glasses. *I know them.* He raised his hand and barked to his troops. "Stay out of this fight." He spotted Virgil running to the Jeep and sending the still dazed human fleeing after his family. *Yes. Save those innocents.*

Ulebos grunted, "Stupid move taking out that crawler. Looks like there's only four of them against a crawler and a platoon of torqued-off Ipis soldiers."

Charon stared at one clone maneuvering stiffly on a prosthetic leg. "Five."

Ulebos scanned the field. "Where?"

"Here." Charon drew a ragged breath. "I'm switching sides."

"You're what?" Ulebos gasped. "Are you crazy?"

"Perhaps I've become sane for the first time in my miserable life." Charon flicked his tail. "The brigade is yours to command." He roared the ancient Centaur battle cry as he galloped toward the firefight. Both the human and the Ipis fighters paused and looked toward him.

A surprised Porthos yelled, "Charon, I knew you were with—" A plasma bolt dropped the clone as eight more crawlers arrived, supported by a full company of Ipis infantry.

"Nooo!" Charon cried. He unlimbered his high-powered sniper weapon from his back and fired at the new arrivals with cold efficiency. But his high-tech defense systems were soon redlining under the return fire.

The ground trembled, and Charon looked over his shoulder when he saw the Ipis soldiers pointing and shooting past him. He whinnied. "My people."

A herd of four thousand charging Centaurs is a terrifying sight. Shouting their ancestral battle cries, they closed on the shocked Ipis scouts. The fight was over in moments. The light armor of the crawlers was no match for the onslaught.

Charon rushed to where Porthos fell and found Virgil, Aramis, and Athos already there.

"What happened?" Porthos winced as he struggled to his feet. His neural-net suit was blackened, and mild burn marks covered his chest.

"You're the luckiest son-of-a-bitch in the galaxy." Virgil broke open a first aid pack and dabbed salve on the worst of Porthos' burns. "We need to get you to a stasis pod." He met

Charon's eyes for a moment, then studied the thousands of Centaurs forming a defensive perimeter. "I wasn't sure which direction your gun was going to point when I saw you running this way."

"You humans have messed my mind," Charon nickered. "Over the years, hundreds have died at my hands. Some deserving, and some not. I never cared." He pawed the damp ground. "Now, I hear my sister's voice in my head. I see her faith in your King Dante. I could no longer be what I was."

Ulebos trotted over. "Commander, we have a small problem. Fifteen thousand Ipis troops are coming along this road and will be here in a few minutes. Another fifteen thousand mercenaries are coming up the road from the south."

Virgil shot Charon a startled look.

Charon nodded. "Keres-ma's plan is to tie down your main force and then hit your exposed rear with a full corps."

Virgil barked into his communicator but was rewarded with only dead air.

Charon reached into his pouch and pressed a button on a small box.

Worried voices were instantly heard on the speaker.

Virgil relayed the information and his face sagged as he heard the responses. "Keres-ma's plan may work. General Cruz is fully engaged against heavy odds. We won't be seeing any help."

"Ya got us. And one Centaur is worth two humans any day," Ulebos chuckled. "Where do you want Commander Charon's brigade placed?"

"Ulebos, you and the boys get out of here." Charon glanced at Virgil. "You know the numbers. This'll be a massacre."

The Centaur soldier shook her maned head. "You're not the only one allowed to switch sides. We all saw the old vids from the first Lethe Sector war. The grand alliance will stand again, and the Centaurs will be part of it. If only for a short time." She whinnied and glanced at Virgil. "Commander Charon has four thousand strong. Where do you want us?"

Virgil turned toward the landscape he knew by heart from studying the American Civil War. He pointed to a rock outcropping. "Dig in over there. That's called 'The Devil's Den'. You'll anchor our right flank." He held his communicator to his ear. "Charon, come with me to the center. You can help Dante coordinate the defenses."

"Certainly. We might as well make the Ipis work for their victory." His haunches twitched as they started jogging. "Besides your communicators, you'll notice that your other gear is functioning again." He coughed. "If anyone's alive after this is over, you really need to harden your military computer firewalls against cyber-attacks."

Virgil gritted his teeth. "Aramis, Athos, carry Porthos to the field hospital."

"Yes, Cap'n," came the identical response from two throats.

Virgil's brows furrowed as he listened to his communicator. "It appears your unit wasn't the only mercenary group to join us. About a thousand Roc light infantry and an armored battalion of Satyr war-wheels are blocking the Ipis mercenaries coming up the BR15." He lengthened his stride and studied Charon cantering beside him. "We didn't even know they were there until the comm-links came back online. Hell, we didn't know you were right in front of us until we ran into you."

"Never get overly dependent on technology for your intel," Charon snorted. "The Ipis have equipment that can negate the most sophisticated systems."

"I'll remember that." Virgil jogged to where Dante stood conferring with Otheth, Quango, and a couple of human officers.

Otheth hissed on spotting Charon. "That one is evil."

"I don't have time for this." Dante scowled. "If Charon intended us harm all he had to do was *nothing*. Right now, I'll take anyone willing to point a gun at the harpies. We're in deep trouble."

"What's the situation?" Virgil asked in an even voice.

Dante rubbed the back of his neck. "The Roc and Satyr units beat back the enemy vanguard to the south, but the harpies are bringing up a full division. I've ordered them back to the Little Round Top. The Satyr armor will be most effective from those heights, and it'll hold down our left flank." He glanced at Charon. "You always seem to pop up when we're in trouble. It's good to see you again. What's your strength?"

Charon pawed the ground. "Four thousand heavy infantry. But it won't be nearly enough. Besides the two Ipis-dis divisions, there's a full mercenary division from the Zintow sector coming in from the west." He cocked his head. "And you only have a single, banged-up human brigade in the center. The defections ruined the Ipis surprise attack, but it doesn't matter. They'll hit with three divisions of hardened veterans. You don't... *we* don't... have the shielding or firepower to withstand them."

Dante touched the statue dedicated to Colonel Chamberlain and the 20th Maine from the fight for Big Round Top during the Civil War. "We cannot retreat. If we do, the war is lost." He shuddered. "General Cruz's force will be cut off and destroyed if this enemy gets past us. We must buy him time to win his battle. We must be stubborn today." He added, "The harpies have no air support, and the approach is narrow and steep. We can do this."

Virgil nodded. "Where do you want me?"

"Take charge of the center. You know a helluva lot more about soldiering than I do." Dante squeezed his friend's shoulder. "Most of them are the survivors of Joe Gentile's marines." He swung his eyes to the other commanders. "Go to your units now. We'll have company shortly."

Chapter XXXVII

By the Rocket's Red Glare

As the morning sun rose into clear skies, burning through the morning mist, the lead edge of the harpy horde swarmed into sight. Spearheaded by hundreds of crawlers, thirty thousand aliens charged the mishmash collection of defenders Dante cobbled together during the predawn.

He scanned his small force with pride. For the first time in over a hundred and twenty years, the humans, Rocs, Satyrs, and Centaurs were standing together against their common enemy.

The assault was vicious, but the defenders were dug in and determined. Forty-five minutes later, the attackers withdrew across the shallow valley. Both sides glared at each other along that expanse now strewn with the wreckage of war machines and dead combatants.

Dante looked at his neural-net suit. It was marred with several blaster burns. He switched on his closed-frequency communicator. "Status report. Virg, you go first."

Virgil powered down his quad-barrel blaster. "The center is holding. Most of the fighting has been on the flanks. But our guns are running low on power."

"King Dante, this is Otheth. The left flank is in trouble. We're down to four Satyr war-wheels and have suffered severe causalities." There was a pause. "Cheepash is dead. He refused to evacuate with the wounded and fell while destroying an Ipis crawler that reached the heights."

Dante's voice became soft. "I only knew him for a short time. He seemed to be a remarkable Roc."

"He was that and also my only love," Otheth cawed. "The human, Gilbert, from the Wild Turkeys was with him at the end. He said my love died valiantly, that he made an ending that every member of the First Order of the Dragon craves."

Dante's shoulders sagged. "Many brave people who did not deserve death fell today."

The communicator speaker crackled. "Your Majesty, my name is Ulebos. I am Charon's second-in-command. Our losses are close to fifty percent on the right flank. Sire, our charge packs are almost depleted. We will not be able to repel another full-scale attack."

Dante tensed. "Where's Charon? Is he injured?"

"No, sire," Ulebos answered. "He said something about evening the odds and slipped away before the fighting started."

The conversation was interrupted by a new voice, "Human king, I bought you some time." There was a chuckle. "This is Charon. I told you not to trust your technology too much. The Ipis should have taken the same advice. Two Ipis divisional commanders and four brigade leaders across the valley are now dead. Their command structure is in chaos."

"What happened?" Dante asked.

"I *am* the most accomplished assassin in the galaxy. I just plied my trade." Charon snorted. "Weeks ago, I planted a tracking device on those generals for my own personal insurance purposes. The plasma darts from my long-range rifle homed in on those signals. Those who were unprepared, died."

"Where are you now?" Dante drew a shuddered breath.

"Right behind you."

Dante spun around and saw Charon squatted on his haunches by a slag heap that was once a memorial statue.

"I could have also killed you about a dozen different times." Charon rose. "You must be far more vigilant."

Virgil moved beside Dante, glaring at Charon. "If anything happens to my friend, I'll hunt you to the ends of the galaxy."

Charon's tail flicked. "In this galaxy, it is easy for the hunter to become the prey."

"Shut up the two of you," Dante said. "In case you haven't noticed, there's a horde of harpies out there waiting to kill us. We're all be the prey if we don't do something." He adjusted the channel on his encrypted communicator. "General Cruz, this is Dante Carloman."

The receiver crackled for several seconds before a voice responded. "King Dante, thank God we have contact again. This is Lieutenant Wells. General Cruz is wounded but still directing the fight. We're completely engaged across our entire front. He's requesting that you send whatever troops you can spare, immediately."

Dante sank to the ground. "Lieutenant, tell the general we're fighting a full corps over here. We don't have the manpower or materiel to hold. I'll buy him until sunset, but he must prepare to fight on two fronts."

"I'll... I'll tell him, Your Majesty," was the somber reply before the line went dead.

Dante's face became resolute. "People, we cannot retreat, and we sure as hell can't attack. So, we stay. Have the men gather whatever energy packs and weapons they can from the wounded and dead." He faced Quango. "Old friend, you're in charge of evacuating the wounded. Stay in the mountains south of here."

"Yes, sire," Quango responded with a husky voice.

Dante turned. "Charon... Where's Charon?"

Virgil answered, "He took off halfway through your radio conversation, mumbling something about 'wasting resources.'"

"Good riddance. I doubt we'll see that backstabber again." Quango limped up the hill. "I'll be back once the ambulance convoy is moving."

Hours slipped by across the quiet battle front.

At midafternoon, thick clouds rolled in, lashed by a chill wind, and a heavy rain that turned the churned field into a muddy morass.

It was late afternoon when they detected the movement of a freshly arrived harpy division.

"Here they come," a frightened soldier yelled.

Dante stood at the center of the front line, beside the water-soaked banner displaying the clenched red fist. He rechecked the charge in his short-barrel ion disrupter and loosened the energy sword in the scabbard hanging from his hip.

His self-appointed bodyguards from the prison world of Carcerem bunched in front of him.

Dante's face twisted into a humorless smile. "No need to shove. There's plenty for all of us. They—"

High-pitched, ululating screeches drowned out his words as thousands of harpies bounded forward, blasting the entrenched positions with their weapons.

They were met by the return fire of the Lethe Sector Alliance. Humans, Centaurs, Satyrs and Rocs united together one more time.

The front ranks of the harpies reached the entrenchments, and the two sides tore at each other with fists and claws and talons.

Dante found himself fighting for his life, swinging his energy sword and firing his small ion disrupter at point-blank range.

After what seemed like an eternity, but was actually only a few minutes, the attackers fell back.

Dante pressed his hand against a ragged wound in his side where his neural-net suit was torn by the last harpy he faced. He spotted the enemy regrouping for another charge but could do nothing about it.

Virgil pointed to an opening through the shattered trees. "They're forming up for another assault."

A female marine with a gashed face, who Dante recognized from the Carcerem prison camp, declared, "All my charge packs are spent."

Several others, with somber voices, added their concurrence.

Moments later, a voice that sounded like it had lost all hope wailed, "For the love of God, look at that!"

Dante spotted motion above him. It was the silhouette of an enormous object half hidden in the clouds. "Oh my God, the harpies have brought in a Striker." He recognized the distinctive quarter-mile-long shape and knew that all three of the still-functioning Strikers the humans had were busy defending the landing base at Niagara Falls. *Our galleys must have been scattered or lost.*

A crackling noise erupted in his earpiece, "Dante, where in this insanity are you?"

He would recognize that voice anywhere. "Tina, what are you doing here?"

"What am I doing here?" her confused voice responded. "You called me and told me to come with the biggest gun platform I could lay my hands on."

"I didn't call you, but I'm sure as hell glad you're here. What are you flying? I thought all our Strikers were tied up screening the supply base in Niagara."

"They are. We got *Reggie* slapped together enough to fly a few hundred miles. We slipped away during a lull in the aerial attacks there."

Another female voice added across the com-link, "I'm not letting my big brother stand alone."

A calm tenor voice interrupted, "I have a rail gun and a plasma battery operational. But my shielding is at eleven percent, and the hull integrity is precarious. To quote the vernacular, I feel like shit." The voice paused. "Dante Carloman, I am not sure how long I can remain airborne. What would you like me to do?"

"Reggie, you're an answer to a prayer," Dante rasped, hope rising in his chest. Tears trickled down his cheek. "The good guys are in a line from the coordinates labeled Big Round Top to The Devil's Den. Blast everything west of there that's moving."

"Roger." Immediately, large gouts of earth erupted across the field, and the rain-soaked, gray afternoon blazed with brilliant light.

The harpies were bunched together for a fresh assault. Their personal shields were no match for the devastating blasts being hurled at them from above. Scores died from each rapid-fire bolt. It became a rout.

Cheers erupted along the line of defenders.

"Reggie, go assist General Cruz's force. They're in trouble too," Dante shouted in excitement.

"Unnecessary," came Reggie's even reply. "The harpy flitters inexplicitly abandoned the area as I arrived. Commander Octavia's fleet of galleys is gathering to provide air support for our main army as we speak." There was a pause. "I need to land. My propulsion systems are redlining again."

"Reggie, park that bucket next to my galley." Virgil's voice was soft.

Dante sank to the ground, wincing at the pain of his wound. "Thanks, Reggie. You saved our lives."

Tina sounded scared, "You're hurt, aren't you?"

"I'll be all right." He gazed around at his ragged force. Tears of pride welled in his eyes. Innumerable dead lay behind the crude barriers. Of the living, many bore injuries far worse than his. The survivors sat, glassy-eyed, beside their fallen comrades. All remained at their positions.

Virgil took in the same sight. "This is truly sacred ground, and we held it."

They both wept.

Shortly after sunset, it was over. The surviving Ipis who were arrayed against Dante's force fled to the main army, leaving their wounded and supply train behind.

* * *

It was after midnight and Dante was still awake. He sat at a camp desk outside a large frame structure at the intersection of Wright Ave. and Route 134. The building and the open field beside it, where the damaged spaceships were parked, had been converted into a field hospital.

The cold night air was kept at bay by a large plastic tarp and a couple of space heaters. The rumble of traffic heading north on Route 15 from military bases in the south could be heard in the distance. The only vehicles heading toward them were the transport convoys bearing severely injured soldiers.

Tina had set up the triage area shortly after *Reggie* landed, using his dozen stasis pods to handle the most critically wounded. Teams of Satyr, Roc, and Centaur medics assisted American doctors on using the new medical equipment.

After a short exchange, Tina walked under the canopy, past the American Secret Service detail and Dante's surviving bodyguards. She sat beside him, too exhausted to talk.

He squeezed her hand as she leaned against him. Dark bags rimmed her eyes.

President Stevenson sat at the other end of the small table with two of her Security Council members. She smiled at the affection the two shared and spoke to Tina, "My Surgeon General tells me your miracle machines are saving many lives."

Tina sat up and nodded. "Not everything the aliens created is evil. There is some good out in the galaxy."

Emma sat on a bench between Virgil and Lieutenant Wells, at the other end of the shelter. She shivered and wrapped an old car blanket tightly around her. "Don't you think the king of the world should have better accommodations?"

Dante's face twisted into a half smile. "Every available structure within a mile of here is being used for the wounded."

Emma pointed at his bandages. "That should include you."

Dante touched his side. "The comfort of a leader counts for little at times like this. It is important that I be seen enduring what I'm asking our soldiers to deal with."

Tina grimaced and added, "We only have a dozen functioning stasis pods in *Reggie*. Only the most critically injured are given time there, and then only until they are stabilized so we can evac them to our base by Niagara Falls."

Virgil cracked his knuckles. "It was an incredible victory. I still don't understand how we pulled it off."

They all had seen the numbers. Once the humans had control of the air space, it became a slaughter. Over a hundred thousand, mostly Ipis-ma, corpses were spread across the battlefront. Their stripped bodies lay thick in the burnt-out fields. About twenty thousand harpies and mercenaries of various species surrendered. The two corps of Ipis-dis troops never reached the battlefield. Lost in the mountains of central Pennsylvania, their commander turned them toward their base in Philadelphia when the aerial cover inexplicably left.

Dante, swathed in bandages, received this information along with the casualty figures for his own forces. Light by comparison, it was still tragic: almost three thousand dead or unaccounted for, and over ten thousand wounded.

"I don't understand it either. But I won't—" There was an angry hubbub outside the perimeter. Dante recognized the voice. "Let him in."

A familiar Centaur cantered into the light.

"Hi, Charon. It appears you missed all the action," Dante said. "What mischief have you been getting into?"

"Missed the action?" Charon snorted. "Who do you think was responsible for the Ipis-dis troops suddenly changing direction, their fighter craft leaving, and *Reggie* flying in unhindered?"

Dante shook his head. "How in the name of God's good green earth did you pull that off in the middle of a raging battle?"

"Actually, I got the idea from you," Charon nickered. "That stunt you pulled on Equitone when you broke into the Ipis Command Center and disoriented their communications, it was brilliant. I just improved on it. Right now, some defenseless icebergs in your North Atlantic are being pulverized. It will take their engineers days to clear the fake orders from their command and control systems."

"Well, your ruse probably saved us from annihilation," Dante rasped and checked his weapons. His disrupter had no charge left, and his energy sword was down to nineteen percent. "We wouldn't have survived another attack."

"You're welcome." Charon shook his maned head.

Dante glanced at the reports in front of him. "There's so much to still do, and no time to do it."

Virgil nodded. "Octavia's recon craft are tracking the harpies fleeing east but can't do much to harass them. Their aerial defense systems around Philly are all active." A smile creased his face. "However, on the bright side, there isn't a harpy combat unit within hundreds of miles of here."

Tina's eyes lit up. "That means the west of here is clear. I can see my folks and let them know I'm alive."

"Me too. My mom's there all alone." A flood of childhood memories rushed through Dante's mind. "We'll go when there's a break in this fighting."

"When will that be?" Tina's voice sounded crestfallen. "This war will never end."

Virgil walked over and grasped Dante's shoulder. "Go now. Take my galley. It's not combat-ready, but I could fly it those few hundred miles. Let the generals manage things without you for a while."

Dante grimaced. "General Cruz will say it's too risky."

"We won't tell him until we're there," Virgil chuckled.

Charon cocked his head. "You'll need a security escort. The Ipis would love to catch the human king alone."

Virgil added, "A small team that can move in and out quickly."

Fear for his mother overwhelmed his sense of responsibility. Dante sprang to his feet, ignoring the sharp pain. "Tina, let's do it."

"I'm coming too. I've been worried sick about Mom." Emma stood and dropped the blanket.

Dante sucked in a deep gulp of air. "We'll go in, grab our families, and get out of there before anyone knows we're gone."

Tina sobbed. "Home."

President Stevenson reached across the table and took his hand. "I pray you both find your families in good health."

Dante rose and limped to the makeshift landing field. His friends and sister followed.

On entering the galley, Dante found Otheth, Quango, Aramis, Athos, and Porthos slumped in the bridge chairs, sound asleep.

"Wake up, sluggards," Virgil shouted. "We got a new mission."

Chapter XXXVIII

The Home Was Still There

Victoria Carloman sat up with a start. A low growl was coming from her old German shepherd, Taz, up and alert at the foot of her bed. "What's the matter, boy?" she whispered as she checked the glowing dial of the wind-up clock on her bed stand. The time was 2:13 in the morning. As with all the houses around Fredonia, the old two-story farmhouse hadn't had electricity or working phone landlines for two days.

Her house was nestled along the edge of the family's large vineyard along Route 20, south of Fredonia, New York. There weren't any nearby neighbors. She glanced out the window into the dark night and didn't see any car headlights in the packed-stone driveway.

The gray-haired woman pulled on her old fleece robe and grabbed the loaded shotgun leaning against the wall. She shoved an LED flashlight in her robe's pocket and lit a kerosene lantern. Taz padded loyally at her side. "If some hooligans are planning on robbing me, they'll get pants full of buckshot for their efforts."

Most of the neighbors and her farm workers fled a few days earlier when the rumor of aliens up near Niagara Falls reached them. She sniffed to her old dog and headed downstairs. "Where would we go anyway? We've no family left."

Victoria reached the downstairs landing and glanced at the three portraits hanging in the hallway. The ones of her husband and son were draped in black ribbon. Fear twisted her gut as she studied the smiling young woman in the third picture. *Emma's always been so good about keeping in touch. Please, God, keep her safe.*

She was startled from her prayer at the sound of an insistent knock on the front door a dozen feet away. She clutched the old pump-action shotgun. "Whoever you are, get out of here. I'm armed and I'll shoot." She checked the load in her late husband's shotgun and released the safety as she approached the door. Taz, sensing her fear, let out a low growl as he moved by her side.

"Mom, for heaven's sake don't shoot. It's me, Emma," came the voice from the other side of the door. "Let us in. It's cold out here."

"Oh, thank you, God." She shook with relief as she leaned the gun against the wall and hurried to unlock the door. "Us?"

"Yeah, Mom. There's someone I know you want to see."

She gasped at what she saw on the porch in the dim light of the kerosene lantern she'd placed in the hallway.

"Mom, it's me, Dante."

Victoria froze as tears welled in her eyes. "My son's been dead for close to seven years."

"Mom, it *is* Dante." Emma ran to her mother and hugged her. "He's back, and boy does he have a story to tell."

Victoria stared for a long moment at the lean young man standing there wearing an open windbreaker, showing thick bandages around his chest. "Sweet Jesus, it is you." She threw herself into his arms.

Dante hugged her, ignoring the pain in his side, as tears seeped from his eyes. "Momma, I'm home. I'm really home." A few moments later, he sniffed. "Mom, there's someone I want you to meet." He turned to the auburn-haired woman standing to the side. "I'm married now."

A very pregnant woman with piecing blue eyes and a soft smile stepped up and stood beside Dante, grasping his hand. "Hello, Mrs. Carloman, I'm Tina, and you're a grandma."

"I'm... I'm a grandma?" Victoria wrapped Tina in a hug. A cold autumn gust blew in from Lake Erie and she became self-conscious about meeting her new daughter-in-law wearing a heavy robe and worn-out slippers. "What are we doing standing out here with you being pregnant? Come inside."

"We can't, Mom." Dante squeezed her shoulder. "We have to leave and want you to come with us. It's not safe for you here. Those aliens will be hunting for you because of me."

"Dante Carloman, you will come inside, sit down, and tell me what happened to you. The government said you were dead."

"Yes, Mom." Dante sighed. He called over his shoulder, "I may be here a little while. Set up a defense perimeter."

"We should not tarry here. You are the human king. Command her to leave," was the irritated rely from the dark.

He pulled out a flashlight and walked to the kitchen mumbling, "Yeah, that'll work. No one tells my mom what to do."

Victoria blinked at the dark. "Dante, don't be rude. Tell your friends they can come in."

"They have a couple jobs to do first." He grimaced. "Mom, don't be scared when you meet them. They're... aliens. Good guys... but aliens."

"Oh dear. Things are happening far too fast." Victoria shook her head, locked arms with Tina, and walked into the house. "I'm sorry there's no lights. We lost power a few days ago. Still have gas though. Useless for the furnace, but the stove works."

Taz wagged his tail as Dante scratched behind his ears while sitting at the kitchen table. "How you doing, boy? You were just a pup when I left." His mother was fumbling through a drawer, holding her flashlight. "Mom, we really have to go."

"Where are we going?" Victoria lit a candle and went to the pantry.

"Not far. Just up to Niagara Falls after we pick up Tina's parents. They live in Dunkirk." Emma followed her mom. "When this is all over, you can come back."

Victoria shook her head. "I heard there're aliens up there. How is Niagara Falls any safer than here?"

"Mom, I have three fully armed spaceships guarding it."

"Spaceships? You have spaceships?" Victoria pulled out a loaf of fresh-baked bread, a large stick of salami, and a round of provolone cheese and placed them on the table.

"It's a long story. I'm sort of king to all humanity now." Dante squinted in the near-dark. "Jeez, I can hardly see in here." He flipped on his communicator. "Mara, get in here. I'd like to see, and this place has no power."

A hum followed on the headset. "Dante, I must finish setting up the perimeter defense first."

Dante rubbed the tabletop as the smells of his home filled him, and tears brimmed in his eyes again. He saw the carefully placed pictures of his father and himself on the wall behind the table. "Emma told me about Dad. I'm so sorry I wasn't here for you."

"He was always very proud of you." Victoria grabbed his hand and squeezed it. "So, you're some sort of astronaut now?"

Dante was still hunting in his mind for a response when Mara floated in, breaking his train of thought. "Mara, plug into a switch and turn on some lights."

"Yes, Your Majesty."

Moments later, all of the overhead lights in the kitchen blazed on.

Victoria gasped at the sight of Mara's titanium cylinder hovering inches above the linoleum with a tentacle extended into a light switch. "Is that one of the aliens?"

"Not really. Mom, this is Mara. She's a robot. Her and her mother are two of my dearest friends and have saved my life a number of times."

"That thing has a mother?" Victoria swallowed and stared.

"I agree. Beatrice is not much of a mother, but I do hold a strong affinity to her," Mara responded. "I am pleased to meet the maker of Dante Carloman. For a biological unit, you produced an excellent entity."

"Thank you. I think." Victoria sighed.

Taz walked over, sniffed Mara, then peed on her.

"Dante, please instruct this beast that I have no need for hydration."

Dante chuckled. "He's just marking you as part of his territory. If—"

"A monster!" Victoria yelped.

Standing in the entrance from the front hallway were Herb Wells and Quango.

"Where?" Quango jumped as he fumbled for his weapon, knocking over a plant stand. He blushed. "Sorry, ma'am."

"What happened?" Virgil burst in through the kitchen door leading to the back yard with his gun drawn. Aramis, Porthos, and Athos charged in behind him.

Dante steadied his mother with a reassuring hug. "These are some of my other friends."

"Oh my." Victoria gasped and took several deep breaths. She gave her son a sidelong look. "This is not going to be a short story, is it?" A leery smile creased her face. "They look no worse than that collection of friends you brought around the house when you were in high school."

Dante looked at the busted door and the smashed planter. "You might as well meet everyone before the house gets destroyed. Charon, Otheth, get in here." He looked at his mom. "Now don't be scared. One is going to look like a little pony with the face of a baboon, and the other will look like one of those raptor dinosaurs, only with feathers and a beak."

"Oh, my," Victoria gasped again.

Otheth and Charon walked in from the front hall, nudging Quango aside. They bowed in unison. Otheth chirped, "Greetings, flock mother. You should have great pride in your hatchling. He has earned much *cou*."

"Thank you." Victoria forced a smile. "Th-this is going to be a v-very interesting night," she stuttered while staring at the Roc, Centaur, and Satyr. "Any friend of Dante's is welcome here." She turned to her son. "Aren't you going to introduce me?"

Virgil grinned as he led the three clones into the crowded kitchen. "Sorry about the door, Mrs. Carloman." He shook her hand. "I'm Virgil Bernius. Originally from the strange world called Hoboken, New Jersey. The triplets who look like NFL linebackers are Aramis, Athos, and Porthos. They're from Dante's *home* planet, Cocytus."

"Cocytus," Victoria repeated.

Dante pointed to the others. "Mom, the dangerous-looking one fumbling with his blaster is Quango. He's a Satyr from Tribulus. Otheth is the one wearing feathers. She's a

Roc from Tannis. The fellow with four legs and a tail is Charon. He's a Centaur from Equitone."

Emma smirked. "And the funny looking one is Lieutenant Herb Wells. He's from a primitive little planet called *Earth*. He's a special friend of mine."

Victoria quirked an eyebrow at her daughter.

Herb blushed. "Pleased to meet you, Mrs. Carloman. I wish it was under better circumstances."

Quango bowed, and Otheth flared her feathers as she chirped, "It is a pleasure to greet the matriarch of the Carloman clan."

Charon glanced around. "This site's not secure. We should leave."

Although Dante was anxious to depart, he spent the next hour explaining to his mother where he had been.

When he finished, Victoria shook her head. "Incredible." She looked around at the strange group. "Thank you all for helping my boy. I hope he wasn't too much of a bother." She rose. "I need to change my clothes." She glanced at her daughter. "Emma, help me pack."

Taz curled up under the table at Dante's feet, lifted his head, then laid it down again.

Fifteen minutes later, Victoria returned to the kitchen and stood awkwardly in the middle of the crowded room. "Will it hurt when I get beamed up."

Dante walked over and kissed his mother. "Mom, this isn't some weirdo science-fiction movie. I have a spaceship parked out behind the wine press."

"Weird." Victoria sighed and glanced at the variety of creatures sitting at her table munching cheese, salami, and bread. "I have a son who cavorts with aliens and has delusions of being the king of the world. I think I can be excused for being a little out of my depth here."

Dante held her arm as they stepped off the porch onto the gravel driveway. As they walked around the wine press building, the galley's ramp slid down and bright external lights illuminated the area.

"Oh my!" Victoria exclaimed.

Taz yipped, peed on the ramp, and dashed inside.

Moments later the lights winked off and they were gone.

The experience at the home of Tina's parents was much the same. It was dawn when the galley finally landed at the Niagara Falls airport.

Chapter XXXIX

Interview with a Special Guest

A week later, Dante sat in his new office in what was once a shoe store in the Niagara Falls Outlet Mall. Much had transpired in that time. His army had grown into a viable fighting force as tens of thousands of American troops, armed with captured weapons, joined the siege of Philadelphia.

As the stranglehold closed, the Ipis-dis commander seized the few transports available and fled to the Eurasian sector with his staff and personal guards. The next day, a few Ipis-ma battalions attempted a breakout on the ground. They did not get far. The unfamiliar land swarmed with hostile human troops and the sky was filled with galley fighters. With no support and exhausted munitions, they were pinned against the Delaware river and obliterated. That afternoon, those left behind surrendered. A treasure trove of heavy weaponry was captured along with close to fifty thousand prisoners.

Dante was very interested in talking to one of those prisoners. He thought it prudent to have the harpy brought to his command center. *If the Americans discover this is the monster responsible for the deaths of millions, they'd kill him on the spot.*

He turned to Mara, who hovered at his side. "Please translate the conversation in real time."

Mara's lights blinked. "Of course, but my services will add little value. You are fully conversant in the empire's language, and the vid-link communication protocols your people are listening on have adequate translators."

"I don't want to give away that I can understand my *guest's* responses. It'll give me an extra second to work on what to say." Dante chuckled as he glanced at the split-screen monitor on his desk. "Any questions from the folks linked in during the interrogation, relay it to me."

The display on his far left showed an open park in Yuma, Arizona. General Cruz was there with his senior commanders, representing Cocytus and America. The display in the middle was Admiral Martinel. The one on the right showed a meeting room that Dante believed was deep in the bowels of the White House, with the American President, the Canadian Prime Minister, and a group of ambassadors from other nations.

He pushed aside the half-eaten slice of his mom's homemade lasagna and signaled Lieutenant Wells, Quango, Otheth, and Charon, who were gobbling up the rest of the dish at a side table. Taz sat on the floor, alert for something to fall from the table.

"Finish that in the back room, but listen in." Dante squinted at Charon. "I know you will anyway. I'll want your opinions afterwards."

Although her feathers were still dyed red to signify her grief over the death of Cheepash, Otheth rose and flared her tail feathers. "It will be an honor to serve, Your Majesty."

The four departed carrying their trays. Taz trotted after them, tail wagging.

When the door closed, Dante gulped. "Here goes." He nodded to the short, wiry man in a torn leather jacket with *Wild Turkeys* emblazoned on the back. "I'll see the prisoner now."

"Yes sir, boss." Rene opened the door. "Bring that piece of shit in now."

A shackled harpy with a prosthetic arm and wearing a mantichoras tail was led in by Aramis, Athos, and Porthos.

Dante pointed to a cushioned stool in front of his desk. "Sit." He was pleased that Mara not only translated the word but put the proper authoritative tone into the command.

Keres-ma hissed but complied.

Dante steepled his fingers. "So, Keres-ma, you're no more successful leading an army than you were running the Carcerem prison camp. What does your Ipis-ma sect say about losing to a collection of simple primates?"

"Some species possess a certain animal cunning that, although limited, can be effective at times. You elves are such a species." Keres-ma glared at Dante. "But in the end, it will not matter. Santa Claus, your identity is now revealed. You do not resemble the caricature in all of your propaganda, but I easily pierced that simple ruse." Keres-ma spat. "Your elvish army won a single battle, but that does not make you victorious in this war."

Santa Claus? Elves? What's this idiot jabbering about? Dante turned to Mara, perplexed.

She responded, after a short pause, directly to the earbud built into his neural-net suit. "With eighty-nine-point-seven percent certainty, given what Charon told us about the invasion plan, I deduce that the Ipis Lethe-Sector leadership collected transmissions from this planet and accepted broadcast fables as reality. It fit their preconceived expectations. It explains the aggressive disposition of a large portion of their invasion force to the polar regions and their lack of credible defensive posturing in the populated sectors of the Earth."

"Ho, ho, ho." A thin smile creased Dante's face, as he returned Keres-ma's glare. "True. It was a single battle. But we will be very successful in this war if all the *harpy* generals are as incompetent as you and Silenus-dis."

"Gloat for the short time you have." Keres-ma sneered as he flexed his claws. "*You* should surrender to me. If you do so immediately, I'll grant you the mercy of a quick death."

Dante arched his brows. "I should surrender to you? You're hardly in a position to dictate terms."

"Am I not?" Keres-ma twisted in the grip of the two marines. "My engineers analyzed the blockade your elvish fleet has around this pestilent world. Within three standard weeks, your grid will collapse and the Ipis armada will reassert its control." He snapped his jaw showing his needle-sharp teeth. "When it does, your pathetically small fleet and ground forces will be crushed."

Dante twitched. "You don't know what I have in reserve."

"If you had a real army, you would have used it by now," Saliva spewed from Keres-ma's fanged mouth. "You were lucky in that last battle. Only a fool would expect to win when outnumbered so badly."

Damn. His analysis of our situation is spot-on. Dante forced a smile onto his face, and he goaded the harpy, "And only a fool of a commander could lose such a battle as you did."

Keres-ma sunk into his stool and hissed.

Mara spoke into Dante's earbud, "General Cruz told me to remind you that we'll gain an additional ninety thousand freshly armed, combat-ready troops thanks to the successful raids on the harpy supply depots in Oceanside, California, and Playa Hermosa, Costa Rica."

Dante rubbed his jaw. "We're still inventorying what we captured in Philly."

"Did you say something?" Keres-ma glanced warily around the room. "Speak in a language a civilized person can understand."

Dante started, unaware that he spoke out loud. He covered up by saying, in Latin, "Your army has lost Silenus-dis and now you. I expect command and control will be problematic."

Keres-ma spat. "What command and control? General Xiroah-dis is treating the landmass labeled Eurasia as his private fiefdom, and Silenus-dis' subcommanders continue to search for you in the arctic region even though you've already revealed yourself."

Mara spoke to Dante again, "General Cruz requests that you keep the prisoner talking. He stated that this information is gold." Her lights blinked. "I must have an incomplete understanding of his words. I comprehend no relationship between the data and an inert metal."

Dante leaned forward. "Perhaps you're right about our capabilities, and perhaps you're not. I do know that without resupply the invincible force you brought to this world will be fighting with sticks and stones a month from now."

Keres-ma's face darkened to a deeper hue of purple and he remained silent.

Dante pushed harder. "If that day comes and we lose to the invaders, I doubt the *harpy* troops will find me cowering in a sewer culvert like you were."

292

Keres-ma glowered and gashed his teeth. "Someday you will pay for these insults."

Dante continued, "And when your relief force breaks through, how do you think they'll regard a commander who lost to us on Carcerem and then here on Earth."

Keres-ma remained silent, but his eyes burned with what Dante perceived as unvarnished hate.

Dante finally pressed his hands on the desk. "I've wasted enough of my time bandying words with you. You and your staff have been charged with the war crimes of murdering millions of innocent civilians." He leaned forward. "The punishment for that barbarism on this planet is death."

"You cannot harm me. I am of the royal blood. Seven hundred and thirty-eighth in line for the imperial throne." Keres-ma's violet skin paled. "I didn't kill any real people. Just humans."

"Take this piece of scum back to his cage." Dante noted the smoldering rage in the three clones' eyes. He added to them, "I don't want him hurt until he faces his accusations."

Aramis grimaced. "Yes, sir. But I volunteer to be his executioner. Monsters like this one shouldn't be breathing."

Dante nodded. "There will be justice."

Keres-ma squirmed as he was dragged from the room, and the clones felt no compunction to treat him gently.

Dante sighed and glanced at the vid-screen on his desk. "You catch all of that?"

Admiral Martinel ground his teeth. "That bastard thinks they can just wait us out, and he's probably right. My scanners indicate that General Xiroah-dis is consolidating his Eurasian forces around three sites: Guangzhou, China; Tehran, Iran; and Madrid, Spain. He's showing every sign of waiting us out."

"What about the other continents?" Dante asked.

"Not detecting any change in behavior there. The forces in the Western Hemisphere, Africa, and Australia are still rampaging, unchecked. And the ones in the polar regions are staying up there."

Dante studied the man on the leftmost vid-screen. "General Cruz, you have to get some rest. Stasis pods are remarkable for healing, but you're stretched way too thin."

"We got to strike while we have the bastards reeling." Cruz sniffed. "As long as the initiative's ours, they won't have an opportunity to counterattack."

Dante nodded. "What's our next move?"

Cruz glanced at the officers around him. "Beyond North America, the harpies still control the air space, so moving massive numbers of troops across the oceans is suicide right now." A feral grin creased the general's face. "But there's a few things we can do. I've been sneaking soldiers and equipment into San Diego Bay on stealth submarines. My troops outside the city are probing the harpy force there. When the army I'm assembling here in Yuma strikes, the besiegers will be the ones trapped."

The general tapped the map in front of him. "Another harpy force is moving north from Mexico and has already crossed into the US at Brownsville. With Philadelphia under control, I'll send the Fourth and Tenth American Army divisions along with the Second Cocytus Division down to Texas to harass them and slow their progress." He rubbed his jaw. "Corpus Christi is probably lost, but I should have the San Diego campaign finished before the enemy reaches Houston, and I can bring most of our forces from the east coast and California over. We stop them there."

Dante nodded. "And then."

Cruz blinked. "And then our time runs out. Either our allies arrive to support us, or the harpy fleet smashes the blockade."

Dante looked at Martinel. "Admiral, any word from the relief fleet?"

Martinel shook his head. "Nary a sign of them, mate." He added, "But I wouldn't know until they make their move. External communications are blocked. The harpy fleet's buzzing around my grid like a swarm of angry hornets."

President Stevenson asked, "These allies of yours, will they come?"

Images of Setteth, Arachne, and Calahas sprang into Dante's mind. He turned to the screen on the right. "My friends will come. But I cannot promise that they'll gather a large enough force in time to make a difference." He rubbed the bridge of his nose. "Madam President, Mister Prime Minister, ambassadors, we do not stand alone in this galaxy, but our opponent has almost limitless resources, and we are very weak."

"Then we must beg for terms," an ambassador cried.

"Surrender would never be accepted. The Ipis goal for humanity is its complete eradication."

"Then what's the solution?"

"We must bloody them and make the cost of a protracted war prohibitively expensive to the Ipis empire." Dante sagged in his chair. "Even with the full might of all four species, I honestly I don't know if we can do that."

Chapter XL

Patience of a Roc

Doctor Esther Easley stood transfixed, staring at the magnified display of the Earth and its moon. Even though their spaceship was drifting in the solar system's asteroid belt, she could see the distinct outlines of the continents. It appeared peaceful, but she knew incredible violence raged across the Earth. She clutched the hand of the five-year-old boy by her side as a tear trickled down her cheek. She had feared this day would come since her abduction almost seven years earlier. She pointed it out to him. "Liam, that's the planet where your mom and dad were born."

"Looks nice," he replied, doubt showing in his voice. "When can I see my mommy and daddy?"

She saw the thousands of tiny flashes of light near the Moon, which she knew was the sun's light reflecting off the Ipis warships. Esther hated the Ipis with every fiber of her being. She sensed someone approach, and Liam's squeal, "Hi, Aunt Setteth," confirmed it. She turned her head slightly in recognition of the old Roc's presence, then bent down to the boy. "Liam, go back to the stateroom. Setteth and I need to have a grownup talk."

The old Roc ruffled Liam's auburn hair.

"Will you play soccer with me later?"

"Of course, I will. I'm the *impregnable* goaltender."

"Okay." Liam laughed and ran off. The bridge crew turned at the sound. Many smiled. The sound of merriment was rare these last few days.

Doctor Easley stared after Dante and Tina's son until the bridge door hissed shut, then turned back to the vid-display of the peaceful-looking planet floating in the blackness of space. "I haven't seen them in years, but my children and grandchildren are down there, waiting for death, and I'm helpless to do anything about it." Her chin trembled. "If they're still alive."

"We will save them," Setteth cooed as she moved to the thin gray-haired woman's side.

Esther wiped a tear from her cheek. "Those children that still live are hiding in their parents' arms, awaiting their end."

"I know well of what you speak. Every day I feel the presence of the dead." Setteth moved to her station on the warship's bridge and studied the tactical displays. "They scream their need to be avenged, and every day I must answer them 'not yet.'" She preened her long neck. "But this morning I gave them a different answer. I told them that, today, the old alliances have been reunited, and the Ipis yoke will be thrown off."

Esther moved beside the Roc's chair and regarded the display panels. It showed hundreds of Roc and human spaceships floating among the countless boulders and space debris orbiting the sun in the asteroid belt. Her heart leapt at the sight, until she compared it to the images close to the Earth. A small warship fleet from Cocytus, under the command of Admiral Martinel, was shielding the planet in a dodecahedron formation from thousands of Ipis warships. "How long can they hold out?" she whispered as she touched the screen.

Setteth glanced over. "The dodecahedron formation is an impenetrable defense. That is, impenetrable until the power for their shields run out." The Roc ruffled her feathers. "Martinel knows what he's doing. The Ipis are focused on him. They can't get past his ships, and he is keeping them from looking too hard in this direction. When the Centaur and Satyr fleets arrive, we attack."

"And if they don't arrive?" Esther asked in a flat voice.

"Then we attack with what we have." Setteth pawed the deck with a taloned foot. "Their forebears were oath breakers and abandoned us at the last battle for the Lethe Sector over Novaroma." She paused. "Hopefully, this generation has more honor."

"I know they'll come in time," a deep baritone voice spoke as iron-hard arms encircled Esther from behind in a gentle hug. "They must. Everybody I've grown to love is trapped on that planet."

"Michael." Esther leaned against his massive chest and stroked his arm. "Or should I call you Admiral. You have a fleet to manage."

"I do." The admiral's brow furrowed. "The plan is set. All we can do now is wait. Without the Centaur and Satyr fleets, we don't have nearly enough capital ships." His eyes drifted across the bridge of his flagship. "Martinel has all of our big ships. The harpy Enforcer-class warships dwarf everything we have except for my flagship." He turned to the Roc. "Captain Setteth, I came to speak to you. Most of the crew have fought the harpies in one manner or another, but never against such odds. They think our foe is invincible. You fought them and survived. I think a few words from you would hearten our people."

"My tale's not a happy one." Setteth hissed, then snapped her beak. "I will tell you the truth, and then you can relay any story you want." Her feathers flattened against her body, and she closed her eyes.

"It was the year 1905 as Earth measures time. As I learned, the humans on Earth were a primitive lot, barely able lift craft a few feet off of their planet's surface. But there were other humans in the galaxy, descendants of a tribe called Romans. They left their planet in a cosmic space-time anomaly and found a way to thrive and prosper among the galaxy's civilizations."

Setteth clucked deep in her throat. "I was perhaps eighteen when I first encountered humans. The Ipis were consolidating their Lethe Sector conquest." She glanced out the ship's portal. "This is a barren area at the rim of the galaxy, with only four sentient species native to it: Humans, Centaurs, Satyrs, and Rocs. We all resisted the Ipis expansion independently and were all being ground to dust. During one disastrous battle, our Roc warbirds were flailing against the Ipis fleet, when the humans appeared with their galley ships. What a magnificent sight. Their tactics were inspiring. Our surviving warbirds rejoined the fight, and together we drove the invaders off. I sang my people's war

298

song as I flew my ship in tandem with a human galley. It was glorious."

Setteth's eyes opened, and she warbled at Michael and Esther. "After that, the human emperor of that time went to each of the other species with a bold plan. He proposed that we unite in a grand alliance to drive off the Ipis. The Rocs readily agreed. We knew our limitations and saw that the human commanders could strategically beat the invaders."

Esther's face twisted in confusion, "Why were they so different? I have never seen bolder fighters than you and your kin."

"It was a limitation of each species." Setteth closed her eyes again. "We Rocs were great individual fighters, but too independent to coordinate a large-scale battle. The Centaurs fought as a pack, always on the attack, with no sense of the defense. The Satyrs fought as a herd, with a bristling defense, but never striking out at their opponent." She glanced at Michael. "The humans walked all three paths and confounded the Ipis at every encounter."

"So, it was successful?" Michael asked.

"For a time," the Roc's voice dropped to a whisper. "I met the human emperor of that time, Marcus Carloman, for a moment. He was magnificent. Bold and shrewd against his enemies, wise and compassionate to those who stood with him." Her voice dropped even lower so that Michael and Esther had to strain to hear her words. "Much like Dante, the Carloman who leads you now." She glanced at the display showing the Earth, and her voice rose. "Dante is down there with a pitifully small force, trying to rally the humans to hang on." Her feathers flared. "Just as in another place and time his predecessor led a similar desperate struggle."

The Roc's voice became shrill, and everyone on the bridge turned to her. "Our victories were many, but the Ipis supply of warships and troops was endless. Our success drew the wrath of the Ipis emperor. We were no longer fighting a frontier army at the edge of the galaxy but the full might of their war machine. Fear overcame the leaders of the Centaurs and Satyrs, and at the decisive battle, the fleets of those two species abandoned us. We were outnumbered ten to one and crushed."

Setteth keened a long wail. "They enslaved my people and attempted to exterminate yours. I do not know which fate was worse." She snapped her beak. "The cowardly Centaurs and Satyrs sued for peace, and Ipis military warlords occupied their planets."

"But what of your story?" Michael crossed his arms. "That is what the crew wants to hear. When we found you, you were a fighter pilot supporting an Ipis Stalker-class warship."

Setteth flattened her feathers again. "After the battle of the Lethe Sector, I was captured, along with many others. The humans were executed. The Rocs were offered a choice to join the Ipis military or die. Most of my people chose the honor of death, but I swore allegiance to the Ipis." She plumed her feathers. "It was a false oath. As I watched my friends die, I swore a sacred vow to avenge them. I waited. For one hundred and twenty years I waited. Serving different Ipis warlords was not difficult. I had no qualms about hunting Centaurs or Satyrs. They were unworthy of honor. The few humans I encountered..." A throaty chuckle escaped the Roc. "...always managed to elude me. I bided my time and waited. So long I waited. My body aged, my feathers molted, and the Ipis forgot I once fought them. I was given minor command positions, high esteem for one not of their species."

Esther stroked her friend's feathers. "I love you as a dear friend, but why do the Rocs follow you? Don't they see you as a traitor for serving the Ipis war machine?"

Setteth stared at her display. "The Order of the Dragon. Dante knows the story, but very few non-Rocs do."

"Excuse me?" Esther's face scrunched in confusion. "Dragon?"

"It is a human concept. Rocs have no myth of such creatures." Setteth's mind focused on that horrible time many decades earlier. "The Ipis collected all of the captured Roc and human prisoners in a single pen where they pronounced our doom. Many of the young Roc warbird pilots

300

gathered in a circle. We decided to kill ourselves rather than give that honor to our captors. While we were talking, Emperor Marcus Carloman..." Setteth glanced at the display showing the Earth. "...came to us and said we must choose life. He said it was our responsibility to keep the spark of freedom alive. He said only through us would the galaxy learn of what happened here."

"It's incredible that he shares the same surname as Dante," Esther gasped.

"Do you still think it was random chance that brought me to you?" Setteth ruffled her feathers. "One hundred and sixty-seven of us declared we would avenge that day. We formed the Order of the Dragon to link us to humanity forever and submitted to the Ipis." She blinked. "Of the original band, I alone still live. Our underground resistance group was an ill-kept secret among my people. Our exploits were mere pinpricks against our occupiers but became legendary. Thousands of Roc fledglings, chafing under Ipis rule, flocked to us and took our vow. I have been their leader for many decades now and have sent many of my people into certain death over that time." She warbled. "They followed my commands with courage and pride."

Setteth eyes softened as she regarded Esther and Michael. "When my last Ipis commander encountered your galley ships over Cocytus, my heart sang with joy. I led the warship's fighters straight into your kill zone, then powered down my craft to watch the show. It took me back to the grand alliance so many decades earlier. The Ipis warship was far more powerful than what you had, but I knew they were doomed. When your soldiers captured me, I saw the anger in their eyes. I wanted to embrace them and tell them that I was one with them before they were even born, but I dared not—"

"Admiral, we just received a signal. The Centaur and Satyr fleets have dropped out of hyperspace into this solar system." The human communications officer's eyes widened. "Sir, the computer has identified over two thousand of them are capital warships. They must have stripped their planets of every hyperdrive vessel they could arm. They'll reach our position in twenty-three minutes."

Michael nodded. "Sound general quarters. I want every weapons system in the fleet online and ready. We attack in a half hour."

Setteth cawed and pressed a single icon on the small pad she clutched in her hand. "The Ipis will soon learn of Roc valor."

Klaxons blared through the ship.

"I will speak to your crew now." Setteth cleared her throat and flipped on the ship-wide intercom. "Warriors, you are all veterans. At Cocytus, Equitone, and Carcerem you were outnumbered and still won." Her eyes closed and she remembered a speech she listened to as a young, scared warbird pilot. *This is my second chance.* Her voice took on a hard edge. "We have lived our entire lives hunted and oppressed by the Ipis. They have subjugated us by keeping us divided. But today we will answer them. Today, we stand together and shout 'never again.' Today, we will be free to live our lives as we choose." She paused. The silence was deafening. "The Ipis have a large armada. They intend to break us forever. But they do not know the heart of the enemy they face." She summoned up the memories of all the horrors she had witnessed and screeched, "Today, we will break the shackles of our slave masters."

As one, the crew cheered.

Images of long-dead friends and comrades swam in Setteth's mind. She turned off the intercom and glanced at Michael.

The big clone chuckled. "I guess we're ready to fight." He walked to the commander's seat.

Thirty minutes later, over thirty-five hundred warships of the reborn alliance, rocketed toward the flashing lights near the Earth's moon. They attacked in a conical formation, with the largest capital ships at the point. Michael grunted in a low voice, "This will be bloody. The harpies have twice our number of capital ships."

The Ipis admiral reacted quickly as he detected the horde of hostile spaceships approaching. He reoriented his fleet using the long-accepted Ipis defensive alignment that had destroyed countless enemies in the past.

Michael studied his computer readouts and glanced at Setteth for confirmation. "It appears our opponent's aligning his fleet in the Ipis textbook standard procedures."

"The Ipis have not changed their tactics in over a hundred years." Setteth stared intently at her displays.

"They haven't had to," Michael responded as he wiped his palms on his leggings.

"They are predictable, and that shall be their undoing," the Roc hissed. "Let's see how they handle the unexpected."

As the alliance ships reached the Ipis fleet's perimeter, a dozen Ipis Enforcers vaporized. The defensive grid was breeched, and the allied fleet poured through the gap.

The harpy ship captains never heard the death chant of the Roc mercenary crew members on those vessels as they opened the power containment cylinders and disabled the regulators. The Rocs never forgot who their true enemy was, and Setteth had no trouble recruiting saboteurs. Small Roc warbirds and human galleys swarmed the now exposed enemy behemoths. More Ipis warships exploded as the Ipis admiral attempted to reform a defense.

The small human fleet that had been defending the Earth broke from their dodecahedron formation and slammed into the exposed Ipis flank, scattering the harpy ships there.

The battle raged on for six more hours, but the balance of power had shifted. An Ipis fleet, for the first time in centuries, had lost the initiative and was being whittled down.

* * *

A human sitting at the communication display on the bridge called out, "Admiral, we have an incoming communication from the Ipis flagship."

Michael smiled and regarded the old Roc sitting a few feet away. "Setteth, would you like to take this call?"

Setteth screeched, surprising everyone in the command center. She clamped her beak closed and bowed to Michael. "Forgive my outburst. I have waited many decades for this moment. For the first time in the living memory of *almost* any sentient being in this galaxy, the Ipis are losing a major battle." She looked at Esther, who stood like a pale statute beside her. "Shall we see what their commander wants?"

Esther nodded, not trusting herself to speak.

Setteth made a deep-throated cooing sound. "Your children and grandchildren are safe now." She turned to the communication officer. "Put the vid-link on my display."

A moment later, a two-dimensional image of a harpy appeared. The purplish-black alien wore the chest stripings of a senior Ipis fleet commander. Smoke and sparking photonic equipment filled the background behind him.

"A Roc," hissed the Ipis admiral as he saw Setteth's face on the screen. "This is a war between humans and us. Your interference is an act of rebellion. There will be consequences for the treaties broken here."

Setteth, with a raptor's eye, glared at her opponent. "For too long have you held sway over this sector of the galaxy. It is not just the humans you fight. The Rocs, Satyrs, and Centaurs stand together as we should have so long ago to oppose you."

"Centaurs and Satyrs are here too?" The Ipis leader bared his fangs. "Allow us to depart and we will consider sparing your home worlds from complete annihilation."

Esther whispered to Setteth, "Why don't they just leave if the battle is going poorly for them?"

Setteth cut the audio on the communication link and faced the old doctor. "It's a limitation of modern technology. No spacecraft can engage a hyperdrive while the energy shields are up. If they shut off their defenses, even our most simplistic weapons would breech their hulls. In a conflict like this, ninety percent of their fleet would be destroyed. As long as they're in normal space, they're committed to this battle."

Esther pursed her lips. "I guess that makes sense."

"Trust me. Our opponent's acutely aware of that problem." A throaty chuckle escaped Setteth as she flipped the audio link back on. "Permission to disengage *denied*. What mercy were you going to show the people on the planet below us?"

The harpy hissed, "That world is infested with humans and some creatures called elves. They must be eliminated."

Setteth glowered at the screen. "I saw your victory over that species at the battle of Novaroma one hundred and twenty years ago, and no quarter was offered them."

"Those monsters fought to the end. Our history reports that they asked for no mercy."

Setteth threw back her head and screamed, "Lies! I was there! I saw hundreds of unarmed transports full of non-combatants callously blown to pieces after the battle was long over."

"Human propaganda," the harpy hissed.

"I saw prisoners butchered with my own eyes." Setteth's voice dropped to a whisper. "The Ipis warlord forced all the Roc captives to watch. I saw my *friends* die that day and vowed to avenge their murder."

"How could you have been there? That was over a century ago." A nervous edge entered the harpy's words.

"Oh, I was not much more than a fledgling, newly assigned to fly my own warbird." Her voice grated like metal on metal. "I am old now, even by the reckoning of my species, but I was there. Rocs are a patient species. To see justice finally done, twelve decades is worth the wait."

"Then die with your vain desire unfulfilled." The Ipis leader paused and listened to someone not visible on the view screen. The harpy appeared to shrink within himself. When he turned back to the screen, his eyes narrowed to slits.

Setteth glanced at her own display and knew the reason for her opponent's consternation. Three more Ipis Enforcer-class spaceships had been obliterated in massive explosions. She clicked her beak in honor of the sacrifice made by the hundreds of Rocs who died in those explosions.

The Ipis had long used Rocs as mercenary fighters. Those warriors had sabotaged many of the Ipis ships and stayed on board to ensure system modifications remained undetected.

This fool still does not know he's fighting an enemy within his own defenses as well as our armada. Setteth's predatory eyes glared at the harpy. "Surrender now or be exterminated. Those are your only options." She glanced at her tactical display again. Without the firepower of the Enforcers, smaller Ipis vessels were rapidly being eliminated under the relentless assault. She cawed in satisfaction.

The Ipis admiral hissed out, "I yield my fleet."

"Unconditionally?"

"Yes, in the name of Fravashi, the all-seeing galactic empress, I yield unconditionally."

Setteth put her frail hand to her chest and wheezed to Michael. "Admiral, you can see to the surrender of the enemy vessels. This battle is concluded."

"It worked. By all that is holy, it worked." Michael sagged in his seat with a haggard face. He gathered himself and opened the fleet broadcast communication link. "Disengage. The Ipis have surrendered. Their unarmed transports will be allowed to depart, but all warships are now our prizes. If you are fired on or they try to power up their warships' hyperdrives, blow the suckers to the hell they came from."

"Yes, sir," numerous excited responses roared over the communicator.

"It is done." Setteth collapsed against the back of her nested chair as her head lolled forward.

The bridge of the flagship became awash in the cheers of Rocs, Humans, Centaurs and Satyrs celebrating.

Only Esther saw Setteth crumple into her seat. She bent to her friend and gently lifted the Roc's head. "Setteth. Setteth, don't die."

Setteth cracked one eye open, "No, not yet. I have too much to savor."

Chapter XLI

On the Edge of a Knife

Two months after the Ipis expeditionary fleet surrendered, the war on the Earth had turned decisively in favor of Dante and his allies. Over most of planet's surface, the Ipis troops, with dwindling supplies and rising causalities, were being routed. Only General Xiroah-dis, fortified behind his bastions in Madrid, Tehran, and Shenzhen was effectively repulsing all efforts to dislodge him. Elsewhere, the harpy units who could not breech the human siege lines to reach Xiroah's enclaves were surrendering en masse.

Tranquility Bay on the Earth's moon, the site of man's first steps off the Earth's surface, was a beehive of activity. Dante had made it his *de facto* capital for coordinating the war efforts and to keep his family safe. Shuttles moved in a constant stream to the base from the allied fleet and the Earth's surface. Workers swarmed the area, throwing up new construction and repairing damaged warships. *Reggie*, with rebuilt engines, was parked at the far edge of the expansive tarmac there.

Michael, although exhausted, chuckled as he leaned back on the cushioned chair. "Good thing little Josh, like his brother Liam, takes after his mom and not you. Otherwise, people would call him a *big ugly*." He stretched out his legs in the nursery. It was previously the captain's stateroom on *Reggie*.

Dante's eyes were red rimmed, but he smiled first at his wife, then the sleeping, month-old infant cradled in his arms. "Mick, just because you're this cute little peanut's godfather doesn't mean you can pick on your king." He reluctantly returned the newborn to Tina, who sat beside him on the couch. "This is the most incredible feeling I've ever experienced."

"Yeah, but I had to do all the work." Tina stroked the baby's cheek. She looked at the giant clone. "Mick, you want to hold him?"

Michael leaned forward, then frowned. "No, I have to return to my ship." He stood. "It's been two months since our victory over the Ipis fleet, but there's still so much to do. Many of the captured spacecraft still need to be crewed and have their operating systems reconfigured."

Dante also rose. "And there's still a few harpy armies that haven't surrendered and need to be dealt with." He leaned over and kissed Tina, then the baby. "I have to go too. Being the all-powerful human king isn't all it's cracked up to be." The smile fled his face. "So much death. So much hate and distrust."

Tina reached over and squeezed his hand. "You saved them... saved *us* from extermination. That must count for something."

"I wish it did. But it's hard for anyone to feel gratitude when they're hungry and no one's there to help." Dante sighed.

Tina's eyes flared. "What can they expect? The harpy EMP blasts wiped out every non-hardened computer chip on the planet, the sea level's risen ten feet, and there's virtually no infrastructure left."

Michael crossed his arms. "Yeah, and I don't think this is the last we'll hear from the Ipis. Hundreds of their transports left. This defeat won't sit well with the empire when they learn of it."

A shiver ran down Dante's spine. "Next time, it won't be mercenaries and cult paramilitaries. It'll be veteran imperial troops with state-of-the-art warships." He stepped to the nursery room exit and leaned his head against the bulkhead. He turned to the concerned look on his wife's face. "I love you. I love you both."

"I know you'll think of something." She forced a confident smile onto her face. It vanished as he walked into the hallway. She held her baby close.

"I'm going to grab a bite to eat in the ship's mess hall before I start the day's meetings. Can I get you something?" he asked.

"No thanks. Your mom and mine have been stuffing me," Tina snickered. "I'm sure they're hovering in the hallway right now, waiting for you and Mick to leave."

Dante was only a few steps into the passageway when his son, Liam, clutching a soccer ball in one hand and Taz's collar in the other, ran to him. "Hi, Dad, Uncle Mick. I've been teaching Taz how to play soccer. What to play with us?"

A sad smile creased Dante's face. "Sorry, squirt. I'll be kinda busy the next few days." He saw the crestfallen look on his five-year-old's face. "Hey, remember I promised to take us to Disney World once the *bad guys* go away."

Liam beamed. "Okay!" He ran into the room. "I think baby Josh needs me."

Dante's mother and mother-in-law followed the youngster, carrying large stuffed animals.

Victoria paused. "If you want any pancakes and bacon, you two better head to the dining mess now. There's a lot of hungry workers coming off the night shift."

Michael slapped him on the back. "I'll eat when I get back to my ship. It'll be quieter there." He turned down the corridor leading to the shuttle bay.

* * *

Dante stood, holding his tray, feeling very alone as he scanned the Striker's expansive dining hall. The happy chatter he heard on entering subsided to a hushed murmur. Quick, fugitive glances and pointed fingers in his direction told him why. *Everyone gives me a wide berth. They either worship or loathe me.*

A chirped call and a waved wing, "Dante over here," caught his attention. He moved to the voice.

Otheth and a couple Rocs sat with about a dozen rough-looking people wearing worn leather jackets emblazoned with *Wild Turkeys* over their neural-net suits. Dante smiled and nodded to their greetings as he joined them.

"I thought you were involved with the Australian campaign," Dante asked Otheth as he poured real maple syrup on his pancakes.

"We weren't needed," Otheth cawed.

Rene's face broke into a feral smile. "The allied forces had the damned harpies bottled up near Darwin. After three days of bombardment, the bastards' energy supplies were exhausted and they surrendered." He ruffled Otheth's feathers. "I'll tell you, those suckers ain't nothing without their fancy toys. There's not one of them that could stand up to a Roc or a human in a fair fight."

"The Centaurs and Satyrs helped too," Otheth warbled.

"Yeah, I guess you're right." Gilbert looked at the Rocs at the table. "But I can see myself cruising on my hog with you guys, and if I got into a bar fight, I know you'd have my back." He raised his coffee mug in the air. "And I never met a better person than Cheepash. God bless him."

The Rocs flared their crest feathers and crowed.

Otheth blinked her glistening eyes. "Finish your repast. We must return to work."

Dante glanced over. "What's your project?"

"There is a dearth of qualified personnel for crewing all of the captured Ipis ships. Admiral Martinel requested that we enlist all trainable Earth humans who are willing to help fill the gap," Otheth warbled.

Rene thumped his chest. "Otheth talked that shiny cylinder named Mara into letting the Wild Turkeys to be part of *Reggie's* crew." He rubbed his beard. "I'll tell ya, once you get past all the high-tech mumbo-jumbo it's not a whole lot harder than restoring a 1948, twelve hundred cc Indian Chief."

"I'll trust you on that point." Dante sipped his coffee. "Thanks. Welcome to the royal fleet."

"Hey, with the damn harpies folding everywhere, any chance of salvaging this year's hockey season?" a burly man with a gray-streaked red beard, sitting to his right, asked.

Dante shook his head. "I think this season's probably shot."

A woman with a long blonde ponytail, sitting on the other side of the man, swatted him. "Show some respect to the king, you overfed lump. He's got more important things to worry about than a bunch of guys sliding a puck around the ice." She smiled at Dante. "I heard you and your wife had a baby. Congratulations."

"Thanks. He's our second." Dante's face grew wistful. "I was with the main army on the push through Italy when Tina went into labor. The Novaromans were infatuated with seeing the place of their ancestors' origin and I couldn't leave. It's important that all humans feel bonded together."

"Hell, yeah!" they shouted. A few of the bikers rose and thumped him on the back as Rene declared, "Ya know, for a high-and-mighty, you're okay."

Dante noticed the careworn look behind their ready smiles. "And thank you for everything you've done. You guys saved my wife... and my baby at Niagara Falls. I won't ever forget that."

"We were in on the supply depot raid in Playa Hermosa too," a voice at the end of the tabled called out.

"And I saw how well you fought at Gettysburg." Dante nodded, then smirked. "Hell, from what I heard, if it wasn't for you, Otheth and her team would still be floundering around the Hudson Bay."

"Damn straight on that one," several voices roared at once.

Otheth rose and crowed in a loud voice as she spread her undersized wings, "These humans are among the greatest warriors I've ever had the pleasure to serve with. And my dearest friends." She paused and cocked her head. "They should be members of the Order of the Dragon and not Wild Turkeys."

Dante's forkful of hash froze halfway to his mouth. He turned to the bikers at the table. "That's high tribute." He glanced at Otheth. "My understanding is that the Order of the Dragon only accepts Rocs, and of them only the best of the bravest."

Otheth snapped her beak. "I have invited the Wild Turkeys to Tannis and will sing of their *cou*. It will be a long chant."

Dante nodded, then motion at the mess hall entrance caught his attention. Herb Wells was there scanning the room. Dante sighed and rose as the lieutenant spotted him and waved. "It looks like duty calls. My guests have arrived. I have a very tricky meeting coming up."

Otheth also stood and cocked her head. "I will go with you. I believe the *tricky* meeting you're leaving for includes my great-grandmother. She asked me to attend with her."

"I have no doubt where Setteth stands. It's the others who I don't know." Dante walked to the exit with Otheth at his side. All eyes followed him, human and non-human alike.

They rode a hyperloop to the new administrative building that dominated the center of Tranquility Bay. It was a four-story, black plexo-steel structure topped by a crystal-clear dome. Powerful generators several levels below the surface provided the interlocked radiation shielding, artificial gravity, and environmental controls.

Dante returned the sharp salute of the two guards, a human and a Centaur, as he cleared the building's airlock. Both had been with him since Carcerem.

As he walked into the spacious meeting room, the hubbub of many conversations subsided. There were over forty dignitaries from the four Lethe Sector species. Some he knew and considered close friends: Calahas, Arachne, and Setteth. But only Setteth led a delegation.

Already seated at the head table, alongside the empty chair reserved for him, were King Prolia of the Centaurs, Guildmistress Drusilla of the Satyrs, Setteth, and the Novaroman Claudia. Dante nodded to Setteth, who bowed her head in return. The others stared impassively, judging him. *Those are the ones I must win over.*

Dante raised his hands in greeting. "Let's begin."

Everyone settled into their assigned seat. *Diplomacy,* Dante noted with disgust. The representatives from the Earth, who had suffered the most in the current strife, were relegated to the fifth table back.

General Cruz picked up his chair and moved to that table, sitting beside the American President, Stevenson. The general winked at Dante's grateful smile.

Dante sighed. "General Cruz, start with an update on the campaign."

Cruz rose to his feet. A color-coded, holographic display of the Earth appeared in the middle of his table. There was much squeaking of chairs as delegates shifted around to view the display. Cruz cleared his throat. "Holding complete dominance in the air and with millions of ground troop reinforcements, all meaningful Ipis resistance has collapsed. There remain Ipis-entrenched strongholds near Madrid, Spain; Tehran, Iran; and Shenzhen, China. But our collective forces have those locations besieged. Those Ipis troops have nowhere to go. It is only a question of time."

The presentation got no further.

Mercantile leader Drusilla leaned forward. "All three of those locations are commanded by General Xiroah-dis. He's a former imperial commander. He won't yield without a bloodbath," she huffed. "Beware. If he hasn't made a move yet, it's for a reason."

King Prolia whinnied. "We Centaurs have met our commitment to the new Lethe Sector Alliance. Equitone is defenseless. How much longer must I remain? These are dangerous times. My fleet is needed back home."

"Fool," Setteth cawed. "The decisive battle awaits us. It will be soon, and it will be *here*." She craned her long neck. "The Imperials will marshal their forces and come. They have no choice, and we must meet them, united."

Dante saw that, although only seconds into the meeting, it was heading in a disastrous direction. He jumped in. "With all of our alliances' warships gathered, plus the captured Lethe Sector paramilitary spacecraft, we have our best, and perhaps only, chance for victory." He met the eyes of the Centaur king. "There is no turning back."

Claudia rose from her seat. "Perhaps we were rash to rush pell-mell into war before being fully prepared."

Dante stood and leaned forward with his knuckles pressing on the table. "When do you think we'd be ready to face the might of the Ipis empire? With every second we delayed, millions of innocents were being butchered. We fought because there was no other recourse." His eyes locked on to her. "No sane person would *ever* claim to be ready to fight the full power of the Ipis empire." He slipped the satchel that hung over his shoulder and dumped the contents on the table.

He lifted two items up for all to see. "This is the sash and medallion Silenus-dis wore when I struck him down. When was the last time an Imperial Sector Governor died at the hands of someone who was not another Ipis noble? It will give the Imperials pause."

Setteth rose to her feet, crest feathers flared. "Never in my lifetime has such a blow been struck. This discourse disgusts me. We fight because we must. A hundred and twenty standard years ago, the Ipis accepted the surrender of the Roc, Satyr, and Centaur species. The enslavement since then has ground our peoples into something that our proud ancestors would not recognize. Today, our home worlds are not even ours. In another generation, we won't even be allowed to live there."

"My commitment here's not open-ended," Drusilla grated. "My troops and ships cannot—"

The holographic image of the Earth in the center of the table was replaced by Admiral Martinel's face. His shouted words resounded over klaxons blaring behind him. "They're here, and there's a lot of them." He gulped. "My long-distance scanners indicate it's the Ipis Imperial First Fleet. The full fleet."

Holographic displays popped up in front of everyone in the conference room.

Dante studied the data. "How much time do we have to prepare?"

"Mate, I've been preparing since we cleaned the clock of that Lethe Sector fleet two months ago." Martinel snorted. "But if you mean 'when will they get here,' the answer is in about two days, somewhat longer if they have a cautious commander." He glanced off-screen, "The intel Charon provided looks to be dead-on accurate so far."

"Charon!" The hackles on King Prolia's back rose, and he snapped, "We move the fleet on the word of a soulless killer? He's been convicted of multiple murders on Equitone, including members of my own family. If he's here, I insist on taking him back to face justice."

Dante pleaded with the Centaur king, "If any of us live through this, we can decide Charon's fate then. Right now, we have only *one* focus, and that is to defeat an enemy that, to my knowledge, has never been defeated."

Prolia locked eyes with Dante for a moment, then bowed his head. "As you say, first things first." He scanned the room. "But I will have justice."

Setteth warbled as she studied the data on her screen. "Interesting. The First Fleet exited hyperspace at the outer reaches of this solar system. Normally that's a tactical blunder because it allows their intended prey ample time to escape. But it's a wise move if they knew their enemy has a large force and is ready to fight." Her crest feathers flattened. "Admiral Yasha-ry is a brilliant strategist."

"The First Fleet." Drusilla paled. "We can't defeat them."

"Yes, we can. We just have to stay a step ahead of him," Martinel snarled. "This Yasha-ry is not all-knowing. Counting noses, we're evenly matched, but the reality is that we're way outgunned. Most of our captured ships only have skeleton crews. If he knew that, he'd charge right in and mop us up with overpowering force." The Aussie tugged at the rim of his battered bushman's hat. "We whittle his fleet down a bit, harassing his flanks. We shift the fighting ships with those that are mostly derelicts. We confuse the hell out of him." He leaned toward the vid-camera. "Then when we get our full strength online, we bust that sucker up and send him packing."

Dante took that as a good time for ending the session. "I'm adjourning this meeting. Its main purpose has just been rendered moot. We all have our tasks. Godspeed." He rose and strode from room without waiting for any responses. He did not want any probing questions of Martinel's dicey plan.

315

Chapter XLII

Hang Together

Yasha-ry entered the private chambers of the Ipis empress on his flagship. "Your Majesty, you were correct. This enemy is far stronger than I expected and are here to fight. You should not have come."

Fravashi smiled and chided him, "My great protector faces a challenge that he cannot meet?"

The admiral scowled. "Your jest is not appreciated. Of course I'll win... eventually. Ipis forces always do. But my opponent has a powerful fleet and is clever. We've been faced off for over a standard week now, and I've yet to dupe him into any rash moves with my feints."

He sat on a stool beside his monarch. "His ships are like phantoms. They strike exposed warships and then disappear. Yesterday, a full squadron was mauled by a surprise attack in this system's asteroid belt. A large number of human galleys and Roc warbirds, hidden in those rocks, caught my ships unaware. They fled to the protective screen of their fleet's capital ships before my commander could react."

"A stalemate then." Empress Fravashi leaned back and regarded the half-finished sculpture she was working on. "Your opposite number is a human named Admiral Martinel."

"I'll remember that." Yasha-ry grunted. "Still, it's only a question of time. I've summoned the Fifth Fleet to come with all dispatch."

"The Fifth Fleet? They're scattered across the Baskra Sector. It'll be at least another week before Admiral Menane-ry even receives your request and at least another month before he can gather his ships." Fravashi put down her chisel and mallet, and the private smile she shared only with her lover vanished. "The human king, Dante Carloman, will not allow us that time."

"Then we fight with what we have." Yasha-ry shrugged. "And I will crush that primate."

"Yes, you will probably win, but the invincible First Fleet would be bloodied beyond recognition." Fravashi sat on a stool beside her consort and closed her eyes. "Word would spread across the galaxy that a ragtag band at the fringe of the empire fought our greatest force to a standstill. It will be the beginning of the end."

"All right then." Yasha-ry shifted in his seat. "I learned to never doubt one of your *seeings*. I will withdraw the fleet until I can return with twice the number of ships."

The empress patted her lover's leg. "That will have the same result. Word will spread that the First Fleet was forced to retreat."

"Then what will you have me do?" Yasha-ry leapt to his feet. "You say I cannot attack and I cannot retreat. What is left?"

"I don't know." Empress Fravashi stood. "Everything my visions show me of the future is the destruction of our people." She tapped her unfinished statue. "The only spot of light I *see* surrounds this human king."

Yasha-ry regarded the sculpture with alarm. "This is the same figure you've been attempting to carve for the last six years."

"Yes. It's the human king, Dante Carloman." Her bony shoulders sagged. "Something about him is the key to *saving* the Ipis." She patted the statue with her gnarled hand. "But I cannot see what it could possibly be or what the path is to reach it."

Yasha-ry squeezed her shoulders. "I guess *seeing* the future isn't the great gift it's cracked up to be."

"It's a curse." She leaned against the admiral's chest. "If only I could solve this riddle. If only I could see—"

The empress spun and looked into the eyes of her longtime lover. "I want you to contact the enemy fleet commander. Propose a truce. Tell him that you wish to parley with their alliance's leadership."

"They'll expect a trap." Yasha-ry's voice sounded worried. "I know I would."

317

"Let them pick the time and place. I don't care." The empress looked at the statue. "I must get close to the human king."

"But... but the risk to you would be enormous." Yasha-ry paled. "How would I be able to ensure your security?"

The empress' clawed feet dug at the steel deck. "My time will not run out *here*."

"But what will I say we wish to negotiate?"

The empress closed her eyes and clenched her fanged jaws. "The lives of everyone they hold dear."

* * *

"Charon, you shouldn't be here." Dante closed the door of the cramped office he maintained off *Reggie's* shuttle dock. "If King Prolia discovers you're around, I'll be forced to turn you over to him."

Charon flicked his tail. "That'll only happen if I grow careless... or am betrayed."

Dante moved behind his desk and sat. "I will not be the one to turn you in." Looking down at his folded hands, his voice was barely above a whisper. "I'm convinced the Centaur king's charges against you are true, and I desperately need to keep him in my alliance." He looked up at Charon's hooded eyes. "But you aided me when my situation was dire and it was in your interest to look the other way. Your choice shifted the balance of that first battle. Without that victory, Earth would have been lost before the war was barely started." He slapped the table. "As God is my witness, I will grant you sanctuary on any world I rule, no matter what the cost."

Charon's withers twitched. "That's a bold promise, but I believe you." He shifted on his feet. "You will recall that I am employed by Admiral Yasha-ry. He has summoned me for a full report on *you*."

"He's looking for the chink in our armor, and you know what it is." Dante paled. "We're just an empty shell, yet he's not aware of that. *You* haven't told him." He gave Charon a level gaze. "Be careful. You're playing a dangerous game. Go. I will not hinder you."

Charon nickered. "That is why you intrigue me. Your mind penetrates the subterfuge. It's a rare talent." He pawed the steel deck. "Rest assured regarding your fleet. Yasha-ry will get little strategic intel from me beyond what his picket ships have already uncovered. But beware. Yasha-ry is clever. He'll see through Martinel's ruse eventually." He shook his maned head. "But there's another topic. He wants all the information I have on *you*." He gave Dante a level stare. "It will be... shaded to your advantage. But beware. If he suspects a weakness, he'll exploit it."

"That makes sense." Dante sat on the edge of his desk. "He's looking for my pressure points at this upcoming parley. What do you make of this offer to negotiate? It's not normal for Ipis, as I've been led to believe."

"What do your allies say?" The Centaur paced the small room.

Dante shook his head. "Setteth says never trust an Ipis and we should attack immediately. Drusilla says our fleet should abandon the Earth and flee to the wastelands. Prolia says we should listen to what the Admiral offers. If it's a trap we're all dead anyway, so it doesn't matter."

Charon abruptly halted his pacing and sat on the only chair in the office that would fit a Centaur's haunches. "And what do you say?"

Dante pressed his forehead against his palms. "For the last seven years, my sole experience with harpies was resisting them with every fiber of my being. But, for the survival of my people, I need to find a way to talk to them and make peace. I don't know how."

Charon nickered. "Seven years ago, were you the human king?"

"Hardly." A sad smile creased Dante's face. "I was a software engineering PhD candidate working on my thesis exploring interfaces between human neural nets and nano-computers."

Charon leaned forward. "So, you became something different for survival of your people."

Dante chuckled as he recalled being elected *president* that night long ago in Beatrice's gardens. "Trust me, I got the job because no one else wanted it."

"False modesty does not become you," Charon snapped. "I have spoken to those you saved on Cocytus and Carcerem, and I saw myself how you inspired those on Equitone and Earth. Do you honestly think anyone else could have accomplished those feats?"

"I was damned lucky and had incredible people helping me," Dante shot back.

Charon snorted. "In my *profession*, I've discovered there's no such thing as luck." He rose and shook his mane. "Those people accomplished the impossible because you believed they could and they believed in *you*."

"Okay, okay." Dante shook his head. "I still don't know what to do about this proposed meeting."

Charon whinnied. "If this meeting was with Admiral Yasha-ry, I'd say no. But that's not who you'll be meeting."

A puzzled look crossed Dante's face. "He's not? I thought he was the First Fleet Commander."

Charon leaned forward. "The Ipis Empress Fravashi is *here*. She is the one who wants to meet. Talk to her, and maybe your species, and mine, will survive." "I have no details besides the fact that she has a strong desire to see *you*." He cocked his head and appeared to be listening to a voice in his ear. "I must take my leave. King Prolia's shuttle is inbound for your meeting. Just remember my words. You changed once to save your friends, and now you must do so again to save your species."

Chapter XLIII

Parley

Dante sat in his customary chair on *Reggie's* bridge as the Striker approached the predetermined landing site in Gale's Crater on Mars. Every key diplomat who arrived with the allied fleet was packed on board. He led the parley delegation but had only a small role in choosing the participants. He knew very few of them.

Although they had no diplomatic credentials, his friends wrangled their way onboard. Quango was the ship's engineer. Virgil headed the security detail, which of course included Aramis, Athos, and Porthos.

Per the negotiated arrangements for the meeting, both the Ipis and allied leadership were allowed to bring a single Striker-class vessel within the agreed upon demilitarized zone. It covered a fifty-million-mile-wide buffer surrounding Mars.

Reggie insisted that he be the Striker used for the daunting responsibility of transporting his king, and friend. He'd made his case directly to Dante three days earlier. "I'll not have one of those mindless lumps of metal carry you. What will they do if something goes wrong?"

Dante nodded. "Glad to have you with us, old friend."

Although an admiral in the allied fleet, Michael would allow no one else to captain *Reggie* for this mission. He glanced over from the pilot's chair. "We'll be on the ground in ten minutes. You ready?"

Dante met Michael's look with steady eyes. "I'm ready as I'm going to be."

Setteth pointed at the view screen. "It appears our Ipis negotiators have also just arrived."

Dante studied the display. He saw an ultramodern class-H Striker touch down fifty feet from a featureless, single-story, circular black dome that was sixty yards in diameter with two airlock entrances at opposite ends of the structure.

Tina, King Prolia, and Guildmistress Drusilla joined him at the screen, and they watched a large, white umbilical cord extend from the harpy ship to the building's airlock.

Mara called over from her console, "I detect twenty entities entering the treaty conference building. None carry any powered equipment other than translator-communicators. They are abiding by the agreement."

"Thanks, Mara. When we're inside, keep me posted of any changes." As Dante rose, Michael gave him a thumbs-up.

Dante returned a nervous smile and directed the delegation out. King Prolia led a team of five Centaurs, which included Prince Calahas. Guildmistress Drusilla headed the Satyr dignitaries and had Arachne at her side. Flock-Mother Setteth was joined by Oteth and three other Rocs. The humans, besides Dante, were Tina, the American President Stevenson, Iucundum, and Claudia.

Although she'd delivered her baby five weeks earlier, Tina insisted on coming. "The lives of our two boys depend on what happens here. I won't sit on the sidelines."

Dante could not talk her out of it.

As he entered the building, Dante was nauseated by the pulsing blue light that encompassed the interior. *Either we negotiate as equals or this conference is doomed.* He moved to the head of his group as they hesitated by the entrance portal and spoke to a control unit embedded in a nearby wall. "Shift lighting to human-normal for our hemisphere."

Immediately, the half of the interior lighting on the side where the allied group stood shifted from blue to a soft golden-yellow. "Testing us," he mumbled.

Dante saw the Ipis delegates scowl but continue to move with their unique gait toward the conference table in the exact center of the open room. Most were large for harpies and wore the sashes of senior Ipis military officers. Their skin coloring ranged from lavender to violet. It was the last harpy who entered that drew his attention. She was much smaller, with scaled flesh the color of eggplant. She wore only a single adornment. Around her neck dangled a wide magenta ribbon embedded with pulsing blue stones. *She's staring at me.*

Dante gazed back and was rewarded with what he understood was the Ipis look of confusion. He quickly strode to one of the five chairs built for a human posterior and found himself sitting directly across from the small harpy.

She flicked her long tongue and spoke in surprisingly good English. "Are humans always so disrespectful?"

"Excuse me?" Dante glanced around and noticed that, besides the small harpy, only he and Tina were sitting. The Ipis officials hissed and glared death at him, while his own delegation stood behind their chairs shifting nervously on their feet. Calahas had grabbed Iucundum and Stevenson before they sat.

The small harpy raised her hand and switched to speaking Ipis. "The transgression is forgiven. Being a primitive savage, he's obviously unaware of who I am." She turned to Dante and splayed her claws. "I am Empress Fravashi, ruler of what you call the Milky Way Galaxy." Eagerness filled her eyes. "And you are the human's king, Dante Carloman. I've waited a long time to meet you."

"Your Majesty, do not lower yourself to speak to these vermin," a large harpy standing behind Fravashi's right shoulder growled. "All I see here are humans, deserters, criminals, and peddlers. They are unworthy to hear your sacred voice."

Fravashi reached back and squeezed the speaker's clawed hand. "Yasha-ry, dearest of my consorts, you make the proposition then. It is a generous offer for rebellious subjects."

"They don't deserve it," Yasha-ry snorted.

"I insist. Make the offer and let's be done with this parley."

Yasha-ry cleared his throat. "Her glorious majesty has decreed that, henceforth, being human is no longer a felony. That species will be allowed to exist on reservations in the polar regions of the planet labeled Earth. All other areas of that world and any additional human-infested planets will revert to imperial ownership for the purpose of Ipis colonization and settlement."

He glared at Setteth. "For the traitorous Rocs, all fledglings will be turned over to the imperial military where they must serve a conscription of thirty years after they complete their indoctrination."

His gaze shifted to Drusilla. "Management of all Satyr mercantile houses will henceforth be controlled by Ipis nobles."

Yasha-ry smiled at King Prolia. "All Centaurs will be quarantined to Equitone, never to leave that planet's surface again."

He spread his clawed hands. "And, of course, this war fleet you've assembled will be confiscated by the Imperium in its entirety. All officers involved with this uprising will surrender. The empress promises that there will be no torture. They will be executed humanely."

Dante glanced along his side of the table. Iucundum's face flushed with rage, and both Setteth and Otheth's feathers flared. Arachne and Calahas glowered, but Stevenson, King Prolia, and Guildmistress Drusilla seemed visibly cowed. Tina studied Fravashi for a few seconds, leaned over, and whispered in Dante's ear. "Someone I dearly love once said, 'The price of vegetables is negotiable and everything is a vegetable.'"

Dante pecked her on the cheek. "Thanks for reminding me." He rose to his feet and gave the harpy standing a head shorter than himself a condescending smile. "You ask a lot before you even blistered any paint off of those fancy ships you brought. You can take that offer and shove it where the sun don't shine." His eyes narrowed. "Let me tell you what the deal will be. You will abandon every military post in the Lethe Sector, and when your soldiers leave, they will take every goddamn *harpy* civilian with them. Then your imperial treasury will pay us recompense for a hundred and twenty years of persecution."

"This is not a negotiation," Yasha-ry sputtered. "I will not stand for these outrageous insults. This parley is over."

"No, it isn't," Fravashi interrupted. "It appears we understand each other's opening positions. Now we talk."

She rose to her feet and studied Dante. "Human king, walk with me while the others discuss things."

Dante looked down his side of the table and only received confused looks and shrugs in response.

Tina squeezed his hand. "Go ahead, it can't hurt. Nothing will come of these negotiations without the empress' approval."

Dante nodded and followed Fravashi to a far corner of the expansive room.

She was the first to speak. "I will be frank. This parley will resolve nothing. There will be a great battle. My fleet will prevail but in the process suffer horrendous losses."

Dante was stunned by those comments. "You seem very dismissive of a meeting your people spent a lot of effort to bring about. If you're so confident of victory, why bother talking?"

"This meeting had only one real purpose." Fravashi tentatively extended a clawed finger and touched Dante's chest. "It was so I could get close to you."

She lowered her hand and sighed. "You are the answer to a riddle that vexes me. I had hoped some clue would reveal itself by seeing you in person, but nothing. My vision of what will be is no clearer."

Dante found curiosity fight with the loathing he had for the entire Ipis species. "So, the rumors are true. You can predict the future?"

"It's a confusing talent." A hissed chuckle escaped her lipless mouth. "I really can't observe the future as one sees things around them. What I divine are the results of different alternative present-day actions. So, following certain paths, I can achieve my desired future realities with no unforeseen loose ends. However, on rare occasions I am confounded." She interlocked her gnarled fingers. "For some inexplicable reason, you are at the core of a significant dilemma. I see you living and breathing before me, but in my mind's eye you are distorted. I see an ever-shifting, glowing version of you, but also utter darkness and death swirl around you. Sometimes your aura is engulfed by the blackness, and sometimes your glow creates a growing island of light."

Dante shook his head. "You better recheck your crystal ball. My only interaction with you people is when they were trying to kill me." He had never had a meaningful conversation with a harpy and found it disconcerting. "You're not quite what I imagined the harpy kingpin would be like."

"I've gotten a translation for that word *harpy*. It's quite derogatory." Fravashi smiled. "Trust me. I *am* as ruthless as you can imagine in your worst nightmares. One must be to rule when every day usurpers plot my demise."

Dante snorted. "So, we have that much in common. Ipis are always trying to do me in also." He rolled his wounded arm that still had not quite healed from his fight with Silenus-dis. "I had to personally take down your governor of this sector when he tried to take my head off."

Fravashi's tongue flicked. "You dueled Silenus-dis and won? He was quite the melee champion in his younger days."

She cocked her head and changed the subject. "I was actually quite innocent once. But the Ipis ethos has a way of changing that." The empress glanced at the conference table where Yasha-ry was shouting at Setteth. A soft smile creased her face. "My peculiar gift was recognized when I was a youth, but none of the royal blood was sure how to exploit it. So, I was kept in isolation. That is when I started sculpting. My only contact with any other Ipis were my wardens, so I carved them. They treated me kindly, especially the handsome prison captain." She pointed at the First Fleet Admiral. "Yasha-ry spent many long hours talking with me as he posed."

She turned to Dante. "One day he came to me, distraught. He told me my execution had been ordered. I knew this moment would come, and I knew what Yasha-ry would choose to do. He freed me from my prison and helped me, one-by-one, to eliminate my rivals until, at a very young age, I assumed the Imperial throne. I was all-powerful and none dared defy me." She sighed, "That was thirty-one years ago, and I haven't been dislodged yet."

Fravashi studied Dante's face. "I must have you pose for my next carving. I cannot get the face right. You humans have such peculiar features."

"You sculpt humans?" Dante asked.

"Only you." She smiled, showing her needle-like fangs. "I've been told you're a software engineer by training." She glanced over at the conference table, where the voices had dropped to low growls. "It appears it's up to us to resolve your dilemma and my riddle."

Dante leaned against the wall's curved surface and a thought struck him. "You probably can't see me in your visions because I'm not supposed to be here."

"Go on." Fravashi sat on her haunches and looked up at Dante with slitted eyes.

He sat beside her and relayed his encounter with the antique Dis-cult computer over six years earlier. "Your people somehow altered an event sixteen hundred years ago. I believe it changed the course of history for my species, and *yours*. I suspect that the threads of time have been attempting to re-weave themselves into the proper pattern ever since."

"Alternative universes explain the overlapping versions of you." Fravashi's eyes glowed. "But I've never seen such extremes in my visions." Her eyes clouded. "Do you bring the destruction of all living things in the galaxy, or are you our salvation?" She touched his chest again. "You are the one I need to solve my quandary."

Dante cocked his ear to the distant debate. "Why can't you just leave us alone? I've never been outside it, but I understand the Lethe Sector is a tiny speck on the fringe of your empire. We can't be that important to you."

"Your thinking is so very provincial," Fravashi chuckled. "Ipis rule of the entire galaxy must be complete. No sector is inconsequential to our racial pride. The governor of a sector must either be one of my consorts, like the late Silenus-dis, or of royal blood. And that rule is absolute."

"Silenus-dis was your mate?" Dante gave the empress a nervous glance.

Fravashi shrugged. "I have, ah... had, eighteen consorts. It's the practical way to buy loyalty and diffuse the power of my ambitious kin." She looked fondly at Yasha-ry. "There's only one of them who I actually love. Most I never see again once the marriage is consummated. They gain prestige and influence; I get a secure sector with a loyal governor. It works well for all parties. I—"

A commotion at the conference table drew their attention. Otheth's crest feathers were fully flared, and a harpy opposite her was poised, ready to spring.

Fravashi sighed. "I think we've done enough talking for one day." She shouted and her voice was amplified through the chamber. "This session is concluded. We will resume again in twenty standard hours." She abruptly rose and walked out without another word. Her harpy minions hurried after her.

The eyes of everyone remaining swung toward Dante.

He shook his head as the last harpy disappeared into the airlock. "We need to compare notes."

Chapter XLIV

Message in a Bottle

Dante slumped in his hard-backed chair, fingering a cold cup of coffee. He sat in *Reggie's* mostly deserted mess hall. After the conference with the Ipis, he'd gathered the allied team of diplomats to consider alternative proposals. They spent four hours arguing. The dignitaries went to bed without developing a new offer they could all agree on.

Tina walked in and sat beside him. "I checked on the boys. They're both sound asleep and Aramis is watching them." She looked around the room. "What are we going to do?"

The only ones still in the mess hall were Dante and Tina's loyal friends, both from the crew and the delegation.

Arachne cleared his throat. "Sire, there may not be anything more we can do. The last Ipis offer spares our lives and doesn't displace anyone from their home worlds. It is generous by their standards."

"In a pig's eye!" Virgil barked. "Every aspect of our lives would be under their control." He started pacing. "I'm a quarter-blood Cherokee. What they are offering us is a chance to atrophy on reservations. We'd devolve into the brute savages they think we are."

"I agree with Virgil," Dante added. "Their assigned planetary administrators would control interstellar commerce, lawmaking, law enforcement. We'd be banned from establishing any kind of independent militia or education system. We'd exist, but that is about it."

"Maybe it won't be that bad." Iucundum steepled his fingers. "Some Ipis administrators tolerate a small level of self-governance. If we—"

Mara interrupted, "Reggie just informed me that he detected some form of digital device has been affixed on the exterior access door by the left rear thruster. The door's seal was breeched but never opened."

Michael was up in a flash. "I knew the goddamn harpies would try some stunt." He raced out of the hall, with Virgil and Quango right behind him.

* * *

Twenty minutes later, the three returned.

Quango held a palm-sized disk. "I scanned this thing. Nothing dangerous. Just a holographic projector."

"Who left it?" Tina asked.

"Don't have the faintest idea." Quango shrugged. "It's imperial equipment is all I can determine. I tried turning it on, but nothing happened."

"Let me have a look." Dante held out his hand. "Someone went to a lot of trouble to put it there and then making sure we found it." As soon as he touched it, a holographic video of Charon appeared right above it.

Calahas hissed "murderer" as Dante placed the projector on the table.

Charon appeared to be in a closet-sized room with no windows and little lighting. His eyes were red rimmed as he spoke to the camera. "Dante Carloman, somehow Admiral Yasha-ry has discovered that your fleet is not nearly as powerful as it appears. He has demanded that he be allowed to attack with his armada. Empress Fravashi acquiesced, with the agreement that he refrains from any action until the parley is concluded. That will be tomorrow." The Centaur's face looked desperate as he moved close to the camera. "I know the First Fleet's capabilities and I know yours. In the name of whatever god you worship, make the best deal you can. The alternative is your extermination." He sighed. "The empress and her visions is the key. Use the wits you've been blessed with and make her an offer she can't refuse. I... I will do what I can from this end. I owe the memory of my sister, Huon, that much. Farewell."

The image disappeared.

"Well, that does it," Arachne sighed. "They called our bluff. This morning's deal is the best we're going to get. If it's even *still* on the table."

"Don't believe anything Charon says!" Calahas shouted. "His whole life is a lie."

Tina pursed her lips. "I believe him."

"I agree with the lass. He wasn't lying." Quango sighed and glanced at Dante. "And I was just starting to get used to you as our grand potentate. Too bad there aren't any harpies like you."

Tina cocked her head. "Why not?"

Quango sputtered. "I was joking. It's not in a harpy's DNA."

Tina crossed her arms. "Why can't we demand that my husband be appointed the Lethe Sector governor?"

Setteth cawed, "That would be magnificent. Only one problem. The Ipis would never agree to a non-Ipis being in charge."

Tina scowled. "Look, even if they know their fleet can best ours, they also have to know that they would suffer some severe losses. We still have that bargaining chip. Why can't Dante be made an honorary harpy?"

Virgil growled, "True. There is only one certainty in war, and that is there are no certainties."

Setteth warbled, "Even if Dante managed to get accepted as a harpy, which in itself is an impossibility, he'd have to be of noble Ipis lineage or a consort of the empress."

Tina crossed her arms. "Fine, then. Dante, volunteer to become one of Fravashi's consorts."

"Wh-what?" Dante sat bolt upright. "You want me to marry a... harpy?"

Tina smiled. "Worse than the one you're already married to?" She chuckled. "Hey, I'm a doctor. So, I know a little bit about biology. You can't have a relationship with that monster. And if you tried, I'd claw your eyes out."

Charon snorted. "Enough of these jests. We have a serious problem and only a short time to come up with a real plan."

The discussion went on for another twenty minutes. Dante did not participate. He was thinking about another discussion he'd had with Charon. *You must become something you are not.* He ventured a question. "Setteth, how *do* governors get replaced in the Ipis empire?"

The old Roc fluffed her feathers and appeared to be thinking for a moment. "The same way they resolve all other ascension situations, by challenging the office holder to a duel and then killing him."

"I see." Dante drummed his fingers on the table. "I killed the Lethe Sector governor in an open duel that was witnessed by many."

"True. But that hardly makes you an Ipis."

Dante leaned forward. "Look, Fravashi wants to keep me alive because of some crystal ball idiocy. I can use that." He glanced at the American President, Stevenson. "There's an old saying where I come from, 'Keep your friends close and your enemies closer.' I can use that too."

A thin smile creased Stevenson's face. "Abraham Lincoln... It did work for him."

Dante slapped the table. "This is what we're going to do."

* * *

The next morning, the allied dignitaries arrived first. Dante, his neural-net suit dyed a dark purple and wearing the sash and medallion he took from the corpse of Silenus-dis, moved to the opposite side of the table from his own delegation and balanced himself on the narrow seat to the left of where Fravashi sat.

There were several shrill screeches when the Ipis entered.

Yasha-ry approached Dante and stared at the signs of office he wore. "Primate, what do you think you're doing?"

Dante smiled and stood. "I erred yesterday. As the Lethe Sector governor, I belong on the same side as my empress." He dipped his head to Fravashi. "I regret the mistake."

Her long tongue flicked out. "Interesting." Her face twisted into a gruesome parody of a smile. "Admiral,... Acting Governor, walk with me."

Dante met Yasha-ry's glare with a steady regard. "Tina, why don't you join us too."

332

A sharp hiss escaped the admiral.

The empress glanced over at Tina. "The human female can accompany the acting governor."

The four walked to the far side of the chamber. The beings at the table stared after them in silence.

Fravashi was the first to speak, "Do you understand the meaning of the symbols you wear?"

Dante touched the medallion and then the sash. "Lethe Sector Governor, Consort to the Empress."

Her tongue flicked. "Only an Ipis noble may become governor."

Dante cleared his throat. "A lowborn can also be raised to that station if the individual is a consort to the empress."

"True." Fravashi snapped her fangs. "But a consort must be Ipis."

Dante gave her a level stare. "Whoever the highest authority in the galaxy declares to be a suitable consort is one by imperial decree."

"True." Fravashi glanced at Tina. "This is your mate?"

"She is my wife. The only woman I'll ever love."

Her nostrils flared. "Do humans understand the concept of love?"

Dante nodded. "For most humans, love is the sole reason to live."

A look of surprise filled Fravashi's eyes. "Really?"

Dante pulled his communicator from a pocket in the neural-net suit and pressed an icon. Immediately a picture of Tina and himself with their two children appeared. "This is my family. I love them more than life itself."

Fravashi scrutinized the picture. "You only have one consort and two spawns? Is that customary for your species?" She glanced at Tina and then Dante. "You do not fear the strife multiple claims on your throne would cause. Have you lost many spawns to assassinations?"

Dante snorted. "I pray my children are smart enough to pursue any profession other than politics. This job sucks. I'd much prefer working in a computer lab than sitting on the surface of Mars negotiating the survival of my species." He gave the empress a hard look. "But if not me, then who? I will find a way to give the next generation a chance to live in peace. I won't fail my people. However, after that, I'm retiring."

"You'd just walk away from the power." Fravashi clicked her fangs.

"In a second. I never wanted this job," Dante responded emphatically. "Being responsible for so many people's lives terrifies me."

Fravashi's words came out slowly as she wrestled with a new concept. "You actually care about the lower castes?"

"There's no such thing to my way of thinking." Dante tapped his forehead and then his chest. "It's only what's in a person's mind and heart that matters. Where they were born and what they look like doesn't count for shit."

Fravashi chuckled. "I would enjoy seeing you at my royal court. I think if they heard you my courtiers' and nobles' heads would explode."

Dante's shoulders slumped. "Are we really that different?"

"I don't know. I've never spoken with a human before." Fravashi's claws clicked on the resilient flooring. "Tell me of your life, and I will tell you mine."

The next three hours flew by. The empress was transfixed as Dante spoke of his life growing up and the horrors he faced over the last seven years. She patted his arm affectionally and then regarded the conference table where both sides were silent and glowering at each other.

"Interesting. You've given me much to think about. I suggest we recess for the day and resume our conversations tomorrow." She gave Yasha-ry a hard look. "You will take no actions until I deem the conference concluded."

Yasha-ry, who remained silent through the entire conversation appraised Dante and grunted. "As you command."

Dante took Tina's arm and they walked out together. Both were trembling.

Fravashi watched until they were out of sight before turning to her admiral. "Come... *my love*. We have much to discuss."

That night, Dante slept fitfully beside Tina.

She finally rolled over and whispered, "Worrying won't change anything. You wake Josh up, you walk him." She sighed. "Why don't you go to the cafeteria and get something to eat. Then at least I can get a little rest before the baby needs to be fed."

Dante kissed her. "I love you." He got up and stumbled to the mess hall deep in thought, reliving the conversation he had with the empress.

Although it was two in the morning as the ship was clocking time, Mara, Setteth, Virgil, Michael, and Quango were sitting at the only occupied table, talking in hushed voices.

On spotting Dante, Virgil called out, "C'mon and join us, boss. I guess we're not the only ones who can't sleep."

Dante poured himself a cup of coffee and sat with them.

"Your debriefing earlier was fascinating," Setteth cooed. "Ipis nobility never reveal anything about themselves. I wonder what that portends."

No one had an answer.

* * *

The next morning, Mars time, the allied negotiators entered the domed building to find the harpies already waiting. Everything was as they had left it, but for one change. A half-carved block of marble stood next to the airlock entrance the Ipis used. Empress Fravashi sat beside it with chisel and mallet in hand.

She beckoned Dante over. "I think best when I'm sculpting, and I've been trying to carve you for six years."

Arachne gave Dante a meaningful glance. "Go for it. I doubt we'll get any further today than we did yesterday." He smiled. "You really must have made an impression. I think she has the hots for you."

Dante went over, but it was close to two hours before Fravashi spoke. He tried to start a discussion whenever the empress paused in her work, but she just scowled.

Dante watched with begrudging admiration as her gnarled hands deftly chipped stone from the eight-foot-tall marble block. *That's an incredible likeness of me.*

He was startled from his reverie when Fravashi dropped her tools and exclaimed, "Done." She regarded him. "What do you think?"

Dante studied the finished product and gulped. "I wish I really looked that good. That face seems courageous and wise."

A childish grin spread across the empress' face. "That's exactly the image I was trying to capture for the last six years, but I didn't see it until we talked yesterday. I worked on the statue most of the night."

"That's great." Dante self-consciously adjusted the medallion and sash he wore. "But could we talk further about a fair peace settlement."

Fravashi absently scratched the floor with her clawed feet. "I have seen enough of the future to know that no blood relative of mine would tolerate continued human existence, and any new consort I would marry and appoint to the role would bend to the will of the cults.

"You do not understand the ramifications of your victory over Silenus-dis." She clicked her teeth. "Your execution of the governor will send shock waves through the Dis and Ma cults. A second expeditionary force will be forged, and any Ipis governor I appoint interested in his own well-being will look the other way. Your species would be driven into extinction."

Dante felt the rage swell within him. "There has to be someone in this empire who would have the courage to stand up to these cults and the capability to resist them."

Fravashi smiled. "You mean, besides yourself?"

"You could make that happen," Dante added pointedly. He then decided to change tact. "Tell me, Your Majesty, since I didn't resolve your riddle, why are we continuing these treaty discussions."

Fravashi remained silent for a long moment. "I'm going to tell you something that I haven't even shared with Yasha-ry." She shifted uncomfortably. "If we're not successful today, we all die."

Dante's eyes flashed. "For all the evil your people have done to mine, I won't mind dying if I take you with me."

"If it were us, I would accept your challenge." Fravashi sank to the floor. "I mean us all: the Ipis, humans... everyone."

Dante reined in his anger. "What are you saying?"

She turned to him. "Being Empress I can move events to the life and death paths of my choosing. But for the last seven years, a new vision has supplanted all others. I don't understand it. In the not-so-distant future, there's a wall of darkness devoid of life." Her clawed hand grasped Dante's. "Tunneling through that black void is a single, slim thread of light. You."

"So, we have a quandary." Dante spread his arms. "You need me, but don't know why, and I need to shelter my people from your empire. The only problem is I'm not Ipis."

"You have a succinct way of phrasing things." Fravashi chuckled as she scanned Dante's captured adornments.

Dante sat beside the empress, fishing for an idea. "It won't bother me if you keep me and my people around until you figure things out."

Fravashi sighed. "I will miss these conversations. They are refreshing."

Dante stared at the statue of himself. "Tell me, Your Majesty, are you limited as to who you take on as a consort?"

"There are no limits," Fravashi replied in an icy voice. "I am the supreme ruler of the galaxy."

Dante hadn't heard "no" yet, so he pushed on. "Then accept me as your consort and make me the governor of the Lethe Sector." The rest of the words spilled out before she could laugh, "You said yourself that I'm the only one who could govern this sector and stand up to the cults. This part of the galaxy is remote. Your First Fleet could be stationed here. That way, Yasha-ry could keep an eye on me for the empire."

"You're so ugly." Fravashi laughed, and then her body went rigid. "You're not blurred anymore. I see the path." She gulped as a tear trickled down her careworn cheek. "I see my death move closer. I see Yasha-ry as an aged Ipis sitting in the sunshine, amiably chatting with friends, friends of many species."

Fravashi grasped Dante's hand. "I accept your proposal, and by royal decree declare that you are Ipis. I will make you my eighteenth consort and governor of the Lethe Sector." She shuddered. "But why does your species have to be so ugly. Promise me we will not have to consummate our union."

"I-I promise." Dante stared at the empress, waiting for more. Nothing came. "That's it?"

The empress regarded him with a look of contentment. "What sect will you declare for?"

"Excuse me?"

"All adult Ipis must claim a cult. Which will be yours?"

Dante cocked his head. "A new one, I think. It will be 'Pax.'"

"What is the significance of that?"

"It is a Latin word meaning 'peace,' but there's an underlying implication that says 'peace through strength.'"

"Dante-pax. I like it." Fravashi's tufted ears twitched. "What will be your cult's creed?"

Dante thought for a moment. "I know just the words. It paraphrases a document I hold sacred." He cleared his throat. "We hold these truths to be self-evident, that all sentient beings are created equal, that they are endowed by their Creator with certain unalienable Rights, that among these are Life, Liberty and the pursuit of Happiness."

Fravashi chuckled. "The nobles' heads will explode when they hear that. I expect you'll get very few adherents." She closed her eyes. "There is a nexus to that thin thread of light now—but also many fluxes that threaten to destroy it."

After several minutes, the Empress shuddered and squeezed Dante's hand. "As my Lethe Sector governor, there are three decisions you must make today. I-I dare not interfere, but I must have the answers, so I-I can prepare."

She told Dante what was needed and glanced at the conference table. "Let's go. In a few moments, your life... my life... will change forever."

As they approached, Tina gave Dante a quizzical look.

He mouthed, "I think we just bought the vegetables."

The negotiators all grew silent as the Ipis empress and Dante approached. Fravashi addressed them, "This is Dante-pax." She exchanged her secret look with Yasha-ry. "He bested Silenus-dis in an open duel. He has forsaken his heritage and is now Ipis. He is my eighteenth consort and the new governor of the Lethe Sector."

Yasha-ry sank into his seat and stared with his mouth open. "You really did it."

Setteth cocked her head and studied Dante.

The empress lightly scratched Dante's cheek and licked the blood. "The union is now complete." She faced Dante. "Governor, I'll leave you to deal with your minions and end this insurgence. I expect you to quell this incipient rebellion."

Fravashi spun around. "Come, Yasha-ry. Our business here is concluded. I have imperial issues to deal with regarding my new consort." She loped to the airlock exit. The other Ipis followed.

While the allied group was still recovering from the shock, Dante collapsed in a chair not built for a human posterior and considered the three issues Fravashi told him her visions revealed needing to be dealt with immediately.

Iucundum recovered first from the shock. "Dante, did what I think just happened, really happen?"

"I made a deal with the devil..." Dante looked around the table. "...and bought us some breathing space. I got us the best deal I could."

Calahas twitched his tail. "What did you agree to?"

"Per the decree of Her Imperial Majesty..." Dante cleared his throat. "Item one: The First Fleet will have basing rights within the Lethe Sector. Their home port will be in and around Bathox, the former governor's administrative planet, and will have unfettered refueling and repair facilities there."

He turned to Drusilla. "Guildmistress, you'll negotiate the lease agreement details."

Drusilla nodded and regarded Dante with an appraising eye. "It will be my pleasure, Governor. The profits from an imperial contract should be significant."

"Money," King Prolia exploded. "We'll have front-line imperial troops occupying our homes instead of cult auxiliaries. We're worse off than before."

"No," Dante shot back. "Item two: The four-native species of the Lethe Sector shall have autonomous administrative and economic management of their home worlds."

Setteth cooed, "I can banish all undesirable squatters on Tannis?"

"Yes. Every damn one of them." Dante set his jaw. "I decree, as the new governor, that the native planetary governments can expel all non-indigenous residents."

"There will be some very unhappy Ipis landowners." Arachne tugged his goatee. "You'll make some very powerful enemies."

"Arachne, the harpies will hate me no matter what I do. Being their administrative and judicial leader will drive them crazy." Dante snorted. "It's another reason why I agreed to have the First Fleet based here. The harpies' living in our sector will flee to Bathox for the Imperials' protection from their 'abomination' of a governor. Let Yasha-ry deal with them."

Dante added, "The titular Sector Governing Center will remain on Bathox, but I'll be living on Cocytus." Dante glanced around. "Questions?"

Otheth fluffed her feathers. "We'll control less than half the sector's habitable planets with this deal. The multispecies worlds are already controlled by the Ipis."

"True." Dante's lips tightened to a slim line. "I can't eject them, and I can't treat them more harshly than any other species. Even worse, I'll have to keep the Ipis cult representatives on the Lethe Sector Advisory Council." He leaned forward. "But for the first time, each native species will also have a seat there."

Setteth cawed, "Now those will be interesting meetings. I'd love to hear some of those discussions."

"Good." Dante smiled. "Because you're all appointed to it."

Otheth clicked her beak. "I well know the home worlds of the Rocs, Satyrs, and Centaurs. But, out of curiosity, what worlds will the humans claim as their own?"

Dante gave Roc a level stare. "Earth, Bathox, and Novaroma." He added, "I'll also directly manage Carcerem."

Arachne tugged his horn. "A cesspool I hope to never see again." He gave Dante a sly look. "But one that has the richest deposits of bi-nexidium in the galaxy. It'll make you quite wealthy."

Dante lips thinned. "And it will require a lot of wealth to rebuild the Earth after the death and destruction Silenus-dis wrought there." He sighed. "Last item: Prisoner exchange. We have over four million Ipis mercenary and cult paramilitary POWs. They'll be turned over to the First Fleet in exchange for every Human, Roc, Satyr, and Centaur currently imprisoned by the Ipis. All of those captives will be repatriated to my jurisdiction within a maximum of six months."

Stevenson's voice turned cold. "We're not letting all of those bastards go. Close to two *billion* innocent people were murdered on Earth."

"You're right." Dante shuddered, remembering the hellish devastation of once vibrant cities. He faced her. "Every senior commander from Silenus-dis' expeditionary force will be tried for war-crime atrocities."

"War crimes. That's an interesting concept." Setteth's feathers flared. "The only crime in war that I'm aware of is to lose. I understand the need for vengeance, but you won't be able to touch Keres-ma."

"Especially Keres-ma," Stevenson shot back.

"Keres-ma is of royal blood and is seven hundred twenty-third in line for the throne. He can only be judged by Empress Fravashi."

Stevenson leaned across the table. "I'll burn in hell before I let that bastard walk away."

"Then you will burn in this place called hell. The Ipis are quite intransigent when it comes to their royal caste," Setteth chirped.

Dante interrupted before the discussion could escalate, "I'll talk to Empress Fravashi. In the meantime, I adjourn this meeting. I believe we all need to confer with our people."

"This has indeed been an interesting day." Setteth eyed Dante. "You realize that your imperial power vanishes the moment Empress dies and there's a new Ipis ruler."

"Fravashi told me something to that effect. If I'm still alive, I'll deal with those issues then." Dante rose to his feet. "That is why my cult Ipis-pax will maintain a large *mercenary* fleet and army." His eyes narrowed. "Closely resembling the one you insurgents have right now."

"A serious war fleet independent of the Imperials." Arachne gave Dante a long hard look. "Are you our savior or ultimate traitor?"

Dante opened his hands. "To do the one, I had to become the other. I expect to be reviled across the galaxy. Few from any species will trust me."

Calahas nickered. "You bought us time. We could ask for no more."

Setteth bowed to Dante. "Dante-pax, it appears I serve an Ipis master again."

The others, one at a time, nodded their assent.

Dante shuddered. "Then it is done. May God have mercy on my soul."

When they returned to *Reggie*, all the negotiators hurried to the communications system.

Dante walked into his stateroom where Tina was nursing their baby. He wiped his cheek. "Honey, did I do the right thing? Did I save humanity?"

Tina stroked Josh's head as tears wet her own cheeks. "You did what you could. Now it's up to all of us to make it work so our children can have a real life."

Dante shifted on his feet. "I'm officially no longer human."

Tina giggled. "I never thought you were. Come here and kiss me, you Ipis overlord."

Liam woke up at the noise. "Daddy you're home." He sprang from his bed into his father's arms.

Dante had time to hug his family for only a few moments before his communicator started buzzing.

Tina sighed. "You better answer it."

It was General Cruz and Admiral Martinel on a joint call.

"Hey, mate, so you're a harpy now?" Martinel laughed. "How the hell did you pull that one off?"

Cruz was more somber. "We have a lot of hard work ahead of us. There are close to six million enemy combatants that we'll need to ship out. General Xiroah-dis may need a bit of convincing to abandon his strongholds."

Dante rose from the couch with Liam hanging on his back. "General Cruz, no more bloodshed. Let Admiral Yasha-ry talk Xiroah-dis out of there."

Tina shooed him out of the room. "You're going to wake the baby."

Dante walked out with the five-year-old's arms tight around his neck. "Liam, daddy has to finish this call." He dislodged the boy and handed him to one of the large guards outside the living quarters. "Porthos, watch Liam for a minute."

"Sure thing. C'mon, little guy. Let's see if there're any goodies in the mess hall."

Dante spent the next hour explaining the settlement over the comm-link.

Martinel concluded with, "I'll talk to this Admiral Yasha-ry. I don't want anything blowing up because of a misunderstanding."

"I'll connect with General Xiroah-dis and work out the enemy combatant evacuation," Cruz added.

"Don't be quick on that one," Dante asserted. "Those enemy combatants are our bargaining chips to free up the humans imprisoned around the galaxy. I want to see repatriation started first."

"Don't worry, mate, we'll work the details." Martinel's voice became soft. "You did good, Dante. Real good."

Dante clicked off and heard a banging against the passageway bulkhead. Liam had returned and was kicking a soccer ball. Porthos was playing goalkeeper in slow motion.

As he slid the communicator into his pocket, Dante saw his son staring at him with big eyes.

Liam asked, "Daddy, can we play soccer... now?"

Dante picked up his son and hugged him. "Yes, we can."

Epilogue

Two days after the conference concluded, half the Ipis Imperial First Fleet departed. Yasha-ry wanted to return the empress to a safe location and lay the groundwork for the new facilities on Bathox.

The warships of Dante's allies departed at the same time per the agreement Martinel hammered out with Yasha-ry. The delegates were impatient to debrief their respective planetary governments on the settlement before rumors became too rampant. They were also anxious to start expelling Ipis from planets designated as home worlds.

In the ruins of Hoboken, Virgil found no trace of what happened to his parents or his sister's family.

* * *

A week later, as Dante stumbled into his office after an arduous three-hour meeting with a collection of Earth political leaders, a voice in a dark corner said, "Zap, you're dead."

Dante turned in alarm and saw Charon sitting in a dark corner watching him. "How the hell did you get in here?"

"Your security sucks." Charon sighed. "I downloaded improvement suggestions to this building's control system."

"Thanks. I guess." Dante rubbed the back of his neck. "What do you want?"

"Just here to say goodbye." Charon smiled. "King Prolia is after me for several murders that I *did* commit, and I can't expect you to interfere. Dante-pax, as governor of the Lethe Sector, you'll collect more enemies than you can imagine. I don't care if Empress Fravashi declared you to be Ipis. The Ma and Dis cults will never accept you."

"What will you do? Where will you go?" Dante asked.

"I'm still in Yasha-ry's employ. I'll ply my trade some-where. There's always a demand for my unique services." Charon smirked. "I've also done you one additional favor. I've 'rescued' Keres-ma from your moon-base prison."

"How's *that* doing me a favor?" Dante snapped. "That bastard murdered millions. He deserves to pay. And how did you know where we were holding him?"

"I *am* the best spy in the galaxy," Charon boasted. "As for Keres-ma, he's a royal. You'd be forced to free him eventually, which will make you appear weak and subservient." His voice dropped. "Governor *Dante-pax*, you *must* succeed. The survival of four species depends on it now."

"Will I see you again?" Dante asked as Charon rose and moved to the stateroom door.

Charon's voice sounded full of regret. "I wish... I wish I would have met you when I was a young colt." His voice hardened. "But I did not. Pray you don't see me again. I'm also a very accomplished imperial assassin."

* * *

Riots erupted across the Earth almost immediately afterward as fear of aliens was replaced by undirected anger. Dante decided to limit the targets for that rage and decreed that all commercial and emigration traffic would be limited to five sites: Niagara Falls, Edwards Air Force Base in California, the Baikonur Cosmodrome in Kazakhstan, Alice Springs in Australia, and Rome, Italy. The last location was forced on him by many of his own people. They viewed Rome as their shrine and started rebuilding the Forum without asking anyone's permission.

Dante declared martial law on Earth and put General Cruz in charge. He allowed the nation-states to continue as countries but reserved all interplanetary military, political, and commercial activities to be solely under the control of his administrators. That authority rested with General Cruz's appointees on the Tranquility Bay Moon Base.

To relieve the overstressed demand for resources on Earth, Dante opened emigration to any who took an oath of allegiance to the Lethe Sector government.

Many of the soldiers who fought in the war developed a yearning to see distant worlds. They gathered their surviving family members and stepped forward to start a new life among the stars. Among the first émigrés were a Canadian motorcycle club who insisted on taking their bikes.

* * *

It was a month before Dante could leave and return home to Cocytus. Desperately needed supplies were finally arriving, and the first batch of harpy POWs were being sent to waiting transports.

All the ground transports were being used for high-priority goods, so the new Lethe Sector governor found himself lugging his mother's luggage. Although it was midwinter in western New York, he was sweating. *Reggie* was parked at the far end of the Niagara Falls Spaceport. Mara was piled high with Carloman family mementos.

Tina was carrying the baby, and Victoria's arms were full, holding her grandson's hand and bags of baby toys. Taz bounded aboard the ship, tail wagging, beside them.

Dante's sister Emma was no help. Her hands were intertwined with another émigré, Herb Wells.

Not all the human traffic was in one direction. The night before, both Dante and Tina cried as they bid farewell to Doctor Easley. She simply said, "My family's here and they need me. Besides, someone has to teach physicians on the proper use of stasis pods."

Although it took two weeks, the return trip to Cocytus was uneventful. As they exited *Reggie* on Heavensgate's tarmac, Dante was greeted by Beatrice shouting from every speaker system she possessed. "My Dante's home, my Mara's home. My Dante's home, my Mara's home." He was leery about introducing Beatrice to his mom. He didn't have to be. His mother threw her arms around the drone that greeted them. "God bless you. You saved my son's life."

"It is my honor to greet the maker of my maker," was the chirped reply. "Please visit my gardens."

"I'd love to have a tour. Dante's told me so much about you and your marvelous valley." Victoria turned to her son.

"Take my bags to Mount Purgatory. I have so much to talk to Beatrice about."

Taz peed on the drone.

The euphoria of the homecoming evaporated at the next session of the legislature.

A majority of the representatives on the Cocytus Planetary Council were incensed by what Dante yielded in the agreement with Empress Fravashi. "He renounced his humanity and aligned himself with our ancient enemy. He's a traitor," Claudia, the leader of the assembly declared. "He surrendered almost all the worlds our ancestors explored and settled without a fight."

Dante had friends in the assembly, like Iucundum, who tried to reason with them. "We would have lost the war and been hunted into extinction. The king achieved the best deal possible. Novaroma, our sacred ancestral home, is now ours again."

Iucundum was shouted down as a puppet.

Dante acknowledged that he could not be both the human king and the Lethe Sector Ipis Governor and abdicated his throne. "I cannot both advocate for humanity and sit in judgement of them."

It did not satisfy his opponents. Within a week, Claudia led an exodus from Cocytus to Novaroma. "We should be as far as we can from this Ipis lackey and choose a leader who will be courageous enough to speak for humanity." She was elected the Novaroma president and became that planet's representative to Dante's Lethe Sector Advisory Council.

At the same time, Gilbert and Rene stood beside Otheth in the center of the Roc Grand Chamber on Tannis. Gilbert played a dirge on his bagpipes, and Rene chanted the story of Cheepash's *cou*. Otheth then sang about the valor of the Wild Turkeys.

At the end, Setteth herself stepped down from her high, nested seat and announced to the gathered Roc warriors, "From this day forward, our Order will not be limited to Rocs. We will add a Fourth Order of the Dragon for humans of courage and honor." She faced the bikers. "You are no longer Wild Turkeys. Henceforth, you'll be known as Dragonmen."

* * *

On her return to Serpens, Fravashi was faced with a palace in an uproar. When it was learned that the Empress had proclaimed the 'abomination' Dante-pax was Ipis and had made him her consort and the new Lethe Sector governor, the nobility went apoplectic. The Ipis-ma declared it a heresy of the highest magnitude. The Ipis-dis leadership called it a dark betrayal.

However, six months after the treaty was concluded, the turmoil evaporated. With a combination of bribes and intimidations, vocal opposition sank to sullen complaints. Relying on her *gift*, she pulled it off flawlessly.

There were still loose ends to tie up. Fravashi sat upon her throne, feeling very alone. Before her stood Keres-ma, waiting for her to speak. He was among the millions repatriated as part of the prisoner exchange.

He fingered the mantichoras tail around his neck and glared at her in defiance. Keres-ma knew there would be no punishment for what transpired on Earth.

Fravashi closed her eyes and watched the thin, frail thread of light twist and turn into the future. *I am content. I've done what I could.* She had read Yasha-ry's dispatches with keen interest over the last couple of months. The First Fleet Admiral had expressed grudging admiration for the fairness and judgement of the new Lethe Sector governor. *I believe my first consort actually likes my eighteenth consort.*

She opened her eyes and glared at Keres-ma derisively. *I wish I could kill you, but I cannot.* "Cousin, I have received a full account of your actions against the insurgency. You are to be *praised* for your efforts in aiding the last Lethe Sector governor in quelling the rebellion that was finally put down by his successor. As a reward for your courage and loyalty to the Imperium, you will be promoted to Admiral of the Ninth Fleet and granted the Anon Sector as your fiefdom."

"Your graciousness has no bounds." Keres-ma pasted a false smile on his face. He knew honoring him was part of the bill she had to pay to defuse the rancor at the imperial court. He bowed to hide the loathing on his face. *The price you paid is not nearly enough. I will have more. Much more.* He turned and walked from the audience room without waiting to be dismissed, shoving aside a lavender-skinned server who was in his path.

He did not notice the small pin attached to the servant's medallion depicting a red human fist with the word "Pax" inscribed below it.

Main Characters

Dante Carloman—American, computer engineer; ruler of planet Cocytus

Tina Phokas—American, third-year medical student; doctor on Cocytus

Rodrigo Cruz—American, Army captain, military commander on Cocytus

Joe Gentile—American, Army lieutenant, Cocytus planet security commander

Virgil Bernius—American, Air Force Pararescue, Cocytus militia leader

Gabrielle Peyago—Argentine novelist, Cocytus ruling council member

Kevin Martinel—Australian, Navy search and rescue pilot; Cocytus fleet commander

Michael—Adult clone, infiltrator clone created by Ipis, Cocytus ruling council member

Aramis—Pre-adult clone, destroyer class, educated by humans

Athos—Pre-adult clone, destroyer class, educated by humans

Porthos—Pre-adult clone, destroyer class, educated by humans

Beatrice—Biomes Ecological Agrarian Test Research Station Three, an artificial intelligence found on Cocytus

Mara—Mobile Articulating Robotic Android, built by Beatrice

Octavia—Human, origin unknown

Iucundum (u-cun-DUM)—Human, origin unknown

Arachne—Satyr, smuggler ship captain

Quango—Satyr, smuggler ship chief engineer

Calahas—Centaur, disgraced noble, smuggler ship security chief

Gesten—Centaur, lover of Calahas, rebel leader on Equitone

Charon—Centaur, mercenary spy, saboteur, assassin.

Setteth—(SET-eth)—Roc, Ipis fighter squadron commander

Otheth—(OTH-eth)—Roc, great-granddaughter of Setteth

Keres-ma (CAR-es-ma)—Ipis, Ipis-ma faction; former magistrate of Carcerem

Silenus-dis (sil-EEN-us-dis)—Ipis, Ipis-dis faction; magistrate of Lethe Sector

Yasha-ry (ya-SHA-ree)—Ipis, Imperial First Fleet Admiral

Fravashi (fra-VASH-ee)—Ipis, Empress of the galaxy, has gift of the third eye

Place Names

Bathox (BATH-ox)—Ipis administrative planet, Lethe Sector

Carcerem (car-CER-em)—Ipis mining and prison planet, Lethe Sector

Cocytus (co-KY-tus)—Human capital world, Lethe Sector

Earth—Human original home world, Lethe Sector

Equitone (e-QUI-tone)—Centaur original home world, Lethe Sector

Serpens (SER-pens)—Ipis Galactic Empire capital world, Capital Sector

Tannis—(TAN-is)—Roc original home world, Lethe Sector

Tribulus (tri-BUL-us)—Satyr original home world, Lethe Sector

You've finished.

Please review this book on Amazon.com!

One of the ways for independent authors and small publishers to get exposure for their books is to receive as many honest, thoughtful reviews as possible.

Thanks in advance!

About the Author

John Caligiuri is a novelist who has a lifelong passion for literature and pens primarily science fiction and fantasy. He blends his fascination with history and his professional background in software engineering to come up with some unusual story twists. His stories emerged from his curiosity about historical watershed events and asking "what if?"

Originally from Buffalo, John lives in Rochester, New York, with his wife Linda. She's been married to him for over forty years and has supported his writing from the beginning. They have three grown children scattered around the country, along with their first grandchild. For relaxation

John enjoys gardening (which stretches his intellect attempting to outwit the rabbits and deer) and distance running. He is a member of the Lilac City Rochester Writers, Greece Writers, and B&N (Greece) writing group.

John is an award-winning author who has published science-fiction novels *Cocytus: Planet of the Damned*, *Cocytus: Sanctuary in Hell*, alternative history novels *The Red Fist of Rome* and *Last Roman's Prayer*, and numerous short stories. He can be contacted at:

johndcaligiuri@gmail.com

For more information visit his website:

http://www.guardiantree.com

For new projects, John is starting a new science-fiction series that merges the *Red Fist Chronicles* with the *Cocytus* series.

www.ingramcontent.com/pod-product-compliance
Lightning Source LLC
Chambersburg PA
CBHW072118250626
47159CB00007B/2487